# STANTON UNCONDITIONAL

T L SWAN

# ALSO BY T L SWAN

My Temptation (Kingston Lane #1)

The Stopover (The Miles High Club #1)

The Takeover (The Miles High Club #2)

The Casanova (The Miles High Club #3)

The Do-over (The Miles High Club #4)

Miles Ever After (The Miles High Club – Extended Epilogue)

Mr. Masters (The Mr. Series #1)

Mr. Spencer (The Mr. Series #2)

Mr. Garcia (The Mr. Series #3)

Our Way (Standalone Book)

Play Along (Standalone Book)

The Italian (The Italians #1)

Ferrara (The Italians #2)

Stanton Adore (Stanton Series #1)

Stanton Unconditional (Stanton Series #2)

Stanton Completely (Stanton Series #3)

Stanton Bliss (Stanton Series #4)

Marx Girl (Stanton Series – set 5 years later)

Gym Junkie (Stanton Series – set 7 years later)

Dr. Stanton (Dr. Stanton – set 10 years later)

Dr. Stantons – The Epilogue (Dr. Stanton – epilogue)

# ACKNOWLEDGMENTS

I would like to sincerely thank the following beautiful people for their friendship, support, encouragement and craziness; I am so blessed to have you in my life. Vicki, Emma, Andy, Jo, Brooke, my beautiful Mum Kerry, Rachel, Nicole, Anne, Renee, Sharon, Carly, Emma G and Keeley. To the amazing people who have embraced me as a new author and purchased my first book, Stanton Adore, thank you so very much. I hope to repay your loyalty with many more books to come.

And to the loves of my life who have sacrificed the most in my search for the perfect story. My beautiful husband, two sons and daughter. I love you all more than words can convey and the support you give to me daily is mind blowing. Writing a book is a team effort and I am so very lucky that you are my precious team. Without you all I wouldn't be able to write about true love because I wouldn't know if it truly existed.

Thank you for believing in me and I love you.

# GRATITUDE

*The quality of being thankful;*
*readiness to show appreciation for, and to return kindness.*

# DEDICATION

*I would like to dedicate this book to the alphabet.*
*For those twenty-six letters have changed my life.*
*Within those twenty-six letters, I found myself*
*and live my dream.*
*Next time you say the alphabet remember its power.*
*I do every day.*

# UNCONDITIONAL

*Unconditional love:*
*does it really exist or is it an urban myth?*
*What does it really mean?*
*Do you love someone because of their flaws?*
*Or in spite of them?*
*And at what point are the conditions more to bear than the love is*
*worth?*
*This is what I'm trying to decipher.*
*This is my story.*
*I'll let you be the judge.*

Brigetta runs into the room and drops to her knees beside him. "Joshua, my boy, it's going to be alright. You need to be strong, the ambulance is on its way." She takes his hand and holds it up to her lips and starts to pray as she wipes the hair from his forehead. "How much has he had?" she asks Ben.

He hunches his shoulders, "I didn't even know he had any drugs in the house. Carson must have left them here."

*"What's taking so damn long?"* I shout. Ben starts doing CPR and I hold my breath. I hear people running in the hallway outside and I realize that the whole house is in an uproar. All of the staff have come inside and are freaking out. I finally hear the ambulance sirens and I put my head in my hands and burst into tears of relief.

They are led into the room by Murray, Joshua's gardener, and the paramedics immediately start to work on him. I am pushed to the back of the room as they take over. My heart is in my chest and Brigetta and I are crying uncontrollably. We embrace and sob into each other's shoulders as Ben runs from the room and vomits in the bathroom. Within seven minutes Joshua is on a stretcher and being wheeled through the house and into the back of the ambulance.

And we are left in shock.

## Natasha

'Cabin crew, crosscheck'.

I sit back in my seat and brace myself for the takeoff. Jeez, I hate this. I sort of thought I would be used to this extreme sport by now, but my stomach is in my throat. I don't know any other twenty-five-year old girls who act like a two-year-old when flying. Max, my right-hand man, is sitting next to me. I have made him sit next to the window just in case.... you know. Glass smashes on impact, so I hear. I give him a weak smile. I have grown quite fond of dear old Max in the last two months. He has been by my side during the most traumatic eight weeks of my life. Joshua left him to guard me when he went back to America. At first, I think it was to guard me from myself and then it was to guard me from Brock, my brother.

I smile as my eyes flick to him, he did that job well. Max and Brock have been hating each other for weeks. Brock blames Joshua for Dad's death and every time Brock even brings up Joshua's name, Max shuts him up with just a look. I'm having a hard time dealing with Brock myself. I blame *him* for Joshua leaving and Dad's death. If he hadn't made it so hard for us, Joshua would have come to the hospital with me on that dreaded day. He would be here with me now and we would be dealing with this mess together as it should be.

*I had an affair and Joshua is another man's child.*

I frown as I go over the words Margaret spoke to me just yesterday. We are not cousins. We do not share DNA. At first, I was ecstatic and hopeful and now the hard cold reality has started to sink in. Joshua is going to be devastated, because he idolizes his father. He is not biologically a Stanton. For him it might be better if we were cousins.

My heart is heavy. I wish to God that Margaret the bitch hadn't told me about her sordid previous life, but then, on the other hand, I would not be on my way to him if she hadn't. I'm so damn confused. It's like his loss is my gain and I feel guilty and torn. I shouldn't be relieved that we are not related ... but I am, in fact I'm ecstatic. I haven't slept but am displaying promising signs. I have been comfort-eating for China since that dreaded meeting in my office yesterday. I have hardly eaten a thing for two months, so this is good, this is real progress. Why have we had to sacrifice both of our beloved fathers to be together? I know my father had an undiagnosed heart condition and that he was a ticking time bomb, but I pulled the pin. I know that, we all know that. It is just not fair and so unrealistic. Talk about a beautiful, tragic love story, ours takes the cake. Loving each other for so long from afar, fighting our social restraints and conscience to be together, trying desperately to resist a deep natural desire.... it doesn't make sense. I've never heard of a couple with so many barriers, not any that have made it anyway. I blow out a breath as I pop two sleeping tablets into my mouth and take a sip of water.

"Wake me up if the plane is going down," I yawn to Max. He smirks. "Sure thing," he replies.

"Meh, actually. Don't. I would rather be asleep as I drown.... or catch on fire." I frown as the disturbing thought rolls through my head.

He pats the back of my hand. "Sleep, worrywart." I return his warm smile and nestle into position. Josh is right, I do feel safer with him around and I can totally be myself. He's seen me at my absolute worst and hasn't resigned yet which is strangely comforting. Max has even been sleeping in the guest room at Mum's while Bridget and I have been staying there. Mum wouldn't let him stay out the front in the car all night.... every night. I think that deep down she feels safer having him around as well. Brock has gone back to Afghanistan for another six-month-deployment so the house is eerily man free. He's refreshing, although he hardly ever says anything. I know he's in my corner and I trust him.

.   .   .

5

"Natasha, put your seat back up."

I frown as I wake and stretch. "What.... I slept the whole time?" Max gives me a smirk as he nods. "Oww, my legs are asleep," I groan as I seep back into consciousness. My heart starts to race as excitement courses through me. I'm going to see him for the first time in two months, my beautiful Josh. My God, I've missed him, I can't wait to hold him in my arms and kiss his beautiful lips. I know he has been suffering like me. This whole ordeal has been a living nightmare.

"How are we getting to Josh's?" I ask.

"Ben is organizing one of the drivers to pick us up. I rang him before we got on the plane."

"You told him I want it to be a surprise, didn't you?"

He nods. "Yes, don't worry."

Thirty minutes later we are at the luggage terminal and Max sees one of Josh's drivers through the crowd. He nods at me as he walks over and starts to quietly talk in Max's ear. I frown. That's odd. What's he saying? Bit rude, whispering.

"Max, I'm going to the bathroom." He nods and then continues talking as I walk away. This is weird, Max doesn't usually leave me alone at all. He must have really missed his friend the driver, they sure are deep in conversation. I exit the bathroom to see Max waiting patiently outside for me. I smile.

"Natasha, I need to talk to you, honey."

I smile and frown, honey.... he's never called me that before.

He looks uncomfortable, "There has been an accident." I frown. "It's Joshua," he whispers.

"What.... what kind of accident?" I gasp. He grabs my arm and I snatch it away from him. "What's happened, Max? Tell me."

He swallows and looks around as if surveying the situation. "Joshua is in the hospital. He has taken a drug overdose."

My eyes widen, "What? What do you mean? What drug?"

He rubs the back of his neck. "Cocaine, honey."

My face drops and I turn and start to sprint toward the door with him hot on my heels. I look around frantically for the Audi. "Where's the car?" I scream.

He grabs my arm, "Natasha, calm down."

I snatch my arm away from his grip. "Take me to him!" I yell, as I start to freak out. This is all my fault. Dear God, no, not this. The car pulls up and I dive in as I angrily swipe the tears from my face. I have had just about as much as I can take.


## Adrian

"I can only speak to immediate family."

Of course, his brother who is also a doctor is in with him now," I reply. He nods and enters the hospital room and I follow. Cameron turns to face us as we walk in. Joshua is in the hospital bed, unconscious and still. He is hooked up to machines in the intensive care ward and nurses are everywhere. I have never been so frightened. Actually, that's a lie. I have, when I was in a hospital ward just like this watching my father lose his battle for life. How did it get to this? I thought he was ok. I knew he was down, but I never thought he would purposely take an overdose. This is my worst nightmare.

"I'm Mark Reynolds. I will be Joshua's doctor."

Cameron nods and holds out his hand to shake the doctor's.

"Cameron Stanton," he replies as he turns back to look at his brother. "What are the stats?" Cameron asks.

Dr Reynolds picks up the chart from the end of the bed.

"We have put him in an induced coma to bring his heart rate and blood pressure down. He is suffering Tachyarrhythmia and at this point we are very concerned about him suffering a cerebral hemorrhage or heart failure."

Cameron drops his head and picks up Joshua's hand. "Christ," he murmurs. "How long until he's out of the woods?"

The doctor shrugs. "Usually about twelve hours, but it could be sooner. If we can just keep his body cool, I think he will make it, but I can't be sure. And then you know of course, depending on how long he went without oxygen, there is a chance he may have sustained brain damage." Cameron nods and drops his head again as I slump into the chair. Why is this happening? "I would suggest you call your family. Is he married?"

Cameron looks at Joshua again. "Yes," he replies softly. "His wife Natasha is on her way."

The doctor rubs Cameron's shoulder. "I suggest you start praying." He gives me a nod before exiting the room.

"Natasha is on her way?" I ask.

Cameron nods, unable to speak past his tears, and slumps onto the floor next to Joshua's bed, his head in his hands. For five hours I sit silently in the corner as I watch Joshua's nurse apply and reapply water cooling blankets directly to his skin and check his vitals and check his vitals. He is hooked up to so many machines but the heartbeat sound echoing through the room is comforting, as long as I hear that beep all is ok. Cameron is a mess. I have never seen him like this. He had to ring his mother and break the news. I feel like I am having an out-of-body experience. I am numb, this can't be real.

"I'm going to get you a drink, Cam." He gives me a weak

smile and nods as I walk back into the hall. Ben is waiting patiently with Pete, Joshua's driver, in the small lounge area opposite Joshua's room. They both immediately stand as I walk toward them, their faces anxious.

"He's still ok, no news." I mutter.

"Thank God," Ben blows out a breath.

I rub my head. "I'm going to get some coffee. Do you want some?"

Ben nods, "Yeah, I'll come with you."

"I'm just going to the bathroom. I won't be a minute." I head through the double doors that lead to the bathrooms.

Two minutes later Ben comes into the bathroom after me. "Do you want the bad news or the bad news?" he asks me.

"Dear God, what's happened?" I stammer.

"No, nothing with Josh.... sorry that was put badly.

Vinegar tits just arrived."

My face drops. "Who in the hell rang her?"

He shrugs, "I don't know."

I am not in the mood for this bitch today. I shake my head, wash my hands and head back out to the lounge area.

She storms over to me. "Why in the hell wasn't I rung?" she snaps.

I narrow my eyes. "Hello Amelie, you weren't rung because you are not immediate family or Joshua's girlfriend, that's why."

She scowls at me. "Last time I looked you were neither of those things either."

I roll my eyes. "Go home, Amelie. Natasha is on her way and I know for a fact that Joshua doesn't want you here. I will call you if there is any news."

"I am here because Margaret, Joshua's mother, called me and I am not going anywhere. Why in the hell was Natasha called? She left him if you care to remember," she snaps.

Cameron walks out of Joshua's room and looks up to see Amelie. His face drops and he quickly turns to go back into the room, hoping to escape her.

"Cameron," she storms over to him before he can make an unnoticed getaway. "Why didn't you call me? I'm furious."

Cameron frowns at her and shakes his head. "I notice you haven't asked me how he is, thanks, Amelie." Cameron's eyes flick to me in disgust. We don't like Amelie. We did at first, but we have watched her manipulate Joshua like a fiddle too many times. She's a conniving two faced bitch but Joshua seems to think she is this gentle pure friend that he has to protect. We decided collectively about two years ago that at least if Joshua spent his weekends with her, he wasn't getting into trouble with Carson. Better the devil you know sort of thing. She is the ultimate player, and she is making a play right for Joshua. Thank God, she's not his type. I think I will kill him if he ever goes there.

Cameron puts his hands in his pockets and glares at her. "Natasha is on her way, so you need to go home. Adrian will call you if there is any change."

"I want to see him," she snaps.

Cameron shakes his head "It's only family at this stage. I will call you when he wakes. Seriously, go home. I promise. Someone will call you."

The doctor walks back up the hall. "Ah, Mrs. Stanton?" he questions.

Cameron's eyes flick to me nervously. "No, this is not his wife. Natasha is on her way." Amelie's eyes widen in shock as the doctor re-enters Joshua's room. Cameron smirks at me and follows him. Oh no.... Great. How am I supposed to explain this shit?

"Joshua and Natasha are married?" she gasps.

I shrug. "Um, yes, not that it is any of your business." Holy shit, she's going to go ape. She shocks me and does the exact opposite, goes deathly pale and slumps silently into the seat. Why in the hell has Cameron told everyone that Joshua is married? It doesn't make sense. I head back down to the cafeteria in the foyer of the hospital to grab our coffee. I am waiting in line when I see her, Natasha sprinting through the hospital hysterical, with Max running to keep up with her. I smile, this is how you act if the person you love is on death's door. Thank God, she is here.

"Natasha," I call out to her. She sees me and runs over and crumples into my arms in a fit of tears. This girl is beautiful, on the inside more than the outside.

"Adrian," she cries. "Where is he? I need to see him."

I wrap her in my arms, even I've missed this beautiful girl. "I'll take you to him, baby." I nod to my bodyguard to take care of the coffee and I take her hand and lead her to the lifts to see him. We approach his room. Amelie lifts her head and glares at Natasha. My anger rises. I could just knock this bitch's head off. Natasha doesn't say anything but frowns at me. I lead her to his room and open the door. The doctor turns to us.

Cameron nervously looks at Natasha. "Dr., this is Joshua's wife Natasha."

She smiles and slightly frowns as she holds out her hand to shake his. "Your husband has taken a cocaine overdose. We have stabilized him and put him into an induced coma but he is not out of the woods just yet." She nods as she tries to hold in the tears. She leans over Joshua and embraces him as she breaks into sobs on his chest. Both Cameron and I tear up at her obvious devastation. This is hard to watch.

## Natasha

"Joshua. My God, what have you done?" I cry into his chest as sobs wrack my body. The doctor leaves and I turn to cuddle Cameron who is just as distraught as me. My eyes flick to Adrian. "What happened, how did this happen?" I sob.

Adrian hunches his shoulders. "We are not sure, but we think it was accidental."

My eyes go back to my broken love. "Does he use cocaine regularly?" I ask as I gently run my hands over his forehead.

Cameron frowns. "No, not regularly. Tash, this was an accident. He has been down lately. He would have just been trying to get through the day."

Realization hits me. "This is all my fault," I sob.

I turn back to Joshua, my beautiful Josh. He is nearly unrecognizable to me. He has tubes coming out of him every- where and is hooked up to machines. He is a lot thinner than when I last saw him and pale, he has no color. He has a beard, probably around two- or three-weeks growth. He's been neglecting himself, as I have. We are as bad as each other, I have never looked like such a sack of shit in my life.

I put my head back down on his chest and sob. "I'm so sorry, Josh. I didn't know what to do. My dad said it was wrong and then he died," I sob out loud. "And then I lost you. I was so deep in grief I couldn't see straight, and now you've done this, and it's all my fault."

Adrian walks over behind me and puts his hand on my

shoulder. "Tash, this isn't your fault, and it has been a terrible string of circumstances. Ones that have been out of your control. Josh doesn't blame you, he understands. He is just not handling things well at the moment, but he will get better and now you are here you can work things out together."

I nod as I wipe my eyes and turn back to look Joshua.

"You're right, he has to get better." A sudden burst of anger breaks through. "Do you hear me, Joshua.... don't you dare think about dying. You can't leave me.... not now. You fight this.... do you hear me? So help me God, Joshua Stanton.... I mean it, listen to me." I break back down into a fit of tears. Dear God, let him be ok, this is such a mess.

Cameron walks back over and pulls me into his arms. "He needs you to be calm, Tash. We are trying to regulate his heartbeat, being irrational will not help the cause."

I nod, he's right. Calm.... I need to keep calm. I nod and pull away from Cameron and immediately pull a chair to sit next to the bed. I need to find some inner strength and I need to find it fast. I grab Joshua's hand and kiss the back of it and put my head down and start to silently pray. Please pull through, please pull through. About three hours later I find myself leaning forward with my head resting on Joshua's upper arm. I am somewhere in between sleep and delirium when I jump with a start as the nurse and doctor enter the room. I quickly stand to allow the doctor greater access. He checks Joshua over and reads his chart.

He gives me a warm smile. "Mrs. Stanton, it seems you have a positive effect on your husband. His vitals indicate a promising result and I think he is going to be ok, he has passed the worst of it. It will be a few days, but it seems all is well. We are going to start bringing him out of his sedation." A wave of gratitude washes over me and my face breaks into a huge smile.

I run immediately to the door and out into the waiting lounge where I see Cameron and Adrian.

"He's going to be ok," I gasp. They both stand in a rush to cuddle me and the three of us stand embracing each other. We stand still, united and exceedingly grateful. It is then I notice Amelie standing in the corner of the room alone.

I turn to her and smile. "He's going to be okn Amelie." She nods nervously and gives me a weak smile. Cameron then picks me up and twirls me around and I laugh out loud. He carries me back into Joshua's room to see the doctor himself. The doctor smiles warmly at Cameron and shakes his hand and Cameron excitedly grabs him in an embrace, forget the handshake. Adrian walks in behind us.

"It looks as though he is through the worst of it. We are going to keep him lightly sedated for the next twenty-four hours just to keep his vitals down. Mrs. Stanton, do you want to stay the night or are you going home?"

"I will be staying, if that's ok," I smile.

He smiles and nods. "I will organize a bed to be brought in for you then."

"Thank you, Dr.," I reply as he leaves the room.

"Why did you tell them we are married?" I ask Cameron.

He looks sullen. "Because I knew if it got bad and they were going to lose him they would have asked you to leave and you wouldn't have had a say in anything. Joshua would want you with him more than anybody else. I did it for him, not for you."

I give him a weak smile. "Sorry, Cam. I haven't dealt with this shit very well, have I?"

He shakes his head. "No, you haven't and neither has he, he's been a total nightmare."

Adrian must have sensed Cameron's underlying anger at how I've treated Joshua and he butts in. "She's here now and everything is going to be fine. Isn't it, Tash?" He puts his arm reassuringly around me.

I smile and turn to Adrian as he wraps his arms around me. "Thank you for looking after him for me. I appreciate you guys being such good friends to Joshua. God, if anything happened to him." I shiver in horror I can't even bear to think of the consequences. My tears start again. "I'm such an idiot. How could I have treated him so terribly? I just left him and told him I never wanted to see him again, after all we had been through to be together." Guilt fills me, I don't deserve him, but to be fair I could never have predicted what the future was going to hold. I was totally blinded by grief. A nurse re-enters the room and injects something into his drip. "What are you giving him?" I ask.

"Diazepam, this will keep him sedated to keep his body temperature down and even."

"Tash, our mum and dad are on their way with our brothers. Prepare yourself, she's going to be fuming mad and I'm pretty sure it will be aimed at you" Cameron sighs.

"She came to Sydney to see me and asked me to come to Joshua. She was worried about him and it seems she had a good reason to be," I whisper. "This is all my fault."

Cameron and Adrian exchange glances. "She asked you to come to Joshua?" Cameron frowns.

"Ripley's believe it or not." I do wide eyes at him. "What's Amelie's problem?" I ask Adrian.

Adrian's eyes drop to Joshua and he hunches his shoulders. "You, I expect. It's no secret she's in love with Joshua."

"Adrian." Cameron snaps. "Stay out of it."

I narrow my eyes. "It's ok. I already know, you don't have to be a rocket scientist to know that. He loves her as well."

Cameron and Adrian frown. "No, he doesn't. He loves you,

Tash," Cameron stammers. My eyes drop to my beautiful unconscious man before me. "I know he loves me, it's ok, boys. I'm ok, I can't blame her for loving him ... loving him is easy. It's the walking away from him that's hard."

They both give me a sad smile and nod. "We will give you some privacy." And with that they disappear out of the room.

# 2

_____

**Natasha**

I LIE on my fold up bed next to my so-called husband. I only wish that he was. A nurse comes and checks on him every thirty minutes. His breathing is regulated, and the monitor's constant beeping is strangely comforting. I know his heart is still beating and he's still with me.

It's late at night and the hospital is silent. Thank heavens for Cameron's quick thinking with the wife thing or I would have been ushered out with the others at ten pm. Cameron is in the hospital somewhere, refusing to go home in case I need him.

My mind wanders back to the night I met his friends at his house when there was a tray of cocaine on the coffee table. Is this Joshua's normal? Is he a cocaine addict? His out-of-control partying and stripper days are a constant reminder of his unruly past but just how deep that runs I have no idea. I know that a lot of wealthy socialites start out taking it to party but because there is no money restraint it very quickly turns into a very real problem in their daily life. Has my beautiful man got an ugly habit that I am unaware of? I troll my brain for any evidence. I knew his friends took cocaine, but I honestly would never have known he would have anything to do with it. He's a fitness fanatic.... mmm, maybe that's why he's a fitness fanatic, to keep him on the straight and narrow, to keep himself on track. He is excessive with it, like.... over dedicated. Why do I have to look for a reason behind everything? Stop thinking like a psychologist, Natasha, don't do it to yourself.

I stand up and lean over him and I smile. He's beautiful, nothing has changed. I lean and gently kiss his lips. "Wake up, sleeping beauty," I whisper. "I want to talk to you. I don't like you being asleep so long." No answer.... why won't he wake up? I gently run my fingers through his facial hair and over the top of his head. I gently pull the sheets back to look at him and I frown at the sight. He is bruised on his torso, quite badly actually. What is that from? Hmm, fighting, he's been cage fighting again. I hate that sport or whatever you call it. I frown as I notice he has a bruise in the shape of a shoe print on his hip bone, as if he has been stomped on or kicked when down. This is no cage-fight bruising, this is real-fight bruising. My heart drops, *Baby, what in the hell have you been doing*? I trace my name on his side with my finger and he flinches. My eyes shoot to his face. He frowns and I hold my breath.

"Joshua," I whisper. "I'm here, baby, wake up." He frowns
again. "Joshua," I repeat. I bend and gently kiss his cheek. "I love you," I whisper. His eyelids start to flutter. I grab his hand and he squeezes it as he slowly opens his eyes. I smile at him. "Hi," I whisper.

He squints as he tries to focus his eyes. "Tash," he whispers.

Tears fill my eyes, "I'm here, baby. It's ok, I'm here." He gives me a weak smile and I lean and gently kiss his cheek.

"What's going on?" he whispers through a husky throat. "You're in the hospital, you took a cocaine overdose." His face drops and he lifts his arm to look at the intravenous drip into the back of his hand, then he shakes his head in shock.

"How long?" he shakes his head again. I buzz for the nurse. He frowns again and I know he is trying to remember what happened. The nurse enters the room and smiles.

"Mr. Stanton, how are you feeling?" He stays silent while staring at me. I think he is in shock. I give him a weak smile.

"She asked you a question," I whisper.

He shakes his head. "I'm ok," he gently answers. Cameron walks into the room and his smile nearly beams me off the bed.

"You ok mate?" He walks over and gently kisses Joshua's forehead and I melt. This is love; Cameron adores Joshua. I smile as my eyes tear up again.

The doctor walks in and nods to us all. "You have given your brother and wife here a hell of a shock, Joshua."

Joshua frowns at me and I smile in return. He's confused, he holds up his hand to look at his ring finger and frowns again. I bite my lip to stifle my smile, he thinks we are married.

"Do you know where you are?" the doctor asks. Joshua nods.

"In the hospital," he huskily replies.

"And why are you here?" he asks.

Joshua casts his eyes down in shame. "Drug overdose," he whispers. He coughs dryly and the nurse pours him a glass of water. He tentatively takes a sip. "Thank you" he whispers. He looks around. "Where's Adrian?" I smile at that question. He's ok. He's going to be ok.

"Only immediate family and spouses," Cameron replies.

The doctor looks into Joshua's eyes with a flashlight.

"I will be keeping you in for observation for a few days but you are a very lucky man. You were close to death and have selfishly put your loved ones through hell."

"You got that right," Cameron interjects.

Joshua's eyes drop again. "Sorry," he murmurs. His eyes find me through the room, and I melt into them. I have so missed this man, it is as if a part of me has been missing. I give him a weak smile and he holds out his hand for me. I gratefully take it and he kisses the back of my hand and rests his cheek against it. Tears fill my eyes as Cameron smiles and rubs Joshua's head. "See you in the morning" and with that he leaves the room. The doctor stays for around another fifteen minutes and I stay silent in the corner waiting patiently for my time with him. A nurse comes and removes his catheter and after what seems like an eternity they leave us alone.

I gently cuddle him as I am overcome with tears. "I'm so sorry, Josh, forgive me, baby. I have done this to you."

He shakes his head. "No, Tash, I did this."

"I will never leave you again, I promise you, Josh. I love you too much to be without you."

He looks down at my hand and frowns. "Did Adrian get your ring from the safe?"

I frown and shake my head. What's he talking about?

There's a ring?

"Cameron just told them we were married to get me access to you."

His face drops. "Oh," he answers quietly. He gives me a weak smile. "I thought we got married."

I smile and bend to gently kiss him. "I wish," I whisper.

He returns my smile. "Me too, though I would like to remember it." I crawl onto the bed next to him and his eyes close.

"I need the bathroom," he whispers. I quickly jump off the bed.

"Let me help you." I grab his elbow to stabilize him as the nurse re-enters the room.

"Back to bed. You are too weak to be standing. When was the last time you ate, young man?"

He shrugs his shoulders. "Not sure" My eyes close in regret. He doesn't even remember eating, what in the hell has he been doing to himself? He lifts himself off the bed and scrunches his eyes closed in pain.

"What's wrong?" I gasp.

"Headache," he winces.

"That's normal," the nurse nods. I blow out a breath in relief.

"Ok," I reply shakily. The nurse and I get on either side of him and help him up as he gingerly walks to the bathroom. I have never seen him like this. It's frightening. So weak, so fragile. I can't believe he nearly died just ten hours ago. I walk into the bathroom behind him as he falls onto the toilet, and I grab him for support. He sits silently with his head down and urinates. As I stand silently beside him it occurs to me that Joshua, my Joshua, would be pulling wisecracks in this situation normally. No way would he sit down to go to the toilet, not without a joke anyway.

He finally finishes and stands. "I need to shower." "Joshua, no, you are going back to bed," I urge. "I'm taking a fucking shower," he snaps.

I beam a full megawatt smile.

"That's more like it," I whisper. He raises an eyebrow in silent question at me. "There's my difficult man," I smile.

Half an hour later he is back in bed and I am feeling much better. After his little snap at me I know he is going to be ok— there isn't a doubt in my mind. He lies with his head facing me as I lie next to him.

"Thank you for coming for me," he whispers. "When did you find out?"

"At LAX airport." He frowns at me, not understanding. "I was already coming to you, Josh. You did this while I was in the air." Should I tell him about the paternity?

His eyes widen. "I thought you said you didn't want to see me again," he frowns.

I kiss the back of his hand. "I'm so sorry, I never meant it. I was blinded from grief, Josh. I felt as though I killed my father. I wasn't thinking straight, you know I would have come back for you eventually. I have mourned the loss of you just as much as my father's." Nerves rise in my stomach. I need to tell him that we are not cousins. Is he strong enough yet? How do you tell someone this kind of information? My heart drops.

He looks down. "I thought you meant it."

I shake my head. "I didn't." Maybe I will wait till he is stronger?

His eyes look to the roof and I can see his brain ticking. "Tash, I thought we were broken up."

Why is he saying this?

"Don't you want me here, Josh?" I ask. "How can you even think that? I love you more than life itself."

And then he frowns. "Stop fucking with my head. I swear to God, Natasha." He starts to get worked up.

"Sshh, Josh, I'm here. I'm not going anywhere, calm down.

It's ok, it's ok." I rise and gently kiss his face. "I'm not leaving again, I'm sorry, baby." He's definitely not strong enough.

The nurse re-enters and takes his vitals. "I'm going to give you another relaxant, Joshua. Your heart rate has gone back up, just something to make you sleep, ok?" He takes a deep breath and nods, and she injects another drug into his drip. I hold his hand and rub his forehead as he peacefully drifts off.

What must it feel like to be in a peaceful sleep? I haven't had one for so long. I keep watch on the silent and still man beside me. On the outside I mirror his calmness; however, the inner turmoil inside my stomach has reached a whole new level. I'm worried.... actually, that's an understatement. I'm panicked. The harsh reality is that Joshua may very well be a cocaine addict. I know that, the doctor knows that. Everybody knows that. He has the motive.... friends and escape and he has the means.... unlimited funds. I have done extensive study on addictions as part of my psychology degree and I know it's a very steep hill to climb to get out of an addiction black hole. Both for the addict and for the ones that love them. I close my eyes. How did it get to this? Was it really an accident or did he try to subconsciously kill himself without realizing? What are the bruises all over him? He has a definite shoe mark on his body, and I know that they don't wear shoes in the fight ring.

Who in the hell has he been fighting and where was Ben, his

Bodyguard, when it happened? I suppose that means nothing. Joshua got into a fight that night at the Ivy and Ben was there then. So, it is possible. I have caused all of this havoc in his life. I wonder what his life was like before I came back into it. What if he has been taking cocaine all along and I didn't realizes it, have I been that blinded by his love? Am I that stupid?

After melting my brain with way too much thought I decide

to ask both him and Cameron tomorrow separately and see how well their answers match up, and maybe even Adrian for that matter. I have a talent to tell when someone is lying and, boy, am I going to put it to use tomorrow. I eventually drift into an unsettled sleep after tossing and turning for hours. Maybe I should have got some of that relaxant put into my veins; I sure could bloody well use it.

I wake to the gentle dusting of lips on my temple and I cuddle into his chest.

"I love you," he whispers. He pulls me into an embrace and wraps his arms around me. Mmm, I've missed this, missed him. I nuzzle into him and drift off as I listen to his breathe regulate. We are both exhausted. Too tired to acknowledge that he has crawled into my fold up bed beside me, too relieved in the comfort of each other to care. The world could stop right now, and I wouldn't give a damn. I'm here with him and that's all I need. How could I have ever thought I could deny myself this? It's impossible and totally unrealistic, we couldn't be apart. Not ever, I need him like oxygen, more than my next breath.

"Look how gorgeous they are," I hear Adrian's voice speak. I frown as I stretch to find Joshua wrapped around me like a blanket. He had even moved his IV so that he could lie with me in my bed. Adrian is standing with a cup of coffee and Cameron is lying on Joshua's bed, reading the paper.

Oh crap. "How long have you been here?" I grumble as I stretch.

Cameron smiles a face-splitting smile as he flicks his paper down to look over the top of it. "Long enough to know you two are pathetic!" He widens his eyes at me to accentuate his point and goes back to his paper.

Joshua inhales a deep breath as he wakes. "This bed is bloody uncomfortable." He groans as he kisses the side of my face from behind.

I smile and roll back to face him. "Good morning, Mr. Stanton"

He smiles and rubs his hand over my behind. "Good morning, Miss Marx," he whispers.

Adrian rolls his eyes. "Hmm, you seem to be feeling a lot better today." Joshua bites his bottom lip to stifle his smile. "And I'm starving. Is there any food in this joint?"

Cameron smiles and winks at Adrian; he obviously sees that as a good sign.

"Josh, why in the hell were you taking cocaine alone like that? That's ridiculous," Cameron asks. I lie still as I listen to their conversation.

Adrian pipes up. "You gave all that shit up years ago. Why in the hell would you do that again?" Joshua's eyes flick to me and I know he doesn't want to have this conversation with me in the room. Too bad, he's having it. I'm just going to come out with it.

"Are you a cocaine addict, Joshua?"

"No. How could you think such a thing?" he stammers. "Probably because we are in hospital after you

overdosed," I reply. "Are you going to take an overdose every time we have a fight?"

He frowns at me and sits up in a rush. "Bit more than a fight, Natasha. We broke up."

I sigh. "Josh, you know I didn't mean that." Cameron and Joshua quickly glance at each other.... silently communicating. Hmm. "Why did you do it?" I ask. "Was it accidental?" He frowns, not understanding the question. "I mean did you purposely take an overdose?"

"No, of course not. I lost track of how much I had had. I just had a really shitty weekend and was trying to perk myself up a bit."

"What happened on the weekend?" I ask.

His face drops and his eyes meet mine and he swallows a large lump in his throat. "Can you get me some breakfast, boys?"

Cameron jumps up and rubs Joshua's shoulder. "Sure mate," he gives him three hard slaps on the back as he and Adrian leave the room. Joshua's eyes search mine and I smile in return.

"Alone at last," I whisper.

He pulls me into an embrace. "I've missed you, Presh. Don't leave me again, ok."

I smile and nod as he runs his lips down the length of my neck.

"Promise me," I smile again. "Natasha, promise me," he repeats.

I shake my head. "Josh, you know I only left you because of my dad and all of that mess. I will never leave you again." I smile as I kiss his neck and he holds me tight.

I run my hands around the back of his nightgown and feel his behind.... he feels good.

He kisses me as he brushes the hair from my face. "Tash.... we need to talk."

My head drops. "I know, Josh. I need to talk to you too." I sigh softly.

"Well, you look much better today." We jump back from each other as the doctor enters the room. Shit, I had my hand on his butt, how embarrassing. Joshua gives the doctor a nod in embarrassment and shakes his hand.

"Thank you, doctor."

The doctor reads his chart and gets his flashlight as he looks into Joshua's eyes. "You are lucky to be alive, young man. You nearly died."

Joshua's eyes find mine and he drops his head. "I know.... I was very frightened." My eyes spring up to his. He's right, that would have been frightening. "You have a lot of people waiting to see you outside. After you shower and eat, I will let them in."

Joshua nods. "When can I go home?"

The doctor narrows his eyes. "Not until you have completed five drug counselling sessions with our rehab team. It will be at least another three to four days before I sign you out."

Joshua frowns. "I don't need counselling."

The doctor looks up from his notes. "I am happy to check you into a three-month rehab program if you refuse.... your choice."

Joshua glares at the doctor.

"Three days is fine. Thanks, doctor," I interrupt. I widen my eyes at Joshua to signify his silence, and he reluctantly nods and heads over to sit on the bed.

"I will be back to check on you each morning around eight. If you need anything just let me know. I think they are moving you upstairs for more privacy. It seems the press has gotten a hold of your overdose and you are making headlines around the world." The doctor sighs and Joshua's head droops. "Upstairs you will be in a private wing so your bodyguards and helpers will have more room. They are making this place a mess," he smiles. "How many do you have?"

Joshua looks embarrassed. "A couple," he whispers. "Natasha, is Max here?"

I smile and nod. "One of them is mine, doctor," I reply. He nods and heads out of the room.

My eyes widen. "Oh shit. I forgot about Max. I have left him out there all night."

Joshua frowns. "And?" he murmurs.

I frown. "I don't do that. Max has been staying with me and Mum since you left."

He frowns as he stands. "What.... in the house with you?" I smile and nod.

"I'm paying him to protect you, not play happy families," he snaps.

I smile. Why is a jealous Joshua Stanton so simply delicious?

"He has been protecting me and helping my family. These last two months have been horrific for me, Josh and he has kept Brock away from me."

"Has Brock been giving you a hard time?"

"No, just making sure everyone knows that he hates you. It isn't as unbearable when Max is with me because he tells him to shut his mouth."

Joshua smirks. "Shut his mouth, hey." I smile and nod. "He might have his mouth wired shut soon if he keeps going," he adds.

I pull him to me. "No, because you love me you are going to let this thing with Brock go. For me and for Mum."

He bends to kiss me. "I really want to kick his ass."

I smile as he nuzzles my neck. "Take it out on my ass instead."

"Hmm," he whispers darkly. "Your ass is going to cop it very soon as well." He nips my neck and I yelp.

"Promises, promises, Stanton," I giggle. God, I love this man. The nurse re-enters. Hmm, this one is young and pretty and I feel a sudden pang of jealousy, especially since I have just felt that he is in full rut under that gown.

"Do you need help to shower?" she asks him.

His eyes dance with delight as he looks at me mischievously. "Maybe," he replies.

I look at him deadpan. "I've got it," I snap.

He gives me a broad beautiful smile and winks at me.

*Bastard.*

"No, my wife will help me shower, but can you take the drip out so I can, please?"

She smiles, knowing exactly what he's playing at. "Yes sure."

I watch as she slowly takes his drip out of the cannula and prepares the bathroom. "I will put a 'do not disturb' sign on the room's door for twenty minutes. Lock the door but there is a buzzer if you need any help, ok?"

I smile and nod. "Ok," I reply. I follow Joshua into the bathroom and he shuts the door and locks it behind us. His eyes drop to my feet and back up again and he ticks his jaw and gently cracks his neck.

I smirk. "Get that look out of your eyes, Joshua. It's not happening. You are here because you are sick."

He drops the gown and puts his head to the side. "Do I look sick?"

My eyes drop to his perfect erect manhood.... my heart drops as I go weak with want, it's been so long.

He gently runs his hands through my hair. "I've missed my beautiful girl," he whispers. His lips meet mine and he blesses me with a tender open-mouthed kiss, his tongue slowly taking what he wants. I hold my breath as he slowly peels off my clothing and pulls me by the hand into the shower. We stand under the strong stream of water kissing and embracing each other. This is home.

I stand under the water with my head on his chest for fifteen minutes, his arms wrapped protectively around me. I've missed his strength, his tenderness, every damn inch of him.

His lips tenderly take mine as he runs his hand over my breast and down my stomach and then further down to between my legs. He closes his eyes at the contact. "There's my beautiful, tight girl," he whispers. His hands are gentle and loving ... tender. I involuntarily throw my head back as he pushes a finger inside me and then another one. His thumb circles on my clitoris in perfect pressure. He knows my body so well, knows exactly how to make me lose all coherent thought.

"My beautiful girl, I love you." He kisses me again as he slowly lifts my leg, so I am standing on one foot to give him greater access to my throbbing center. His fingers start to slowly pulse inside me and my eyes roll back in my head.... this is what I need.

"I can't wait, Presh.... I have to be inside you. Now."

My breathing catches. "Josh, we are in a hospital room. No."

He smiles as his eyes drop to my lips. "You don't have a say in it. You told the nurse you were going to look after me and she can't come back in here when I'm in this state."

I smile. "I know what you are doing," I whisper. He smiles into my neck.

"What am I doing?"

"Trying to make me jealous," I reply.

He bites my neck again. "I'm too hard. It's not going to go down and you don't want the nurse to see me like this, do you, baby?"

I smile and narrow my eyes. He's really not playing fair. "Tash, I need to be inside you, it's been too long. I can't wait. Look, I'll sit, and you can do all the work." His skin is covered in water beads, his large erection hangs heavily between his legs, his eyes are dark and his big, beautiful lips are open with want. I've never seen anything quite so erotic in my life. He gestures to the bench seat in the shower. My eyes flick to the seat and back to his mouth. This is unbearable, I can't stop. I grab him and kiss him hard as I push him into the seat, and he groans out loud. Then he is lifting me over him and rubbing the side of his shaft through my flesh. Our breathing is heavy and the steam in the room is starting to run down the walls. He slowly brings his hand up to his lips and puts some saliva onto his fingertips which he then rubs into my weeping sex as a lubricant, like I need any. He holds his thick length up and, with the other hand, pulls my hip down. We both groan as he enters me.... we stay still, panting. My eyes close, my heart races and I'm scared if he moves a muscle, I am going to explode into orgasm. He rests his forehead against mine and looks into my eyes.

"I love you," he whispers as he brings both of his hands up to my cheeks.

My eyes cloud over with tears. "I love you, Josh."

He smiles and then kisses me, probably the most beautiful kiss he has ever given me. The depth of emotion behind it gives me goosebumps and I slowly lift myself to move.

"Presh, I'm not going to last. You just feel too good, baby."

I smile. "It's ok, me too." He lifts me once and my legs fall wider open.

"Fuck it." He snaps as he lifts me again. He slams me back down and circles my hips on the upstroke and groans as he comes hard, his body doubling over in orgasm. I feel his thick length throb deeply inside as his body empties into me and I know I can't make him keep going. He's not well enough. Damn.... I needed that orgasm. I shake my head and lift myself to pull him out of me as we both scramble for air.

His forehead rests on mine as he pants. "Sorry, precious. I couldn't last."

There's a first, I am so in love with this man. I smile broadly as I kiss him again. "Shh, it doesn't matter." I whisper. "We have the rest of our lives, Joshua." His eyes search mine, and he smiles gently.

Knock, knock, knock....

"Joshua, are you ok?" Joshua and I glance at each other in shock.

"My mother's here."

# 3

## Natasha

HOLY CRAP, Margaret, why did she have to come now of all times? We are both wet, overheated and out of breath, it is blatantly obvious what we have been doing. I wanted Joshua to myself for a few tender moments. She bloody ruins everything.

He breaks into a full-blown smile as his eyes drop to my lips. His two hands clasp my face to pull my head back to give him greater access to my neck. "Shall I invite her in to watch round two?" he whispers as he slowly pumps his hips into mine, his open mouth skimming the length of my neck down to my shoulder blade. I widen my eyes and slap him on the chest.

"Stop it, you idiot. She's going to go ape." He bends and kisses me slowly as if we have all the time in the world.

"Let her, I'm done with what people think. I only care what you think." He smirks.

I smile shyly at him and pull back to look at his face. "Well, I love you, Mr. Stanton, that's what I think."

His face mirrors mine. "That's all I need to be happy. My mother can go to hell on her broomstick for all I care." I bite my bottom lip to stifle my smile at the thought of her on a broom stick. That analogy is so very fitting.

"Joshua, stop it," I scowl. "This isn't a joke."

Knock, knock, knock.... "Joshua," she calls.

"In a minute, Mum, I'm showering with Natasha." My mouth drops open in shock and I hold my hands over my eyes.

"Sshh, shut up," I whisper as I shake my hands in a nervous gesture. "Stop it. She's going to go crazy."

He smiles a full beaming smile and raises his eyebrows at me. "I told you I don't care anymore; she can like it or lump it." I jump out of the shower and start drying myself double time.

"She's going to lump it.... you know that." He turns off the shower and starts to dry himself. He stands still while I hurriedly dress. I quickly brush my hair and exit the bathroom. This is just so uncomfortable, what must I look like? He's in the hospital, for Pete's sake. I walk out into the room to find Cameron sitting on the bed smirking at me.

"Really...hospital sex?" He raises an eyebrow in question. I screw my face up in embarrassment and turn to see Joshua saunter out of the bathroom in a towel, proud as punch. My stomach drops. God, this looks bad.

Cameron shakes his head at Joshua. "You look," he smirks as he raises an eyebrow, "better."

Joshua smiles at him as his eyes flick to me, "Yes, I'm feeling much better, thank you." Please, earth, swallow me up, I'm like a hospital sex stalker taking advantage of the sick. "Where's Mother?" Joshua asks.

Cameron smiles. "Your little 'I'm showering with Natasha comment' scared her off."

I put my head into my hands. "Oh God, Josh, you're making it worse. She hates me enough." I pull a worried face at Cam.

Joshua saunters over and embraces me from behind. "Presh, let me take care of my mother." He kisses my cheek over my shoulder. "I told you I'm done with her making me feel guilty for loving you. Hasn't this last two months shown you to not worry about anyone but me?"

Cameron interjects. "And me.... and Adrian," he winks.

I smile warmly at him. In all honesty, they're the only three people worth worrying about on his side anyway.

"I will handle my mother and if she can't handle us being together then," he shrugs his shoulders, "I don't know what role she will have in my life."

I shake my head and pull away from him. "Joshua, you are not fighting with your mother over me. I will not let you cut her out of your life. She deserves more respect. You wouldn't even be here if it wasn't for her. I will try to make this right and stop

... all this nonsense. But I need you to stop antagonizing her. You're just making it harder for me." He smiles and gives me a quick kiss on the cheek before he walks over to his drawer of belongings, he pulls out some clothes and starts to dress. "Can we talk about this later, please?" I ask as my eyes flick to Cameron and I notice he is in a white coat. "Oh my God Cam, you're in your doctor's get up. Is this the hospital you work at?" He nods and smiles as he looks down at his coat.

"Yeah, I start at ten," he replies.

I hunch my shoulders up like a little kid. "Ohh, this is so exciting." I bound over to give him a cuddle and he laughs out loud.

"Shit, I'm getting a photo." I run to my bag and get my phone and turn to see a proud as punch Cameron. Probably nobody took a photo of him on his first day. I start to click away. "I'll send this one to the girls, so try to look hot," I smile.

"That won't be hard, I am hot," he replies.

Joshua rolls his eyes. "Yeah, smoking." I smirk at Joshua who is now sitting on the bed watching the photo shoot.

"Tash, I have an idea. Why don't you go and find a nurse's outfit and then let me take some photos of you looking hot," Joshua whispers.

I fake scowl at him and shake my head.

"Cam, where's Murph?" Joshua's eyes flick to Cameron.

Cameron frowns, "I don't think he is coming until later. The press have gotten a hold of your overdose and the office is swamped with reporters."

Margaret enters the room. "Joshua," she runs to him and breaks into tears and I know the fun conversations are over. This is about to get heavy. "You could have died. What were you thinking, you stupid boy?" She nervously smiles at me and I fake a smile in return. They embrace as she cries. "I thought I was going to lose you. Don't ever put me through that again. You have no idea how terrifying the flight was, not knowing if you were going to be alive when I got off at the other end."

"Sorry, it was an accident. I didn't mean it," he replies.

She pulls back from the embrace. "Why were you taking cocaine, Joshua?"

Joshua hangs his head. "I don't know."

"Dear God, Cameron, do you take cocaine?" she stammers as her eyes flick to him.

"No, Joshua has never done it before either. It was a one-off thing. It just got out of hand," Cameron sighs.

Mmm, even I can see he is lying. What the hell? Cameron too. This partying lifestyle is coming to a stop right now for the both of them. Cameron is now a doctor, for heaven's sake, and

Joshua is a frigging millionaire. This is just ridiculous. My mind flicks back to that asshole Carson. I hate him even more now if that's possible.

I give a weak smile. "I will give you some privacy and get some coffee. I will be back later."

Joshua looks at me and frowns. "Ben can get you that. You are not leaving the room every time my mother enters it. I thought we were in this together." His eyes challenge me.

Shit, I swallow uncomfortably. "We are but.... Josh, spend some alone time with your mother. I want to go and see Max and ring the girls anyway." He holds out his hand for me and my eyes flick nervously to Margaret who is watching me attentively.

"Natasha, dear, we need to talk," Margaret says quietly. I bite my bottom lip and look at the ground. I so don't want to talk to this bitch, I despise her.... every damn thing about her, and now I know she is a lying adulterer, I hate her even more if that's possible.

Joshua picks up my hand and kisses the back of it as his eyes plead with me to make peace with his mother.

I give a resigned smile. "Yes, okay, I will make some calls and be back in about fifteen minutes." Joshua smiles warmly and kisses my hand again. "Take Max with you, baby. I don't want you walking around here on your own." I roll my eyes, Cam smiles and pulls me into a headlock.

"Come on, Marx, I will show you the hot nurses on level four." I pull a disgusted face. "Jeez, I can't wait."

An hour later I am in the lounge area talking to Max. "So, have you called Holly?"

He smiles. "Yes, but she worked last night and now it's the

middle of the night there, so I have just left her a message for when she wakes up." I nod. Max has met an Australian woman and is really quite smitten with her. She is thirty-four and widowed with two kids. She lives in the building next to mine. They would speak when they ran into each other in the front yard and it went from there. I have met her, and she seems nice and very attractive. She's a radiologist at the hospital and does shift work. I hope it works out for him. His first wife left him because he worked too much. He came home one day, and the house was wiped out with a note saying she had met someone else. Poor guy, he says she was obviously the wrong woman anyway if that's how she respected marriage.

I can't imagine how horrific that would be. We have actually become quite good... I don't know what you would call it... friends maybe. He's cranky but honest with a dry sense of humor and I hate to admit it but I kind of like having him around. If the truth be known I would have told Max to return to America weeks ago if it wasn't for this little romance, he has going on. I figure Joshua has the money to pay him so why not stretch it out and see where it goes. It is weighing heavily on my mind now though, because I will obviously be moving back here.

"How are things going?" Max asks as we walk up the corridor to the room together.

I hunch my shoulders like a little kid. "Pretty good, I feel like we haven't been apart."

"And that's good?" He smiles.

I smile and widen my eyes. "Yes, that's very good." He nods his crooked smile.

I knock tentatively on Joshua's hospital room door. The door opens in a rush as Joshua opens it. "Here's my girl," he smiles as he bends to kiss me. My eyes glance around the room.

"Mother has left." I blow out a breath in relief and put my hand up to my chest. Joshua narrows his eyes at me. Oh shit, busted... mother hating. "Where did you go?" he asks as he raises his eyebrows. "Cam gave me a tour of the emergency department where he is working and introduced me to the head of the psych ward," I reply as I walk into the room.

He nods and sits on the bed. "I don't really want you working when you move here."

I drop my handbag onto the chair and put my hands on my hips in question. "What do you mean?" I frown.

"I thought I would take six months off and we could go travelling."

I smile in excitement. "Really? Where would we go?"

"Where wouldn't we go is the question." He smirks.

"I thought you said you were in the middle of a big project and couldn't leave work," I reply.

He hunches his shoulders. "My priorities have changed."

"What does that mean? What are your priorities now?" I ask.

He bends and gives me a gentle kiss. "You.... making you happy is my only priority."

Relief fills me. I like that answer.... I like it a lot. "If you want to make me happy, Josh, can you please not take cocaine again," I murmur into his chest.

"Don't worry about that. I scared the hell out of myself. I will never touch that shit again."

"And Cam, can you tell him not to do it either?" I ask.

He bends and kisses my neck, "Stop worrying, Presh. Cameron is a big boy, and he is only young. I'm not being a fun cop for him."

"Well, I'm going to be, and I don't care what you say," I scowl.

He raises an eyebrow at me in silent disapproval but keeps his opinion to himself.

"You don't think I should work for six months to secure a good job before we leave?" I question.

"No," he answers deadpan. "I don't want you doing sexual psychology at all Natasha." I frown and step back from him in question.

"Tash, I don't want you dealing with sexually fucked up deviants that are just dying to bang you and add you to their sex addiction," he replies flatly as he takes a sip of his water.

"Is that a joke?" I snap. "How dare you say that to me? I did six fucking years at university, Joshua. It is my chosen career, and you will have no say in what I do!" I snap. He raises his eyebrows in a silent dare and sits on the bed.

"We'll see."

I scowl at him and head into the bathroom. He's bloody lucky he's in the hospital because I feel like chucking a total wobbly right now. I take my time going to the bathroom while trying to calm my anger and reminding myself about compromise. When I come out there is a young man sitting in the chair next to Joshua's bed.

He stands. "Hi, I'm Peter. I'm from the rehab team. I will be working with Joshua for the next few days. Joshua just told me you are also a psychologist."

I fake a smile at Joshua. "Yes, I am. Sex psychologist, actually." Put that in your pipe and smoke it, asshole.

Peter raises his eyebrows, "Wow, interesting line of work."

I smile again. "Yes, very." Joshua purses his lips in disapproval.

"I will leave you two to it then," I smile. I give Joshua a brief kiss on the lips and go to head out the door.

"Tash, my mother is coming to take you out for coffee at four."

My face drops but I quickly recover and smile. "Great, I will look forward to four o'clock."

Four o'clock and I am dreading the coffee date like the plague. Margaret smiles like a Cheshire cat on heat as she walks down the corridor toward me.

"Hello, thank you for agreeing to meet me," she purrs.

My skin prickles in contempt. "I'm only here for Joshua, Margaret. It has nothing to do with you," I snap. I inwardly cringe because that came out harsher than I intended it to.

She nods nervously. "Right," she replies. "There is a café across the road. Would that be ok?" she asks. Why in the hell is she being so nice? It's giving me the creeps.

I nod and we walk to the café in uncomfortable silence. "Max, can you wait outside the café for us?" I ask. He nods and takes a seat on the sidewalk.

Ten minutes later we are seated and waiting for our order without speaking. I have nothing to say to Margaret. Last time I saw her, I nearly slapped her face off. I can't believe I actually hit her. What in the hell is going on with me and the bitch slapping lately? I frown as I try to forget the disturbing thought.

Margaret grabs my hand over the table, and I bite my lip to stop myself from speaking.

"Natasha... can we please call a truce... for Joshua's sake?"

I force out a nod. "Margaret, I have never wanted to fight with you. You are the one who hates me."

"I have never hated you, dear. Please understand it from my point of view. My nineteen-year old son comes home and tells me he's fallen in love with his seventeen-year old first cousin.

That he has been having sex with her every day for a month and that he is going to marry her."

I look down and smile as my heart melts. "He said that?" I ask. "He said he wanted to marry me?"

She sits back and frowns. "From that whole sentence that's the only information you took?"

I nod, embarrassed. "Sorry, carry on."

"And then, not two weeks later, she sleeps with someone else and breaks his heart and I have to put him on a plane to go to the other side of the world alone.... and devastated."

I swallow the lump in my throat as the horrible taste of guilt rises from my stomach. I look her in the eyes. "I never slept with another man, Margaret. I lied so that Joshua wouldn't throw his life away on me. I knew he would never let me leave him unless I told him that and it has haunted me ever since. To this day, I have never had sex with another man."

She goes silent and sits back in her chair in shock. "What, never?" I shake my head. Her face drops.

"I know this sounds strange to you, but Joshua and I are truly in love, and you have made us miserable with your venom. Joshua should never have to choose between us, Margaret. It is just not fair to put him in that position. I would never do that to him but you seem to do it easily."

She drops her head. "I know."

"And then you come to me after I let my father die telling me that we are not even related, when you have hated me for all these years. How do you expect me to react?"

She tears up as she looks at me. "Natasha.... I'm so sorry. I felt you were dangerous to Joshua. His love for you is all-consuming and I know that in all honesty if you left him again it would break him... and I was right. He took a cocaine overdose. But in the end when I saw him so miserable, I couldn't do it to him any longer. I had to tell you the truth."

I sit back in my chair. "Tell me, are you going to tell your son the truth about his paternity?" I ask as I raise an eyebrow in contempt.

Her face drops. "Natasha, please don't judge me. After I had Scott," she looks around the café to make sure nobody is listening, "Robert was working all the time and lost interest in me sexually. I was only twenty-two years old. He was away three weeks out of four and I was pretty sure he was having an affair. I was miserable." The waitress arrives with our coffee. Margaret stops talking immediately. "Thank you," she smiles. "We had a friend that used to come to the house regularly to check on me and Scott, at Robert's request. He was my only friend at the time, and I came to depend on him. His marriage had temporarily broken up and we leaned on each other for support. We talked a lot, and often he would come over and then stay for dinner. We were both very lonely. One night after a few wines he told me that he used to fantasize about me.... sexually.... when he was alone in bed." My eyes widen as I imagine the situation she is setting for me. "I was totally shocked and asked him to leave immediately. But I couldn't stop thinking about it. It haunted me, Natasha. I was in my sexual prime and I was married to a man who saw me as a mother to his child and nothing more. It was a very difficult time for me."

"I can't imagine what it would be like to be married to someone like that," I whisper. She smiles. "You will never have to worry about that. The chemistry you have with Joshua runs too deep." I give her a thankful smile, she didn't have to say that. "Anyway, I thought about it for two whole months and in the end, I was fantasizing about him in my bed as well. I wanted to feel wanted, I wanted to feel desired. Robert went away for four months and as usual our friend would call daily to check on me. The sexual tension between us became unbearable and one night he kissed me on the lips goodnight. I got nervous and asked him to leave, but he didn't. He stayed out in his car for four hours while I paced inside, distraught at what I was about to do. When he knocked again at two in the morning, I didn't have any resistance left.

I broke Natasha, I gave into temptation. We made passionate love every day and night for a month. I fell totally in love with him and when Robert was due home in a few weeks I told this man of my intentions to leave Robert so we could be together." I sit back in shock, this is not the story I expected. "He told me to not be a fool and that he was going back to his wife." She tears up at the memory.

My stomach drops and I actually feel... pity for her. "He told me that we could never be together and that he would not choose me over his friend and that if I told Robert he would make my life misery. I was heartbroken, how could I have been so stupid? I threw away my marriage vows on a man who was using me for sex." She wipes her tears with a tissue and takes a sip of her coffee. "When Robert got back, he was different. The man I married was back and he admitted that he had in fact had an affair and wanted us to start again. To try and be a family unit for Scott's sake. How could I say no when I had been just as deceitful? I jumped at the chance to stay with the man who I had previously been deeply in love with." She wipes her eyes again with her tissue. "Anyway, to cut a long story short I found out two months later that I was pregnant, but I didn't think the child could be through the affair as we had always used condoms. And, besides, Robert and I had fallen back in love and a child was a blessing. My beautiful Joshua was a gift. He brought me so much happiness and I thanked

God every day that I had been given a second chance at happiness."

Empathy wins and I smile and grab her hand over the table. "Margaret, I know how it feels to give into temptation. I fell in love with my first cousin, remember. Every night we would fight our conscience to be together. It was dreadful."

She nods and smiles as if understanding. "When Joshua was sixteen, he fell off a horse and lost a lot of blood." I frown as the next part of the story unfolds. "Anyway, his father was away at the time overseas and Joshua ended up needing a blood transfusion. When the doctors tested his blood type it came back that he had a very rare blood type and that it was not genetically possible that he could be a full sibling to his brothers. I have never been so crushed. Joshua was the son of another man. How could I have done this to Joshua and his beloved father?" My eyes cloud over now as I realize this was a terrible mistake. I actually feel sorry for her.

"To make matters worse I had to go to this man who is still a friend of Robert's and tell him the truth so he could donate the lifesaving blood Joshua needed. He was mortified and if the truth came out, he would lose everything, his wife, his kids, and his best friend. He has threatened me with violence if I ever told anybody."

I frown. "Margaret, is this man dangerous?" I whisper.

She nods. "Unfortunately, yes, and unstable." She wipes her eyes again with her tissue. "It was he who brought it to my attention that the only way this secret would come out is if you and Joshua stayed together and had genetic testing.... for pregnancy and things." My eyes widen as I understand. She sobs out loud.

"I knew I had to keep you apart.... at all costs." I nod as I grab her hand, and she squeezes it.

"Natasha, will you keep my secret.... please? No good can come of this getting out. Joshua will be devastated, Robert will be devastated. This man will lose everything and take vengeance on me. Robert will probably leave me, and Joshua will not be a Stanton." I frown as my tears threaten again.

"Margaret, you are asking me to lie to the man I love. I can't do that," I whisper.

She shakes her head. "No, not lie.... just not mention it and then if it comes to him having to know, I will tell him and I will pretend that you didn't know anything about it.... I swear I will never implicate you in any of this mess."

I rub my hands through my hair. "Margaret, I wish you hadn't told me," I whisper angrily.

She nods. "I know but I had to, you were both so devastated. I have never seen a love like yours, Natasha. You really are soul mates... I believe that... you believe that... Joshua knows that. How could I keep it from you? Keep you from each other when I knew the truth?"

I frown as I drain my coffee cup. I put my head into my hands on the table. "This is fucked up, Margaret, and I'm a psychologist.... I deal with fucked up well."

She smiles and grabs my hand. "I know, dear. I'm sorry to put you in this situation but what choice do I honestly have? If you can think of another way out of this where Joshua doesn't get hurt, please let me know. I'll be all for it." I sit in silence for ten minutes quietly drinking my second coffee as I wrack my brain for another avenue to follow. I've got nothing. I nod as I blow out a heavy breath in resignation. She's right.... there is no way out of it. I have no choice but to lie. Joshua deserves better.

# 4

---

**Natasha**

AT FIVE THIRTY I return to Joshua's room to find it empty. His belongings, my fold up bed, everything.... gone.

Max and I are puzzled until a nurse approaches us. "Are you Natasha Stanton?" she asks.

I smile proudly. "Yes"

"Your husband has been moved upstairs to the private wing and asked me to let you know where he is."

"Oh okay, thank you," I reply.

"Take the lift up to level seven and then you will see a large set of grey doors with a security code on your right. Push the buzzer and you will be buzzed in," she answers.

I smile again. "Ok thanks." We ride the lift in silence. My mind is heavily weighed down by Margaret's story. I can't believe I actually feel sorry for her. Can you imagine what it must be like to hold a secret like that in for twenty-seven.... actually, no, she said she found out when he was sixteen, so eleven years. And it is such a bad secret.... my poor baby, he has no idea. God, this is such a mess. Have I done the right thing agreeing to keep this quiet? What if he finds out later that I knew all along and then leaves me for deceiving him? It's entirely possible.

I'm just as bad as his mother.... but what choice do we have? It's him we are protecting. *What a fucking nightmare.*

We arrive at the security doors and a janitor is cleaning the foyer near the double doors.

Max speaks first. "Natasha Stanton to see her husband." I smile at the floor, that sounds really, really good.

The bored receptionist's voice echoes through the speaker. "Yes, come in." The doors open. We reach the

receptionist's desk.

"I would like to see my husband. Which room is he in?"

"Of course, the last door on the right." I smile at Max and we head down the corridor towards the last door on the right and it opens to a large private lounge area complete with television, cable and a kitchen.

I frown at Max. "This is random." He smiles and nods.

There is a cleaner in there restocking the kitchen. "Hello," I smile. She smiles. "Hello."

I frown at her. "What are these large rooms? Where are the hospital rooms?"

"This is the private wing for celebrities who need more privacy from the press, and more room for their bodyguards and things."

My eyes widen. "Oh," I reply, shocked. Jeez.... this is so.... over the top Hollywood.

"Yes, most of the LA celebrities have been in here at one point or another for substance abuse issues." My eyes drop to the floor. Yes, like my so-called husband.

"Hmm I see, where is my husband?" This gossipy bitch is starting to piss me off.

"The door to his room is around the corner next to the television." I nod and head in that direction.

"Tash, I will just stay out here tonight, okay?" Max states.

I turn and frown at him.

"Max, that's not necessary. Go home honey. I will be fine. Nobody can get in here. There is security. It's safe here."

Max narrows his eyes. "No, I will be staying. I'm good. I will watch the game on the screen." My eyes flick to the gossipy kitchen girl who is now listening to our conversation. *Buzz off, big ears.*

"I will be out to see you soon," I reply as he flops into the lounge chair. I walk into the room and my jaw drops. Bloody hell, this room looks like a luxury hotel suite. There is even a double bed. *What in the world?* Joshua walks out of the bathroom and throws me a swoon worthy smile.

"There's my beautiful girl. I was starting to get worried. I thought that maybe you and my mother may have killed each other. I was going to send out a search party." He bends and tenderly wipes the hair back from my face. I smile and put my arms around his neck and inhale his wonderful scent. I feel better just being in his vicinity.... I need to put this paternity shit out of my head.

He kisses me gently. "So...." he steps back to scan my face.

He wants to know what was said between his mother and me.

Guilt fills my stomach ... I can do this. "We are calling a truce, for your sake, Joshua. Only because we both love you."

His eyes light up and he smiles warmly. "Thank you.... I really appreciate you doing this for me." He bends and kisses my neck. "I will make it up to you, Presh. It will be well worth your while." He grabs my behind and grinds me forward onto him.

My eyes close instinctively. "That's great, big boy, but stop.

We are in a hospital. No fun for you until we get home," I smirk.

He sits on the chair and pulls me onto his lap.

"I'm hungry for you," he whispers darkly. I smile. God, me too actually. The little two pumps I got yesterday have only heightened my need for a long hard sex session.

"Patience, baby.... later." I smile into the top of his head.

"Prick tease," he whispers into my neck.

"Baby, I am going to tease that prick until you're crying with want. You have no idea." I gently run my tongue through his lips and pull back to smirk at him.

"There's my beautiful slut. I've missed that filthy mouth of yours, Natasha." His eyes darken as they drop to my lips.

Just him calling me beautiful slut awakens memories that send a throb of arousal to my center. "Well, I've missed that beautiful strong tongue of yours, so we are even," I whisper.

"If you are trying to get yourself fucked you are going the right way about it." He licks my neck.

My eyes close as I feel my legs start to open by themselves. Mmm, I need to be fucked...hard. "It's working then," I whisper.

He pats the bed next to him. "Come and lie with me."

"How did your session go with the rehab guy?" I ask to try and change the subject.

He shrugs his shoulders. "Embarrassing. I felt like a junkie." "To them you are," I reply.

He nods and flops onto his back. "I hate that I have done this. How could I have been so stupid?"

I nod and my eyes tear up. "Josh, what if you had died...it

would have killed me. I wouldn't have been able to go on. How could you be so selfish?"

He kisses my forehead as he pulls me tightly into his arms.

"I know, Presh. I'm so sorry. I swear I didn't mean it. I was watching the movie of us on repeat all weekend."

I frown in horror. "What, the porno?"

He smiles and nods. "Yeah, you look smoking hot by the way." He kisses my forehead again. I bring my hand up to my face in embarrassment. What must I look like?

"And then what happened?" I ask.

He blows out a breath. "I was down on myself for letting you down."

I turn to look at him. "How have you let me down, Josh?"

He drops his eyes. "I just have Tash. I am supposed to be the one to take care of you and I can't even do that."

"Josh, it wasn't your fault my dad died. We had no idea that Brock was going to go crazy." His eyes are still downcast. "Josh, he had an underlying heart condition." I sigh.

"Why did you cut me like that? We are supposed to be in this together. In the worst time of your life, I am supposed to be the one who takes care of you and you wouldn't even speak to me. I had to have Cameron check on you daily to see if you were alright. In the end it was him that told me you weren't coming back any time soon and that I should return to America," he murmurs in a hurt voice.

"Josh," I whisper.

"It fucking killed me to get on that plane without you." His eyes tear up and guilt fills me as we touch foreheads and stay silent. There are no words for this moment, nothing that accurately describes the amount of remorse that I have, for my father's death...for leaving Josh. What was I thinking? For a long time, we lie silently together enclosed in regret, lost deep in our own thoughts and holding each other tight. I feel sick in my stomach. I should tell him the truth about his father.

"Joshua, we will never be apart again, I promise you. Our hard times are over with." I smile through the lump of guilt in my throat. He nods as if not believing me. "What about when Brock finds out? What are you going to do then?" he says in a flat voice as if not believing me.

"Josh, Brock has been a horrible cold brother to me since Dad died. He has no regard for my feelings. Even Mum has told him to wake up to himself. I have my mother's blessing to be with you and now, that your mum and dad are on board we will be ok, baby. We love each other, right?"

He nods.

"Let's just concentrate on today.... being happy today." I smile softly.

He kisses my lips gently. "Deal," he whispers. "I will spend every day ensuring a happy one for you." I smile and kiss him gently as a knock comes to the door.

"Come in," he snaps angrily at being interrupted.

Cameron walks into the room with a beaming smile. "Hello lovebirds." I smile and pull out of Joshua's embrace to lie on my back.

"Hello Doctor Love." I smile.

"Hmm, Doctor Love has a ring to it. Although I would rather be known as Doctor Multiple."

Joshua laughs out loud, "You really are a tool you know?" Cameron bites his lip to stifle a smile and winks at me.

"How are you feeling today?" he asks Joshua.

"Much better," he replies. Cameron picks up Joshua's file and starts to read it as he stands at the end of the bed. It still freaks me out that he is actually a qualified doctor. He reads something and frowns.

"What's Murph doing?" Josh asks.

Cameron is still frowning and looking down at the file answers. "He's busy working again. The media has got a hold of your overdose and the phones and website are apparently going crazy."

"I'm going outside to see Max," I whisper to give them some privacy.

Josh narrows his eyes at me and grabs my hand. "What's with the sudden interest in Max?"

I frown at him. "You can't be serious.... he's my bodyguard." Josh raises an eyebrow and continues to hold my hand in silent disapproval.

"Joshua, you are the one making him follow me around. He can go any time you like."

My eyes flick back to Cameron who is still frowning at Joshua's file. What is he looking at?

"Why are you frowning like that? Is something wrong?" I ask.

Cameron's eyes shoot up as if distracted. "Huh?" He has no idea what I just said. He is distracted.

"What's wrong, why do you look like that?" I repeat.

He bites his bottom lip in concentration. "No reason, just a lot on my mind. I need to go. I will catch you both later." He leaves the room in a rush.

I walk to the end of the bed and pick up the file. I wonder.... what was in the file?

Shit.

*Joshua Mark Stanton Blood type AB– DOB 12/11/87*

*Fuck.* Blood type. Was Cameron looking at Joshua's blood type?

Is he onto something? What type of blood does everybody else have? How do I find this information out?

"Go and find a naughty nurse outfit and come back in here and give me some sexual healing," Joshua says in a low sexy voice.

I smirk as I look up from his file. "Really, sexual healing? That's very eighties." I raise my brow in question.

He smiles and a nurse opens the door. "Mr. Stanton, we need to run some tests." I jump at the chance to exit unnoticed.

"I'm going to get a coffee, babe. Back in a moment," I stammer.

He kisses the back of my hand. "Take Max." I smile and give him a quick peck on the cheek.

Ten minutes later, I am sitting at the café consulting Doctor Google. Shit, this stuff is confusing. I decide to ring Mum.

"Hi Mum"

"Hello darling, how is our patient?" She smiles down the phone.

"He's going ok, thanks. Listen Mum I can't talk long. They need some blood at the hospital, and I was going to donate. Do you know what blood type I am?"

"Yes O+ like me," she answers. I stay silent as I think. Mmm. "Do you know what type of blood Robert has? He is not

here but I can ring him if he has the right type," I ask.

"Yes, he is O+ like me and you. What type do they need?"

"AB –" I snap. Holy shit, this is bad and my eyes close in a panic.

"Mmm, Tash, that's a very rare type. I think only a person who has A or B could donate."

I rub my face as I type double-time on my iPad.

"Do you know what type of blood Margaret has?" I ask.

She hesitates, "I think she's A. But I could be wrong. Do you want me to ring her?" she replies.

"No!" I snap. "I mean that's ok." Holy shit, what if she says something to Margaret? "Umm, I will see her when she gets back," I reply nervously. I need to get off the phone before I totally let the cat out of the bag.

"Ok love. Call me when you have more time to talk," she replies cheerfully.

"Ok, love you," I whisper.

"You too, love, goodbye." And with that she is gone.

I type in: can a woman with A blood and a man with O+ create a child with AB- blood?

The answer comes straight back.... Negative. Check paternity.

Fuck.... Cameron could know. I put my head into my hands on the table. This is a fucking disaster. I hate this. Do I tell Margaret that Cameron knows or at least I suspect that Cameron is suspicious? Is he suspicious? Or am I imagining this? Bloody hell, how did I get roped into this shit? Perhaps my mind is playing tricks on me? I stand and walk to the fridge and see Max standing outside the door waiting for me. He is on his phone. I open the door, distracted, looking at him and get out an Iced Coffee Milk. As I turn, I run headfirst into a man and drop my drink.

"Oh, I'm so sorry," I stammer. I look up and step back. This man is in a bad way, his whole face is bruised. Two black eyes, cut lips, broken nose. Jeez he must have had one hell of a car accident. He has red dreadlocks. Freaky looking.

He smiles and bows his head. "No problem."

I smile at Max who is now looking at me, shaking his head. Why am I so damn clumsy? Max shakes his head and laughs at me. Hmm, he's getting accustomed to my klutziness.

. . .

TWO HOURS later I am lying on Joshua's bed when Cameron comes in. "I'm heading off for the day. Do you want me to bring you anything from home?"

I stretch and stand. "I will come with you, Cam. I will sleep at the house tonight."

Joshua looks at me, mortified. "You don't want to stay with me?"

"Yes, I want to stay with you. I think it will be better if I stay at your house tonight. This looks bad," I reply.

He smiles shyly. "But we are married. It doesn't look bad at all. I sleep better with you."

I smile. He really is adorable.

"It doesn't look bad, Tash, just stay. No one gives a rat's ass here anyway." Cam smiles.

I frown. "Are you sure?"

"Positive," he smiles. He gives me a kiss and leaves us.

I have a burning hot shower and I have to say this is the most relaxed I have felt since before we separated. I feel like things are finally returning to normal. The hospital is finally dead quiet and still and our room is darkened and only dimly lit up by the side lamp. As I exit the bathroom Joshua's eyes follow me through the room as I walk over to the bed slowly. He holds out his hand for me, alone at last.

"I've been waiting for bedtime all day," he whispers.

I smile a shy smile. "Josh, we are in a hospital. Nothing can happen, what if a nurse comes in?"

"Then she will be in for one hell of a show," he replies softly as his eyes drop down my body and he gently cracks his neck. I feel my insides start to liquefy as he grabs my hand and pulls me onto the bed. He flicks the television on and spoons me from behind. He inhales my hair deeply. "I've missed these pajamas."

I smile. He really is easily pleased if checkered men's flannel pajamas do it for him. We lie in silence watching TV. His fingers lightly skim my body from behind, his lips dust up and down my neck, and he gently kisses my earlobe. I can feel the exchange of power happening moment by moment, inch by inch. His body gently dominates me from behind and as I feel his erection grow against my lower back, my body gently submits with want. Eventually, after half an hour of him touching me he turns me into his arms. I'm aching for him, nearly to the point where I can't lie still. He rolls me onto my back and slowly lifts my pajama top over my head and removes my pants while not breaking eye contact.

"Fuck, I've missed your body," he whispers as his large hands run freely over me and his eyes close at the contact. His tongue gently swipes through my mouth, his hand under my jaw. Holding me the way he wants me. This is when he sends me wild. Crazy with lust. When he takes me the way he wants me. Total control, total domination. His other hand pushes my legs apart and his strong fingers go directly to my wet center. He runs the backs of his fingers back and forth through my lips.

God, I've missed this, I've missed him. He cracks his neck hard and kisses me again, more urgent, harder. He slowly pushes one finger inside me as he twists his hand. We both groan as my heart rate reaches fever pitch. I'm not going to last, I'm so close to orgasm. Two then three fingers stretch my flesh and my legs fall wider open, seeking more. He twists me so we are lying on our sides. He is behind me and he lifts my top leg up toward my shoulder, my knee falls behind my ear. His strong fingers are plunging in and out of my body from behind. Our eyes are both closed. We are running on pure instinct.

His kisses turn aggressive over my shoulder and my body starts to ride up the bed as his hand turns almost violent. He grabs my hips and slams me back down the bed toward the penetration. Fuck, this feels...he's so good at this. He removes his fingers and changes the pressure completely by running the tips of his four fingers gently over my clitoris. I nearly jump off the bed. The sound of my wet arousal hangs thick in the air and my legs fall open as far as they will go. He kisses me gently, his tongue rimming around my lips. I can't take much more; I need to come. Like. Now. He brings his hand up and tenderly holds my face as he kisses me softly. This is how he drives me insane, the tempo change...hard and aggressive and then gentle and loving. When he is being hard on me, I crave the tenderness and then when he is being tender and loving I crave the hard dominance. I can't take any more. I try to move so I can mount him, but he stops me.

"Don't move," he snaps. I swallow as I pant and close my eyes. He continues the onslaught with his fingers from behind, his tongue mirroring his fingers. Taking everything I have. There isn't a doubt in either of our minds why we are so sexually suited. His body controls mine with such force that my body quivers with need. The harder he dominates, the higher my arousal level. He's the same, the more I submit the harder he gets.

"I need to taste you," he whispers.

"Josh, no. Not tonight, anybody could walk in. When we get home, baby. Not here." He closes his eyes and nods in understanding. His bottom arm is under my head and I am twisted so we are kissing over my shoulder. Actually, he's kissing, I'm lying here with my mouth open, way too distracted by what his body is doing to mine. He pulls his fingers slowly out and I groan at the loss. He rubs the palm of his hand over my swollen sex spreading my arousal and I think trying to calm himself as I lose all coherent thought. He slowly starts to stretch my lips open with his fingers. I lean my head back into his chest as he rubs his hard length through my creamy arousal. "Fuck, you feel good, precious. I'm going to come so hard inside you, baby. I'm aching for it." My mouth hangs open as he slowly feeds his large length into my sex. We both groan at the pressure. Holy shit I've needed this. His mouth falls to my neck and he sucks. My eyes roll back into my head as his hand comes across my body up to my breasts. His engorged length slides slowly in and out of me and his hands run from my clitoris to my hipbone to my breasts to my stomach. His open mouth slides from my mouth to my neck to my collarbone. Our kissing turns aggressive as our arousal hits fever pitch and he grabs my hipbone to bring me down hard onto his brutal length.

"You are such a hot fuck, precious girl. You turn me inside out, do you know that? I've fucking missed you," he growls into my ear.

If I could answer I would, but I can't...I'm in the pleasure dome, one where I can't think or speak. His hips start to pump at piston pace. His hands pulling me onto him with such force it's painful. My top leg is being held back by his large strong hands. He bends and kisses the side of my knee with an open mouth, his hard cock still turning me inside out with every deep plunge. He kisses me again and I can't hold it. I scream into his mouth and I lurch forward as an orgasm wave hits me like a train. He closes his eyes and holds himself deep and I feel his hot semen burn me from the inside out as his cock quivers as it empties. He hooks my top leg over his body and grabs my face and kisses me deeply. I can feel his heart beating so hard inside his chest. We both pant as we try to come off the high. Who am I kidding? I will never come off this high.

Joshua Stanton is too damn beautiful for words. We lie in comfortable silence as the perspiration sticks our bodies together, still slowly kissing. His body still inside mine.

"Josh," I whisper.

"Mmm."

"I can't live without you. I love you so very much."

He smiles softly.

"That makes two of us, Presh."

# 5

## Natasha

*I STRUGGLE TO BREAK FREE. The sound of Joshua groaning as they hit him echoes through the dark wet tunnel. Three men are holding him while three others are taking turns hitting him.*

*"Stop it! You're going to fucking kill him. Please let him go," I sob out loud...."Please, what do you want?" They start to kick him repeatedly in the stomach and I scream. "NO! You are going to kill him! Please, stop it!" I sob while I desperately fight to escape the two men holding me. They throw me onto the ground and one of them kicks me in the stomach. I scream in pain and I hear Joshua go crazy again as he tries to break free.*

*"Let her go," he screams. "Kill me.... just let her go. It's me you want."*

*They pick up a metal bar and hit him across the face and a cold metallic thud echoes through the space.*

*"Noooooooooo!" I scream.*

*"We are not letting her go. Who will we take turns in fucking with her gone? There are nine of us to please you know."*

*Joshua goes crazy. "I'll fucking kill you when I get free," he screams. "I swear to God if you touch her, you gutless pricks, you're fucking dead."*

*I look to the corner where Ben's dead body is slumped in the corner. I close my eyes, the sound, the sight.... the pain too much to bear.*

*They continually hit him until he slips into unconsciousness and my heart breaks.*

*Dear God, no!*

*One of them hits me hard across the face and I fall to the ground. They gather around and one of them unzips his pants.*

"Tash. Baby, wake up." He shakes me.

I scream as I sit up in a rush. Heart racing, my body is covered in perspiration.

"Jesus, Tash. What were you dreaming about?" Joshua grabs me in an embrace and pulls me into his chest as I sob.

The door opens and a bodyguard bursts in. "Is everything alright in here? I heard screaming."

"Natasha just had a nightmare. Can you give us some privacy, please?" Joshua says flatly, obviously annoyed at the intrusion.

"Yes, sorry." He leaves immediately. I cry into his chest as I shake in fear.

"It's ok, baby. I'm here. Don't be frightened," he whispers into the top of my head.

I continue sobbing.

"Were you dreaming about your father?" he asks in a defeated voice.

I shake my head. I don't want to say it out loud in case it makes it come true.

"Tell me sweetheart. What were you dreaming about?"

"I have been having the same dream over and over," I sob. "What dream?"

"They kill you." My chest heaves. "Who kills me?" he gasps.

I sob out loud again as I bring my face up to his. "They hold me and make me watch the men taking turns bashing you to death and then they gang rape me."

His expression drops. "Christ...it's not real, Tash. It's just a bad dream."

I pull back to look at him "I am scared it's a premonition, Josh. What if my dad is trying to warn me? It's so real, always exactly the same dream. They started two days after Dad's death."

He smiles sympathetically. "It's a nightmare, baby. Let's have a shower. You always feel better after a shower."

I nod nervously and let him help me to the shower. We stand in an embrace as I cry into his chest, and the fear eventually subsides as the water washes away my nightmare from hell.

"I'm scared, Josh," I whisper.

He gently kisses my face. "It's ok, baby, nothing is going to happen to me. You're safe now, I'm here."


I WAKE WITH A START, my heart is racing through an orgasm. Joshua is on top of me and inside me. He kisses me as he pulls out and rolls me onto my side to face him.

He smiles as he leans in and kisses me gently again.

"Good morning, Mr. Stanton," I sigh happily. "Helping your- self?" I smirk.

"You love it when I take you in your sleep."

I smile broadly at the beautiful specimen in front of me. It's true. I do love it when he takes me in my sleep. "Yes, but why do you love it so much?" I've never asked him before why it gets him so amped up.

He bites his lip as he contemplates his answer. "I don't know. I think that it's the way your body responds to mine, even when you're not conscious. You have no idea what a turn-on it is to know that your body wants mine. I don't know actually." He shrugs. "I think it's that I realize we connect on many different levels and the fact that you know about it and give me permission. I don't know what it is, but it's fucking hot."

"Have you ever done that to anybody else?" I ask.

He frowns at me. "Natasha, I don't fuck you while you sleep, I make love to you while you sleep. I've never made love to anyone, but you and I have definitely never stayed next to someone as they slept. What we have is a deeper connection. There is no way in hell I would want to do that with anybody. It's actually creepy thinking of doing that with someone else." He fakes a shiver.

I smirk. "And it's not creepy when you do it to me?"

He frowns. "No, I adore you. I love you. Nothing could ever be creepy between us." His eyes widen. "Do you think it's creepy?"

I smile. "No, Josh, I think it's beyond hot and it tells me how deeply I trust you."

His face drops.

I frown. "Why did your face just drop?" I question.

He takes my face tenderly in his hands. "Kiss me." I smile into him.

Knock, knock.

"Shit." Joshua spits. "Just a minute," he yells. I jump from the bed and sprint to the bathroom with him hot on my heels.

"Just get dressed," I snap. "I don't want them to know you are in the shower with me."

"No, I need a shower too. I smell like sex." He pushes me to the side and turns the shower on and dives in before the water heats up. I stand naked with my arms crossed looking at the beautiful sex god in front of me.

"What?" He smiles as he quickly soaps up.

"The nurses are going to think you're a nympho."

He smirks. "Then they would be right, wouldn't they?"

I smirk and in two minutes flat Joshua is dressed and heading out of the bathroom to answer the door. I take my time and twenty minutes later I emerge from the bathroom to find the doctor and Cameron in the room talking to Joshua. Cameron's eyes shoot up to me and he bites his lip to stifle his smile. Boy, this is uncomfortable. They know exactly what we have been doing.

"I'm going to get a coffee, Josh," I whisper uncomfortably.

His eyes lock on mine and he smiles a knowing smile. His eyes gently drop from my head to my toes and he runs his tongue over his bottom lip. I feel a familiar throb of arousal as his gaze burns holes through my clothes.

"Take Max, Presh. Can you get me and Cam one as well?" he says gently.

I nod and he holds out his hand for me. As I take it, he pulls me in for a quick peck on the lips.

Cameron rolls his eyes. As I am grabbing my purse there's a knock on the door.

"Come in," Cameron yells.

Ben sticks his head through the door. "Josh, there are two policemen here to see you."

Josh's eyes flick straight to me. I frown.

"Give me a minute," he replies. He turns to me, "Go and get the coffee, Presh. I will be about twenty minutes. Call your mum or the girls."

I smile and nod as I leave the room. He is trying to get rid of me. What in the hell is this about? Two policemen are waiting outside. Ben, along with Joshua's other two bodyguards, all enter the room after the police. I frown. That's weird, why do the bodyguards have to hear what is said. Actually, what is being said?

I turn to Max, "What's going on?"

"Let's go for a walk, honey," he sighs.

One thing that I am becoming increasingly aware of is that Max only calls me honey when he feels pity for me.

## Joshua

"This is Constable Mathews and Detective Stevens," Ben introduces the two policemen.

I shake both of their hands and stay silent as I wait for them to speak.

"Mr. Stanton, we have found your car."

Relief fills me. "Oh good. Is it a write off?" I reply.

The detective frowns at me. "It seems we have bigger problems than your car being stolen."

I frown, "What does that mean? Where was my car?"

Ben and the officer trade glances. "Your car was found parked in the parking garage of your offices."

I frown. "But why?"

"We think that Friday night was not just a random car robbery. We think it was supposed to be a premeditated hit."

"Hit?" Cameron interjects. "Why do you think that?"

"Because your Aston Martin is worth $220,000 and it was returned without a scratch."

I drop to sit on the bed as the information sinks in.

"That's ridiculous," spits Cameron. "Who in the hell would order a hit on Joshua?"

My eyes flick over to Ben. "Ben, can you go and make sure Natasha is ok. She's at the cafeteria."

He nods and leaves the room, understanding my fear. I don't really care if they order a hit on me. My fear is for Natasha. The only way to hurt me is to hurt her. Bile rises in my stomach.

"Let's go through Friday night's events again," the detective says.

I blow out a breath and nod. "I was at Willowvale and I decided to leave."

"What time was that?" he asks as he scribbles down some notes.

I shrug, "About ten."

"Where was your security?"

"They had gone to bed and I just needed to get home." My eyes flick to Cam and he gives me a small smile.

"Okay, what happened then?" he asks as he scribbles notes on a pad.

"I pulled in for gas and then when I went to pay, I was jumped by three men. We scuffled and then they got a hold of me and we fought a bit. I don't know for how long. The service station attendant must have called the police because a police siren came and then they all ran off and jumped in my car and took off."

The policeman smiles. "We watched the security footage. You gave two of them a hiding. Where did you learn to fight like that?"

I shake my head, "I cage fight for sport."

The detective raises his eyebrows, "I think that sport may

have saved your life. They had a gun, the guy at the back in the footage pulled it out just before the police came."

I run my hand over my face.

"A fucking gun," Cameron snaps. "This is bullshit, who in the hell would want him dead? You're the police. Do something about this. What are you going to do about this?"

I blow out a breath as my nerves hit a new level. "Peter, can you go and check on Natasha. Why is she taking so long?"

"Yeah, sure man." He leaves the room.

"Did you get a look at any of them?" the second police officer asks.

"No, only what I told you the other night. It was filtered light. One of them had dreadlocks. I think his hair was red."

"Yes, we saw that. Anything else you can think of?" I hunch my shoulders, "No."

"I would keep a close eye on your wife if I was you. Until we get this under control, she is not safe either."

I frown as my eyes flick to Cameron. "How do you know I am married?"

"It's on the front page of today's newspaper. Headlines read you married your sex therapist."

I drop my head to my hands. "This is a nightmare. How does this shit get out?"

The policeman shrugs. "You are in a hospital with hundreds of staff and visitors. It was only a matter of time. Don't go anywhere without your bodyguards and like I said I wouldn't let your wife out of your sight if I was you. If you think of anything, no matter how small, give us a call. I have given my business card to Ben."

I nod as I look at the floor while the policemen leave.

"What's Natasha going to say?" Cameron sighs. "Natasha

is not to know about this. Not a word," I snap. "Are you kidding?" Cameron gasps.

I shake my head. "No, I said no! She has been through enough, she lost her father and now she's been having nightmares where I get murdered. She had one just last night. I have never seen anyone so terrified. It took me half an hour to calm her down."

"Bloody hell. This is a total fuck up," Cameron snaps. "What the hell does she dream about?"

I sit on the bed as her fear runs through my mind. "She said it's the same dream every time. They have us underground in a wet tunnel. It's nighttime. Ben's body is slumped on the floor and she is tied up and forced to watch me get bashed to death by a group of men. Then they gang-rape her."

"Bloody hell, no wonder she's terrified." Cameron runs his hands through his hair. "We need to get Adrian in here."

I blow out a breath and nod, "Give him a call."

"Give who a call?" Adrian asks as he walks into the room with a beaming smile. I turn, smile and embrace him in relief.

He pulls back and frowns at me. "Ok...What's going on? Why are you cuddling me?"

Cameron holds his hand in the air in exasperation. "Where shall we start? Oh, I know, how about Joshua

nearly got murdered on Friday night in an ordered hit. Now the police think he and Natasha are in danger and Joshua doesn't want to tell Natasha because the poor petal is having scary dreams."

I glare at Cameron. "How about I shut that smart mouth for you," I snap. He fakes a smile.

Adrian's eyes widen. "How do we know it was a hit?"

"It seems my car was returned to the work parking garage on Friday night. The keys were on the passenger seat."

"My God," Adrian whispers as he slumps into the chair. "We also have another problem." He pulls his newspaper from under his arm. He opens it and shows me the front page, a huge picture of Natasha with the heading 'Joshua Stanton secretly marries his sex therapist'.

I angrily snatch the paper from him. It is a picture of Natasha and Max crossing the road out the front of the hospital. Natasha is laughing and looking gorgeous and Max has his hand in the small of her back guiding her across the street. The story reads:

---

*Joshua Stanton, the infamous wealthy LA playboy, has secretly married his Australian sex therapist. They met in Sydney on his recent stay after she treated him for his sex addiction. Natasha Stanton has rushed to his side from Australia after he took a cocaine overdose over the weekend. The handsome playboy who formerly dated Heidi Mills and Vanessa Shortland...*

---

I stop reading the dribble in front of me. "The fucking paparazzi, they just make this shit up," I snap. "This is just perfect, at a time when I need her to be in disguise, she's on the front of the fucking paper." I put my head into my hands. "What am I going to do? She has been through enough. I don't want her frightened," I sigh.

"What's with the nightmares?" Adrian asks.

"She's been having the same recurring dream where she

is tied up and forced to watch me get bashed to death and then they gang-rape her."

"Gang-rape? Christ," Adrian gasps.

"Let's not forget that they kill Ben," Cameron snaps. I nod and Adrian screws up his face. "You don't want to tell her?"

I shake my head. "Not yet. She's been through enough." Ben walks through the door.

"Where's Tash?" I snap.

"Talking to your mother. She's safe. Relax."

"Ben, I want the security doubled around Joshua and Natasha. Natasha is to have four bodyguards with her at all times," Adrian asserts.

This is why I love this man, he's a micromanager. He takes control of any situation and has the ability to make important decisions quickly. I smile, feeling better just having him here.

I look at Ben. "I want Max taken off guarding Natasha. You swap with him and I only want trusted long-term staff with her."

"Why? Max is the best bodyguard we have. He is more qualified than me. Why can't he guard Natasha?" Ben frowns.

"He just can't," I snap.

"Fuck off. Are you jealous?" Cameron spits.

I narrow my eyes at him. "Did you know that he has been staying in the house with Natasha? I am paying him to guard her, not cut my fucking grass."

Ben bites his lip to stifle his smile.

"Yeah, this is hilarious, Ben...you ass," I spit.

My phone rings and Cameron picks it up, glances at the screen and hands it to me, the name Amelie on the screen. I push reject and Cameron shakes his head.

"Have you had that conversation yet?" he asks.

I shake my head. "No, I haven't had time."

"How's that going to go?"

"How do you fucking think?" I snap.

Adrian shakes his head. "You, Stanton, are a tosser. You're jealous of her bodyguard, when you are the one who makes her have one. And now that she actually needs one, you want to take the best man off the job because you're insecure."

"I am not insecure. He's just too.... familiar."

"He's twenty years older than her. Grow up," Adrian replies flatly.

The door opens and Natasha breezes in. Her warm smile cuts through me. What if something happens to her because of me? I couldn't bear it. She sits next to me on the bed.

"What did the police want?" she asks.

"Umm...nothing. They were inquiring where I got the drugs from the other night."

Her eyes hold mine. She knows I'm lying but is staying silent while the others are in the room.

"Tash, Ben will be swapping with Max to guard you," I mutter. She frowns as I pick up her hand and hold it in mine. She looks nervously at Ben. "Ben, I don't mean to be rude, but I would rather stay with Max. I am only comfortable with Max."

Ben and Cameron both smirk at me. I narrow my eyes at them.

"Then Max can stay with you, baby, that's ok," Adrian interjects. "Now that you are in the States, Tash, you need more protection that's all. There is a nasty story in the paper today about you and you will be followed by photographers. They are really pushy. You cannot go anywhere without protection."

"What kind of story?" Her eyes widen as Adrian hands her the paper. She slumps into the chair to read it.

A nurse enters the room. "Nurse, please let the doctor know I am checking out this afternoon."

"Joshua," Natasha snaps. "Your treatment."

"Tash, I need to go home." She frowns at me.

"I am going to find the doctor." Cameron stands and leaves the room.

"Josh, I want you to do this drug rehab, it's really important."

"I know, Presh. I promise I will continue the treatment from home." My eyes flick nervously to Ben. "The pap has access to me in here, baby. We are safer in a more protected environment."

She rolls her eyes. "I think you are being a bit of a drama queen, Josh."

"It is safer at Joshua's house, Natasha. I will go and make arrangements for the transfer," says Ben as he leaves the room.

I pull her to lie down next to me on the bed and I hold her tight. "You ok, baby? That was a pretty awful nightmare you had last night."

She smiles warmly and kisses me, and her lips linger on mine. "The wake-up call I got has erased all bad memories, thank you Mr. Stanton."

I squeeze her tightly. "Good...Tash do you want to go travelling for a while? Take a couple of months off, see the world."

Her eyes widen. "You are serious about this? Could you take time off?"

"I don't see why not." I smile warmly.

"Oh, I have to go back to Australia this weekend. I need to be back at work on Monday."

My eyes widen, "Well that's not happening. I need you with me."

"Joshua, I am going back to resign and there is not a thing you can do about it. My boss has been so good to me and two other staff are on holidays and I am booked solid all week. I will come back in two weeks."

"I will come with you then. I am not letting you out of my sight." Bloody hell, this is a logistical nightmare.

The doctor enters the room. "Cameron has just explained the situation to me. I understand you are checking out."

"Yes, I have to go to Sydney on the weekend, Doctor, so I will just pick up my treatment over there."

"I'm afraid that won't be possible. You are unable to fly for at least two weeks, your heartbeat is too erratic. Let's not forget that you almost died three days ago. You will risk a heart attack at that altitude."

"Josh, I will just come back in two weeks. It will be okay," Natasha urges as she picks up my hand again.

"I will send a nurse in to put a drip in for a couple of hours to rehydrate you and then I will hook you up to an angiogram for an hour and if the results are all good, I will check you out this afternoon. Definitely, no flying for two weeks."

Natasha

It's four o'clock. Josh has been hooked up to a drip for three hours. I'm tired and I just want to get the hell out of here. I stand and stretch, the nurse pushes in the heart rate thingy and starts to stick things to Joshua's chest.

"I'm going to go to the bathroom outside in the waiting room, Josh."

He frowns and mouths the words, "Just go in here," as he gestures to his bathroom with his chin.

I smile and shake my head. "The private rooms outside are riddled with guards. I will just be a minute." He shakes his head apprehensively. "Be quick."

I smile and leave the room. I head through the lounge area and I see Max.

"Max, I think I want a coffee. Let's go for a walk."

He frowns. "You can't leave the room till the other guards get back."

"Where are they?"

"They have gone back to check Joshua's house and prepare for the transfer."

I roll my eyes. "This is ridiculous: prepare for the transfer.

This isn't an episode of bloody *Star Trek* you know."

He smiles. "I will go get the coffee. Do not leave this room."

I give him a salute. "Aye, aye captain." As he leaves the room, security buzz through.

"We have an Amelie Richards here to see Joshua Stanton." Max looks at me for approval and I nod as I head into the bathroom. *Great, bitchface is here.* I suppose it is better she comes here rather than to the house to see him.

I finish up in the bathroom and am washing my hands when she walks in.

"Hello Natasha." She smiles.

"Hi Amelie. Thank you for coming. He's in the room. Just go in."

"I didn't come here to see Joshua. I came to see you."

I frown. "Really, what about?"

"What has Joshua told you about him and me?" she replies flatly.

My stomach drops and my heart rate picks up speed. "What do you mean?"

"I mean exactly what I said. What do you think Joshua's and my relationship is?"

"That you are close friends," I whisper as dread creeps through me.

She tutts. "Did he tell you that we have been sleeping together since he got back from Australia?"

I stumble back from her in shock. "You're lying," I snap.

"Go ask him yourself. You see Joshua is confused. He thinks it is you that he wants but the reality is he can't let me go. We made passionate love as recently as Friday."

Pain lances through me as I step back from her in shock.

*That's five days ago.*

"I don't believe you!" I whisper.

"Natasha, I think it's time you realize the harsh truth. You cannot make him happy like I can. He is only with you out of obligation. Wake up and smell the coffee, dear girl. Joshua is in love with me."

# 6

## Natasha

I SCURRY out of the bathroom in a daze and find myself entering Joshua's room. The nurse is still in there adjusting his machines. He smiles warmly at me as I stand at the end of the bed, my face is blank and expressionless, and I fall into the chair against the wall as I keep staring at him in shock. This can't be true. I don't believe her. He frowns and puts his head on the side in a question as he looks at me. My eyes fall to the floor as I go over the words Amelie has just relayed to me: *He's only with you out of obligation. He loves me. We made passionate love as recently as Friday.*

The nurse smiles and leaves the room and he holds his hand out for me.

"Come and lic with me, Presh."

My heart stops, I stand and walk to the end of his bed. "Did you sleep with Amelie?" I breathe.

His face falls and he starts to pull the cannula out of the back of his hand.

"Natasha," he whispers.

"Did you or not?" I cry. He lunges for me and I jump back.

"You've been sleeping with her all along?" My eyes fill with tears.

"No!" He shakes his head. "So, she is lying?" I ask.

"Tash, baby. Listen to me."

"Answer the fucking question!" I scream. "She told me you're in love with her." I sob.

He shakes his head urgently. "No, Tash. I'm not. Listen to me." He rips the cannula out and starts to frantically try to remove the suction things attached to his chest. An alarm from the heart-rate monitor sounds through the room.

"*DID YOU?*" I scream.

"I love you, Natasha. I made a terrible mistake ... It was just once."

I step back from him in shock. Dear God.

"Tash, listen to me!" He struggles to break free from the machine. "Cameron. Get in here," he yells.

I turn to the door as adrenaline courses through my body. He lunges off the bed to grab me again but is held back by the wires on the machine that he can't remove. I dive away from him.

The door opens and Amelie walks in.

His eyes flick to her. "Get out!" Joshua screams.

I step back again. It's true, she was telling the truth. I look at her deadpan. "He's all yours," I whisper through my tears... and I run. Joshua dives for me. The machine alarms echo through the room and nurses come running from everywhere. I duck past them out the door and sprint for my life down the corridor.

"Natasha...Natasha, come back. Get the fuck out of here, Amelie!" I hear Joshua scream from behind me.

"Nataaaaashhhhhha."

"Where are the fucking bodyguards?" he yells at the nurse.

I run around the corner, dive into the waiting lift and push the button. I quickly look up at the numbers. Come on. Come on. The doors slowly close and I run my hands through my hair. Oh fuck, it's going up, wrong way. The lift stops at the next floor and two nurses get in. I step to the back. What am I going to do? What am I going to do? My heart is beating so hard in my chest. He will be going off his brain, I remember Max told me that security has gone back to his house. I need to get out of this hospital before they get back or they won't let me go, I will be cornered.

The lift stops on the next floor and I step out into the corridor. My eyes shoot around as I look for an exit. I'm panicked, I just need to get away. I see a sign for a fire exit, the stairwell. I open the door and start to sprint down the stairs two at a time as I sob uncontrollably. I desperately need to get out of here. He fucking slept with her and then he slept with me. After everything we have been through...he slept with her. I probably have AIDS now or some other STD. I dry-retch as the thought poisons me from the inside out as I keep running. I scramble for air as my lungs burn from the exertion. Finally, I hit the bottom and burst out the door. Sunlight beams onto my cold face and I feel a wave of relief hit me. Daylight at last. I run to the road like a mad woman and flag down a cab as I half run in front of it.

"Stop...please...Please, just stop," I cry. The tears run freely down my face as I pant in exhaustion.

The cabbie frowns at me and stops. "Get in. Are you alright?" His eyes shoot around as he looks to see who's chasing me. I dive into the backseat and nod nervously as I run my hands through my hair.

"Where to?" he asks.

I look at him in the rearview mirror and my eyes fill with tears again. Where to? I don't even fucking know. Away from him...and his... deceit.

Shit. I don't have my purse. I quickly feel my pockets. I have twenty dollars coffee change from this morning.

My eyes dart around. "How far is the closest McDonalds?" "Two blocks around the corner," he says flatly with his wrist draped over the steering wheel.

I nod nervously. "Take me there."

He nods, puts on the blinker and pulls into the traffic and moments later we arrive at my safe haven. I look around frantically as I walk in and my phone rings and I jump.

Joshua... his name lights up the screen. My heart sinks and I start to sob uncontrollably. Everything I thought I knew is a lie. It's not real. I run to the bathroom and put my phone on silent. It rings again. Oh shit... stop fucking calling me, I sob again. I burst into the cubicle and throw the lid down. I sit and put my head into my hands. My foot taps double time as I think. The phone rings again. I press reject. Fuck, what am I going to do? My passport and bag are back in the room. My phone rings again. I instantly reject it. I stand, turn and vomit into the toilet. The phone rings again. I press reject instantly. It beeps a text.

**Baby. Where are you? It's not how it looks.
Please. You are not safe alone**

I sob into my hands. Not safe, what does that mean? Nobody could hurt me as much as you have.

**Natasha, please.**
**You have no money.**

My lip quivers as I realize the sick truth: he is right. But if I go back, he is going to feed me some bullshit story. Lie some more. Amelie can fucking have him, they deserve each other.

**Please, Natasha. I'm frantic.**
**I love you more than anything**

I stand and start to shake my hands. Should I go back? Maybe I should just listen to him? *It was just once.* I cry out loud as the pain lances through my chest. Once is one too many times, asshole.

**Natasha, please tell me you are alright.**
**Where are you?**

I pull my feet up into a fetal position. My phone beeps a message. I look at the screen. It's Max.

**Natasha, it's me.**
**Let me come get you**

Can I trust him? I put my hand over my mouth as I think. He texts again.

**Where are you?**
**I will not tell him.**

I stand as I exit the stall and start to pace. I catch sight of myself in the mirror. Bloody hell, I look like something from a Halloween movie. Makeup is smeared all over my face.

**Natasha, trust me.**
**You have my word.**

Fucking hell. What am I going to do? My hands shake as I put them over my mouth to think. My phone beeps again. Joshua.

**Tash, I'm begging you.**
**Come back.**
**Let me explain**

I grab my head in my hands. How can you explain having sex with someone else? There is no explanation. The harsh reality is that while I hit rock bottom on the other side of the world, after murdering my father, he was making passionate love to another woman. A woman he swore he had no feelings for. A woman who I know he loves and could no longer resist.

A text beeps. It's Max.

**Natasha, listen to me.**
**He is tracking your phone as we speak.**
**You need to tell me where to meet you.**
**I have your passport and ID with me.**

Holy shit. He's tracking my phone. Why does he have to be so damn smart? Fuck, Fuck, Fuck. I shake my hands as my body courses with adrenaline.

I text.

**I need to get back to Australia**

He replies.

**I know, honey.**
**He has men on the way to the airport.**
**He's beside himself.**
**Are you sure you want to do this?**

I text.

**He's been sleeping with Amelie**

He replies.

**I'm not sure if that's true.**

I text back.

**Forget it. I don't want your help.**

He replies.

**Meet me at the Greyhound bus station**
**1716 E 7TH Street, Los Angeles**
**Take out your sim card**
**and put it in the trash.**

Holy crap. Sim card in the trash. What do I need from my phone?

I quickly run to the counter and ask the attendant. "Have you got a pen, please?"

She smiles and nods. "Sure." Her eyes scan my face and I can see her brain ticking at my frantic appearance.

I quickly take it and copy the address from Max's text onto the back of my hand. And write down Bridget and Abbie's phone numbers. I hand back the pen. "Thank you." My stomach fills with dread as I remove the sim card and put it into the trash. I then turn and, running on total autopilot, walk straight out the door and hail a cab.

## Joshua

Natasha's haunted eyes search mine, the door opens and we both look in its direction. Amelie walks in.

"Get out!" I scream.

"He's all yours." Natasha cries as her face falls.

I lunge for her as she dives out of the way. "Natasha... Natasha, come back." She bursts out of the door and runs down the corridor.

The heart-rate monitor starts to scream as the nurses burst through the door. "Get the fuck out of here, Amelie." She looks at me in shock. "Where the fuck are the body-guards?" I scream at the nurses.

"What the hell is going on with you? You're acting crazy," the nurse snaps.

"Unhook me...please hurry." I glare at Amelie. How could she do this to Natasha?

"And so she runs again," Amelie whispers as she folds her arms in front of her.

My anger hits a new level. "So help me God if you don't get out of my sight I'm going to fucking kill you!" I scream and the nurses gasp at my threat. I am finally unhooked and run down the hall looking for her. I'm frantic, and my heart rate is going through the roof. I find myself close to tears as I run up and down the corridor desperately searching the rooms for my love. She's hurt...and it's my fault...again. The lift opens and Cameron walks out. He frowns as he sees me shirtless frantically running down the hall.

"What the hell are you doing?" he frowns.

I put my head into my hands. "Amelie told Natasha. She made it sound like I was in love with her."

Cameron's eyes widen. "Where's Tash?"

"I don't know. She ran off before I could explain. She's alone and she has no money. This is my worst fucking nightmare. She has been gone for ten minutes."

"Have you called her?" Cameron asks.

My eyes widen. Shit, why didn't I think of that? I run back to the room to retrieve my phone. Amelie is sitting on the bed.

"Why are you still fucking here? I told you I want nothing to do with you. I told you that on Friday night," I scream.

"Joshua. You love me, I know you do," she cries.

"No, I don't, you're delusional." I shake my head and dial Natasha's number as Cameron walks into the room.

"I've had enough of you. What a bitch you are. How could you do that to Natasha?" Cameron yells.

It rings out and I start freaking out. Pick up. baby... please, pick up, my heart starts to thump through my chest. "Where are the guards? Where's Max?" I yell

Cameron shakes his head as he grabs Amelie by the arm. "I said get out."

"I only listen to Joshua," she snaps as she rips her arm from his grip. I dial the number again... it rings out again.

What am I going to do? My glare turns to Amelie. When

Tash comes back, I do not want her here. Max walks through the door with three coffees.

"Here we go." He smiles.

My eyes widen. "Where is Natasha?"

He frowns. "When I left, she was in the bathroom. Is she not here?"

My anger turns back to Amelie. "I am going to say this once and once only. Get out of my room, get out of my life, and get your ass out of my horse farm. You no longer work for me. I never want to see you again."

"Joshua, no," she cries. "We love each other. Don't let her come between us."

I screw my face up in disbelief. "I don't love you. How many times do I have to tell you that? You forced yourself onto me on Friday night and when I realized what the hell was happening, I pushed you off me. I'm beyond mortified at what happened between us. I'm in love with Natasha.... and now you've fucked that up too. If anything happens to her, I swear to God, I will strangle you!" I scream.

She starts to cry. "Enough of the waterworks, bitch. Just go," Cameron snaps.

"Where the hell is Ben?" I yell at Cameron. He runs his hands through his hair in frustration.

I start texting Natasha as Cameron grabs Amelie by the arm and pulls her out of the room. I walk over to the window. Tash... baby. Please come back. I look on the chair and I see her bag. I rush to it and realize her purse is inside. She has no money. Dear God.... where is she?

"What the hell is going on?" Max asks.

"She told Natasha a bunch of lies and now she thinks I have been sleeping with Amelie and she's run off. She has no money. She's alone and she's not safe in this city." I quickly pull on some clothes. "I'm going looking for her. Call the others. Get them back here now. I want her found."

"Joshua, you can't go out there without protection," Max snaps.

"Are you kidding me? She thinks I have been sleeping around on her. You know how emotional she is. She will be freaking out somewhere. Get your ass into gear and find her. I told you not to leave her alone. Where were you?" I run down the hall and start to text her again as I wait for the lift.

Cameron is hot on my heels. "I will go down. You go up," he asserts. The lift opens and the four bodyguards come out.

"Where in the hell have you been? Natasha is missing!" I scream.

Ben's face drops. "What?"

"We had a misunderstanding, and she has run off."

"Did you track her phone?"

Why didn't I think of that? I run back to the room to grab my laptop and see Max texting someone. "Is that Natasha?" I ask in desperation.

"No, I was looking up the hospital security system so we can check the surveillance tapes."

"Good thinking." I start to type double time, initiating a track on her cell. My heart is in my chest. Please...please, Tash, pick up. I call her again...no answer.

Adrian walks through the door, smiling. "Hey, I brought you coffee."

My eyes flick up to him. "Do you have your laptop with you?"

He frowns. "Yes, in the car. Why?"

I drop my head in shame. "I need it to find Natasha."

"What do you mean?" He puts the coffee down so hastily it spills. "Where is she?"

"Amelie told her that I slept with her and Tash has freaked and taken off."

"You slept with Amelie!?" he gasps.

I drop my head. "Sort of."

"What the hell does that mean? You can't sort of sleep with someone, you idiot!"

I nod as I type. "It just happened and then I realized what I was doing and I stopped it midway."

"You are the biggest fuckwit I know. Why in the hell would you give that stupid bitch ammunition against you?" He sighs as he runs his hands through his hair in frustration.

I keep typing.

"She won't come back. You've done it this time. She will never forgive you." He shakes his head in disgust.

"Shut the fuck up and get your computer!" I yell as my heart starts to speed with panic.

He runs out of the room. Cameron comes through the door and throws me a piece of paper. "This is the hospital security system. I brought my laptop for you." He throws it onto the bed.

"Thanks. Cameron, what if those people have her? What if she is danger?" I stammer nervously.

Cameron puts his hand on my back. "I thought you were going to tell her. She would have understood if you just had told her."

My lip quivers in regret. "How do you tell someone you love that you had sex with someone else? I tried. A couple of times I tried, but the words wouldn't come out of my mouth."

"They came out of Amelie's mouth easily enough though," he says, void of emotion.

"I thought...," I sit back and put my head into my hands. "This is all my fault."

"You are an...," he shakes his head, "imbecile."

Max walks back into the room. "I'm going to go outside on the street and ask a few questions. See if anybody saw anything."

"I don't think she would have left the hospital. She has no money on her. I am tracking her now. I will hack the security system to check the exits and see if she left. This hospital is so huge. How in the hell are we going to find her?" I say, defeated.

Max walks over and puts his hand on my shoulder. "She will be ok. She's tougher than you think. When she calms down, she will hopefully come back."

My eyes meet his. "She doesn't deserve this, Max. I've totally messed up. It just happened. I didn't mean to hurt her. I thought we were broken up. She left me."

He gives me a sympathetic smile and nods. "I know. Shit happens." With that he leaves the room.

Adrian runs into the room and starts to set up his computer on the table.

I quickly start to hack the hospital security on his computer as I track her phone on mine. My heart is in my throat...Where are you, Tash?

Ben comes rushing in as I crack the security code and he starts to watch the replays of the last twenty minutes on all doors of the hospital. I send the immediate visual to Adrian's laptop. Once again, I try to text Natasha.

> Natasha, please. We need to talk.
> It's not how it looks.
> I love you.

Why isn't she returning my call? What if she is in danger?

She is so trusting. She would go with anyone to try and get away from me without any money. I should have told her about the attack. I should have told her about Amelie. Regret slices through me...she deserves better. Amelie. What a bitch, she has turned this totally around to make Natasha think that I am in love with her. It looks as though I have been sleeping with Amelie all along. I close my eyes and put my hand over my mouth as I wait for the track to kick in. My God, please be ok, please come back to me.

Ben gasps from the other side of the room. "What is it?" I ask.

"We have a bigger problem," he says.

I frown. "Not possible. Natasha running off takes the cake." Cameron walks over to Ben and watches his screen. "Hell! Joshua, get over here."

I walk over to see what they are looking at and watch the footage that Ben is replaying. Two men walking into the hospital. One with short dark hair and an arm cast, the other a man with red dreadlocks and two black eyes entering the hospital. Horror dawns.

"How long ago was this?" I rub my hands through my hair.

Ben pushes some buttons and the tape rewinds. "Thirty minutes."

"What! Holy shit. They have her. That's them, two of the dudes from Friday night."

"Calm down, you don't know that. This could be coincidental," Ben asserts.

Adrian runs back into the room. "Any sign?"

"It is not fucking coincidental. Call the police, Adrian," I yell frantically

"Huh, what's going on?"

"The guys that attacked Joshua on Friday night are in the hospital. We just saw them on the CCTV footage. Call the police," Cameron stammers.

Adrian's mouth drops open. "They are here now to... hurt you... Like in this hospital? Do these kinds of people do this kind of thing in a public place?" he stammers, wide eyed.

Ben shrugs as he continues to watch the screens.

Adrian dials the police. "Hello, I would like to speak to Detective Johnston, please. Hurry, it's urgent."

"Josh, I have her," Ben snaps.

We all run back to his screen and he hits replay. It's a fire escape, the door bursts open, and she runs out. She's crying... actually, she's hysterical, gasping for air. She looks around frantically and runs for the road. Our eyes are all locked onto the horror opening before us. My heart sinks again. Look at her. She's openly devastated...what have I done? She runs in front of a cab and it stops, and she dives into the back seat. It slowly drives away. My head drops in shame as my heart rips in two. The only woman in the world I love is the only woman in the world that I hurt. What in the hell is wrong with me?

My computer beeps and I rush back to it. It's an aerial shot and a red cross shows where her phone is. I quickly scribble down the address. "She's at McDonald's just two blocks away. Hurry." Ben, Cameron and I run for the door.

"What will I do?" Adrian asks while still waiting on the phone.

"Wait here for the police. Keep the door locked."

"What if the hit guys come and get me?" he shrieks.

I shake my head in disgust. "It's hit men, not hit guys. Wimp. Keep the door locked."

"This isn't funny, Stanton," he yells as I run down the hall.

## Natasha

I sit in the back of the bus shelter, curled in a ball in the corner chair, my legs tucked under my body. I know if Max has betrayed me and Joshua turns up, I will have no choice but to go with him. But what choice do I have? I don't know who to trust anymore.

At this point in my life if I can't trust Max, I really have no one on my side. I feel like a vulnerable child, so lost and home-sick. The tears run freely down my face as the reality hits home. My worst fear has become my reality. I know he loves her, I felt it in the barn that day. She said that he was with me out of obligation. Is that true? My mind goes back to when we started hooking up. *I can't be monogamous, so I guess it's not fair.* Why did I think he was different to other men? Why did I think I could turn the ultimate player into husband material? My mind goes over our relationship so far. I have always been the pursuer; it has always been me. I am an idiot; how did I not see this coming? I even had to bribe him with sex to be monogamous while he was in Sydney and that didn't even work.

My memory brings forth the prostitute that Abbie calls TC which is short for tunnel cunt. I sob out loud as I realize he didn't even tell me he loved me until I told him I hadn't slept with anyone else. Amelie is right; he is with me out of obliga-tion and even if he's not I am definitely not strong enough to deal with this at the moment. I need time to think. Was he really with me out of guilt? He thinks he wants me...but deep down is he really in love with her? Do they share a bond that I can't compete with? They have common interests, and they are close friends, companions.

He and I share amazing sexual chemistry, but we fight like cat and dog. I hate horses, know nothing about computers and if I am honest with myself, I want to stay living in Australia. We were never going to work. I just wish I had never killed my father in pursuit of the ultimate happiness. Joshua's unobtainable love. I just need to get home and forget I ever met this destructive man. They say everything in life happens for a reason. What in the world could be the reason for the amount of hurt I have endured in the last two months? What have I done that is just so bad that it deserves this kind of punishment?

Max walks through the double doors and I half expect to see Joshua behind him, but he's not. Max has stayed true to his word. I sit still as he walks over to me.

"Come on, crybaby. Up," he whispers.

I smile as I shakily take the hand, he is holding out for me. He pulls me into an embrace, and I burst into full blown sobs. I hate it when people are nice to you when you are on the edge, it makes you fall apart. I stand for a minute in his arms crying hysterically.

"Tash, let's go back. Try and work this out with him. He loves you. He's frantic," he whispers into my hair.

I shake my head. "He has been sleeping with Amelie," I sob. "Honey, you left him. Remember. I don't think he was sleeping with her all the time. I think it was just one time from what I heard."

"What did you hear?" I sob.

"He was screaming at her and telling her that he loved you and that he was going to kill her if she didn't get away from him."

I start to really sob. "What was she doing?"

"She was crying, and then she went outside, and Cameron and she had a big fight. When I was leaving Adrian had asked the bodyguards to escort her from the building."

I cry again, out of pity for her. I put my head into my hands and slump back into the chair. Maybe he does love her, and she knows it and yet he is denying them a future together out of obligation to me. This is my worst fucking nightmare. He's sacrificing his own happiness to give me mine.

"Get me back to Australia, Max, I need to get out of here.

This isn't my happy ever after I dreamt about." "But Tash."

"No... are you going to help me or not, because if not you can fuck off right now too!"

He smirks. "Really, fuck off?"

I smirk back. "Basically."

"So, you want me to basically fuck off." I smile through my tears as I nod.

"I will go and buy us some bus tickets to another state and then we will get on a plane back to Australia. But I want you to call Joshua and tell him you are safe first."

My eyes widen with horror. "I am not calling him Max; he will just talk me around. I have no resistance against him. Please, you text him and tell him you are coming with me and that I'm safe."

He rubs his face in frustration. "Tash, you are asking too much of me. I will lose my job."

"Please, Max, I'm begging. I need your help. I have no other options."

His eyes hold mine as he thinks. "Let me buy the tickets and then we will go for a walk and text him before we dump the sim." An hour later we have caught a cab to the other side of town and Max takes out his phone. He blows out a heavy breath as he types the text.

**I have found her.**
**She's safe.**

He rubs his forehead in frustration and a text bounces immediately back.

**Thank God.**
**Where are you?**
**I will come and get you.**

"Natasha, honestly. Can't you just talk to him? He will never forgive me if I do this. Joshua has been very good to me," he urges. "Please, Max, he's confused and is only with me out of obligation. He just wants me to be safe and in time this is what is best for him. He will eventually understand." My lip quivers with unshed tears again.

**I'm sorry.**
**She won't come back.**
**I am taking her home to Australia.**
**I will call you when we land.**
**Once again, I'm really sorry.**

With that he pulls his phone apart, takes the sim out and throws it into the bin. He looks at me solemnly. "Our bus to San Diego comes in two hours. From there we will get a plane to Honolulu and then fly direct to Sydney. I hope you know what you are doing, Natasha. Are you sure you won't regret this decision?"

My eyes fill with tears as pain lances my heart. "Every day," I whisper.

# 7

---

**Natasha**

"TASH, PUT UP YOUR SEAT," I force my bleary eyes open. "We are in Sydney, honey."

I nod gratefully, unable to speak. Only five days ago I boarded a flight to LA filled with such hope, such joy in my heart. Now I am returning empty and tired. I am emotionally exhausted. I have nothing left.

AN HOUR LATER, I stare out the window in silence as Max maneuvers his Audi through the city. We are both lost in thought. What am I going to tell work? Where do I start? I fell in love with my cousin who turned out not to be my cousin, murdered my beloved father and left my so-called boyfriend. He then took a drug overdose because he may be a cocaine addict and he nearly died so I went to him and then found out he is sleeping with the other woman he's in love with. This is like the world's worst James Bond film...on steroids. I frown as I summarize the events so far. I am so being punked, where are the fucking TV cameras? They are going to think I am the world's biggest loser...and guess what? They're right, I am. We park out the front of my building and Max parks the car.

"I'm going to text him now." He pulls out a phone we have just stopped and purchased. I swallow and nod as he starts to type.

**We are out the front of Natasha's house now.**
**She's home safe**

He pushes send and blows out a breath. We both sit still, waiting for a response. It beeps a message.

**You're fired**
**Another guard will take over in three days.**
**I am giving you one month's notice**

Max closes his eyes in regret and my eyes fill with tears as the lump in my throat burns. "I'm sorry, Max. I had to get home. I couldn't stay there with him," I sob.

He nods but doesn't speak. He gets out of the car and retrieves our things, and we head upstairs. As we get to the front door, we hear a noise inside and Max pushes me behind him. He holds his finger to his mouth signifying silence.

I roll my eyes. "You should take up acting you know, you really are good with the dramatics," I mutter under my breath.

He bursts open the door like in an episode of *NCIS*. Mum, Bridget and Abbie are all lying on the lounge and scream in fright. Mum falls off the lounge in fear. "Shit!" she screams.

I laugh out loud. Honestly, what has my life come to... this is just totally fucked up.

"What the hell!" Abbie yells. "Are you trying to frighten us to frigging death Max?"

He relaxes. "Sorry." He gives a stifled smile.

"How did you guys know I was coming home?" I mutter flatly. "Joshua called me," Mum says as she pulls me into an embrace.

I pull back to look at her face. "Joshua called you. Did he tell you what happened?"

She smiles sympathetically. "Yes, love, he did. Can you call him? He's distraught, Natasha."

I screw up my face. "Did he tell you he slept with Amelie?" She nods again. "Yes."

My eyes flick to Bridget and Abbie.

"Natasha, you left him. He thought you weren't coming back," Bridget sighs.

"What? You're on his side? You're taking his side?" I frown as I pull out of her embrace. I need support, not a fucking lecture.

"No, love, there are no sides. But I know Joshua has had just as hard a time as you and I understand. We all understand. He's suffering too, Natasha," Mum says as she rubs my arm.

I stand still in shock as my eyes hold hers. I can hear my heartbeat in my ears as my anger hits a crescendo.

"Get out! All three of you. Get the fuck out! You may condone my boyfriend playing up on me, but I don't. And I never will." I storm to the bathroom and lock the door.

I run the water as hot as I can stand it, get in and sink to the bottom of the shower as silent acid tears roll down my face and the distinct taste of betrayal burns my stomach and lines my mouth.

· · ·

AN HOUR AND A HALF LATER, I leave the steamy bathroom to find the girls all lying on my lounge watching *True Blood*. The girls are filling Mum in on the storyline, which she doesn't seem to be getting. Hmm. I walk past them in silence and into my kitchen to make a cup of tea. Shit, I don't have any bloody milk. I open the fridge to find it stocked with groceries.

"Who went shopping?" I yell from the kitchen.

"I did," yells Abbie.

"Thanks," I reply flatly.

"Does that get me out of the bad books?" she yells again.

I narrow my eyes. "Just," I snap. "Does anyone want coffee?" I ask.

"Yes, I do. Milky Milo actually," calls Bridget.

"Can I have one of those Latte Sachet thingies?"

Abbie yells. "I want a chai latte, or do you have any lemon tea?"

I roll my eyes. "Fuck off, this isn't a cafe. I'm serving coffee, plain fucking coffee! If you don't like it leave."

I hear them all giggle. *Bitches.*

Ten minutes later, I walk into the lounge room with a tray of coffees, they all take them in silence and smile.

The thing is, I know that they know that I'm a donkey on the edge. But what they don't know is that I am so on the edge, I don't even care anymore. Anyone who messes with me tonight is going down.

"Where's Max?" I ask.

"We gave him the night off to go and see his girlfriend. We are going to stay with you for a couple of days."

I roll my eyes. "Can you keep your *Joshua sleazebag loving* mouths shut?"

They all stifle a smile and nod.

"Good, then fast forward it to the Alcide bits. Only Jo Manganiello can get me out of this funk. And nobody talk, I'm not in the mood to listen to your shit."

The three of them exchange small smiles and lie back in comfortable silence.

I WAKE to the sound of the jug boiling and Mum talking to Max, toaster popping, and Bridget and Abbie talking about some boring subject on a way too high decibel. I blow out a breath. How is it that the rest of the world is just carrying on as normal when my world is literally crashing around my feet? I feel different today...I'm angry. So angry, at myself mostly. I am a psychologist, and I ignored every warning sign. Went against everything I preach in order to hold a man that was never actually mine to hold. I was totally delusional. Joshua Stanton is not my happy ending; he is not my soul- mate as I once previously thought. What a load of shit that term is...soulmate. I don't even believe in that word anymore.

He has brought me nothing but heartbreak and you know

what? It's time to grow up and get on with it. I need to pick myself up and dust myself off. My heart is safe as long as I am away from him... so that's how I am going to keep it. I'm done. I get up and walk out into the lounge room.

"Hi love, how are you today?" asks Mum

I smile. "Better. Max, you don't need to guard me anymore. Joshua and I are finished so I am not in danger of being stabbed or something equally ridiculous. I'm going to the gym. Go back to your girlfriend's house," I announce confidently.

He narrows his eyes at me. "Natasha, I am not leaving you unaccompanied until I get the go ahead, so you can forget the spoilt brat routine. I'm not copping it," he snaps.

Abbie bites her lip to stifle a smile. "You should use that as a pickup line, Max. It sounded totally hot."

He shakes his head in frustration. "I agree actually, Abbs." Mum laughs.

"God...you girls are ridiculous," he sighs.

Two hours later, we have been to the gym. Max worked out with me so that was...different. I want to call into work to pick up my laptop. I have some patient notes to go over before the court case I am going to next week.

We walk through reception and I smile at our secretary. "Hi Belinda, I just need to get my laptop from my office."

"Oh, you're back already. I thought you were away till Sunday." She raises her eyebrows in question.

I fake a smile. "No, got back last night." I grab my laptop and am walking out of the office with Max when Nicholas Anastas walks out of Henry's office. I stop dead in my tracks. Lordy Lord, he is one delicious man, once again I am stunned to silence.

His eyes light up when he sees me. "Hello ... Natasha, isn't it?" I hunch my shoulders like a juvenile delinquent. Holy shit, he remembered my name.

"I was hoping to see you today." He smiles.

"You were?" I smile as my brain turns to mush.

"Yes, can I have a private word?"

My eyes widen. "Of course, come into my office." Max frowns at me. "It's ok, Max, I know this man."

Nicholas frowns at our exchange. "Why are you so heavily guarded?" he asks as we walk into my office.

I shake my head in embarrassment. "My boyfriend...ex-boyfriend is a little on the protective side."

He nods. "Was that your boyfriend I met at the restaurant that day? Joshua Stanton."

I nod glumly. "Yes, that's him." *Fucking scumbuckett.*

"Oh, right. So, you had another man with you, Adrian Murphy." I smile, oh my God, I know where this is going."

"Yes." I can't hold the smile that is splitting my cheeks.

He looks around in embarrassment. "I am going to America for a couple of weeks and I wondered if I could get his number off you. I thought we might hook up."

I give him a resigned smile as I frown. How do I put this? "Umm, Adrian...isn't really the kind of guy that hooks up."

He frowns. "Sorry, that came out wrong, I meant catch up." He raises his eyebrow as he contemplates asking me a question. "Not that kind of guy, hey?" he adds with a trace of a smile on his lips.

I smile broadly as I picture the beautiful Adrian. "Adrian is a romantic, he believes in love. Trust me, he doesn't hook up with random people."

I can almost see his brain ticking as he licks his scrumptious lips. His eyes hold mine with renewed determination. "So... can I have his number then?"

Hmm ok, I'm going to make Adrian a little hard to get.

Right, what would Abbie do in this situation?

"Look, I don't know, he doesn't like me giving his number to anyone. I get asked for it a lot." I inwardly cringe, oh boy was that too cheesy?

He nods and passes me his phone. "Call him. See what he says." I smile as I look at his hand outstretched with his phone in it. Determination in a man is so damn hot.

"No, I am not calling him on your phone because then you will have his number in the call register." I smirk.

He smiles as his ploy to trick me is uncovered. "Touché," he whispers as he raises an eyebrow. He passes me his business card. "Call him tonight and then call me back and tell me what he said."

Hmm... so dominant. So bloody sexy. "Why don't I just tell him to call you?"

"I'm pretty sure we both know if we leave it up to him, I won't be getting a call anytime soon." He smirks.

I scrunch up my face in uncomfortableness. "I wouldn't take it personally. He doesn't call anybody back." God... I should shut up now, I'm blowing it.

He nods. "Yeah, I get it. I will speak to you tonight." He smiles and leaves my office.

I blow out a breath that I didn't even realize I was holding. If Adrian doesn't go out with him, he's crazy. That man is frigging hot. I regain my composure and leave my office. "Ready to go?" I smile at Max.

He nods and we leave the building. Suddenly cameras start flashing and two men start to scream. "Natasha Stanton, is your husband going to make a full recovery?" Huh?

"Is your husband still a sex addict, Mrs. Stanton?"

What the hell? My horrified eyes meet Max's.

"Is he still currently in rehab, Mrs. Stanton?"

Max steps in front of me and holds out his arm to shield me, obviously much more accustomed to this than me. We make a run for his car with them chasing us. This is ridiculous, is this really what the world has come to? How could anyone be interested in this trivial nonsense?

"Is your husband a sex addict and a cocaine addict, Mrs. Stanton?"

I get into the passenger seat of Max's car and he speeds away. He looks into the rearview mirror to check we are not being followed.

"Shit, that was intense," I whisper to Max wide-eyed.

He nods. "I was wondering how long it would take for them to find you. Just make sure you don't give them a reaction when they ask you any questions. It just amps the assholes up."

"I would really like to answer their questions with 'yes, he is a sex addict, possibly a cocaine addict and a total adulterer prick and I'm not his fucking wife, asshole'. Not even close," I snap as I throw my handbag into the backseat.

He smirks at me. "Tough." He smiles.

I rearrange my cardigan and fold my arms as my anger rises again. I can't believe I am now being followed, by his paparazzi. For his mistakes. This has got to take the cake.

"I am going to call Joshua and tell him you need extra protection for a while." Max mutters while watching the road, and the wipers come on automatically as it starts to sprinkle rain.

My heart sinks. I wish I could call Joshua. I would dearly love to hear his velvety deep voice. I miss him... already. My sad eyes stare out the window; this is so unfair. He has made this painful bed for me and now unfortunately I have to lie in it...alone.

"You can tell him that you are the only bodyguard I will have, or he can forget it."

Max's eyes flick to me. "I'm not telling him that, you should call him if you have something to say."

I fake a smile. "Nice try, Max, I am not calling him. I am not texting him and I am definitely not thinking about him. If you don't tell him that then I won't have a bodyguard at all. I don't care, it's up to you."

"Natasha, you have cost me my job already. Do not start pulling your two-year-old tantrums now, because I won't stand for it," he snaps.

I narrow my eyes as my temperature rises. Now even Max is

pissing me off. Actually, is there anything in the world that doesn't piss me off? I nearly punched the screen on the treadmill today when it wouldn't give me my calories burned. I have some serious anger issues going on. It will be better when I get back to work next week, I just need to keep busy.

## 8

Natasha

I'M CUT. So deep that I can feel myself bleeding out, gasping for air... for life. If I was hooked up to a heartrate monitor it would show the weakening of my heartbeat every hour, every minute without him. The sound of the beep would be getting softer beat by beat. I feel like a plant that has been starved of the sun, in total darkness.

I don't know how to not love Joshua Stanton. I have loved him for every minute of every hour of every day since I was a seventeen-year old girl. He was my life, my every dream and until now I didn't realize what an ingrained part of my psyche he was. I dream of him nearly every night. Horrible nightmares, ones where we are in the tunnel and he is being beaten to death and I am raped, or the other dream, the one where I am forced to watch him make tender passionate love to Amelie. It's so real that I can see the sheen of perspiration on his body, hear his cries as his orgasms rip through him. Feel him quiver with need, kiss her lips as they both gasp for air. I don't know which dream I dread the most, they are both horrific. But it's the vision of Joshua and Amelie making love that haunts me throughout my working day. Are they making love right now?

I sit in my office staring out the window, lost in my own regret.

It's 7 am. I have been working ridiculous hours to escape the small-talk of the girls in my apartment. Max is across the road in the park, Ben has asked him to stay with me until the media circus dies down. Except now there are three other guards as well, and I don't have a minute of privacy. I should just issue a statement saying we are not or never have been married, but I just can't do it. It's the final nail in my coffin that I don't have the strength to hammer in. How did it get to this? I have been back at work for a week and my mind is far from being on the job. I still haven't gotten a new phone, I'm too scared. Scared he will call, scared that he won't. I can't have him in my life, I know that. But the thought that he could move on with her tears my heart wide open.

I am dreading the weekend like the plague. I can't even pretend not to be sad and I feel bad for the girls who are constantly trying to cheer me up and pull me out of this funk.

Now I have to call Adrian as Nicholas Anastas is on my case. He has come into work twice this week. He's keen, I will give him that. My little hard to get act was very effective. Abbie is right, this shit actually works.

I feel sick knowing I have to make this call, I slowly dial his number. It rings.

He picks up. "Adrian Murphy."

I panic and hang up as tears rush to my eyes. Who am I

kidding? I can't talk to Adrian, he's Joshua's best friend. I need to distance myself from everybody in his circle. Too bad, I'm making an executive decision. Nicholas can have Adrian's number. I text it to him immediately from my work phone before I can second guess myself, the way I feel at the moment the bloody grim reaper can have his number.

## Adrian

I sit on my deck chair beside Cameron as I feel the warmth of the sun dance on my skin. We both watch him glide through the water in silence. It's 1 pm and Cam and I are on our second beer as we ponder how in the hell to keep him occupied for the weekend.

"How many laps can he actually do?" Cameron asks. I shrug.

"A lot, it seems. More than us anyway." Cameron smirks. "That wouldn't be hard."

It has been eight days since we lost Natasha and she consequently returned to Australia. Joshua has been a fucking nightmare. He's training like a man possessed, his way of burning that extra energy, extra anger. He still can't fly for another six days.

"What do you want to do tonight?" I ask.

Cameron shrugs. "Has Ben finished the security tapes yet?"

"No, still no idea of what hospital that guy got his cast on at."

"At least when we find the hospital, we will have a name to track." Cameron sighs as he lays back and closes his eyes as his face tilts to the sun.

"Didn't you say you had to go into work today?" I frown.

He nods as he takes a sip of his beer. "I was just going into pathology to get some blood tests, but now that I've been drinking that's not going to happen."

"What are the blood tests for?"

Cameron shrugs. "Just routine stuff. Tell me, Murph. What happens if this trip to Australia doesn't go well? What then?"

I shrug. "The thought has crossed my mind. Tash will understand, she loves him. They were broken up; she can't hold it against him... surely."

"You know, I've been thinking and the fact that Natasha has never slept with anyone else is going to work against him." Cameron sighs.

I frown. "What do you mean?"

"You knew that, right?"

"Knew what?" I ask.

"Natasha has never slept with anyone else. She waited for Josh for seven years." His eyes hold mine as he takes another sip of his beer.

"What the fuck! What never? Not one person?" I frown. Cameron shakes his head.

I close my eyes and put my head back against my chair in regret. "This is all my fault, Cam. I knew Amelie couldn't be trusted and yet I never warned him. And now he's lost the girl that actually really loves him."

"You didn't know the stupid prick was going to sleep with her."

"How did that even happen?" I shake my head.

Joshua silences our conversation by swimming to the edge and taking the stairs of the pool. He dries himself and wraps the towel around his waist.

"Anyone want a protein shake?" he asks as he heads to the pool bar.

Cameron frowns at me. "As if. You freak."

"What's wrong with protein?" Joshua replies.

"Nothing if you don't have taste buds," I mutter.

He makes his shake and flops onto the deck chair next to me. "Don't you think you're training a bit much? It can't be good for you," I say as I close my eyes and put my head back to feel the sun on my face.

"I tell you what's not healthy. Being trapped in this fucking house like a stale bottle of piss," he snaps.

Cameron gives him a sad smile as he reaches over and rubs his hand roughly through Joshua's hair. "It'll work out, mate. No use worrying about it, stop stressing."

"Why don't you call Tash?" I ask.

"No, I need to see her in person. She will just hang up on me if I call her."

I smile. "She's a ballsy little bitch...isn't she?"

Joshua rolls his eyes as he takes a sip of his drink. "Hmm, much to my detriment."

We sit in silence for a few minutes and my phone rings. "Adrian Murphy," I answer

A deep male voice with an Australian accent. "Umm, hello Adrian."

"Yes." I frown, who in the hell is this?

"I'm not sure if you remember me. It's Nicholas Anastas.

We met in a restaurant a couple of months ago." My eyes widen and I sit up suddenly.

"Oh yes, I remember." I start waving my hand around in the air at Joshua frantically.

He frowns at me and takes a sip of his shake. "Nicholas Anastas, what a pleasant surprise."

Joshua's mouth drops open and he hits Cameron in the stomach. Cameron has his eyes closed and was not expecting the hit, so he doubles over as he groans.

"Natasha Marx gave me your number."

I look at Joshua. "Oh, Natasha did…right."

Joshua puts his head in his hands at the mention of her name.

Fuck, what will I say? I stay silent as nerves steal my ability to speak.

"I hope you don't mind me calling."

I swallow nervously. "No, it's nice to hear from you."

"I was wondering if you wanted to catch up for a drink tonight," he asks.

Cameron throws a piece of ice at me from the ice bucket sitting next to him. It hits me hard in the face. I hold my hand up in a fist to him as he and Joshua break into laughter.

"Are you in LA?" I ask, wide-eyed, as I rub my face. "Yes, I'm here for business. How about that drink?"

Holy shit. "Um, look, I'm not sure I can make it tonight," I answer. Joshua hits me hard in the stomach.

"You're fucking going," he mouths at me.

I shake my head as I cover the phone with my hand. I stand to get away from my two idiot friends.

"Ok. Fine. Never mind, at least I tried," he snaps. Oh shit, he's pissed. What will I say?

I scrunch my eyes up as the next words escape my mouth. "I'm staying with friends. Why don't you come here for dinner? Cameron can cook." I bite my lip to stifle my smile. This time Cameron holds out his hand in a fist to me. "Joshua makes a mean cocktail," I add. Joshua rolls his eyes at me as he takes another sip of his shake.

"Who are the friends?" he asks.

"Joshua, the man you met at the restaurant with me and my other friend Cameron." I can hear him thinking through the phone. "They are nice guys. Fun. Cam is an amazing cook." Cameron walks past to the bar and gives me a shove, hoping I will fall into the pool. Joshua smirks.

"Okay. What time?" he asks.

Oh fuck. Now I've done it. I start to shake my arm around in the air as I freak out.

"About seven. I will text you the address," I answer nervously. His deep velvety voice rasps through the phone. "I look forward to it, Adrian." He hangs up and I put my head in my hands. "Oh my fucking God. He's coming here." I start to panic.

"Who?" Cameron frowns.

"That dude we met in Australia. Psychologist, author," Joshua replies.

"Oh, yeah, that one. You went on about him for a week, looks like you might be getting some head tonight after all." Cameron smiles, making Joshua laugh.

"This is not funny. Does everything come back to head with you?" I stammer, exasperated.

Cameron smiles and shrugs his shoulders. "Basically," he replies.

"How did I rope myself into this? I don't want him to come over here. What was I thinking?"

Joshua's eyes light up. "You were thinking that Cameron and I needed some comedy entertainment tonight." He smiles broadly as he winks.

"Stop it," I snap. "You two had better be on your best behavior. Or I fucking mean it, you are both dead."

Cameron laughs. "We will be on our best behavior. Naked, but well behaved."

I roll my eyes. "Great, something to look forward to," I say deadpan. "I don't even remember what he looks like."

"I do. He's hot." Joshua smirks. "Give me your phone." He takes my phone off me and starts to google him.

"Why did you say I would cook, asshole? Why don't you fucking cook?" Cameron throws me a dirty look.

"Because that's just too try hardish. What, so he sits at the bench while I cook in the kitchen? I'm not fucking Nigella Lawson."

"Why didn't you say I would cook?" Joshua smirks as he scrolls through my phone.

"Probably because you can't cook, dumbass."

Joshua laughs as he hands me the phone. "Yep. Like I said."

My eyes scroll down the length of the screen as I feel my nerves rise. He is more than hot, he's damn delicious. "What the hell will I wear?" I splutter.

"Naked on first dates always works for me." Cameron lays his head back to the sun to catch the rays on his face as he swigs his beer.

I roll my eyes at Josh. "Can you be fucking serious for one minute, Cameron? Why is everything a joke to you?"

"Probably because you are always so serious, and Joshua is so fucking boring at the moment with his little broken heart routine. Someone around here has to have some fun."

"Fair call," Joshua replies.

"What's the look you are going for?" Cameron sighs.

"Not trying."

Joshua smiles. "That's easy then. You should wear flannel pyjamas." He takes a drink from his shake.

My eyes widen in horror. "You've lost the plot. You like Natasha in flannelette pajamas."

He smiles as he folds his arms behind his head. "Yep, that's what's so hot about Tash. She doesn't try to be sexy at all. She looks sexiest to me when she is wearing flannel pajamas, her pink fluffy slippers and her hair in pigtails with her glasses on."

Cameron pulls a disgusted face and I nod in agreement with him.

"Sounds like a bad Taylor Swift film clip." I do a fake shiver.

"I never thought I would like that either," he replies wistfully. "There is a certain level of comfort when you realize it's not the packaging you want in someone."

Cameron rolls his eyes. "Oh God, your soppy shit is driving me fucking nuts. Man the fuck up," he snaps, bringing a smile to my face.

"What are you cooking, Cameron?" I ask.

"I don't know, whatever. Who cares?" he says matter-of-factly. Joshua laughs again as he puts his head back onto the chair.

"Sounds delicious."

I shake my head. This is going to be a long night.


## Natasha

It's Wednesday, another word for hump day and, in my case, shit day, annoying day and fucking depressing day. I am going to my first court case at the jail. Coby Allender is having his first appeal hearing today. I have been witnessing his visits for the last couple of months from the private box. Today, though, I will actually be in the same room as him for the first time. The man completely freaks me out. I am just so intimidated by his intelligence and the fact that his behavior is motivated by evil only adds to the horror of dealing with a suspected serial killer. I think those nightmares I have been having are making me crazy, my imagination is running away with me. We are at the jail's private courthouse; this is a closed hearing. Henry, my boss, has gone to check on some details and I am waiting alone in the corridor to go in when Mr. Cheeky walks up behind me.

"Hey, Doc." He pokes me in the ribs from behind.

I turn and smile. Oh shit, it's the guy who told me to think of him when I had sex with Joshua, my face falls.

"Don't look so pleased to see me." He smirks. His messy blond hair hangs over his forehead and his dark brown eyes twinkle with mischief. He's tall and buff with a full sleeve of tatts. He has the whole naughty boy thing going on. Hmm.

I shake my head as I smile. "You're a dick, you know that?"

He raises his eyebrows at me. "I've been called worse." He smiles. "How's your tool of a boyfriend?"

"Ex," I snap. "You're lucky he didn't kill you that night by the way."

He scrunches up his face. "Hmm. Good." He smiles.

I can't help but smile at this conceited fool.

"Why is that good?"

"Because you are still totally into me, I can tell. And he's an ex, so." He shrugs his shoulders.

I roll my eyes. "You've been fighting too much. I think you're punch drunk."

He smiles broadly. "I thought you were coming back for more witness dates. What happened? Are you chicken shit?"

I frown. "No, am not." I smile. "I've been back, and you haven't been here. Who still says that anyway...chicken shit? I haven't heard that since first grade." I shake my head as I readjust my jacket.

He winks. "I do. Chicken shit."

I narrow my eyes at him. "Stop calling me that," I whisper. This guy's confidence is starting to piss me off. "I am far from chicken shit," I snap.

"Prove it." He smiles. "Give me your number."

I roll my eyes. "God, give me a break. Is that the best pick-up line you've got?"

He laughs. "Pretty much, are you going to fall for it?"

I frown. "No."

He smiles again. "We'll see...Persistence pays."

I smile as I bite my lip. He's definitely cute, I will give him that. Maybe I should just break out and have wild rebound sex right here, right now. "What's your name again?" I ask.

He smiles. "Jesten Miller."

"Do you want to know my name?" I ask.

He shrugs. "Not really, I'll just call you Hot Doc." I roll my eyes. "I'm not a doctor."

He shrugs again and then smiles as Henry and Richard, my work colleague, come out of the doorway and we walk into the room together. There are four rows of eight chairs on each side with mahogany large benches at the front of the room. We all take our seats. There are only ten people in the room. Three psychologists, three lawyers and four prison wardens.

I am achingly aware I am the only woman present. Jesten is at the right of the room in my peripheral vision and for some reason that is strangely comforting. The judge arrives and we all stand in silence as he enters the room and sits. Coby Allender is led into the room in handcuffs. He looks around the room and then his eyes connect with mine, they bore through me and then he smiles icily. I drop my eyes immediately. I'm too fragile for this shit. The court case carries on, but I am too distracted by the fact that the suspected serial killer's eyes have not left me since he entered the room, and I can feel the evil emanating from his every pore. How long has it been since he has seen a woman? I can feel my heart rate picking up as fear starts to send me into a panic. Between nightmares, philandering boyfriends and heartbreak I am very fragile indeed. Why is he still looking at me? Don't look at him, don't look at him, I chastise myself. I know he's trying to freak me out, and it's fucking working. I'm starting to sweat here.

Henry leans over and whispers. "He's just trying to scare you. Don't look at him."

I nod and put my head down. He's right, just look down. Stop freaking out. The court case carries on and my mind starts to wander. What's Joshua doing now? Who's he with? I must be in a daydream because before I realize the court case finishes. My eyes flick to the psychopath in front of me. His eyes are still locked on me, he smiles, slowly licks his lips and blows me a kiss. I drop my head again. Forget criminology, this is fucked up shit I don't need messing with my head. Who was I kidding? I can't deal with criminals; I would end up a head case. He is led out of the room by the handcuffs and I blow out a breath I didn't know I was holding. Let this day be over!

THE DRIVE HOME from work is long...and silent. Max doesn't feel the need to talk and I don't have one positive thing to say, so why bother. I hate negativity. I never imagined I would have so much of it coursing through my veins...where does it come from? And more importantly, how do I get rid of it?

My headache is back, and it's starting to thump. In the two months since Dad's death, I have had six migraines, what a bitch those things are, I had no idea. On a few occasions Max and Bridget have called the doctor to my house and he has given me a shot to knock me out for two days. Stress related is what he called it; I call it toxic information overload. The poison from my heart seeping into my brain cells, one by one. It's the weekend so at least I can just relax and sleep. It's funny, through the day when I should be doing things that are constructive all I want to do is sleep but at night when I should be sleeping all I can do is think...about him... with her. It's poisoning me.

I am riddled with guilt as my mind goes over the patients I have treated and how I have analyzed them void of emotion. Bethany. Beautiful, smart Bethany, I saw her just today. She is also in love with an adulterer, she refused to give up and she stayed for love. But at what cost? She has no self-esteem, no sexual confidence and an inability to orgasm. She has children with him... so, in effect she is trapped. So even though she stayed for love, she has been rewarded with hate...for herself. Today I sat and listened to her talk and looked deep into the mirror. I felt like I was having an out of body experience. I could relate to everything she told me, every emotion, every fear. When she cried... I cried; the tears weren't for her. They were for me. If I go back to my beloved Joshua, in five years I will be Bethany. Petrified that every time he walks out the front door, he is going to meet up with her. Petrified that I am not pretty enough, funny enough...sexy enough.

In all honesty, I don't think any woman could hold my beautiful Joshua forever, he's just not wired that way, even though I know he desperately wants to be. He tried...and failed. I gave everything to him and still in the end it wasn't enough.

I don't trust him. I have lost all faith in his words. I never trusted her. But I trusted him with my heart, and he broke it. I know I will never love again like I did him... and that's ok, I don't want to.

We pull in and Max turns and looks at me.

He frowns, "You okay?" I nod as I look into my lap. "Yeah, I can feel another migraine coming. It will pass." I

smile at him. "What doesn't kill you makes you stronger right?" I whisper.

He gives me a sad smile and sits silently, watching me. I can tell he wants to say something but is holding his tongue. He's leaving me, I know it. He just doesn't know how to tell me. He and Mum have become good friends and I know they talk about me. I can hear them late at night when they think I am asleep. He's worried about me...I'm worried about me. I need to snap out of this...shitty time I'm having.

We get out of the car and walk quietly up the stairs.

"Tash, take your phone out of your bag, honey," he whispers as we get to my door.

I frown at him.

"Do it," he whispers. I do as he asks.

"I will stand right here ok. You call me if you need me. I'll be right at the door."

I frown at him as I open the door and step back in shock. Joshua is standing front and center in my lounge room. His haunted eyes meet mine. My eyes immediately fill with tears and I close the door silently behind me.

Dear God...he's so beautiful. A wave of affection rolls over me. Why? Why has he come? I can't take this, I'm not strong enough.

He is wearing his three-piece navy suit, his armor from the outside world. His dark hair and skin are in contrast to his white shirt. His hands are in his pockets. I stand still, rooted to the spot.

"Natasha," he whispers.

Instantly my lip quivers and my tears fall onto my cheeks.

He rushes me and grabs me into an embrace, where I fall

against his chest. We stand still and silent. His arms around me and my arms straight at my sides. I sob out loud. I want to stay in his arms...I can't say goodbye. I'm not strong enough, I can't do this. He kisses my temple. "Tash... I've missed you."

The lump in my throat forms and I can't speak. I want to tell him I've missed him too, but I can't. I need to be strong for the both of us. I need to set him free so he can be with Amelie...I know he loves her. He just doesn't realize it yet and he won't, until I release him. He kisses my face again, his eyes close in reverence. I need to do this; I need to get it over with.

I pull out of his embrace and fold my arms in front of me in defense. He bites his bottom lip as he thinks.

"Natasha, let me explain. I need to tell you what happened that night," he whispers. I want to scream at him to get out, but I need to hear this.

I nod nervously.

"Tash, I was...so sad. I didn't think you were coming back to me. Cameron and Adrian had sat me down that day and told me I needed to snap out of it, and they didn't think you were coming back either." He shakes his head in regret as his eyes fill with tears. "I went to Willowvale. I hadn't been there since I came back to America. I wanted to see Jasper."

I stand still as I picture what he is telling me, my face expressionless.

He swallows again. "I had dinner with Amelie and a few glasses of wine."

He shakes his head too quickly. "I finished up and went to my room. I had a shower and I had come out of the bathroom with a towel around me."

My eyes close in pain.

He frowns as he relives the memory. "Amelie was in my room, and she had a robe on."

I hold my hand up in a stop signal. I can't hear this.

"Tash...I don't know what happened. One minute I was sitting on the bed, the next thing she was on top of me."

I slam my hands over my ears. Stop it...stop it...stop it. "Tash, I promise you. As soon as I realized what was happening I pushed her off me. I told her I was in love with you."

I stand still with my hands over my ears and yet I can hear every sordid detail he is explaining to me in IMAX.

The caustic tears burn my face as they roll down my cheeks. "Natasha, I swear to you. It was just once, and it went for one minute. There was no emotion. She lied to hurt you...which in turn hurts me."

My head drops as I think.

"I was furious with her. I trusted her and she...she forced herself onto me. Tash...please," he whispers.

I can't talk. If I say anything, I know I will take him back. I love him just too much.

"Natasha...please talk to me." I shake my head.

"I had a massive fight with Amelie. I was so mad at her. I got dressed and got the hell out of there. Then I went home. I was so disgusted with myself, I watched the movies of the two of us together all weekend and then I took drugs like a fucking idiot.

I had no idea you were coming back and yet I was still mortified at what I had done."

My eyes hold his, but I hold my tongue. Don't say anything ...don't say anything.

"Tash. Please," he whispers again.

I turn and walk to the bathroom and close the door behind me. I get my phone from my back pocket and I text Cameron.

**Get the hell over here.**

I try to calm myself for a minute and then I flush the toilet, wash my hands and re-enter the room.

He rushes me again and holds me tight in an embrace. "Precious, I swear. I love you more than anything. We can get over this. We can go to counselling, whatever it takes. We are stronger than this. We love each other too much. We have been through too much."

I sob out loud onto his chest. How do women do this? How do they find the strength to walk away from someone they love so desperately?

"Speak to me," he asks. I stay silent. "Tash, please. Speak to me."

I shake my head into his chest. If I say anything...it will be I love you, I need you. He holds me silently in his arms, and for a long time, we say nothing.

A knock sounds at the door. His head snaps to the direction of the door.

"Come in," I yell.

He frowns at me. "Natasha... no," he whispers as I close my eyes in pain.

Cameron opens the door. His eyes find Joshua. "Cameron, get the fuck out of here!" Joshua yells.

I start to cry. "Max," I sob. He and Ben walk through the door, and their haunted eyes meet mine.

"Can you please show Joshua out?"

"No! Natasha, no." His eyes snap back to the two bodyguards. "Get the fuck out of here or you are both fucking fired!" He screams.

I'm close to being hysterical. I sob loudly.

Cameron turns to the boys solemnly. "Give us a minute," he whispers.

They both look to me for approval. I nod silently. They turn and close the door behind them.

"Natasha...speak to me. Please," he sobs. "What's wrong with you? Say something." The tears run freely down his face.

"We are stronger than this...Please, listen to me...I'm begging. You told me you loved me unconditionally. Prove it. Please. I need you to forgive me."

The sight of my beautiful powerful man in tears is catastrophic. I sob out loud. My eyes flick to Cameron who is standing with his hands in his pockets looking down at the ground. He lifts his tear-filled eyes to meet mine. Oh God, Cameron's in tears too. I can't imagine witnessing someone I love go through this. I drop my head.

"Natasha. I love you. *FUCKING SAY SOMETHING*," he screams.

I sob again.

"Goodbye, Joshua," I whisper as pain slices my heart wide open. He shakes his head frantically. "No... no, no. Don't say that. You don't mean that," he cries as he dives for me. I jump to escape him.

"I love you...you can't do this to us. We are stronger than this, Tash."

I sob as I hold my hands up to him in defense. I can no longer handle this torture, I need to get away. He tries to grab me again and I run for the door. Joshua dives for me and Cameron steps in front of him and holds him back.

"Cameron...let me go. Please," he sobs as he breaks into full blown tears.

I run out the door as I hear him screaming my name. Max is hot on my heels, we run down the stairs and burst out the front door and I collapse from the sheer grief of this situation. Max picks me up and carries me in his arms and loads me into the car where I fall into the seat.

The car trip to my mum's is made in complete silence... complete grief.


TODAY WAS the worst day of my life.

# 9

Natasha

THE CALL of the kookaburra echoes through the still street outside as my eyes slowly open. I look to the window and see the faint red glow of the sunset peek through the closed blinds. Jeez, I feel like shit. I rub my eyes as I try to focus. I slowly look around. I'm in my darkened childhood bedroom. The door is ajar, and I can faintly hear the television from the lounge room.

"It's ok, love, I'm here."

My eyes flick to my mother who I now see sitting in the corner in my armchair reading a book by the lamp.

"Hi Mum." I smile weakly. She walks over and sits next to me on the side of the bed and brushes the hair back from my forehead as she leans to kiss me on the cheek.

"You ok, baby?" she asks. I nod. "Yes," I whisper. "Tash… you're scaring me." Her eyes search mine. I nod as
my eyes fill with tears. "What time is it?"

"It's 7 pm on Sunday night."

I frown. "Sunday. What do you mean? What happened to Saturday?"

"On Friday when you came back here...you were so upset, hysterical. Your headache progressed and you started to vomit so we called the doctor. He gave you a sedative again."

I frown as I take in the information. "Tash, talk to me. Tell me what's in your head," she whispers as she starts to push the hair back from my forehead again. I shrug. "Scoot over, let me in." She smiles.

I smile and shimmy over. I love it when Mum gets into bed with me. Some things never get old. I roll over and she cuddles my back and kisses my shoulder from behind.

"Is Joshua okay?" I whisper.

She shrugs. "I'm not sure, baby. Bridget and Abbie have gone over to see him tonight." My heart drops, I want to go and see him.

She kisses the side of my face. "Explain it to me, Tash. I don't understand, why can't you forget these last few months and start fresh?"

"Mum, it's complicated."

"Please, Tash, I'm worried sick over you. I need to know what's going on in that brain of yours. If I understand why you feel like this, I might be able to help you, honey, you need to talk to someone. And if you won't talk to Joshua, talk to me."

I shrug as I look at the ceiling. "Natasha," she whispers, "please."

'I love Joshua, Mum, you know that."

"Why won't you talk this through with him? Anything can be worked out, Tash, but you need to talk to him. Cutting him out is not the answer," she sighs.

"Mum, I can't talk to him. If I talk to him, I will forgive him and I am not strong enough yet to do that."

She lies silent behind me. I can hear her thinking. "Why are you not strong enough to go back to him?" she whispers.

"I can't explain it, Mum. I don't know if it's the fact that Dad has died or my own mind playing tricks on me."

"What do you mean?"

I swallow as I contemplate whether to tell her or not. "Since Dad's death I have been having horrible nightmares about Joshua being murdered in front of me."

"What?" she whispers.

I nod. "I have them at least four times a week and I know it's the reason I have been having these migraine headaches. I'm so stressed about going to sleep that I am wound up all the time."

"Tash, why haven't you told me this?"

"Mum," I start to silently cry, "haven't I worried you enough? I killed your husband, for Pete's sake. I blame myself for your grief, for all our grief and I can't forgive myself. No matter how hard I try. I'm so terrified that I am going to lose Joshua to death that I dream about it, it's not normal. I have been seeing a psychologist at work and she feels that I need to get stronger before I can give myself totally to someone who I don't trust."

"Natasha, that's enough. I won't have you saying that you killed your father. It was a terrible accident, he had an undiag-nosed heart problem and it was just bad timing that it happened when it did."

"I know," I whisper unconvinced.

"Do you think you can't trust Joshua?"

I shake my head. "Mum, Joshua loves me. I know that, but on some level, he also loves Amelie, and I don't blame him for that. She's beautiful and sweet and they have a connection. If he had slept with someone else, I would have been upset but I would have understood. I know I left him, but I was grief stricken. If he had been honest and told me that he slept with her before he slept with me, I maybe would have been able to handle it better. He thought I would never have found out and he was just going to lie to me forever. I was in the same room with her and she knew he hadn't told me that he had slept with her just three days before. I'm ashamed to be so stupid. I thought I would have been able to tell if he was hiding something and I didn't have a frigging clue. I was totally blindsided," I whisper in a rush.

"Tash, I don't think he would be here if he wanted Amelie."

I nod my head. "Yes, he would, Mum, he feels obligated to make me happy."

She frowns. "Why do you keep saying that? It doesn't make sense."

I stay silent as I think. "I never told you this before, but I have never slept with anyone else but Joshua."

She frowns. "What about Christopher?" I shake my head. "No."

"Tash, baby." She pulls me into an embrace and cuddles me tightly. "Is that why you think Joshua wants to be with you, because he owes you?"

I nod as I cry into her chest.

"Tash, tell me what you want to do. How can I help you through this? I don't know what to do," she sighs empathetically.

I wipe my tears away. "I want to let Joshua go and hopefully, in time he will decide that it is me that he loves, and he will come back for me and we will live happily ever after. If I go with him now, I will never know if, given the chance, he would have married Amelie."

"Tash...you might lose him. This could backfire," she whispers.

I nod. "I know, but if I do, he wasn't mine in the first place...was he?"

"What will you do?" she asks.

I give her a sad smile. "Try to work on myself. Stop being so insecure, stop having nightmares. Mum, if I go with Joshua now, I am just so insecure we will break up in two months anyway. I don't like who I have turned into and in all honesty if I go with him and he does decide he wants her...I don't think I would survive it. I'm so weak."

She holds me tight. "Don't say that love, I don't like you speaking like that."

"I am only doing this so that Joshua and I can have a real hope of a future together. I need to know that our love is real and not just a teenage tragic love story that ends in divorce in two years."

"Can you tell Joshua this? When you put it like this, it makes sense Natasha. Make him understand why you are doing this," she pleads.

Tears fall again. "I can't Mum, he needs to think that he is free to go to her if that is what he wants. If he knows I still want him, he's not really free, is he?" I sob.

"Oh baby. Why are you such a deep thinker? Why are you sacrificing your happiness for his?" she whispers into my hair.

I break into sobs. "Because I fear that is what he is doing for me and I love him too deeply to let him do it."

"Tash... he doesn't understand why you are doing this. He thinks this is about him sleeping with Amelie."

I nod. "I know, it's not. That was just the straw that broke the camel's back."

She kisses my forehead and brushes my hair back again. "Do you believe in fate, Mum?" I question.

She nods as her eyes well with tears. "Yes," she whispers. "Me too. If Joshua is the man I am meant to be with, then

we will eventually work it out. I just pray to God that he comes back to me and I learn to trust him and build some faith in myself," I whisper.

"Natasha...my beautiful brave girl. If he has any brains in that pretty head of his...he will never let you go." She smiles sadly as she kisses my forehead.

I nod my head. "I need him to let me go. Every time I have to hurt him, I die a little inside. I'm not wired to hurt him, I can't physically do it."

"Tash, I still think you should talk to him. Arrange to meet up in twelve months and tell him you love him."

A weight of sadness sits heavily on my shoulders. "No. And don't tell a soul about this conversation. At this point I can't even trust the girls because I know they will tell Joshua or Cameron and then he won't go. I'm setting him free. I want an unencumbered future with him, one where I am strong and confident and know for certain that he is with me for the woman I am now and not the girl he fell in love with seven years ago."

Max walks up the hall and stands in the semi-lit doorway. "You finally wake up, sleepyhead?" He smirks.

I smile broadly. "What? Did you miss me or something?" I tease.

He tutts. "Yeah, like a hole in the head." He winks, turns and walks back up the hall. "Promise me something, Tash." I nod.

"If Joshua turns up here you will be honest with him."

**I am sorry**
**It meant nothing.**
**You're overreacting.**

My stomach drops. "He won't. I know he won't. He would be beyond mortified that his staff and brother saw him in tears the other day. His pride will keep him away." I sigh sadly.

"Does that bother you?" she asks.

I shrug my shoulders as I contemplate her question. "That's Joshua, he's a proud man. He won't beg again, I know that. His upset will turn to anger soon, and he will return to LA." My eyes tear up at the painful thought.

"Please go to him, Tash," Mum whispers.

I shake my head. "We just talked about this. I told you what I am doing. I am not giving up on us. I am just putting it on the backburner for a while."

She shakes her head. "You are going to lose him," she sighs

I pull my eyes away from hers in anger. "Like I said, if I do, he was never mine to start with."


It's WEDNESDAY, 2.00 pm, and I am sitting in my office staring at my computer monitor trying desperately to rein in my grief. Thirty-two emails from Joshua just today and each day that number has risen. On the first day I got one with the subject 'Joshua', when I clicked on it I realized he had a read receipt on it so I couldn't open it. I'm dying to know what he is trying to say, is he hurting as much as I am? Each day since then though the pattern has changed. He has started speaking to me through the subject line:

**Natasha, listen to me.**
**Speak to me.**
**Say something!!!!**
**I love you.**
**Please.**

I smirk as I read the subjects of today's email in bold print. Can't hold a good temper down for long, that's my man. I'm glad he's angry. It means he's close to leaving Australia. He won't put up with being ignored for too much longer. It's not in his nature. I know he's too proud to come over here and beg or make me listen. He probably would though if there wasn't security everywhere. I now have four men trailing me at all times. It's totally ridiculous. His irate email headings read:

**Fucking speak to me.**
**You left me. Remember.**
**Sorry I am not as perfect as you.**
**You are going to regret this.**
**Speak to me or I will never forgive you.**
**Your last words to me were, I never want to see...**
**I fucking mean it.**
**You owe it to me to listen.**
**Call me. Now!!!!**

"Oh baby, just go." I whisper as my heart fills with hurt. I link my hands on top of my head and sit back in my chair. I blow out a deep breath of regret as I go over the words 'Speak to me or I will never forgive you'. What if he really never forgives me and I lose him...forever. Would we make it if I went with him? I know I'm not good girlfriend material at the moment. I'm just too insecure and that trait doesn't sit well with me. He deserves someone stronger and in the life that he leads insecurity would poison anything beautiful we ever had between us.

No. Sacrifice now for payment later. I have made the right decision. If we are meant to be it will work out in the end and if not... who knows and who cares for that matter? A life alone with ten cats sounds good at the moment. I'm so sick of my head being filled with all this pressure. I'm twenty-five. I should be tarting around town without a care in the world... like Abbie. Not suffering terrifying nightmares and migraine headaches not to mention the inability to eat or sleep. I don't need this shit in my life. It's just not worth it. I've been summoned to Oscars tonight by the girls. They had dinner again last night with the boys so I know I am going to get a lecture. They have been blissfully silent up until this point and not wanting to upset me but that will all end tonight.

I walk sheepishly into Oscar's with Max at eight fifteen. I

have been staying with my mother but tonight I am going to go home after this. I need to get back to some normality. I see the girls sitting in our regular seats and smile and wave on my way over to them. I flop into the large leather chair and Max goes and sits in the corner on the other side of the café at a table and pulls out his iPad to start reading his book.

"Hi." I smile.

The girls smile and exchange glances. "We've ordered for you." Bridget smiles.

I nod. "Thanks, can we have cake?"

"Umm, yeah. Cameron is just getting us some." Abbie winces.

My eyes snap to the counter where, sure enough, I see Cameron picking out cake.

"Are you fucking kidding me?" I snap.

"Tash, Cameron is our friend too. He's done nothing wrong.

Why can't you talk to him?"

I screw up my face. "You two are totally fucked. How dare you ask him here without telling me? What, is Joshua hiding in the toilet?" My eyes fly around the restaurant.

"No, he wouldn't come. We asked him."

"God, I'm off you two. You're unbelievable," I whisper angrily. Cameron rejoins the table. "Tash." He nods.

I smile slightly at him. He's furious with me for hurting his brother. I can feel the animosity from here. This is a disaster. I glare at my two friends who are openly uncomfortable. The waitress brings over the coffee and cake.

"Thank you," I whisper as she passes me the cake. I take a massive slurp of my coffee, anything so I don't have to talk. I gasp in pain. Shit, I burnt my tongue. What in the hell temperature is this, 200 fucking degrees? Everybody watches me silently as they drink their coffee. *Awkward.*

"So, when are you going back to LA, Cam?" Abbie asks. "Sunday, I go back to work on Monday," he answers flatly.

Everybody nods and takes another drink of their coffee in silence. *God, I'm furious.*

"How are you Natasha?" Cameron asks.

I swallow the lump in my throat. "I've been better," I reply flatly.

He nods but stays silent, his eyes locked on mine. I'm not taking your shit either. Bring it on, I feel like fighting with you asshole.

"Where is Adrian?" I ask

"Back in the hotel with Joshua."

I nod and take another sip of my gazillion-degree coffee.

Why did I ask that?

"Did Nicholas Anastas ever call him? He hassled me for his number and I never heard anything," I splutter through my burnt tongue.

Cameron shrugs his shoulders and shakes his head. "Yeah, he came over for dinner at Joshua's last week."

My eyes widen and I smile. "Oh my God, really. How did it go?"

"Great, they totally hit it off. The LUST was ridiculous. Josh and I were worried we were going to be forced to watch gay porn when they finally got it on, but it didn't happen."

My face falls. "What? Not even a kiss?"

He shakes his head. "Nope."

"Why not?" Bridget asks.

Cameron shakes his head. "No idea, they had a great night laughing and talking and then Murph walked him out at the end of the night and came back ten minutes later to announce to us that he isn't interested, something about living too far away from each other." He shrugs as he takes a sip of his coffee. "I don't know what's going on in anyone's head at the moment, everyone's fucked up." His gaze comes back to me in insinuation.

I narrow my eyes. "Cameron, why don't you just come out with it?" I reply sarcastically.

"Out with what?" he snaps.

"Oh I don't know, maybe Joshua for one."

"I just don't see why you can't talk to him. Listen to what he has to say."

I roll my eyes. "You know what Cameron? The time for talking was in the hospital before he slept with me. Before he lied to me."

"Tash," he stammers.

I cut him off. "Don't you dare Tash me! I sat in that hospital room with a woman who he was sleeping with five meters away and you all knew it. You were all keeping his sordid little secret for him. You all make me sick."

"I make you sick?" he snaps.

I raise my eyebrows as I take another sip of my coffee. "Yes, you do actually."

He sits forward in anger and Bridget pipes up. "Let's calm down, shall we?"

"Well, you make me sick," he snaps. "You are the one that broke up with him and broke his fucking heart and then he fucks up once and you dump him again. What the hell is that?"

Abbie puts her hands on her head in a panic.

Steam starts to pour from my ears. "Fucking up, Cameron, is forgetting to pick up the dry cleaning, forgetting an anniversary or maybe forgetting to pick the kids up from soccer practice. Putting your dick inside another woman is a bit more than fucking up, asshole!" I sneer as my anger hits crescendo.

"Sssshhh," Bridget snaps as she looks around the room to see if anyone can hear us.

"You, shush Bridget. How did you think this conversation was going to go? You all are taking his side and blaming me for this. I did nothing wrong. I demand honesty because that's what I give and I damn well deserve better," I stammer.

They all sit silent, their eyes planted firmly on me. "Tash, we are not taking his side. This is not a cut-and-dry case," Bridget whispers.

"I know that." I lean back on the chair and put my hands over my face in frustration.

"Tash, he hadn't heard from you in over two months," Bridget whispers.

"Because I was devastated. I had just killed my father. Cameron, you were there with me, you saw how I was when you would visit. Was I really in my sound mind?" I demand.

He drops his head. "No," he whispers. "You didn't kill him, Natasha."

"I know you all love Joshua and you are trying to help. I love Joshua, I will always love Joshua, but he doesn't love me the way I need to be loved."

"That's bullshit and you know it," Cameron snaps.

"I tell you what love is, Cameron. I went out with a man for two and a half years who loved me, and I could not bring myself to physically have sex with him," I whisper.

His silent eyes watch me as he drinks his coffee. "You want to know why?"

"Enlighten me," he sneers as he raises an eyebrow.

"Because I was still in love with Joshua. I stupidly felt that my body belonged to him and I could never betray him like that. Seven years. Seven fucking years, Cameron, I watched him sleep with every woman in the United States and still I couldn't even sleep with my own boyfriend," I snap.

"That's not his fault. That was your decision," he asserts. "Precisely, just like this is my decision. I don't want the life Joshua is offering. The women, the partying, the coke friends. It's all bullshit, I don't want any part of it."

"Joshua can't help his past. That's not what he wants now." Cameron shakes his head in frustration.

"For now, Cameron, that's not what he wants for now. You know when I was a little girl, I dreamt of a man that *loved me*, Cameron. Never once in my dream did my hero say to me, sorry I slept with that other women...it was an accident. The sex meant nothing. Sex does mean something to me and if I'm unforgiving to someone who gives it away so easily then that is my decision and I expect you all to support me as your friend and not just Joshua. You have no idea the suffering I am going through and for you all to sit there and judge me and call me cold breaks my heart." My eyes tear up.

Bridget puts her arm around me. "Tash, we don't think you're cold. We are just trying to understand."

I stand as I try to hold in my tears. "Then I want you all to understand this. Tell Joshua I want him to go home to Amelie.

She wants the money and the lifestyle...she can have it. I want nothing to do with it. I want him to move on with his life without me." I sob. "This is one of those sad cases in life where love simply isn't enough. I don't want his lifestyle or his money or those fucking horses. I just wanted him to love me...but he didn't." I sob again. "Joshua and I have different morals now and I can't change that, I only wish that I could. I would give anything to be with him, but he is better off with someone else who is more like him and will understand his infidelities. I'm not that girl and I never will be." I stand and turn and shrug my shoulders. "Who knows? Perhaps in ten years when I've slept with half of Sydney and Joshua is onto his third wife maybe we will understand each other's point of view, but at this point I don't." I stand and walk out of the café with Max hot on my heels. I walk out of the front door where once again those stupid tears fall down my face and Max tries to comfort me as we walk down the street to his car.

## Joshua

Darkness surrounds the car. It intermittently rocks as each car speeds past us on the busy street. I sit behind the wheel diagonally opposite Oscar's café. We are waiting for Cameron who is having coffee with the girls. They don't know we are here. My elbow is on the window and I swipe the side of my pointer back and forth over my lips as I think.

"What do you think they are talking about?" Adrian sighs from the passenger seat as he stretches and puts his feet onto the dash.

I shrug without answering.

"I know...I've got a plan." He holds his hands up in karate style. "How about we just bowl over there and, like, kidnap her or something." I look over at him and he smirks. "We could take her, I reckon. I'll handle Max and you take Tash."

"Don't tempt me," I reply dryly as my eyes flick back to the café. "Don't think I haven't thought about it."

I link my hands on the top of my head in impatience. "Why don't you just walk over there and just...I don't

know." He shrugs. "Do something Hollywood." I roll my eyes. "Like what, Einstein?"

"I don't know. Drop to your knee and propose."

I blow out a breath. "If I had some fucking privacy I probably would and besides this isn't the time or place."

He stays silent for a while. "Josh, this privacy thing. I know it's driving you crazy, but it will pass, as soon as they get them you can have your life back." Adrian sighs.

"It will be too late then, she will be gone. Because we can't have a fucking minute's peace."

Adrian rolls his eyes. "You're being melodramatic now." "Am I?" I snap. "You should have seen me the other day,

Adrian, crying like a baby. Begging for her to listen to me. The guards would be in their element, loving this gossip." I run my hands over my face in frustration.

"Josh, your staff love you. They are just as sad about this split as you are."

I raise my eyebrows at him.

"Ok, that's an overstatement. I mean they don't like it either." He shakes his head as he corrects himself.

"I just want a normal life without drama, without bodyguards. The money is not worth this shit. I have zero privacy; all I want to do is follow her around till she listens to me but I can't because I might be photographed with her and then she will be a target for the sick fuck who is after me. You have no idea how frustrated I am," I snap.

"Here she comes," Adrian whispers.

We both sit up in silence as we watch Natasha and Max briskly exit the café. She's crying, Max puts his hand around her shoulders and pulls her into him. They walk quickly down the street where he opens her door, and she climbs into the car.

Jealousy rips through me as I grip the steering wheel with both hands and brute force.

"Fucking Max. I swear to God I am going to..."

"Stop it. You're being crazy. This is Natasha. You know she's not like that," Adrian comforts.

"I know exactly what's in that fucker's head," I growl. "Bullshit," he snaps. Their car pulls out and the two other

cars of guards pull out after them. My heart rate speeds with anger. "See, she's gone again, and I could do nothing but sit in this car and watch her go." I punch the steering wheel hard. Adrian jumps in his seat.

"Be careful. This is a bloody rental car you know."

"Shut up," I snap.

We sit in silence for another ten minutes and Cameron exits, walks over to the car and gets into the back seat. My eyes meet his in the rear-view mirror.

"Sorry, mate, it didn't go well," he whispers. I drop my head into my hands. He passes his phone through the seat to Adrian. "I taped it."

"Huh."

"I taped the conversation on my phone. I had it sitting on the table in front of us."

"Oh yes," Adrian snaps. "Inspector Gadget strikes back." He quickly scrolls through the phone and plays back the conversation.

"Hi," Natasha whispers. "We've ordered for you." "Thanks, can we have cake?"

My eyes meet Cameron's again in the mirror and he links his hands on top of his head as he listens.

"This is good shit Cam." Adrian smiles as he bites his lip. "Umm, yeah. Cameron is just getting us some."

"Are you fucking kidding me?" Natasha snaps

"Tash, Cameron is our friend too. He's done nothing wrong. Why can't you talk to him?"

"You two are totally fucked. How dare you ask him here without telling me? What, is Joshua hiding in the toilet?"

"That's a good idea. You so should have hidden in the toilet," Adrian whispers as he raises his eyebrows.

"Sshh," I snap. "I can't fucking hear."

"No, he wouldn't come. We asked him."

"God, I'm off you two. You're unbelievable," Natasha whispers angrily.

"Tash." Cameron's voice replays. "Thank you," she whispers.

"So when are you going back to LA, Cam?" Abbie asks.

"Sunday, I go back to work on Monday," he answers flatly. "How are you Natasha?" Cameron asks.

"I've been better. Where is Adrian?" she asks.

"Back in the hotel with Joshua."

"Did Nicholas Anastas ever ring him? He hassled me for his number and I never heard anything."

Adrian punches me at the mention of Nicholas's name. "Shut. Up." I snap. "I can't hear a thing."

"Yeah, he came over for dinner at Joshua's last week."

"Oh my God, really. How did it go?" she replies.

"Great, they totally hit it off. The LUST was ridiculous. Josh and I were worried we were going to be forced to watch gay porn when they finally got it on, but it didn't happen." Adrian glares at Cameron.

"What? Not even a kiss?" she asks.

"Nope."

"Why not?" Bridget chimes in.

"No idea, they had a great night laughing and talking and then Murph walked him out at the end of the night and came back ten minutes later to announce to us that he isn't interested, something about living too far away from each other. I don't know what's going on in anyone's head at the moment, everyone's fucked up," Cameron says flatly.

**Adrian turns to the back seat and holds up his fist. "You are a bona fide fuckwit, Cameron."**

**"Shut the hell up," I snap again**

"Cameron, why don't you just come out with it?" Natasha replies angrily.

"Out with what?" he snaps.

"Oh I don't know, maybe Joshua for one."

**My eyes widen at Adrian who is holding his lips while looking at the phone.**

"I just don't see why you can't talk to him. Listen to what he has to say."

"You know what Cameron? The time for talking was in the hospital before he slept with me. Before he lied to me."

**"Shit," I whisper as I run my hands through my hair.**
"Tash," Cameron whispers.

"Don't you dare Tash me! I sat in that hospital room with a woman who he was sleeping with five meters away and you all knew it and you were all keeping his sordid little secret for him. You all make me sick."

"I make you sick?" he snaps.

"Yes, you do actually."

"Let's calm down, shall we?" Bridget whispers.

"Well, you make me sick," he snaps. "You are the one that broke up with him and broke his fucking heart and then he fucks up once and you dump him again. What the hell is that?"

Adrian smiles and puts his hand up for Cameron to high five it. Cameron hits it from the back seat.

*"Fucking up, Cameron, is forgetting to pick up the dry cleaning, forgetting an anniversary or maybe forgetting to pick the kids up from soccer practice. Putting your dick inside another woman is a bit more than fucking up, asshole!"*

"Mmm, that is a really good point," Adrian whispers as he nods at me.

*"Sssshhh," Bridget snaps.*

*"You, shush Bridget. How did you think this conversation was going to go? You all are taking his side and blaming me for this. I did nothing wrong. I demand honesty because that's what I give, and I damn well deserve better."*

I can hear the hurt in Natasha's voice, and it cuts me like a knife.

*"Tash, we are not taking his side. This is not a cut-and-dry case," Bridget whispers.*

*"I know that," Natasha snaps.*

*"Tash, he hadn't heard from you in over two months," Bridget sighs.*

*"Because I was devastated. I had just killed my father. Cameron, you were there with me, you saw how I was when you would visit. Was I really in my sound mind?"*

*"No," he whispers.*

*"I know you all love Joshua and you are trying to help. I love Joshua, I will always love Joshua, but he doesn't love me the way I need to be loved."*

*"That's bullshit and you know it," Cameron snaps.*

*"I tell you what love is, Cameron. I went out with a man for two*

*and a half years who loved me, and I could not bring myself to physically have sex with him," she replies softly.*

**I put my head in my hands as I listen.**

*"You want to know why?"*

*"Enlighten me," Cameron sneers.*

*"Because I was still in love with Joshua. I stupidly felt that my body belonged to him and I could never betray him like that. Seven years. Seven fucking years, Cameron, I watched him sleep with every woman in the United States and still I couldn't even sleep with my own boyfriend."*

*"That's not his fault. That was your decision," he snaps. "Precisely, just like this is my decision. I don't want the life*

*Joshua is offering. The women, the partying, the coke friends. It's all bullshit, I don't want any part of it."*

*"Joshua can't help his past. That's not what he wants now,"* *Cameron snaps.*

**"Another good point." Adrian points at Cameron who nods and smiles.**

*"For now, Cameron, that's not what he wants for now. You know when I was a little girl, I dreamt of a man that loved me, Cameron. Never once in my dream did my hero say to me, sorry I slept with that other women...it was an accident. The sex meant nothing.*

*Sex does mean something to me and if I'm unforgiving to someone who gives it away so easily then that is my decision and I expect you all to support me as your friend and not just Joshua. You have no idea the suffering I am going through and for you all to sit there and judge me and call me cold breaks my heart."*

**I can hear she's crying. I close my eyes in regret. God, I'm a total fuck up.**

*"Tash, we don't think you're cold. We are just trying to understand," Abbie whispers.*

*"Then I want you all to understand this. Tell Joshua I want him*

*to go home to Amelie. She wants the money and the lifestyle... she can have it. I want nothing to do with it. I want him to move on with his life without me."* She sobs. *"This is one of those sad cases in life where love simply isn't enough. I don't want his lifestyle or his money or those fucking horses. I just wanted him to love me...but he didn't."* She sobs again. *"Joshua and I have different morals now and I can't change that, I only wish that I could. I would give anything to be with him, but he is better off with someone else who is more like him and will understand his infidelities. I'm not that girl and I never will be."*

*"Who knows? Maybe in ten years when I've slept with half of Sydney and Joshua is onto his third wife maybe we will understand each other's point of view, but at this point I don't."*

It goes silent. I sit and stare out of the windscreen in shock. "I've lost her, she's not coming back," I whisper.

Adrian turns around to Cameron in the back seat. "Those were good arguments, Cam, she did leave him, and he can't help his past."

"I know," Cameron snaps.

The voices come back on and Cameron dives for the phone.

I snatch it off the console before he can grab it.

*"Fucking hell, she's a stubborn bitch,"* Cameron snaps.

*"I don't know what she is doing. She cries herself to sleep every night. I've never seen her so miserable,"* Bridget whispers.

My haunted eyes meet Adrian's, and he swallows as he listens.

"Turn it off," Cameron stammers.

*"You know what she needs? She needs to fuck around. Whore it up a bit. She has unrealistic expectations of men. What was with the fairy tale shit? I'm thinking she needs a good threesome with two frigging...hot men,"* Abbie whispers.

"*That's what I would do, anyway,*" Bridget cuts in. "*She seriously has every man who meets her in love with her.*"

"*I'm telling you, she needs to be tag teamed. I know the two men I am going to set her up with too. They will make her forget her name let alone Joshua Stanton,*" Abbie replies.

"*Fuck off,*" Cameron snaps. "*Don't even say that about Tash.*"
"*Yeah don't,*" Bridget whispers. "*You're gross.*"

"*So you are into threesomes, hey Abbs?*" Cameron's voice smiles.

Adrian rolls his eyes. "Oh God. Get it off." He snaps as his eyes shoot to Cameron in the back seat. "You never miss a chance to try and pick up, do you, wanker?"

Cameron holds his hands up in the air. "How could I let that slip? I had to comment."

I sit silently, staring out the window, lost in thought. I get the fairy tale stuff and she's right. She's too good for me. I need to let her go.

"Adrian, call the pilot in the morning. We are leaving on Saturday." I start the car and pull out into the traffic. The two security cars trailing us follow behind. The car falls deathly silent as I fall back into my pool of depression.

## Natasha

The car trip home is silent. At least I get to sleep in my own bed tonight. I wonder where Joshua is. Is he ok? We walk up to the lift as Max carries my bag. I have my laptop, my pillow and blanket bundled in my arms.

"Are you sure you don't want to go over to Joshua's?" Max asks.

"No and stop asking me. You are not helping the situation," I reply. "I just don't get it. You love him. Why are you letting him go?" he sighs.

"Because I'm not an idiot." I shake my head and storm to my door. I stop dead in my tracks.

The lock has been broken and the door is ajar. Max immediately drops the bags and texts someone. My eyes widen as he ushers me back to the lift where we wait for a moment. The other guards run up the stairs and into my apartment. Max grabs me and pushes me into the lift and pulls out a gun.

What the fuck is happening now?

# 10

**Natasha**

I SHUFFLE to the wall as Max pushes me aside. My eyes widen with fear.

"What's going on Max?" I whisper. "Sshh," he answers as he listens. "Clear," one man says.

"Clear," another yells.

"Max, tell me what's going on," I whisper again more urgently. "Joshua has a hit man after him. He might be here," he replies as his grip on his gun readjusts. His eyes don't leave the door.

"What?" I shriek.

"Hit man, what hit man?" My heart rate picks up as my eyes bulge.

"He was attacked just before we got to LA in what the police think was an organized hit." My eyes widen.

I drop my head as I think... the bruises.

"Why wasn't I told? This is total bullshit," I whisper angrily.

"Sshh. Listen," he says as he cranes his neck around the corner to see what is going on.

I pull my arm out of his grip. "You explain this right now." My whispered voice rises as I start to panic.

"Shut up," he snaps. "Joshua didn't want to frighten you," he whispers as his eyes stay firmly on the door. "That's why the security has been upped but it could also be just a case of simple carjacking. We are not sure."

I frown in horror as I watch his face. "Why aren't you sure? He pays you to be sure. What kind of security people are not sure?" I put my hands over my mouth as I start to hyperventilate. Oh my God, oh my God, *oh my fucking God.*

Max's eyes flick to me. "Stop it. Don't even think about freaking out right now. I don't have the time."

I hold my hand over my mouth in shock and I nod. He's right, we don't have time for my dramatics.

We both stand deathly still and listen as Max stands defensively in front of me, gun drawn. This really is *NCIS* action, if ever I saw it. I bite my bottom lip as I think. Hit man... my beautiful boy has someone after him. I drop my face into my hands.

"It's clear," the bodyguard snaps as he leaves the apartment and walks toward us. Max nods and drops his gun.

"Looks like an interrupted robbery."

Max immediately gets his phone out and starts to dial the police. "Are you sure they are gone?" I whisper to the guard as I grip my bottom lip.

"Yes, no one is in there. We checked everything."

I nod, still deep in thought. Who would want to kill Joshua?

Is this really happening?

"Hi, Ben," Max snaps down the phone. My eyes search his face and I punch him in the stomach. I shake my head angrily at him. I don't want fucking Ben here.

"Natasha's house has been robbed," he snaps down the phone.

His eyes flick to me and he shakes his head.

I cross my arms angrily and narrow my eyes at him. This is bullshit!

"Okay, see you soon." He hangs up. I open my mouth to speak but he cuts me off.

"Don't you dare say one thing. I work for Joshua Stanton. He pays my wage. Not you. I am here to protect you at his insistence and I will be informing him if I think you are in danger in any way. So, don't waste your breath."

He storms past me and into my unit. Hmm...*asshole*.

The other guard shuffles on his feet uncomfortably and gives me a stifled smile. I push past him and walk into my apartment. My eyes shoot around the room, everything seems in order. Television, DVD player, laptop on my coffee table. I wring my hands in front of me as I am wracked with nerves. Someone has been in my apartment...looking through my things, probably a drugged person...maybe a murderer. My eyes widen in fear as the thought crosses my mind. *Stop it.*

"Go and check out the other apartments and see if anything else is amiss," Max asserts to the other guards. They all nod and file out of the room. I slowly start to walk through the apartment. Kitchen, my eyes look around, seems fine. Hallway, I wring my hands in front of me as I walk down it, seems fine. My bedroom, I stand still at the door, someone has been in here I can feel it. My bed has a mark where someone has sat on the bed... or maybe that was me before I left last week. Oh jeez, I don't know, I can't remember.

Max walks in behind me. "Don't touch anything."

I nod as I bite my lip. "I think someone has been in here," I whisper.

"Me too," he answers as he looks around.

Max's phone beeps a message and he looks at it and passes me the phone. It's from Joshua.

**Is Natasha ok?**

I immediately text back.

**Yes, she's fine.**

A text comes back.

**Do not scare her, keep her calm.
Don't tell her anything**

*Always lying.* I throw the phone at Max and storm into the bathroom as the tears of fury start again. I stand with my hands on the bathroom sink as I look at myself in the mirror. I can hear my heartbeat in my ears as anger seeps into my bone marrow. Don't tell her anything. Is that what he told all of his staff about him sleeping with Amelie? Don't tell Natasha anything...he must have. Nobody said a fucking word...except Amelie of course. He probably said the same thing to her. I bet he did, *the asshole*. I shake my head in disbelief at myself in the mirror.

Every time I think I might be making the wrong decision he proves me right again, every damn time. He is making me look like a total idiot in front of all these people. It's not even between me and him anymore. There are about ten people who know more about our relationship than I do. This has got to stop.

"Where is Natasha?" I hear Ben's South African accent snap through my apartment.

"She's in the bathroom," I hear Max reply flatly.

"Is she ok?" Ben asks.

"Yes, shaken up, but ok."

I put my ear to the door to hear what they are saying. "Joshua doesn't want her frightened," Ben replies.

I can't hear Max's reply.

"No, don't call the police until we know what we are up against." What? They are not calling the police? This is ridiculous. I will not be controlled by these men for one minute longer. I open the door and storm down the hall.

"Get out!" I snap at Ben as I point to the door.

"Hello Natasha," he replies calmly.

Embarrassment heats my cheeks. "Hello. I do not want you here so you can go and tell your boss the sooner he returns to America, the fucking better."

"Natasha," Max whispers as he grabs my arm and tries to calm me down.

I rip my arm from his grip as my furious eyes flick to him. "You can leave too, Max. I will not be deceived by all of you for one minute longer. Nobody is here. I am safe and I am calling the police now. So get out!" I scream. I'm totally losing it.

The guard comes back through the door.

"Looks like the unit above and below on this side have been robbed too."

Max puts his hand around the back of his neck.

"Thank God," he mutters as he looks at the ground.

I pick up my phone and dial the police.

"Hello, I would like to report a robbery."

Max and Ben are talking in the kitchen quietly. I walk in sheepishly.

"Sorry, Ben, I'm on edge," I whisper, embarrassed at my previous outburst.

He nods and gives me a crooked smile.

"I have been under a lot of stress and I am not handling things very well," I stammer. He nods again but stays silent. The poor bastard is probably too scared to speak.

"Max, I don't need protecting anymore. Go home with Ben and back to America where you belong."

"Natasha, you need to be guarded," Ben whispers.

I screw up my face in frustration. "Ben, the only person who can hurt me is Joshua and he has done just that. In fact, I would say he's excelled at it. You and Max being here is just putting salt on my wounds. Leave me alone, I can't take much more." My eyes fill with tears as I shake my head in disbelief.

"We are not trying to upset you, Tash," Max whispers as he puts his arm around me sympathetically.

"Well, you are. Ben, go home and guard Joshua, he needs you to keep him safe. Stop wasting your time on me, this isn't a movie scene. I need you to keep him safe for me. Promise me you will keep him safe," I splutter through my tears.

He smiles sympathetically at me. "I will." "Make him go home to America, please!" I sob.

Ben walks to the door and turns, his eyes hold mine for a moment. He wants to say something but holds his tongue.

"What is it?" I snap.

"You're making a mistake, Natasha," he sighs.

I screw up my face as pain lances through my chest. "What?" I shriek. Is he fucking kidding? "Tell me, Ben, did you say the same thing to Joshua when you watched him walk into Amelie's room that night or was that ok because your boss was about to get some action? Did you boys all stand outside his door and listen? Did you place bets on what would happen next?" I sob.

"Natasha," Max whispers in a hurt voice.

I step back and shake my head at the two of them. "This whole entourage bullshit you all have going on makes me sick. You both know more about my relationship than I do. So, you know what? You can have it, because I want nothing to do with it. If you care about Joshua go and find him a woman who is prepared to go to bed with the ten of you, seeing as you're all as thick as thieves. I am sure that will suit him just fine."

"Natasha, you're just upset," Max whispers.

"Stop saying that. I'm more than upset. I'm furious!" I scream. A knock sounds at the door and we turn to see two policemen.

I smile uncomfortably. Oh boy, did they just hear that? "Come in," I stammer.

"Are we interrupting?" one of the policemen says as his eyes flick to Ben.

Ben frowns and shakes his head. "No"

I look at Ben, signifying for him to go, but he raises his eyebrows and walks into the kitchen defiantly. "Does anybody want a cup of coffee?" he asks.

"Actually, I will have a coffee if that's ok," one of the policemen remarks.

Oh great, now a scabby cop who wants coffee. Shouldn't he be taking fingerprints or, I don't know, catching fucking robbers?

The policeman who wants coffee walks into the kitchen and the other one gets out his pen and notepad.

"Tell me what happened."

"We came home," I whisper as I wipe the tears from my face.

He cuts me off. "Is this your husband?" he points to Max in the kitchen.

I frown. "No...definitely not. He is my...bodyguard."

His eyes raise from his notepad as he frowns.

"Why do you have a bodyguard?"

"Umm...my ex-boyfriend is overprotective and he is wealthy so," I shrug, embarrassed.

"I see." His eyes drop and he continues writing. "So, you came home and then?"

"We noticed that the lock was broken so Max checked the apartment and then we called the police."

He nods. "What was taken?"

I look around the room and shrug. "Not really sure, nothing really."

His eyes scan the room. "They may have been interrupted before they got a chance to take anything."

I nod. "Hmm, probably."

"So, the television, stereo and laptop are all here. What about jewelry? Do you have any?"

"Oh, I didn't check." I walk into my bedroom and over to my side tables. I pull out the top drawer. I frown and pull out the bottom two drawers in a rush. I sit down onto the bed as I try to think. My underwear... it's all gone, *what the hell?*

I trace through my previous steps; no, everything should be in these three drawers. I slowly walk around to the other side of the bed and look into the drawers on that side of the bed. I pull them out in a rush, nope everything is still here. Photos, junk, moisturizers, make up. Nothing is missing, only my underwear. My eyes widen. Fuck!

My vibrator, *how embarrassing*. I run back around to the other side of the bed and pull out the drawers again in a panic, no still nothing in there. Who in the hell would want to steal my underwear? Oh boy, this is creepy. The policeman walks into the bedroom.

"Is everything ok?"

"Um." I hold my hands over my mouth as I try to make sense of this.

"My underwear is missing...my vibrator," I whisper embarrassed.

He frowns as Max walks into the room. "You alright?" Max asks me.

I nod as I bite my lip in mortification. "Can you please give us some privacy, Max?"

He frowns and stands still. "What's going on?" he asks.

I shake my head in embarrassment. I don't want Joshua finding out about this. "Nothing, I just want to talk privately with the policeman."

He stands still and narrows his eyes. "If something has been taken, I want to know about it."

The policeman's eyes flick between the two of us as he tries to work out the dynamics of our relationship.

"Max, I will say this just once, leave the room while I talk to the policeman."

He glares at me and leaves the room.

The policeman frowns at me. "Are you being kept here against your will?"

I shake my head. "No, I'm being guarded against my will. My boyfriend is a very wealthy man and was attacked so the security has been escalated to a ridiculous level. Max and I have been arguing about him watching over me."

He nods as he thinks. "So, what exactly has been taken?" He gets his notepad out again.

"My underwear and..." This is appalling, not so confident talking sex toys now, am I?

"Can I have a description?" He keeps his eyes cast down as he tries to not embarrass me any further.

Jeez, I have hit the bottom of the barrel. "Pink," I whisper, mortified.

He bites his lip to stifle his smile. "Pink," he repeats. I nod. "Yes, pale pink."

"Pale pink vibrator, anything else to add?" "Underwear."

"Anything about the vibrator that is identifiable?" He lifts his eyes to meet mine in question.

Good grief, I've had enough. "Regular size, regular shape. Pink!" I snap.

"I see," he answers as he smirks.

I smile broadly at him as I raise my eyebrows. "Do you have any idea how embarrassing this is? This is every woman's worst nightmare." I rub my forehead as I giggle at this ridiculous turn of events. He smiles. "Looks like you might have to return to your boyfriend, it seems his opposition has disappeared. Maybe he took it to get you back."

I fake a smile. "You're hilarious. I didn't realize police do stand up."

He laughs. "Trust me, in this job if you don't laugh, you will cry."

We walk back into the lounge room where I see Max sitting at the kitchen counter glaring at me. *Oh crap, I forgot about him.*

The other policeman comes back through the front door. "Two other apartments have also been robbed."

I nod, relieved, it was just a crazy coincidence.

"I will be in touch if we find anything and a fingerprint team will be around to do the door handle but I'll bet any money that they wore gloves so we will wait and see."

I nod and smile as Max shows them out. I walk back into my bedroom and a creepy feeling oozes over me. Who would want a secondhand vibrator? Surely a criminal wouldn't go home and use it on his wife...would he? Who knows, they are the dregs of society so it wouldn't surprise me. A cold shiver runs up my spine as the disgusting thought rolls through my head.

Max walks back up to my door. "You okay, Tash?"

I slowly nod. "Yeah, sorry I've been a bitch tonight. I can't handle all of you guys ganging up on me," I reply softly.

He puts a reassuring hand on my shoulder. "Tash, we don't try to gang up on you. We care about Joshua. He's in love with you. We want him to be happy."

My eyes tear up. "Can you stay in here in the spare room tonight? I'm a bit freaked out," I whisper.

He nods. "What did they take from your bedroom that you're not telling me?"

I shrug. "Nothing. I just wanted some privacy."

He reluctantly nods and walks over to the door to leave, then he turns. "Tash."

My eyes meet his. "Yes."

"For the record, Amelie went to Joshua's room that night, not the other way around. He was so upset about it he left without any guards and then nearly got killed by a hit man on the way home. He didn't tell you this because he doesn't want you frightened, not because he's trying to keep secrets. He's trying to protect you."

I drop my head as I listen.

"We were all as shocked as you. Joshua tells us nothing, he only speaks to Cameron and Adrian. You underestimate him. He doesn't talk about his private life to anyone."

I nod with my eyes on the ground. "Thanks, Max," I whisper through my tears as the hard lump of hurt balls in my throat.

I wait for Max to come around to the front of the building to pick me up for lunch. How is it I have come to depend on Max?

We have become friends by default. I have been forced to hang out with him and it's strangely...comforting. He has been the only constant male in my close circle since Dad's death. We walk in comfortable silence to his car.

"Joshua is leaving tomorrow night," he says matter of factly.

I stop and look at him as I get to the door, and my stomach drops.

My eyes flick around to the two cars full of men watching us. I get into the car and slam the door hard.

"How do you know?" I ask.

"Ben called me this morning and asked me to come around for a meeting this afternoon."

I chuck my bag onto the floor of the car. "And?" I snap as I flick my hair around my shoulders, annoyed.

"And I think, that if you are going to call him, you have twenty-four hours left to do it."

I roll my eyes as I look out the window.

"Well, I wish he would go today, that's what I think," I snap angrily.

"No, you don't. You think you have everyone fooled but I know what's really going on here. You are pushing him away to protect yourself."

I frown in disgust. "You know you are very opinionated for someone who is supposed to be invisible."

He smiles broadly and I find myself mirroring his stupid grin. "What's funny?" I snap.

He shakes his head. "Nothing. I didn't realize you thought you were hanging out with the invisible man."

"Yeah, well I am. A very annoying, big-mouthed invisible man...who, actually, isn't that invisible." I sigh as we pull into the traffic.

We buy our lunch and eat in silence. My mind is racing a

million miles per minute. Am I doing the right thing? What if I do really lose him? Oh God, please let me not lose him.

"What does Ben want to see you about?" I ask with a mouth full of food.

He continues chewing and shrugs. "I think I'm getting a finishing date."

My eyes widen as I chew. "Finishing date." I repeat as I wipe my mouth with my napkin.

"Pretty much."

I frown. "What will you do?"

He shrugs. "Go back to America," he says dryly.

"But I thought your romance was going well. She's lovely. Are you just going to leave her?"

"It is going well. Too well, but I'm not allowed to stay here if I'm not employed. You know how strict Australian immigration laws are."

"Oh," I whisper. "Do you want to stay?"

He nods. "Yes, I would love to see how this goes. I haven't liked anyone like this for a very long time." He frowns. "I even like her kids."

I chew as I think. It's not that bad having him around, is it?

Maybe I could stretch this out a bit for him.

"Tell Joshua that I feel unsafe after the robbery and that you need to stay and guard me for a while."

He wipes his mouth with a napkin as he frowns in question.

I shrug. "Why not? It's not like he can't afford to pay you."

"But I thought you didn't want to be guarded permanently?" he asks.

"I don't, but I can put up with it if you get rid of the other dickheads." I flick my head towards the corner.

His eyes flick over to the table of four guards sitting at the front of the restaurant waiting for us and he smirks.

"If he thinks you don't feel safe, he won't leave me alone with you, he will want at least another guard left."

"Fine, just one," I sigh.

He smiles. "You know he will probably sack me anyway because he knows we get along well."

"Tell him I won't have anybody else and if he doesn't like it then I will be scared stiff and it's all his fault."

He smiles. "You drive a hard bargain, Miss Marx, but you know what? He might just fall for it."

It's six o'clock Friday night and dark, the building is dead silent, and I am in the office alone. Max and the other guards are in their cars out the front of the building. I can see them from my window. I'm procrastinating because I don't want to go home. Joshua leaves Australia tomorrow and I desperately want to see him. I want to say goodbye...Hello...I love you. Why am I doing this to myself? I stare into space for about the fourth hour today; my last appointment was two o'clock. I lean my elbows on my desk and put my face into my hands as dread seeps into my every pore. How am I going to stay away from him tonight? How in the hell am I going to find the strength to do this? I just want to talk to him...I miss him desperately. I want to tell him about this terrible person who has hurt me so deeply. I want him to protect me from him and I know he would be outraged if someone hurt me like this. But then I remember the cold reality that he is that person and I am the only one who can protect myself. He offers no protection, only hurt. I blow out a breath as I start to slowly close the programs on my computer and my computer pings. A YouTube tab comes up in the middle of my screen. I frown, what's this? Don't tell me I've got a computer virus now.

A curser flashes on my screen...huh. I watch in wide eyed horror as a message starts to type on my screen.

**Precious girl, please talk to me.**

I bite my lip and my eyes instantly fill with tears as I realize that Joshua is hacking my computer. How long has he been sitting there waiting for me to close the programs? The cursor is flashing, waiting for a reply. I type.

**Josh... I can't. I'm sorry.**

I break into full blown sobs and hold my hands over my mouth as I cry out loud and stare at the screen. He types again.

**I love you.**
**Please see me.**

I sob uncontrollably as the reality of this horrible situation crushes my heart. The cursor flashes again and I reply.

**I can't, Josh.**
**I'm not strong enough to be with you.**
**Just know that I will always love you.**
**Remember me**

I cry out loud as I grip my stomach in pain. The picture flashes and I click on it. Oh dear God, no. Not this...not this song. I try desperately to click out of it, but it won't let me, and the film clip of the song 'Say Something' by A Great Big World and Christina Aguilera starts to play. Every time I hear this song I burst into tears.

Why is he sending me this shit? Is he trying to send me round the twist? I bang on the buttons, but I can't get out of it and I become hysterical as the depressing song blares through my office.

In desperation to stop it I bend to the floor, grab the electrical cord and rip it out of the wall, and the computer goes dead...just like my heart. I slump to the floor and lean up against the wall and sob. He needs to leave the country...I won't survive much longer.

## Joshua

I sit at the airport staring into space as we wait to board my jet. I am utterly gutted. The silence that surrounds me is stifling.

I look towards the doors for the ten thousandth time in the last hour.

"She's not coming, mate," Cameron whispers as his eyes hold mine.

I nod as I drop my head. "I know," I whisper in monotone. Adrian puts his arm around me. "You will feel better when we get back to LA." He shakes my shoulder in a reassuring gesture.

I sit slumped in my chair as I nod sadly, I don't even have it in me to speak. The blistering memory of the last time I felt like this poisons me from within, when I was nineteen and heartbroken, sitting in an airport just like this waiting for a flight to LA...trying desperately to escape her love...or lack of it.

Ben sits opposite us, and his eyes search mine. "Do you want a coffee?" he asks as he raises his eyebrows.

"Yes," I reply.

He stands and walks over to the stewardess. "How much longer?" he asks.

"Not long," she replies.

"Good," he mutters under his breath as he storms through the double doors.


## Natasha

It's Friday and I have survived Joshua leaving the country...just. I don't even know if you can call it surviving. I'm running on auto pilot like a zombie. If I think, I will crack...it's easier to function with no feeling...block the hurt...block the pain...if only I could block the memories. I've been listening to 'With or Without You' by U2 on repeat for days...it seems so fitting to my situation. I honestly can't live with or without him, how am I going to do this?

I've been throwing myself into work to try and get on with it. I just wish I didn't have to come to this stupid jail anymore. My job is really starting to piss me off. I think I need a change. Coby Allender totally freaked me out on my last visit to the court-house when he stared at me like his next meal the whole time, he's a frigging scary son of a bitch. Henry has assured me I am in the safe room today and he can't see me, so I guess that's a bonus. I wait in the observation room in a daydream, with a prison warden sitting next to me. Where is that spunky boy anyway? Jaxon...Jasper...Johnathon, what's his name again? At least his annoying flirting keeps my mind occupied and off serial killers and my beautiful Lamborghini. I'm starting to think of Joshua with fondness again: six days...it didn't take long. The door opens behind me and I keep my eyes firmly on the window in front.

"Swap seats," I hear a husky whispered voice say.

I turn to see Mr. Cheeky falling into the seat beside me. "Hey, Doc. Did you miss me?"

I smirk at him and turn my eyes back to the window. "Yes, totally." I frown as I try to remember his name.

"Jesten," he smirks.

"Oh, right, sorry. I'm hopeless with names," I whisper so the other guard can't hear me.

"Yeah, I noticed." He smirks. "Most girls remember mine though. How come you don't?"

I roll my eyes. "I see you're still full of

yourself." He laughs out loud and raises an eyebrow.

We watch as the door opens and Coby Allender is led into the room, my blood runs cold just seeing the creep. I wonder if he really is a serial killer or is just so insane that he likes the game of fooling everyone into thinking he is. They still think he has an accomplice, but I'm not so sure.

"Are you giving me your number today?" Jesten whispers in my ear.

"Sshh," I whisper. "I'm listening," I reply as I keep my eyes firmly on the screen.

"This guy is boring. Listen to me instead," he whispers back.

I giggle, this guy really is a dick. "No, I'm not giving you my number. I told you I'm not into you," I whisper.

"Fuck off, all girls are into me."

I giggle again. Total idiot. "Not me."

"Do you always lie compulsively? Or is it just when you're in the presence of greatness?" he whispers as his eyes stay on the screen.

I smirk at his ridiculous confidence. "No...only to losers. Aren't you going out with short and slutty Barbie anyway?"

He burst out laughing. "Not that I know of."

"Oh," I smirk. "What happened to her?"

"I sort of told this other hot girl to think of me while she had sex with her boyfriend to piss him off, not realizing it would also piss her off."

I giggle as I shake my head. "You are an idiot," I whisper. "Yeah, funny, she said that too."

I have to admit this stupid banter really does get my mind off things. The interview begins and we fall silent. I sit riveted to my seat.

"Are we being watched today?" Coby asks he looks at the double sided glass.

"Yes," Henry replies.

"Is Natasha here today?" he sneers.

I frown. How does he know my name?

"It is none of your concern who is here as a witness today," Henry replies calmly.

Coby smiles at the screen. "Natasha, dear, I have something of yours in my possession."

I frown and Jesten leans over to me. "Don't listen to him, he's trying to mess with you. He does it to everyone."

I nod as I swallow the lump in my throat. "Ok, thanks," I whisper. He smiles at the screen again. "It smells divine, Natasha." God, he's creepy. I start to sweat as fear grips me.

"It's pink and perfect. Tell me dear...was it a tight fit?" he questions.

Huh...what the hell? My eyes widen in horror as his sick eyes look straight through me.

"Tell me, how many orgasms have you had on that vibrator, Natasha? Do they feel good? Do they feel like cock?"

My face drops. *Holy fuck.* I stand in a rush and run for the door. Oh my God...it was him. He's got it. How...how did he even know who I am? Who was in my apartment? I run into the hallway and feel Jesten's arm around my waist.

"What's wrong?" he whispers.

My eyes are wide and before I can think what I am saying I blurt out. "My house was robbed last week, and my vibrator was stolen and he has it."

He frowns. "What?"

I nod frantically. "It was pink, and he just asked me how many orgasms I had on it. What the hell is that about?" I snap.

"Jesus, stay in here. I will go and get someone," he mutters.

"No, don't leave me. What if he gets me?" I stammer as I grab onto his shirt in fright.

"He's not getting you, Doc. Calm down." He runs off somewhere.

I wring my hands in front of me and I ring Max's number in a panic.

"Hello, Max, come and get me," I stammer. "Sure, I'm out front. What's up?" he replies.

"Just wait there. I'm coming out," I cry.

"Ok, what's wrong?" he snaps. I hang up in a panic.

I burst out of the bathroom and run straight into Jesten. "Jesus," he snaps as he grabs my arms. "Hey, calm down," he whispers as he pulls me into an embrace.

My heart is racing as I am gripped with anguish. I am wrapped in his embrace as he tries to comfort my fear. My arms are wrapped around his broad back, he smells good, masculine, warm. I feel a frisson of arousal sweep through me and I pull back in shock as I frown.

He sweeps the hair back from my damp forehead and looks down at me...*huh?*

Henry comes through the door in a rush. "Natasha, are you okay?" he asks.

Oh God, embarrassment sweeps over me and I pull out of

Jesten's grip. I do not want all of these people knowing I have a vibrator.

"Can we talk in private please, Henry?"

He smiles sympathetically. "Sure, dear. Meet me in the office at reception."

I nod. "Okay, I just want to freshen up." I walk into the bathroom and put my face into my hands. The James Bond movie has now turned into Quentin Tarantino...fucked up horror movie. I start to giggle uncontrollably. Even if I imagined this shit, I couldn't fucking imagine it. I need a strong drink.

Jesten walks into the bathroom. "You ok?" I smile, embarrassed.

"Yes, sorry."

He cuddles me and for some reason I melt into his arms again.

*What am I doing?*

He smirks at me. "Why in the hell does a chick as hot as you need a vibrator?" He smiles into my forehead.

I feel my face go bright red and I pull out of his grip, that just feels too familiar. I scratch my head in horror.

"No comment."

He giggles. "Don't worry, when you're my girl you won't need one. Don't bother replacing it."

"Stop it," I snap. "I am not your girl and I am not going to be your girl. Stop deluding yourself."

I walk out of the bathroom in a huff and down to the office to have the most embarrassing conversation of my life.


**Joshua**

I sit in my office as the intercom speaks. "Amelie is here to see you," the receptionist's bored voice echoes through the room. My eyes close in regret. I knew this was coming. I have been back in LA for two weeks and I haven't heard from her. I was hoping that I wouldn't. I put the heel of my palms into my eye sockets. "Send her in," I reply flatly.

I swivel on my chair with my eyes down. I'm furious with her. I know she's hurt but the pain she has brought me is unforgivable. I never meant for any of this shit to happen.

The sound of her heels click on the marble through the huge room and I raise my eyes slowly to meet hers.

"Hello, Joshua," she whispers nervously.

My eyes stare through her and I run my tongue over my front top teeth. "Hello, Amelie."

She stands still and waits for me to speak. I don't.

"Are you going to speak to me?" she asks as her eyes fill with tears.

"I have nothing to say to you," I reply coldly as I twist on my chair.

"Joshua, please." She bursts into tears. "I love you, I had to tell Natasha. I couldn't be dishonest." She sobs.

I frown in disgust. "I would have told her, it wasn't your place to hurt her like that." My anger rises.

She frowns. "You weren't going to tell her," she snaps. "Why didn't you tell her you love me?"

I screw up my face. "Because I don't. You're delusional, it was five minutes of shit sex Amelie. I have never regretted something so much in my life!" I shout.

Her face falls. "You regret it?" she questions.

"Of course!" I yell. "I make myself fucking sick that I have hurt her like this. She is a good person, and she didn't deserve any of this. I will never, ever forgive you for the way you treated her."

"Stop lying," I snap as my skin starts to crawl.

"Think about it, Joshua, she leaves you at the drop of a hat. She has no regards for your feelings. It doesn't sound like she loves you at all or that she ever did."

"Shut up!" I scream as I jump from my chair.

"She actually gets off on your pain," she sneers.

"Get out!" I scream.

I turn my back on her and look out the window.

"Tell me, Joshua, how many times have you tried to contact her and been ignored?"

I don't answer.

"She will never make you happy, Joshua."

"Get out!" I reply with my back to her. "I'm done."


## Natasha

"So, what did they say then?" Abbie frowns and I shrug. "Apparently he has done this before. He reads the police reports and tries to scare people."

"Get a new job, this shit is too weird," Bridget gasps. I nod. "I know."

We are at Milson's, a bar in Pitt Street. We can't go to any of our normal hangouts because Abbie is hiding from army guy, the man Abbie is sort of dating. Apparently, he's getting all possessive and jealous and she's not coping, it was only a matter of time. The music has a distinct R&B feel, very different to our normal dance kind of places.

The walls are painted gold and it has big brass pendant lights that hang over huge wooden benches, and you sit on what could possibly be the most uncomfortable stools in the history of the world.

"So, the police think he has read the police report about the robbery and then has purposely tried to scare you," Bridget sips her margarita as she listens.

"Aha, they accessed his computer, and he was looking up some illegal website of local crime and he had also googled me," I shiver at the thought.

"Shit. Thank God you don't have any social media."

"This is why I don't. Do you think he really does have my vibrator? What if he was telling the truth?" I sip my drink again. "He's in maximum security, he doesn't have your damn vibrator." Abbie pulls a disgusted face.

I blow out a breath as I scull my margarita and Bridget bubbles up a giggle.

"What?" I say deadpan.

"This is actually funny, this last week you have been having. Just how many black cats have you run over?" Bridget asks.

I smile and shrug. "I don't know...maybe a huge one. Like a fucking Jaguar or something." We all giggle and our next round of drinks arrive. I hand over my credit card.

"I would like to propose a toast." Bridget smiles and we all raise our glasses.

"To no more sadness." Their eyes meet mine.

I smile sheepishly. "Sorry girls, I know I have been a nightmare lately."

"Not to mention fucking boring," Abbie snaps.

I nod and smile as I lick the salt from my glass. "I will endeavor to be more fun, just for you, Abbie." I raise my glass to her.

She does an exaggerated nod. "Good...about time. I would hate to have to trade you in."

The waitress returns. "Excuse me, your credit card has been declined." She hands me the card.

"Oh God," I stammer. "I will have to transfer money, I'm so broke."

Bridget hands over her credit card and I start to log into my internet banking on my phone.

"It's good to have a phone again," I remark as I concentrate on the screen. I'm having trouble reading it without my glasses, so I hand my phone to Bridget.

"Here, can you transfer $300 for me onto my credit card?" She takes the phone off me and I take a sip of my drink. "Check out the fabulous shoulders on that guy at the bar," Abbie smirks.

I turn and look. "Hmm, not bad. Seven."

"No way, nine," she replies.

I smile as my eyes flick back to Bridget who is frowning at my phone.

"What?" I frown.

"How much is seven zeros?"

"Huh, what do you mean?" I ask.

"I think you have three million dollars in your account."

I frown as I snatch my phone from her, and I look at the screen. "Huh."

Abbie snatches the phone from me. "Fuck off. No way.

That's thirty million."

I look at the screen

$30 000 000.00.

*What the hell is that?*

"How many drinks have we had?" I stammer. I scroll through to transactions:

**Deposit - $30 000 000.00 - Stanton**

"Fuck off, what's that?" Abbie asks, wide-eyed.

I scull my drink and Abbie immediately puts her hand in the air to order another round.

My heart drops. "I'm guessing it's my divorce settlement," I whisper as my eyes fill with tears, and the finality of the situation sinks in. I don't want his money, I want him.

"How long were you with him?" Abbie snaps.

"Three months," I whisper as I stare at the screen.

"That's ten million a month, that's two and a half million a week." Bridget frowns.

The waitress comes over and Abbie snaps. "We will have nine margaritas, and do you have any cigars?" Bridget and I frown at her.

"Yes," the waitress replies.

"We will have three cigars and a lighter, please," Abbie asks the waitress.

I raise my eyebrows at her in question.

"He's a stupid fuck, let's spend the lot," Abbie sneers. I sit with my head resting in my hands. *What the hell.* I immediately text Joshua.

**I don't want your money.**

A text bounces immediately back.

**Liar**

"Liar," I snap. "He's such an asshole. He's calling me a liar because I said I don't want his money." The waitress arrives with our cigars and Abbie lights hers immediately.

"Oh, get off it. What an idiot," she tutts as she takes a drag of her cigar. "He could have broken my heart for a hundred grand."

Bridget laughs out loud and chokes on her drink. "I would have done it for fifty."

I text.

**For what it's worth, Joshua.**
**You will always be the love of my life.**

"What are you texting?" Bridget tries to grab my phone from me. It beeps again.

**Liar.**
**If that was the case,**
**you would be here with me now.**

I scull my drink and light my cigar as I try to think of a comeback. I'm not with you, Joshua, because I love you.

"What time is it in LA?" I ask the girls as I narrow my eyes. "Um, it's Friday night midnight...so in LA it's...nineteen hours behind us. Five in the morning," Bridget answers.

**You know I would be with you if I could.**
**We want different things, Josh.**
**It doesn't mean I don't love you.**

A message bounces back.

**You don't get to say that to me anymore.**
**You have brought me to my knees for the last time.**
**Stay the fuck out of my life.**
**I never want to see you again.**

# CHAPTER 11

## Natasha

*JULY 14<sup>TH</sup> DEAR DIARY,*

*It has been three weeks since my beautiful Joshua left Australia, and his absence has left a massive hole in my heart, in my life. I have a sick feeling in my stomach all the time.*

*Every time I eat, I have to run to the bathroom. I can't even vomit effectively now, I just dry-retch continually. What can I do right? I'm a mess. I have lost so much weight I look like a skeleton. I never knew the effects of stress could be so damn horrific. The nightmares, the migraines, the insomnia. I have seen my psychologist three times this week. I need to get on top of these nightmares. I'm a walking petrified time bomb. What if they are true? What if they are a premonition? What if I lose my love to death and I never get to tell him how desperately I love him? I wish I could call him. I want to tell him that I am desperate to share my life with him, but I need him to be sure that it is me that he wants, before he wrecks our love completely. He is the only man I will ever love and if I can't have* him, I will have no one. My psychologist is the only one who under-stands why I have done this to myself. I love Joshua so much that I fear it's abnormal. How can I turn my life around?

JULY 29*TH* DEAR *Diary*

   I went to the bank today. I feel sick. I don't want his money. The cheque that was written in my blood. The more I think about it the more I know he has moved on with Amelie. He put that money into my account in guilt. His last words to me were 'I never want to see you again'. At Amelie's insistence, I'm sure. I don't want his money; I want his love. I want him to love me like he did when he was just my Josh, my beautiful Josh. I want to remove the last twelve months of my life. I want my dad back, like a do-over. I can't bear this pain.

AUGUST 17*TH* DEAR *Diary*

   I went out clubbing for the first time last night, a total disaster. I had three drinks, burst into tears and left. I was in bed before eleven. Max is the only one who understands my level of grief. He gave the other guard the night off so he could come out. He knew I wouldn't handle things well. What's wrong with me?

   Will I ever recover?

NOVEMBER 12*TH* DEAR *Diary*

   I have been in tears all day and couldn't go to work. It's Joshua's birthday today. Did she make him a cake? Did she sing 'Happy Birthday' to him? I went to Oscar's today while Max stayed outside, ordered a cupcake and then sat on my own and cried as I ate it. I'm fucking losing it.

   Happy Birthday, my beautiful Lamborghini. I miss you.

. . .

DECEMBER 17<sup>TH</sup> DEAR Diary

*It is one week till Christmas. I heard Mum crying tonight when she went to bed. Her heart is broken because of me. I killed my father, I pushed away the love of my life and now he's with her. I hope he's happy. Are you happy, Joshua? I hope this has all been worth it. I have to put up the Christmas tree tomorrow and all I really want to do is burn the fucking thing down. Maybe I might move to London, I need a change.*

DECEMBER 26<sup>TH</sup> DEAR Diary

*I cried most of yesterday, it was a bad day for all concerned. I have started eating for China or Willy Wonka...not sure. I rang Joshua last night, but he didn't answer, as if he would. I need to move on. I need to get over this. Millions of people go through relationship breakdowns every day and they get through it. I thought Cameron and Adrian might have called me, they didn't. Figures. Bridget and Abbie and I are going to the beach today with Abbie's army guy. Can't bloody wait. I'm thinking of getting a kitten.*

DECEMBER 31<sup>ST</sup> DEAR Diary

*It's New Year's Eve and I know he's fucking with her. I hate him. His life has not changed and mine is in tatters. I have been dancing all night with Gran and Mum to Beyonce. Tomorrow, I start a new year and I am not doing another year like this one.*

*Bridget just called me and tried to get me to go the Ivy but I'm going to bed. It's 12.30. Bring on the next year.*

. . .

*JANUARY 15<sup>TH</sup> DEAR Diary*

*I have been going out, it's actually ok. I have even had coffee with Jes a few times. It's been fun. It feels good to laugh again. Jeremy admitted he has been seeing someone from work and he and Bridget broke up. She went on a date with someone else a week later, why can't I do that? I need to sleep with somebody else.*

*FEBRUARY 14<sup>TH</sup>*

*It's Valentine's Day. Who invented this shit? I got roses from Jes and got asked on three dates. It's been six months since I last saw Joshua, but I am still not ready, I'm staying home and eating Ben and Jerry's instead. Joshua will probably propose to bitch vet today. She can have him.*

## Six months later, August 19th

## Adrian

Cameron pulls the car into Joshua's driveway. It's eight in the morning and we have just trained at the gym after Cam finished a nightshift. It's a habit we have gotten into, get it out of the way early. "Seriously, my arms are shaking. There is no way he can lift that." Cameron shakes his head.

"He does. I watched him the other night," I murmur as I open the back car door to retrieve my bag.

"He has to be juiced up. No one can bench-press that." "Probably, where do we get some of that shit? You're a

doctor, write us a prescription," I say dryly as I start toward the house.

Cameron rolls his eyes. "I can't wait to go to jail, so you can have bigger biceps. Dick."

I turn back to face him as he walks behind me. "Can that happen? Just say you write a dodgy prescription, would you go to jail?"

Cam screws up his face. "Yes, of course. What do you think?"

I raise my eyebrows as we continue up the drive. "Huh, I never knew that. So, what if your prescription pad gets stolen?"

"Then you're basically screwed," he replies.

"Hmm."

We walk up the steps and the front door opens in front of us. Heidi Mills smiles as she steps out into the sun. Her long sandy blonde hair is messed up and she is wearing a skimpy gold dress and high strappy stilettos.

"Miss Mills, ravishing as always," Cameron smiles as his eyes drop down her perfect body. He holds both of his hands up to accentuate his compliment.

She smirks at him. "You know it, Cam. Not happening." She walks past us without stopping.

He turns and smacks her on the ass as she passes him. I laugh and we head into the foyer where we see two more gorgeous women walking down the hall out of the party room.

"Heelloooo." Cameron smiles as he raises his eyebrows. "We haven't met." He holds out his hand to the tall brunette and she takes it as she smiles.

"Carmen." She bites her lip to stifle her mischievous grin as she shakes his hand.

"Cameron, I'm Joshua's brother and this is Murph." He smiles as he gestures to me.

I look her up and down and nod. "Hi," I mutter deadpan. "I'm Allegra." The dark blonde steps forward.

Cameron smiles as he looks her up and down. "All legs alright." Both the girls burst into giggles.

My eyes flick to him and I smirk. "You did not just say that." He laughs and then winks at me. I shake my head and head down to the party room. The door on the other side of the room into the pool area is open. I can see Joshua in the

pool so I head back to the kitchen to make myself a coffee.

Cameron walks in after me. "Meeeooow," he snaps. "Fucking hot."

I smile and shake my head. "Coffee?"

"Yep." He sits at the kitchen island, opens the paper and starts to read.

I continue making three coffees as Joshua walks into the room from outside in a towel.

"Hey," he murmurs as he continues to the cupboard and starts to make a protein shake.

"Fucking yessssss," Cameron snaps. "Pussy trifecta."

Joshua smirks as he keeps looking down at the shake he's making, and I laugh out loud.

"Did you go to the gym?" Joshua asks into his shake. "Yeah. Did you know that black haired guy can deadlift

100 kg?" Cameron asks.

Joshua looks at him and replies flatly. "So?" "You reckon he's on the juice?"

Joshua shrugs. "Who fucking cares? What are you checking him out?"

Cameron frowns. "No...Murph was." He shoots me a stupid smile. I shake my head and take another sip.

Joshua walks over to Cameron. "Give me your phone."

Cameron hands it over without looking up from the paper and Joshua goes and lies on the lounge and starts to log into Cameron's Facebook page.

"So, what happened last night? Get any action?" Cameron asks as he turns the page.

I shake my head. "No, not into him. Bit of a toss actually, he told the waitress off. Rude bastard."

"Who is this prick?" Joshua snaps.

My eyes meet Cameron's as he rolls them. "What prick?" I reply monotone.

"The same guy was in a photo with them two weeks ago." "Are you kidding?" I snap.

"You just banged Charlie's Angels in the hot pussy trifecta and you are worried about some loser sitting next to Natasha in a photo on Bridget's Facebook page?" I shake my head at him as I drink my coffee.

"Here, look at this photo. He has his hand on her leg. See, under the table." He points to the screen.

I walk over to him and take the phone from his hand and study the photo.

"Who cares? It's been six months," Cameron snaps. "Natasha's a bitch...he can have her."

Joshua's eyes shoot up. "Watch your fucking mouth," he snaps. I smirk at Cameron and throw a cushion at him which hits him hard in the head as I walk back toward the kitchen island.

"Blasphemy, Cameron. Never try to dethrone the queen." "Go home, both of you," Joshua says flatly.

"Bullshit," Cameron snaps. "You're a soft cock. You have the hottest chicks on the planet lining up for you and you're stalking your ex-girlfriend from my Facebook page."

Joshua smirks as he keeps scrolling through the screen.

"So, anyway," Cameron continues, "you know that hot nurse I've been banging from the hospital."

Joshua's eyes stay planted on the screen. "Which one?" "The blonde one."

"Elaborate. I think you're banging about ten blondes at the moment," I mutter flatly as I drink my coffee.

"Anyway, word on the street is she's married, and she just left her husband for me." He scratches his head in frustration.

Joshua laughs, his eyes not leaving the screen. "Ha, sucked in."

"How do you not know she's married?" I ask in horror. "Murph, I hardly know her name. How would I know

she's married?"

"You're a cock. I hope someone screws your wife when you get married," I stammer.

"No one will be screwing my wife because I will be marrying a virgin...like Nat." He realizes what he is saying and stops immediately. Joshua's eyes lift from the screen and he glares at Cameron. "Sorry mate... I didn't mean," Cameron whispers uncomfortably.

"I know what you fucking meant," Joshua snaps. He stands and throws the phone onto the lounge and walks upstairs. We hear the shower turn on.

I put my fingers in the shape of a gun and pretend to shoot Cameron as he slumps back into his chair.

"You know you really are stupid," I mutter.

"Tell me something I don't know."

## Natasha

The morning sun warms me through the windscreen as I sit in my car. I watch Max slowly walk across the pedestrian crossing with the two little girls, one in each hand. We are dropping them off at school for his girlfriend Hallie, who had an early shift this morning. I watch attentively as the girls point and talk in over-animation as they show him things around the playground. One of them bounces on the spot, full of excited energy. He looks and smiles as he comments, then he laughs out loud. I smile broadly.

Max is happy when he's with his girls, carefree even. I myself have a huge soft spot for the two of them, their beautiful little personalities ooze honesty. Their father died when they were just one and three. Cancer. I cannot imagine the horror of not having my dad alive and around as I grew up, and yet they can't even remember what he looks like, or the sound of his voice. Tragic.

Speaking of tragedy. It has been nine long months since I lost my beautiful dad. I miss him. Christmas was the hardest. I don't know whether the dread of the impending day was worse than Christmas Day itself. Brock was still in Afghanistan, so it was just Mum, Bridge, Grandma and me. The Stantons graciously invited us to their house in Melbourne but Mum declined, because Josh and Cam were not going to be there and it was too far to travel with Gran, not to mention the small matter of us all not being able to stand Margaret. I have kept her sordid secret... regrettably.

Joshua and Cameron had Christmas in LA with Adrian. I know if Joshua had been in Australia, Mum would have been in matchmaking heaven, she hasn't given up, nor have the girls. I'm not so sure though, maybe I have.

On Christmas night after an afternoon of silently crying in my bed, I did the unthinkable. I rang him. He didn't pick up. And yet he knew how desperately sad I would have been about my dad; he still didn't pick up. I've blown it. I have no doubt he has moved on, with who though I'm unsure. The girls speak to Cameron and Adrian on Facebook every couple of days and they told me Joshua hasn't seen Amelie since the Armageddon day at the hospital. I find that hard to believe. Cameron asks about me every time he speaks to Bridget. I know this because unbeknownst to him, half the time he is speaking to me.

On New Year's Eve with a few margaritas under my belt I texted Cam, Josh and Adrian.

**Happy New Year Thinking of you X**

I remember smiling and tearing up when Cameron's message bounced straight back. He must have been really drunk.

**Happy New Year, baby.**
**I love you**

I waited again and when my phone beeped a message, I excitedly grabbed it...Adrian, who must also be inebriated, as his text didn't even make sense.

**Happy New Year, Cinderella.**
**We miss you.**
**Read the message!**

Read the fucking message. I wanted a message from Joshua...not you, not Cameron. I wanted him, only him, to miss me. After realizing that Joshua was probably on a secluded island like he has been for the last five years with bitch vet, I had no choice. I did what any self-respecting girl with a broken heart would do in this situation. You know the situation...staying home to watch the fireworks on television with my mother and grandmother on New Year's Eve. I threw my back into those margaritas, put on Beyonce and danced for two hours while Gran and Mum sat on the lounge and watched me, and of course pretended I was a good dancer. I think the term was bootylicious to be exact. Jeez, if that's not love, I don't know what is. What a way to ring in the New Year. I frown as the memory crosses my mind. I'm such a loser.

Max pulls me out of my daydream as he jumps back into the car. "Ready for your first day?" He widens his eyes at me as he smiles.

"Not really." I frown. I'm starting a new job today and I'm nervous as hell. I'm going to be working in the public hospital system as a psychologist. A regular straight psychologist and it's only for thirty hours a week. After Joshua's divorce settlement, thankfully money is no longer a problem for me. I haven't touched the money, but the interest isn't bad. The girls and my psychologist have been on my case about the fact that my job as a sex therapist was perhaps affecting my personal life and in the end, I had to agree with them. I still suffer from the night-mares but I'm so nervous about starting this job that I haven't had one in five days, a record. Maybe the change is working already.

"Are you still going out tonight?" Max asks.

"Yeah, is Steven coming?" I murmur, as I check my makeup in the sun-visor mirror for the tenth time since we left home.

"Yes, he starts at nine. What time will you be leaving?"

I shrug. "Not sure, we will wait till he starts if you want."
"Okay. Good."

Max has become over-protective and I have to say it's rather comforting. The whole Coby Allender episode and the knowledge that the authorities still don't know if he has an accomplice on the outside totally freaks me out. Twelve young women raped and murdered in cold blood...disturbing. In the end, I had to tell Max about the whole embarrassing vibrator theft and threatened him with death if he told Joshua, Ben or Adrian. He has thankfully stayed silent but has hired two more bodyguards.

Steven is young and good-looking. He comes out with us at night...and Abbie is conspiring to sleep with him. Surprise, surprise. Mark is older and he works Saturdays and Sundays through the day and Max hangs with me through the week. It works out well because Max gets to spend time with his girlfriend and her girls and Joshua is still footing the bill. Not sure about why...but who cares...it's not like he can't afford it.

He pulls into the hospital parking lot. "Good luck, boss lady." He smirks

I screw up my face. "Thanks. I'm freaking out. What if I break into sex talk? I'm so desensitized to sexual therapy I fear I don't know what's normal psychologist talk anymore."

He laughs. "Just try to not say the words vibrator, semen or prostitute." He bites his lip to stifle his smile.

I nod and smile broadly. "I kind of like those words. What about Viagra...can I say Viagra?" I tease.

"Yeah, if you get me a script." He giggles.

"Ewww, gross." I frown. "Too much information."

"See, it's working already. You never say 'Ewww, gross'."

I laugh and hunch my shoulders. "Hey...you're right. See you tonight. Wish me luck."

## 1 am Cargo Bar

We sit at the huge wooden high tables on our cane high back stools. The cream Chinese lanterns glow a warm light throughout the space and the sound of loud laughter and voices echo throughout the room. David Guetta plays in the background. We are celebrating the completion of my first week in my new job. It seems we have found a new hangout for Friday nights. Bridget was asked here a couple of weeks ago to meet this guy she fancied and we sort of became instantly hooked. This place definitely deserves the title, Dry Cleaners. Never have you seen so many beautiful men in suits under one roof, Friday night work drinks of course. It's like shooting fish in a barrel, they don't stand a chance. I have to say, I myself stand a very good chance of being picked for the Australian Olympic team...in prick teasing. I seem to have mastered the art of, as Abbie says, not giving a shit. I give them fake names, fake jobs and fake phone numbers, not to mention my fake intentions. Just last week my name was Gertrude, and I was a taxidermist.

Tonight, my name is Cheetah, and I am a contortionist. I

have never laughed so much in my life. Bridget broke up with Jeremy and for the first time in history the three of us are actually on the same page when it comes to men. Who cares... whatever. While Didge and I spend our nights lying and club kissing, Abbie spends hers running away from army guy, aka Tristan. It seems he thinks he is in love with her and she is running for her life, scared. We can only go to the Ivy now when we have had enough fun and Abbie turns into a pumpkin and is ready to go home with Tristan, otherwise she has to behave and act all girlfriendy. Hilarious. It's so fun teasing her for a change. We are talking to four guys we met here a couple of weeks ago. They are all gorgeous and slightly younger than us, stockbrokers...or so they say.

"So, Felicity," one of the guys says. My eyes look around as I wave to another man we met earlier tonight.

"Felicity," he repeats. I keep looking around.

"Fuck off. Your name is not Felicity, is it?" He pokes me.

"Oh, you're talking to me?" I giggle.

Bridget laughs. "Ahh der Felicity, who else would he be talking to?" She rolls her eyes around in her head like a freak.

I giggle into my drink.

"And what's your name again?" he asks Bridget.

"What do you want it to be?" She laughs.

"Threesome." He laughs as his friend chokes on his drink in shock.

We all giggle, we really are very pissy.

"What's your name?" the tall guy asks Abbie.

"Lemon, lime and soda," she coos. God...such floozies, men are so stupid.

"I'll get you one." He runs to the bar and she winks at us. "Right, free drinks for the girl who can get these guys to kiss."

Abbie smirks into her glass.

I burst out laughing. "Margaritas, can I get margaritas?" "Of course," Bridget snaps. "I want Martinis."

The tall nob returns with her drink.

"Thank you," Abbie whispers as she shrugs shyly. Oh boy... get off it! This guy is as dumb as dog shit if he falls for that crap. Abbie doesn't have a shy bone in her body.

"So," Bridget smiles at the four men, "we thought we might go to another bar."

"Can we come with you?" the cute curly haired brunette with brown eyes asks innocently as he leans forward on the table.

"Yes, I suppose, but you have to do an initiation test if you want to party with us."

Abbie and I hide our laughter behind our glasses.

"Yeah, okay." The tall guy smiles. "What is this initiation?" The boys all laugh and start flexing their biceps like freaks as we giggle. "I want you." She points at the guy who just brought Abbie a drink. "And you." She points to the tall guy with dark hair. "To kiss."

Their eyes widen in shock.

We all hide our giggles and Abbie's eyes light up with mischief. "Tongue kiss," she whispers as she widens her eyes.

"No way." They start to shake their heads nervously as their friends start to nod.

"It's just, we are team players...if you know what I mean." She licks her lips for effect. Bridget and I are nearly wetting ourselves as we try to act serious.

"And we want to know that the boys we party with like to... team play too."

Their eyes widen as they realize that she is perhaps talking about a gang bang. They exchange looks and the two men that don't have to kiss start to tell their friends.

"Just do it. We want to party. Fucking do it."

The whole group of seven of us are in fits of laughter as they try to decide if they are going to do it.

"Seriously, fucking kiss now. Actually, give him a head job if that's what it takes," blond guy snaps to his two friends. The poor two men under pressure don't know whether to laugh or cry.

"What do we do if they actually go through with this challenge?" Bridget whispers.

Abbie takes a scull of her drink. "Run."

I spit my drink out as I laugh out loud. Where do we come up with this shit?

The two un-kissing men start to chant to their friends to kiss and we are all in fits of laughter when I feel an arm come around me from behind. I turn as I feel lips on my temple.

"Hey Doc," Jesten smiles.

I turn and smile broadly at him. "Hi, Jes."

"*Kiss, kiss, kiss, kiss,*" the group chant from behind us.

Jesten frowns. "What's going on?"

The curly haired guy sits forward. "These girls are going to stack us on...if we kiss."

Jesten bursts out laughing and shakes his head at us.

"You girls are bitches." Jesten laughs as he shakes his head. "I knew it," the guys yell collectively as they point at us.

Bridget, Abbie and I clink glasses as we laugh. "You guys were totally going to kiss," Abbie laughs as she points at them.

"Were not," they start to scream. "Were not."

Jesten tucks my hair behind my ear. "I'm going to another bar. Do you want me to swing back and pick you up on the way home?"

I shake my head and frown. "No, what for?"

He smiles mischievously. "Hot sex Doc, what else?"

Abbie chokes on her drink. "Yes, she's coming. You're going!" She points at me.

I shake my head, smiling. "No Jes, for the ten thousandth time, I'm saying no."

"You know all this resistance is just making you hotter." He bends and kisses me quickly on the lips. "See you later."

I turn and watch him leave the bar with his three friends. His broad shoulders and muscular back look edible in that white t-shirt, not to mention the faded tight denim jeans around his cute tight ass. He has that thing. You know the thing, some men have it and others don't. Like an X-factor. That very same thing that I find ridiculously attractive in a man. Only one other man I know has it and we are so not talking about him. I've been trying to analyze it, it's the domination thing. After twenty-five years, I have finally worked out that I'm sexually attracted to dominant men...too bad I have only ever met two of the bastards. Both hot, both players. One rich, one poor. Both way too dangerous for my sanity. Nope, not going there again, grown out of bastard-player-lover-syndrome. If only I could get my body to keep up with my brain.

"He's so hot," Bridget snaps.

"If you don't tap that you're an idiot," Abbie slurs.

"Change the subject. Jesten is off limits," I snap.

"Good, I might go home with him then," Abbie smiles.

"Don't you dare," I narrow my eyes. "He's on the bench."

"Ha, I knew you liked him." She laughs.

I roll my eyes. "Shut the hell up and buy me a drink, bitch."

THE DAY after is always hell. Why do I do this to myself? I have to wash clothes and grocery shop...hungover. Again. It would be such a great society if we just popped a pill to eat and threw our clothes out after we wore them once, or better yet went naked. No grocery shopping, no cooking, no washing, no folding or ironing...the very bane of my existence. I hate house-work with a passion. I wish I was one of those Martha Stewart types who gets off on it. I just don't like it. I like my house clean but, boy, it shits me doing it every damn spare minute I have. Imagine having messy kids living with me. I shiver at the thought.

I'm in my local grocery store, trudging up the aisles with my cart and my guard is at the front drinking his coffee. The aroma of the deli is rolling my nauseated stomach. Who in the hell eats that like vomit smelling cheese? I rub my face and try to stop myself from dry-retching, this is totally shit. I'm not drinking again. I start to perspire as I fight the wave of nausea. Kill me now. I pull out my phone and text Abbie.

**Call me an ambulance.**

She immediately texts back.

**Can't.**
**I'm in the mortuary.**
**Dead.**

An hour later I am at home unpacking my groceries when my phone rings. I got one less problem without you! I got one less problem without you! Rihanna's 'Diamonds' is out and 'Problem' by Ariana Grande's is in. The words to this song somehow ring true in my life...wonder why?

I used to cry when my phone would ring 'Diamonds' and now when I hear those words I smile.

"Hello."

"Hi Tash."

"Oh, hi Mum."

"Love, can you come with me to the hospital? Something is up with Gran."

I frown and immediately stop what I am doing. "What do you mean?"

"I don't know, she just rang me and said she needed to go to the hospital and could we take her."

"Oh...okay." I answer wide-eyed. "I'll get over to Didge's house and you pick me up from there." I start to panic and run around frantically to try and find my keys in amongst the shopping bags on the counter. Why do I only lose my damn keys when I'm in a hurry? I quickly put away the meat and milk and head to the car.

Fifteen minutes later, Bridget and I stand out the front of her house as we wait for Mum to pick us up.

"So, then what did she say?" Bridget frowns.

I hunch my shoulders. "I don't know. Just that. Gran needed to go to the hospital, and she thought we should come."

"Yes. But what's the problem?"

"I don't know. For the tenth time!" I scream. Honestly, I'm too sick for this shit.

"Calm down, you crazy bitch," Bridget snaps.

"You know what, when we get to the hospital, book me in. I'm dying from alcohol poisoning and it's your bloody fault. Stop making me drink so much!"

She laughs as she looks at me. "You do look like shit actually, come to think of it."

I fake a smile at her as the car pulls up and we pile into the back seat. Gran is seated in the front seat and smiling calmly.

I lean over her seat from the back and put my arms around her neck. "What's wrong, Gran?" I ask. "Are you ok?"

She nods and puts her two hands over my two hands around her neck. "Darling, yes, I have just been having these terrible stomach pains for a couple of days."

Bridget screws up her face to me in question.

"What does that mean?" she mouths at me. I shrug again. I see Mum's worried eyes flick to her as she drives. I sit back and worriedly assess the situation.

We arrive at the hospital and are walking up the stairs when Gran doubles over in pain.

"Mum, what's wrong?" My mother frantically rushes to her side. Bridget holds her hand over her mouth in fear.

"Go and get someone," Mum snaps.

"Right." I run through the doors and up to reception.

"My grandmother is in pain outside and can't get in here." "Ok, I will get someone." She picks up the phone and makes a call as she smiles calmly at me. "Won't be long, go back to her and someone will be out to help you."

"Ok, we are on the front steps," I nod before I run back through the reception area where I see a nurse already attending Gran and helping her through the double electric doors. Bridget is as pale as a ghost and walking slowly behind them. They usher her into the casualty consultation room with Mum by her side and the doors close behind them.

BRIDGET and I wait for three hours, where in the hell is Mum? Why doesn't she come and tell us what's happening? What *is* happening?

"Why did we go out last night? I feel so bad," Bridget groans.

"You look worse," I mutter.

"You can talk."

Mum walks through the doors and we both jump up immediately and rush to her.

"They are admitting her overnight to run some tests."

I frown. "What for?"

"It seems her stomach and some of her organs are swollen. They have just called in an ultrasound person and we will know more after they do some tests." She pulls out her phone. "I have to ring Robert." She walks away from us and starts dialing his number.

"What do you think is going on?" Bridget asks.

I shrug. "I'm not sure but I don't like it."

For the next six hours Bridget and I sit in the waiting room with Mum, worried sick, and eating every hangover treating grease-trap food we can find in the cafeteria. I'm never drinking again; this is intolerable.

AT SEVEN O'CLOCK that evening the doctor comes out. "Mrs. Marx?"

"Yes," my mother answers as she stands. The doctor is about fifty, greying and kind-looking. He shakes her hand. "I'm Robert Walton. I have been looking after your mother today."

"Is she ok?" my mother asks.

"Yes, we have sedated her, and she is sleeping like a baby." He smiles and gestures to the offices at the end of the corridor. "Would you like to come into the conference room so we can talk privately?"

Bridget and I exchange looks, that doesn't sound good. "Umm, sure," my mother answers in a quiet voice. She looks nervously at us.

The kind doctor smiles. "Are you girls Netta's granddaughters?" We both nod. "You're welcome to come too if you wish." We follow him down the hall and into the conference room and we all sit nervously on the lounge.

Mum swallows. "What's going on?"

"I'm sorry, your mother and grandmother has advanced stage four cancer."

"What?" Mum gasps.

Bridget silently grabs my hand as we sit still in shock.

"We think it may have started as bone cancer, but it has now spread to her pancreas," the doctor says sympathetically. "We will make sure that she doesn't suffer any pain but to be realistic I don't think that she will leave the hospital."

Mum frowns. "But she has been so well, there haven't been any signs. I am with her at least three times a week, surely there would have been some signs if she was unwell." Mum's voice is rising as the reality of the situation starts to hit her full force.

"There must be something that you can do. Money is no object, my brother, Robert Stanton, is a very wealthy man. Some treatment, overseas?"

The doctor sighs, shakes his head and pulls out the X-rays and puts them onto the light box. We all gasp as the obvious shadows cloud the screen.

The doctor points and explains the shadows as the three of us sit in silent horror.

"Please remember that your mother is eighty-four, her body cannot be cured of the cancer at this late stage of diagnosis. I'm sorry there is nothing we can do."

Mum puts her head in her hands and starts to weep. I feel like I am having an out of body experience and this is not really happening...I feel detached, with no emotion. This can't be real.

"How long does she have, Doctor?" Mum whispers through her tears.

He puts his hand on her shoulder as he stands. "Not long... a few weeks, maybe less."

Bridget pulls Mum into an embrace and they both cry as the doctor leaves the room.

I sit back in the chair, devoid of any feeling. More hurt is coming for my beautiful mother and sister. How much more can one family take? When is enough, literally enough?

. . .

THE NEXT THREE days is a blur of waiting rooms in the hospital, only leaving to sleep. Robert and Margaret arrive with Wilson, Scott and his wife Alyssa. We sit camped in the waiting room outside the palliative care unit, the most depressing place on Earth. I thought the intensive care waiting room was depressing, but at least people there have a chance of getting better.

Every visitor has come to this ward to say goodbye to their loved one, there is no chance of getting out of here alive. Bridget is so tired she doesn't care anymore and is asleep on the lounge, spread eagled, perhaps even dribbling. I am sitting on the floor next to the vending machine with Wilson. My legs are curled up and my arms are around my knees. I am lost in thought. Margaret, Scott and Alyssa are on the lounges. My mother and Robert are in with Gran, they haven't left her side. How do you say goodbye to your parent? It's something nobody should have to do. Cancer. How many beautiful people have to die of this insidious disease before they find a cure? Why in the hell are the world's leaders spending billions of dollars every year on space exploration when we have a disaster on Earth to explore? I know every taxpayer on Earth wants a cure for cancer. The governments need to find one...quickly.

Max is here, sitting in the corner reading on his iPad. It's

strangely comforting having him here. I think back to when he first started guarding me at Joshua's insistence and how much I hated it, but now I understand what poor Joshua deals with every day and why he is like he is and why Ben is so obsessive about Joshua's safety.

Apparently, about three years ago Joshua's company designed an app and sold it in a multimillion dollar deal to a major company who was in talks with another man about his app. Unbeknownst to Adrian and Joshua, the company dumped the other man and bought Josh's app instead. The man then went berserk, claiming Joshua's company stole his app idea and that in effect Joshua had stolen millions of dollars from him, costing him his wife and family.

The man is mentally unstable and is obviously not taking his medication. Max said that not long after that the man broke into Joshua's house and was waiting there when Joshua got home after a night out. Luckily, he had Carson and the boys with him and a security guard. The man had a gun and was going crazy, threatening to kill him, but they managed to wrestle him to the ground and hold him there until the police came and arrested him.

He was ordered into psychiatric care and an AVO was placed on him but then eighteen months ago Joshua was walking into a restaurant one Saturday night with Adrian and Ben and the same man turned up with a gun and fired a shot at them. Luckily, he can't shoot, and he missed, but he escaped and is still at large. Max won't tell me his name. I think he is scared that I can look him up on the system or something. I can't, mental health records are not accessible to just anyone. But I would love to see his psychometric testing so I could see how dangerous I think he is. They live in constant fear that he will turn up and try to kill again. He has since threatened to kill Adrian and I guess they think that I am in danger because I was photographed with Joshua...that and the fact that the world still thinks we are married.

The carjacking thing in LA though is still baffling to me. If this man is so unstable, he probably doesn't hold down a permanent job, which means he wouldn't have the money to hire a hit man. I have discussed my theory with Max, and he agrees with me. We think it's highly unlikely that this is the same man but the police are sure it is...so, I don't know. The police have footage of the hit men that attacked Joshua in the petrol station that night and are just waiting to get a name and then they will be able to trace his bank accounts to find out any info or perhaps the person who hired the hit. Either way, my nightmares are warranted. My beautiful man has crazy people who want him dead and he is heavily guarded. I know he hates it. I am pulled from my nightmare as the doors at the end of the corridor open. My heart stops and I gasp when I see first Ben walk in, then another guard. Cameron walks in front, wearing jeans and a white shirt, his hair curled and unruly, and behind them Joshua.

Two guards walk behind him. I feel like I am watching this in slow motion. He's wearing a navy suit and pale pink shirt, navy tie. His height and stance dominate the men around him. His dark chocolate hair is super short which only accentuates his strong jaw line, dark skin and beautiful large lips...Dear God! My eyes close in pain and I drop my head.

I had forgotten how beautiful he is.

He walks gracefully down the corridor without noticing us tucked in the corner. My heart has stopped as I watch him from across the room. How can any human being hold so much sexual energy? It's unfair.

I am immediately overcome with a wave of affection for him and my eyes fill with tears. *Stop it. Stop it. Stop it.* Ben sees us and heads in our direction. I don't know if I am going to wet myself or jump up and down and scream like a groupie. Bridget is now sitting sleepily in her chair and her eyes are about to bulge from her head as she looks at me. *Yes, Bridget, I fucking see it.* They walk over to us and Cameron immediately cuddles his mother and kisses her cheek. I am overcome with emotion as I scramble to my feet. I don't know whether to laugh or cry. I stand at the back of the group like a child waiting for my turn. Joshua then turns and kisses my mum who has come out of the hospital room. He pulls her into an embrace and then Bridget, then Margaret. I stand still, frozen. *My turn, my turn.*

Cameron walks over to me. "Hi Tash," he whispers as he kisses my cheek gently and puts his arm around me, but my eyes are firmly set on Joshua who hasn't even looked in my direction. The family collectively hold their breath as I walk over to him. His hands are in his pockets and he is looking down at the ground.

"Hello, Joshua," I whisper as I lean up to kiss him on the cheek.

His cold eyes meet mine and he turns his head to avoid my kiss.

"Don't touch me," he whispers.

# CHAPTER 12

**Natasha**

I STEP BACK from him in shock and Bridget puts her arm around me gently in pity, as my heart drops. Don't touch him...he told me not to touch him. I look at the ground immediately as I try to pull myself together, my world spinning on its axis. Robert, Joshua's father, enters the room and laughs out loud at the sight of his two sons. He embraces them both. Bridget grabs my hand in support. I stand still, head down. I don't know what I expected, but it wasn't that. Wilson and Scott walk over and the family start talking. Cameron is asking Robert about the prognosis when I see something catch Joshua's eye over my shoulder. He runs his tongue over the front of his top teeth.

"Excuse me for a moment," he snaps as he brushes past me. I turn to see what he is doing, and I see him marching towards Max on the other side of the large room. *Oh shit*. I take off after him and catch up just in time to hear him snap, "Leave, before I kick your ass." Max narrows his eyes and glares at Joshua.

"Joshua, don't speak to him like that!" I gasp.

He turns on me like the devil himself. "I will speak to him any damn way I want to, Natasha. I will not sit here in the same room as this," he looks him up and down, "traitor."

"Joshua, just because Max helped me get home to Australia does not mean he is a traitor to you. He tried to get me to go back to you continually," I reply nervously.

He steps back in disgust and Ben walks over. "Is there a problem here?" Ben asks as he gently grabs the back of Joshua's elbow.

Joshua runs his tongue over his front teeth again as he glares at Max, then he turns back to the others. "Get rid of him," he snaps as he walks off.

Max glares after him.

"You had better leave," Ben remarks quietly to Max as he scratches the back of his neck.

Max's eyes flick to me for approval. I can't believe he just said that. I look over to Joshua who is blatantly furious. His hands are in his pockets, his legs wide, still glaring at Max while his brothers try to talk to him.

My eyes flick nervously between the two men. "Max, maybe you should go, there is enough security. I don't need any more drama than I've got. Sorry," I whisper.

Max bites his lip and nods. "Make sure Natasha has a guard with her till she gets home," he says to Ben.

Ben nods and shakes Max's hand, "Good to see you man." He smiles.

Max then walks over to the lift and disappears downstairs. I stare at the closed doors behind him. Who in the hell does this guy think he is? He marches in here like Fabio, refuses my kiss, tells me not to touch him and then tells my bodyguard he's going to kick his ass if he doesn't leave. I stomp back to the others where Wilson grabs me affectionately around the neck in a headlock. Joshua stands still, his hands in his pockets, glares at him and raises a brow. Wilson immediately drops his arm from me. Oh right, so Wilson isn't allowed to touch me either. *Unbelievable.*

"I'm getting coffee," I snap.

"I'll come too," Bridget smiles as she grabs her bag. As soon as we get into the lift Bridget starts to jump up and down. "Oh my God. I have to ring Abbie." She pulls out her phone and starts to text. She reads out what she texts: "Hot. Hot. Hot. Smoking fucking hot." She laughs out loud for the first time in days. She continues to text as she reads out loud: "Mr. Stanton is back in town." She wobbles her stupid head around to accentuate her point.

I glare at her deadpan. "You're such a loser. Did you hear the attitude he was giving me? Hello...Newsflash. He cheated on me, *the asshole*. He can't come back here throwing me orders. Who in the hell does he think he is?"

Bridget smiles and bites her lip as she hunches her shoulders. "But you are in the same room as him."

"So," I answer flatly.

"So, who knows what could happen? You could be having passionate make up sex. Maybe later tonight even." She widens her eyes as she puts her hands above her head and does sparkle fingers in excitement.

I roll my eyes. "Are you on crack?" I snap. The doors open and I march into the foyer. I find two security guards waiting for me. Bloody hell, I am sick to death of these guards everywhere.

Half an hour, a huge chocolate and a cup of tea later, I have calmed myself down to simply just rage and have devised a making-it-through-strategy with Bridget. I'm going to wait for him to talk to me. I tried to kiss him first and he brushed me off.

I am not going to appear needy. So, the ball is in his court, I'm not begging. No fucking way. I am going to be cool, calm, collected and totally self-absorbed...just like him.

————

THE THING about waiting for a mule to apologize is that it's ridiculous. I have never met a more stubborn...more annoying, pig headed, utterly gorgeous bastard in my entire life. He has not made eye contact with me in four days. I'm not talking passing each other in a corridor and looking the other way kind of eye contact, I mean sitting opposite each other in a circular lounge in a hospital waiting room, where he refuses point blank to even look at me. I sit on the floor next to the coke machine with Wilson as I watch Bridget and Joshua talking on the lounge. She's telling a story and being all animated, he is leaning back on his chair with his head on the cushion, his legs are spread wide and he's laughing. Cameron, who is sitting opposite them, is laughing too, what are they talking about?

Wilson's eyes gaze at where I am looking. "You okay, chick?" he asks quietly.

I nod and smile. "Yeah." I bump him with my shoulder. "You?"

He smiles and bumps me back. "Yeah, I'm ok." His eyes look over at Josh. "Have you spoken to him?"

I drop my head. "No. He won't even look at me." He nods solemnly.

"He will come round."

"I never wanted to hurt him, Wils, I loved him," I sigh. He gives me a sad smile. "Past tense?"

I shrug as I drop my eyes. I look back over at Joshua who looks relaxed and gentle. Beautiful. Bridget does that to everybody she talks to, especially me. I'm jealous that the boys still want to spend time with her and yet neither Cameron nor Joshua have hardly said a word to me. It's blatantly obvious that Cam is harboring a grudge. I'm waiting to get him alone so I can have it out with him. I hear the electric lift doors in the background.

"Have you been to LA since we broke up?" Wilson nods and smiles.

"Is Josh with Amelie?" I ask. I know I sound desperate, but I need to know. Wilson will tell me the truth; he's probably the only non-player in the Stanton family.

He shakes his head and slings his arm around my shoulder. "No."

"Is he seeing anyone?" I ask. I silently cringe at the loser coming out in me.

He shrugs. "Josh has just been being Josh, no one special, in love with Natasha Marx from afar."

I blow out a breath and raise my eyebrows. "So in love, he won't even speak to her?" I stammer.

"So in love, he *can't* speak to her," he whispers.

"Where's my girl?" Adrian's voice echoes through the room and my eyes snap up.

"There she is." He laughs as he spots me in the corner. Oh thank God, Adrian is glad to see me.

He marches over and scoops me up into his arms.

"My beautiful chick, I've missed you." He smiles.

My eyes fill with tears as I cuddle him. We stand still in an embrace for a moment. When I pull back my eyes flick to Joshua, who's silently watching. Wilson is right, he is hurt. I can see it in his eyes. Adrian flops onto the lounge over in the corner and pulls me with him, holding my hand on his lap. Joshua's eyes flick to our entwined hands across the room.

"How have you been?" he smiles.

I nod. "Ok, I guess. I could be better." I smile.

"This is a terrible thing, huh?" Adrian sighs.

"It is," I sigh. "Not to mention Joshua and Cameron have decided not to speak to me so it's just shitty all round actually," I whisper as I smile sadly.

Adrian's eyes fly to the boys and he raises an eyebrow. "Are you that ridiculous you are not talking to her?" he snaps loudly. Oh shit, how embarrassing, please be quiet.

"I am talking to you, you haven't talked to me," Cameron gasps.

I drop my eyes in embarrassment.

Joshua raises his eyebrows. "The time for talking was six months ago, now I have nothing to say," he sneers.

I don't believe this, my blood starts to boil. "Actually, if we are keeping score the time for talking was in the hospital," I snap.

"Let's get some coffee," Bridget frowns at me, desperately trying to make a distraction. She stands, and Cameron and Joshua follow.

I stay seated and Adrian pulls me up by the hand. "Let's go, Cinderella, coffee time. Enough," he snaps.

We get down to the cafeteria and the stupid idiots behind the counter nearly wet their pants at the sight of the three boys. "I've got it," purrs fish face. "Two double shot lattes. One with sugar. See, I remembered your order." She points at Cameron and giggles. Joshua smirks. Bridget, Adrian and I all look at each other deadpan. *Get off it, stupids.* Bridget does cross eyes and I giggle.

"I'll have what I have twice a day, too," Bridget replies as she fakes a smile at the waitress. She rolls her fingers in a tap on the counter.

The waitress appears uncomfortable and looks at the other girls working who are all giggling. "I can't actually remember your order, love," she smiles.

"Of course not. I can tell you don't have a very big memory," Bridget snaps. "Or brain," she mouths to Adrian and me. We put our heads down to hide our smiles.

"Meeeooow," Cameron snickers.

"Sshh," Bridget snaps.

We take a seat by the window that overlooks the outside garden, this is uncomfortable. Joshua's large blue eyes glare at me as he runs his tongue over the front of his top teeth in contempt.

My eyes hold his. "Yes, Joshua. What is it you want to say?" I snap. I have been playing nice for four days and, you know what, I can't do it one minute longer. I wish he would just come out with it and yell at me.

He is making me feel so uncomfortable with my own friends and I have done nothing wrong. He shakes his head and looks down angrily. This silent treatment is killing me, and I start to perspire as fury heats my blood.

Cameron and Adrian discuss the hotel they are staying at and Bridget starts telling them about some new place they should have stayed at. Joshua's eyes stay fixed firmly on me. The thing is I should be jumping for joy that he is even looking in my direction and all I really want to do is climb over the table and strangle him. He comes back here, tells Max off, ignores me and then gives me dirty looks over the coffee table. Asshole.

"Here you go," fish face coos as she puts the coffees down in front of everybody.

Bridget looks at the coffees and narrows her eyes at me.

"Excuse me," she calls after the waitress.

"Yes," fish face answers.

"Can you take back these two coffees?" She points to hers and mine. The waitress frowns.

"We would like love hearts in our froth as well. And where are our marshmallows? Do you have to be good-looking and have a penis to qualify for the optional extras?" Bridget asks way too sweetly as she fakes a smile.

The boys all choke on their coffees and I cringe in embarrassment. She glares at Bridget and I hold my hand over my coffee. "I'm good," I smile as I wave her away. She nods and takes Bridget's coffee out the back.

"You idiot," I snap. "She's going out there to spit in your coffee."

Everyone laughs. "She so is," Cameron stammers.

*I got one less problem without you. I got one less problem without you.* My phone rings on the table. Joshua stops with his coffee midair and glares at me.

"New ringtone. What happened to 'Diamonds'?" he snaps.

Bridget laughs out loud. Oh crap, he remembered. "I thought this song was more suitable," I stammer embarrassed.

"That should be my ringtone. Not yours," he scowls.

"This is going well. Don't you think?" Cameron smiles into his coffee as he raises his eyebrows.

Shut up, Cameron. Dick. You're pissing me off too.

I drink my coffee while I watch him...them. It's no wonder every woman here is ogling these three men, they are utterly gorgeous. If Joshua was any more alpha male and virile, he would impregnate women just by being in the same room as them. So not fair, why can't he be ugly and weedy? He gets a message and he picks his phone up and smiles as he reads it.

Who was it from? Is it her? That sick insecure feeling seeps into my stomach. Why do I do this to myself? I can't sit here, I need

to get away. Why does he make me feel like this? What's wrong

with me? I stand in a rush. "I'm going back to the room."

"But you haven't touched your coffee," Adrian murmurs. "You have it, Bridge, I wouldn't be touching yours after your

Tantrum. I will see you back there," she nods and smiles.

Half an hour later, I exit Gran's room and go over to my bag that I left sitting on the lounge. I turn to the boys and Bridget who are sitting together in a large group. "I'm going to head out." I point with my thumb at the door. "I will see you all tomorrow," I sigh, defeated. Adrian must have left as he is not here.

Joshua's eyes flick up at mine and he drops his head immediately. My stomach drops, still not a word, not even goodbye. I turn and start making my way up the corridor.

"Tash, I will walk you out," Cameron calls as he runs after me.

Huh, what now? Just leave me alone.

"I am talking to you anyway," he snaps. I find I speed up as my anger starts to return. "That's great, how big of you," I mutter.

I keep walking at a quick pace, and he follows.

"I just don't understand you, that's all. So, it pisses me off."

I stop as I frown at him. "So, you are pissed off with me?" I point at my chest.

He nods angrily.

"Why in the hell are you pissed off with me?" I snap. "I don't like the way you treat Joshua."

Oh, the gall. "My past relationship with your brother has

nothing to do with your and my relationship. I thought we were close."

He puts his lips together. "Yes, we were. Are," he corrects.

I screw up my face as tears threaten. "You know what? Forget it. I don't need your fake friendship, Cameron. When I texted you on New Year's and you sent me that nice reply, I thought we were ok. I guess I didn't realize you are so shoved up Joshua's ass that you can't even think for yourself."

"Don't start your crap with me. You didn't even text me on New Year's, so how would you know I wasn't angry with you?" he spits.

I screw up my face again and shake my head. "You must have been drunk. You called me baby and told me you loved me. I was sober Cameron, I remember."

He steps back and narrows his eyes. "I never wrote you a text, Natasha. I have had no contact with you since we left that coffee shop that night."

I put my hand on my hip. "Then who wrote it?" I snap.

He narrows his eyes and shakes his head. "A fucking idiot that I know too damn well."

He storms off in anger. I stand and watch him walk back up the corridor and around the corner. My mind is in overdrive. If he didn't write the text, who bloody did? Please tell me it was Joshua.

# CHAPTER 13

## Natasha

TODAY WAS my first day back at work since we found out about Gran. I worked from eight until four and have just arrived at the hospital to see her. I have purposely worn my black high-waist skirt and my cream silk blouse, sheer stockings, patent pumps. Hair up, glasses on. Going for the secretary thing I know he likes so much. If he's going to hate me anyway, I may as well look good and rub his damn face in it.

Last night I wracked my brain all night about that text on New Year's. Did he send it from Cameron's phone? Is that true, does he still love me? Maybe Adrian sent it playing matchmaker. Only one way to find out. Test him and, boy, is he going to be tested. I undo my top button. I'm feeling more myself today, more confident. I think I had an epiphany in the shower this morning. Finally, it's only taken six painful months. I have had enough of trying to hold us together. If he really doesn't care, why should I? Next time Jesten asks me out, I'm going. Stuff it, stuff him.

I walk down the corridor and see everyone sitting in a group, their backs to me. Bridget turns and sees me first, her eyes widen, and she smirks a knowing smile. You got it sister, I'm back.

I walk up gracefully and take out my phone. "Hi," I smile at the group.

Cameron smiles. "Hi, Tash." "Hi," the others collectively say.

Joshua looks up the length of my body and snaps his eyes away angrily. Robert walks over and puts his arm around me. "How is my beautiful Natasha today?" he smiles broadly.

I smile. "Good thanks, back at my new job today. Glad to return to some normalcy."

"New job?" He frowns. "Where are you working now?"

I smile and from the corner of my eye see Joshua's head snap back to me. "I have left the Sexual Psychology Clinic. I now work in the hospital system, just regular psychology."

He smiles. "Really?"

Cameron butts in. "Wow, Tash, big move. What made you move from what you were doing?"

I shrug. "Sick to death of dealing with infidelity and broken relationships."

My eyes flick to Bridget and she winks at me. Take that, asshole.

My phone rings. *I got one less problem without you. I got one less problem without you.*

"Excuse me, Robert." I pull away to answer my phone as I look at the screen. Abbie, let's play one of her charades. Game on.

"Hello, Natasha Marx," I purr as I hold my finger up to Robert. I walk away from the group and fake laugh.

"What are you doing?" Abbie snaps.

"Being you," I smile.

"What?"

"I'm doing a little market research, seeing if you know who is still interested or not," I whisper as I turn away from the group and face the window.

"Oh my God. Loving it sick. Fake laugh, make him think you are talking to a guy."

I frown. "Oh God, so desperate," I whisper.

"Trust me, this shit works." She giggles. I laugh out loud. "Now make sure he can hear you and say yes you will see me on Saturday night if you're there because you don't know what you are doing yet, but thanks for the invite."

"What, that's ridiculous," I whisper as I frown.

"Just say it," she snaps.

I turn and walk back to the group, on the way saying, "I'm not sure yet. I might see you Saturday night. Thanks for the invite. Bye." Oh shit, I stuffed it up. My phone immediately beeps a text and I stop mid step to check it.

It's Bridget.

**Joshua just cracked his neck at you.**

I smirk and take a seat. One can never underestimate the power of a naughty secretary outfit. I sit opposite Bridget and she smirks at me. I look away so I don't laugh or high five her or something equally ridiculous.

Robert stands. "This weekend all of Mum's friends are coming from everywhere, so you kids have the weekend off. We can't take up the whole waiting area, go out and blow off some steam. After you see her tonight, don't come back until

Monday." Everybody nods solemnly. My heart drops, I won't see him all weekend. Bridget must be able to read my mind.

"Tash, Abbs and I are going to the Ivy tomorrow night. Why don't you all come?" she asks innocently.

Cameron and Wilson nod. "Yeah, okay." "I'm busy," Joshua snaps.

This is backfiring. I pretend not to care and take out my wallet and for a distraction I walk over to the coke machine to get a bottle of water. Joshua leans back on his chair and throws his arm along its back in annoyance. His eyes scan down the length of my body and he cracks his neck again. Ha, got you. You are still attracted to me. I take the lid off my water, put my hand on my hip and put my head back to take a sip, deliberately licking my lips. Yep, now I'm acting like some loser off a Coke ad, but who cares? Joshua's eyes run down the length of my body again and back up to my face. This time he doesn't even pretend not to be aroused. His eyes penetrate mine, he's giving me that look. The one I love, fuck me it screams, and boy it's smoking hot. I can start to feel the heat from his stare burning a hole in my shirt, through my underpants. Oh God, I need some serious...it's been a long time. I start to hear my pulse in my ears. Everybody else in the room has disappeared and just as I picture myself walking over, hitching up my skirt and straddling the magnificent beast, I am brought back to the present.

"Tash, Gran wants to see you and Joshua together," Mum smiles. My eyes snap to her as I pull out of my fantasy. "Huh?" I frown.

"She specifically asked to see you two together."

My eyes shoot to Joshua and he runs his tongue over the front of his top teeth, his angry sign. He stands in a rush and walks to the door. He turns to me. "Coming," he snaps as he raises his eyebrows. Oh shit, I swallow the lump in my throat, and we walk together tentatively into Gran's room where she lies peacefully in her bed surrounded by flowers. She smiles when she sees me and holds out her hand affectionately. I grab it and smile as I kiss the back of it.

Oh Gran, I love you. My eyes fill with tears at the reality of this situation. How many more times will I get to see her? Spend time with her, laugh with her?

We both gently kiss her on the cheek. "Are you ok, Gran?" I whisper.

"I want you two to make an old lady happy," she whispers as she smiles.

I nod. "Yes, Gran, of course."

"I know you two are desperately in love. I want you to both stop this ludicrous charade and get back together."

My eyes widen and Joshua shakes his head. "Gran," he whispers.

Oh no, what's he going to say? He might upset her. I can't stand it. I butt in. "It's ok, Gran. Joshua and I are working it out, we are trying to get back together." He narrows his eyes at me and shakes his head.

She smiles broadly. "Really? I didn't know. This is great news. I knew it. I always knew you would find your way back to each other," she whispers.

I walk over to Joshua and put my arm around him to cement my story. Crap, he feels good. Why does he feel so damn good? Warm and hard, I feel my body soften with arousal.

His eyes flick to me in contempt. He grabs my hand, picks it up and kisses the back of it. I'm half scared he's going to bite my finger off in anger. Oh shit, what am I doing? My eyes widen in fear. The door opens and two nurses walk in with a doctor and a trolley. "Sorry to interrupt, we will just be five minutes," the doctor smiles.

Joshua and I smile politely and move to the back corner of the room, and he stands behind me. We both watch silently for a minute, and then I feel it. Joshua runs his finger from the base of my neck down my spine to my bottom where he grabs a handful of my behind. Holding onto my hips tightly, he slowly pulls my hair around my neck and he moves so he can whisper in my ear.

"So, you want to play happy family, do you, Natasha?" He gently nips my ear from behind and goosebumps scatter up my arms.

My eyes close as I am filled with desire.

"Do you want to go to pound town, baby?" He bites me gently again.

Oh, yes, I do. Yes, I do. He pulls my hips back so I can feel his erection digging into my behind and he gently bites my neck again.

"Are you aching to be filled, beautiful girl?"

YES. YES. YES. My body starts to pump with arousal. "Answer me," he whispers.

My eyes close as I lose all coherent thought. "Yes," I whisper.

"What do you want?" He kisses my neck again as he grinds his hips into me. Oh shit, I lose control as goosebumps scatter across my skin.

"You. Everything," I whisper as I turn to kiss him.

He pulls back and smiles at me, as he raises an eyebrow. "You are like liquid nitrogen, Natasha," he whispers.

"Burning hot on the outside. Freezing cold on the inside. Christopher was right, you are the fucking ice queen," he sneers.

My eyes widen at his harsh words and I immediately step back from him in shock. He pulls away from me and rushes out of the room. My fury ignites. What!

"We will be back later, Gran," I snap.

"Okay, dear." She smiles as she looks at the nurse, oblivious to her asshole grandson and his bastard antics.

I storm out of the room and see Joshua standing over near the coke machine. I storm over.

"What the hell was that?" I snap. "Shut up," he sneers.

"I will not shut up. Who in the hell do you think you are?" "Who in the hell do you think you are?" he snaps.

"I'm over it," I yell.

"Stop this immediately." Robert's voice cracks through the room. Oh shit, we both look around to see we have an audience. Joshua narrows his eyes and pulls me by the arm into the fire escape stairway door.

"I'm not finished with this conversation," he yells as the door slams behind us.

"I am," I yell.

"Listen here, you spoilt little bitch. You will not tell me you are over it, because I am the one who is fucking over it." He jerks me with his grip on my arm, so I am up against the wall. He leans into my face. "I will not lie to my dying grandmother about our fucked-up relationship." He jerks me closer again.

His proximity steals my ability to speak and my eyes flick to his lips. He jerks me again but says nothing; his eyes widening, he feels it too. I can feel the heat emanating from his strong body. I put my head back up against the wall as I am filled with want, want for him and what his body can give to me. I've so missed this beautiful man. He bends and, starting at the base of my neck, licks up to my jaw. His hand is still painfully tight on my arm, his other hand moves up to my breast and he kneads it as he bites again. His lips linger on my neck. Oh boy, mechanical meltdown.

The sound of our heavy breathing echoes through the space. He bites me again and a whimper escapes my mouth. And then he is on me, his strong lips take possession of my mouth, his tongue swipes against mine. He pushes his hips into me, and I am rewarded with the feeling of his large erection up against my stomach. His hands move down to my behind where he grinds me onto his hips as he kisses me aggressively. He's so big, so hard. So fucking perfect. I'm like putty in his dominant hands. His hands run up and down my body as if he can't get enough, as if he doesn't know where to feel first. I can't help it, I need to feel him. It's a need, not want. I run my hand down over his chest where I feel his heart going crazy, down over his rippled abdomen. I have missed this man and his perfect body. He puts his head back as his eyes hold mine and I keep going lower, lower. Oh shit, I am instantly rushed with a wave of wet arousal and my knees nearly buckle from under me. I run my hand over his huge throbbing erection through his pants, and his eyes close at the contact. I gently stroke it upwards as I lean forward and bite his neck. I kiss him again and this time I don't hold back. I kiss him with everything I have as I stroke him again. "Does that feel good, baby?" I whisper. I am desperate to please him.

His eyes snap open in realization. He pulls away from me in disgust and my body cries out in withdrawal.

"I'm not your baby," he snaps, as he stands still looking at me while panting. With that he opens the door and leaves the stairwell in a rush. Huh...what the hell happened? Come back. Oh shit, how embarrassing. I can't go back out there now. My heart is still racing, and I'm so aroused that if the wind blows and hits me I will burst into orgasm any second. Damn that robber taking my vibrator, this is all his fault. I'm like a dog on heat. With security following me every minute I haven't been able to replace it, six months without an orgasm is un-fuckin-natural.

I rub my hands over my face as I think, what am I going to do? I look up and then down the stairwell. I will go downstairs, then outside and get some fresh air. I don't know whether to laugh or cry at what just happened. In excitement I start running down the stairs as adrenaline pumps through me. He's still attracted to me. This outfit is fabulous, I'm wearing it all week.

When I get to the bottom, I open the doors tentatively, as I don't know where they are opening up to. I peek around the door. Oh good, around the side of the hospital. I exit and start to walk around the front of the hospital. There is thick hedging that surrounds a path along the side of the building. I turn the corner to the front of the hospital. Up in front is the large stair-case leading into the main entrance and on the other side of the hedge is the grass going down to the road and parking lot. I am walking along the path back to the front steps when I see Joshua leave the hospital in a rush. Cameron is hot on his heels. "What in the hell is the matter with you?" Cameron asks as he follows Joshua down the steps. Ben is just behind them.

"I'm a fucking idiot. Glutton for punishment," Joshua snaps as he runs his hands through his hair in frustration.

"What happened?"

"I just kissed her, actually more than that I dry humped her up against the wall."

"What?" Cameron squeaks.

They get to the bottom of the stairs.

"Where are the cars?" Joshua angrily snaps at Ben as he looks around.

"At the back of the parking lot. I will call them now." He pulls out his phone and starts dialing.

Oh shit, this is bad. I'm on the path minding my own business and now I find I am a Russian spy hiding in the hedge. My eyes bulge, what if they see me? Joshua will go feral. I sink deeper into the bush. Shit, shit, shit.

"Why are you acting so crazy?" Cameron asks.

Joshua glares at him. "Because I'm not fucking going there." "You already went there, dumbass."

"Shut up," Joshua screams, and Ben raises his eyebrows at Cameron, signifying psycho chicken.

"Book the VIP room tonight, Ben," Joshua snaps. "I need to get laid."

Ben smiles. "Yes," he mouths at Cameron while he starts dialing another number.

The three cars pull up and they jump in and drive away.

I stand in the bush with my hand on my hips. Are you kidding me? He's not going there. *I'm* not frigging going there. VIP room. My blood boils. I should blow up that bloody place. I narrow my eyes and storm back upstairs with renewed vigor. Right, when I get home, I'm calling Jes and I am going to tell him that it's on, baby...and, yes, I fuck on first dates. Mr. Stanton is going to miss the boat. Tough luck. And if anyone around here needs to get laid, it's bloody me!

I walk back upstairs and over to the scattered group.

Bridget is sitting with Wilson. She smiles when she sees me. "What did you do to Joshua?" She raises her eyebrows.

I narrow my eyes. "Nothing...yet." I glare at her.

Wilson smiles. "He ran out of here like a scared puppy."

"He should be scared. I'm going, Bridget. Binge drinking at my house at eight." I pick up my bag and make my way to the door.

She nods and smiles at Wilson. "Jeez, binge drinking at eight, could get messy."

————

"SO THEN WHAT DID YOU DO?" Abbie asks. "I kept hiding," I mutter into my drink.

She rolls her eyes. "You should have jumped out of the bush and punched him straight in the nose."

I nod as I run my hand over my face. "Yeah, I know," I reply.

We are sitting in my lounge room. It's ten o'clock. I am in my pajamas and we are drinking wine.

"You should have seen him when he came back through the stairwell door. He was totally freaked out." Bridget smiles.

Abbie points her glass at me. "How was he anyway?" "Ridiculously hot. On fire." I sigh.

"Hotter than that guy you kissed last week?"

I pull a disgusted face. "You are kidding, right? No one compares to Joshua Stanton. How in the hell do I get him out of my system?"

We sit in silence as we think.

"Screw it out," Bridget smiles as she flops back onto the lounge.

"What?" I screw my face up.

"Just have sex. Some poor unsuspecting random guy. Have sex with him. Trust me. Things will be different once you have been with someone else. Broaden your horizons."

"I do need sex," I whisper.

"Then JFDI." Abbie raises her eyebrows at me.

"Huh?" I frown.

"Just fucking do it," she snaps.

"Right. Tomorrow we are having a girly day. Pedicures,

facials and then a massage, then we are going to the Ivy and you," she points her wine glass at me, "are going to score, hopefully with Jesten." She raises her eyebrows.

"No, not Jesten," I reply as I shake my head. "We are friends, not Jes. He's too like Mr. Stanton. Someone completely different. Maybe a big beautiful black man."

"Ohh, yeah," Bridget laughs. "Now we are talking."

WHAT A DAY OF PAMPERING. We have just left our beautician where we had facials, pedicures, waxing and bleaching, squeezed in around a beautiful lunch, and now we are going to Abbie's massage parlor. She comes here once a month.

It is in an industrial area. We pull up out the front of a four story dark glass building.

I frown as I look out of the car window and to the bodyguards in the car behind us. "How do they get business out here? Nobody is around."

Abbie smiles as she closes her car door. "Trust me, the massages are so good, repeat business isn't a problem."

Bridget and I smile and hunch our shoulders. "My last massage was three years ago at the physiotherapist."

Abbie smiles and bites her lip.

We walk through the large glass doors. My eyes and those of Bridget are instantly lifted to the opulent surroundings. Wow, this place is beautiful. It's all cream with huge mirrors and plush carpet. The smell of aromatic massage oil hangs heavy in the air and piped music echoes through the space. This is female opulence at its best.

I feel a wave of excitement run through me. Yes, I do need a massage. Good thinking, Abbs.

We wait in the grand reception area and Bridget grabs my hand and giggles. "Wow, check this place out."

"I know," I mouth. "Who knew?"

A tall blond muscled up man, wearing all white, walks into the room. His eyes light up when he sees Abbie.

"Hi, Abbs." He walks around the counter and gives her a kiss on the cheek. She runs her hand up his muscly arm. What the hell? My eyes widen.

"Hi Adam," she purrs.

"Why did you cancel your last appointment? I was looking forward to it," he smiles.

Bridget's eyes and my eyes meet in horror. Holy shit, she's banging her masseur. Now I have seen it all.

She shrugs. "I had a lot of stuff going on. I'm here now, so you can make it up to me."

He gives her a carnal smile. "Are these your two friends you were telling me about?" His eyes flick over to us.

"Yes," she smiles at us as she bites her bottom lip.

"I will go and get their masseurs. Back in a minute." He smiles at us and leaves the room.

Bridget smacks Abbie hard on the arm. "Oh my fuck," she whispers. "You're banging your masseur. Who are you?" I start to giggle uncontrollably, what next?

"You can thank me later," Abbie whispers.

We stand in silence as we wait. Adam returns moments later with two men also dressed in white. Oh shit, they are both gorgeous. Bridget's eyes meet mine and I swallow uncomfortably. One has brown hair and large brown eyes, and the other is tall and well built, maybe Italian or something. Dark eyes, dark hair. Holy shit.

Bridget widens her eyes at me, and I nod uncomfortably as I smile. Jeez.

"This is Markus," Adam holds up his hand to the man with brown hair and gestures to Bridget. "He will be looking after you today." Bridget smiles nervously at Markus and he gestures to the hallway which he leads her down. I swallow the lump in my throat and my eyes flick back to the Adonis in front of me. "This is Antonio, he will be looking after you today." He raises his eyebrows in question.

"Natasha," I whisper.

Adam smiles kindly at me. "Enjoy." He then grabs Abbie's hand, and they walk off together down the hall. My eyes follow them as they disappear into a room. Bloody hell, what on earth do Abbie and I have in common?

My nervous eyes flick to Antonio who looks at me gently. "Your name is Natasha?" he asks in a heavy accent. Oh boy, he sounds good. His voice is velvety and enticing, definitely Italian. Shit, next shop we go to is going to be an adult warehouse. No doubt about it, I'm becoming desperate. I'm checking out the damn masseur now, what's wrong with me?

He leads me to the massage room.

It's large and all white with a huge expensive brightly colored bunch of flowers sitting on the counter. The room is immaculate, a huge extra wide white massage table is in the middle of the room and a white leather lounge sits in the corner. This place is swish.

"Natasha, just change in here," he says kindly as he opens the door to a bathroom off the massage room.

I nod nervously. "What do you want me to wear?" I stammer nervously. Maybe I should have worn a swim suit.

He smiles as his eyes drop down my body. "Nothing, I need you naked."

"What?" I stammer as my eyes go wide.

He smiles broadly. "Darling, I can't massage you properly

with clothes on. Trust me, you are in safe hands. You are in control here. Just lie on the table on your stomach and then I will come back in and we will get started."

I nod and smile nervously. Can't I have a granny masseur? This guy is too hot for my overheated condition. I quickly undress, and practically run and dive on the table. Bloody Abbie, what has she gotten us into now? He walks back into the room.

"That's better," he coos. I am feeling very naked, so I stick my face so far into the face hole in the table to hide my embarrassment he might need pliers to free me.

He warms the oil between his hands, as he is standing down at my feet. He starts to slowly slide his hands up my calf muscles, both hands on one leg at the same time. Oh, that feels good.

"Nice," he whispers.

I smile into the face hole. "Yes," I answer meekly.

"Natasha, this massage is about deep relaxation. I want you to let go completely."

I smile into the face hole again. "Hmm," I answer as I start to unwind.

"The beauty about Tantric massage is the energy that is released into your system," he whispers.

His hands slide up one leg to my thigh and back down to my feet and around the bottom of my foot.

"Hmm," I sigh. Hang on, what did he say?

"The energy I will release from your body is a natural high and your stress will be released instantly."

Oh my God, oh my God. I swallow the lump in my throat. "Did you say Tantric massage?" I whisper as horror dawns and I instantly tense.

"Sshh, just feel. Stop thinking. Close your eyes, sshh," he

coos. "I won't push you farther than you can go, you are in control, Natasha. Let's start with the massage. Stop thinking."

He pours oil onto my back and I feel my eyes close against my will. This really is divine. His expert fingers roam up and down my body, massaging spots I didn't even know were sore. For over an hour he massages my back, my butt and my legs, my arms and fingers. He's right I do need this, I haven't felt this relaxed since I don't know when. He moves my legs a little further apart and starts to massage the inside of my thighs. This feels so nice, unthreatening and natural. This is actually pretty good. I think I can do this. His fingertips on the upstroke gently start to skim the lips of my sex. What? Mmm, that feels...unexpectedly good.

"That's it darling. I want you to start to breathe deeply for me. When I stroke up, I want you to breathe out and then in on the downstroke."

"Ok," I whisper nervously. I really want to go through with this. Abbie will never let me live it down.

His hands go up my legs again and I breathe out, they slide down and I breathe in. He does this for what must be twenty minutes. His fingers start to linger on the lips of my sex and his fingers circle firmly before they slide back down my legs. I find on the top of the upstroke I stop breathing altogether. My body is starting to rise to meet his fingertips as my body craves a deeper massage.

"That's it, sshh. Relax. Let me release your tension." This is damn hot.

"Roll over," he whispers gently.

Oh no, now he has to see my body but for some reason I'm so relaxed I don't seem to care. I tentatively roll over, where I am greeted by the sight of a large erection through his white pants. Oh fuck! My eyes widen in fear.

He smiles warmly. "Sshh. Relax." I nod nervously.

"Close your eyes." He stands behind me and starts to massage my chest, his hands running over my breasts in a circular motion and then down over my stomach and then back up around the backs of my hips and back around to my breasts.

My eyes close as I feel a deep relaxation sweep over me. "Sshh," he coos. The beautiful aroma of the massage oil

only heightens my level of relaxation. The music blocks out the outside world. Am I really here, doing this?

"Release," he whispers. "Sshh." His heavy velvety accent permeates my senses as his hands go to my legs.

This really is...I can feel myself reaching a new level of, oh shit.

He sits on the bed between my legs and they fall open at his touch. My eyes flick up to him and he smiles warmly at me as he picks up my foot and rests it on his shoulder, he starts to massage my hamstring muscle then down to my butt. His fingers once again circle the outer lips of my sex on the upstroke.

"Does this feel nice?" he coos as his eyes lock on mine. "Yes," I whisper as I bite my bottom lip to stop myself from groaning out loud.

He does the other leg, and once again his fingertips explore my sex. Still in a non-threatening way. This is different to the way Joshua touches me. Patient, medicinal even. I am not threatened by this man at all. He's not being sleazy or pushy and I find I am very quickly falling into an almost trance like state.

He swings his legs over the massage bed, so he is seated straddling it and he picks up my other leg and puts my foot onto his chest next to the other one. His fingers and hands massage my hamstring muscles, then move up to my hipbones where he rubs my hipbones. For some reason the way he is touching my hipbones start to raise my arousal to a new level. I don't know if it's the fact that I am naked with my legs up on a hot man or if this has something to do with the Tantric technique, but I feel my knees start to try to fall open by themselves. Oh shit.

"Sshh, don't fight it. Let your body release. This is totally natural. Sshh," he whispers again.

Holy crap. I start to breathe heavily as his hands rub more deeply over my hipbones. My knees have absolutely no strength and have fallen to the bed. His eyes are on my glistening open sex as he pushes deeper into my hipbones.

"Sshh, let yourself go. Relax, Natasha," he whispers. "Breathe deeply."

I shudder as an orgasm runs gently through me. He immediately goes back to massaging my hamstrings.

"Did that feel good?" he whispers.

"Yes," I nod nervously. Holy shit...what am I doing?

# CHAPTER 14

Joshua

I WALK into the Ivy behind Cameron and Adrian at 11.50 pm. Our security trails behind us. I've been pissed off all day. We went to the VIP room last night and I had to leave suddenly. I was faced with a situation that has never happened to me before and I'm in shock.

Adrian turns to me. "Come on, soft cock." He smiles.

I glare at him. "Shut up before I punch your ugly face in. I'm not even joking."

He and Cameron laugh. They think this is hilarious. All day I have been copping it. I couldn't get it up last night. A beautiful woman was pulsating on my lap naked and...nothing. I had to leave in embarrassment with my tail between my legs.

"Were you hard when Tash kissed you yesterday?" Cameron smiles as we wait at the bar for our drinks.

"What do you reckon?" I snap. I rub my face in frustration. "Now the fucking bitch has made me impotent as well."

They both laugh out loud.

"How long till we get this job finished? I need to get out of here," I murmur.

"Oh shit," Cameron murmurs as he drops his head, "Two o'clock."

Adrian's eyes and mine follow where his direction is indicating.

"Oh great," Adrian whispers. "I didn't bring a leash."

The beautiful prostitute that I slept with before I got back with Tash is here. Great, more ammunition for her to fire my way.

We turn and head to our regular lounging hangout upstairs. "How did you get me here anyway? I told you I wasn't coming," I say flatly.

"Um, I think I said, are you coming to the Ivy? And you said are the girls still coming? And I said yes. And you said, what time?" Cameron smirks.

"Hilarious," I mouth at him as I take a sip of my drink.

Bridget and Abbie come through the crowd. Bridget smiles and sits on the arm of my chair.

"Hi," she smiles as she runs her hand over the top of my head.

"Hi," I smile. Abbie and Cameron immediately start to talk.

"Where is Tash?" Adrian asks.

"Oh my God, she's so drunk. We left her downstairs with her bodyguard. I give it half an hour and she will have to go home."

My eyes flick to Adrian and he stands. "I will go and get her." He disappears through the club.

"Who is the guard she has with her?" I ask.

"Mine," Abbie laughs. Hmm, she's really drunk too. "Where have you been? Why are you so drunk?" I ask. "We went out for dinner to celebrate," Bridget smiles into

her drink as she tips her head back to scull.

"Celebrate what?" Cameron asks as he flops into the chair beside me.

Bridget and Abbie burst into laughter as their eyes meet. "Just stuff," Bridget murmurs.

Hmm. Then I see her. A bright yellow short backless dress and gold strappy high heels. Her hair is out and messy. I snap my eyes away from her. Stop it. Why is she so damn perfect?

"Jooosshhhua," she coos drunkenly. My eyes flick to her. She is really drunk. I've never seen her like this. She giggles and walks over to me. "I've been waiting for you, my beautiful Lamborghini." She runs her hand over my head affectionately.

My eyes flick to Cameron and Adrian who have been rendered speechless. I sit still as I hold my breath.

She walks around in front of me, hitches her dress up and straddles me in my seat. I sit back in shock.

She puts her arms around my neck and leans in and kisses me. My eyes flick to Cameron and he smirks. Good grief.

"I need you to take me home and fill me up, big boy," she purrs. Cameron chokes on his drink as he laughs.

"Christ, Natasha, what are you doing?" I stammer.

"I'm about to have sex," she smiles as she takes my drink from me and sculls it, "with you." She points the glass at me.

Bridget and Abbie start to laugh as they high five each other. She leans over and starts to suck on my neck and runs her tongue along my jaw and into my mouth and then gifts me with a deep kiss.

"Stop," I stammer as I pull back from her. "What are you doing?"

"Taking back what's mine," she slurs.

She starts to untuck my shirt from my pants, and she runs her hand over my lower stomach.

"Jesus, Natasha. Stop it."

She goes back to my neck and starts to suck on it again.

Cameron laughs out loud. "How's that big dick of yours now bro, still soft?"

"Shut up," I snap. I will never admit it but I'm rock hard. "Natasha. Stop it." I pull back and take my drink from her. "Do you want to taste me? Do it here, right now on this lounge." I choke on my drink in shock.

"Excuse me." We look around to see a bouncer standing over us. "She needs to stop that behavior or she needs to leave," he says flatly.

I nod. "Tash, get off me."

She stands and glares at the bouncer. "Party pooper." She sticks out her tongue at him and we all laugh at her ridiculousness.

She grabs my hand. "Come and dance and then take me home, baby." She kisses the back of my hand.

Why does she have to be such a beautiful deceiver? I'd give anything to go with her. How am I supposed to resist this?

I shake my head. "No."

She stands back and glares at me. "No," she repeats as she puts her hand on her hip.

"That's what I said," I repeat.

"Fine, I will find someone who will then, you can come and watch if you like. It's going to be a great show tonight."

I hear Cameron and Adrian snicker at each other.

"Is that a threat?" I snap.

She smiles sweetly. "No, that's a promise." She raises her eyebrows, blows me a kiss and then walks off sexily through the crowd. Her guard turns and follows her.

"Joshua, you had better go with her. She's not joking," Bridget snaps.

I screw my face up at her.

"I'm just saying, she hasn't had sex since you and she is seriously good to go." She widens her eyes at me to accentuate her point.

Cameron puts his hands over his eyes. "Oh my fucking God, she still hasn't had sex. It's been over a year. Are you stupid? Get your ass down there."

"No." I sit back in my seat in defiance.

Two hours later I am in a near silent panic. I haven't seen Tash since she told me she was going to sleep with someone else. The girls haven't been back either. What in the hell is going on downstairs? It's unusual. Usually, they come back every half hour or so for drinks between dancing. Not tonight.

Adrian is talking to some ugly guy at the bar and two girls are sitting so close to Cam they are almost on his lap. Ben is against the wall with the other security guards. He's too neurotic to drink at the moment. He blames himself for the attack three weeks ago at my office when he had the week off. I sit next to them, detached from their conversation. The side of my pointer slides back and forth across my lips as I think.

She still hasn't slept with anyone...why?

It can't have anything to do with me. She didn't love me when we were together, so she definitely doesn't love me now. Why hasn't she slept with anyone? She's obviously gagging for it. I've never been with a woman who is so sexually raw and untamed. My mind goes back to her body yesterday in the stairwell and a wave of arousal sweeps over me, and I harden. I scrub my hand over my face in frustration and lean back in my seat. Oh, the irony. I had a hot naked stripper rubbing herself all over me last night and nothing and yet just the thought of Natasha and her beautiful tight body sends my hormones into overdrive. Why am I so physically attracted to the ultimate deceiver? I need to break free from this stupid obsession. Cam's right, why can't I be attracted to one of the beautiful women from home? Am I ever going to feel something? I make myself sick. I need to go home. Now.

Cameron returns with drinks. I hadn't even realized he had left. "Here." He places them in front of me. "Thanks," I murmur, distracted.

"Hello Joshua." A voice from behind me sneers.

It's that blonde prostitute. I don't even know her name. I make eye contact with Ben and slightly nod, he nods in reply and walks slowly over to us.

"Let's get out of here." She signals to the stairs.

I roll my eyes. "Let's not," I reply flatly. "Go away, I'm not interested."

She puts her hand on her hip. "That's very rude."

I raise an eyebrow at her in contempt. "No, if you want rude, I will rephrase it, get out of my fucking sight."

Cameron smiles and sits back as he watches our interaction. He's loving this.

"I didn't hear you complain when we were together," she purrs.

I roll my eyes. "Go away. I'm done." I signal to Ben who walks over and stands behind her.

"Move," Ben snaps.

"Don't you dare put your ghouls onto me. Who do you think you are?"

"Over this boring conversation. That's who." I scratch my head in frustration. I don't want Natasha to see her talking to me.

Ben grabs the back of her elbow and she rips it away from him.

"Don't touch me," she yells. People around us start to notice the disturbance and I drop my head in embarrassment.

"You will be sorry, Joshua."

I laugh. "Actually, trust me. No, I won't." I raise my eyebrows.

She smiles. "I wonder if your little princess would like the movies sent to her private or personal email."

My eyes slowly rise to meet hers.

"Natasha Marx, Psychologist. Just changed jobs right. Email is natashamarx@sydneyhospital.com.au." She folds her arms in front of her and smiles at me.

Ben grabs her again and I hold up my hand to him to signify for him to stop. Cameron sits up in his seat immediately.

"Got your attention now, haven't I?" she sneers. "That's right. I filmed our nights together and I am only too happy to pass on the happy memories to the boring little wife and kiddies."

"What do you want?" Cameron snaps angrily. "I will let you know." She storms off.

"Son of a bitch, you attract crazies," Cameron stammers as he holds his forehead with one hand.

Adrian walks over. "What did she want?"

"Nob jockey here was filmed by the prostitute and now she wants money, or she is going to send the movies to Natasha."

Adrian's eyes snap to me. "Tell me you are not that stupid." I drop my head. "This just gets better by the day."

My phone beeps a text. It's Natasha.

Hello xx

I sit back in my seat and smile. This brings back memories.

I reply.

Hello

My phone beeps again.

Are you coming down here to kiss me?

I smile, I wish. I reply.

No

For fifteen minutes I watch my phone while I wait for her reply, but it doesn't come. What is she doing?

"What if that chick goes and sees Natasha and tells her about the movies?" Cameron remarks over his drink.

I frown and stand in a rush. "Let's go downstairs," I stammer. Adrian smiles broadly as he stands. He nods and signals to Ben.

We start to make our way over to the staircase.

"What's happening with Tash?" Cam smirks over his shoulder as he takes the first step down.

I shrug as I follow. "Nothing, why do you say that?"

He turns back to look at me. "Well, if you were finished with her you wouldn't care what that chick has to show her." He smirks at me.

My eyes meet his.

"Would you?" He breaks into a broad smile as he raises his eyebrows.

I roll my eyes.

"He's right." Adrian laughs. "Inspector Morse doesn't miss a trick."

I shake my head and we get to the bottom of the stairs where I am greeted by the sight of Abbie kissing a guy to the side of the bar.

Cameron smirks again as he turns back to me. "Figures," he mouths at me and I raise a brow.

My eyes instinctively search the space. I don't see her anywhere. Bridget comes through the crowd.

"Hi." She kisses me on the cheek, and I put my arm around her affectionately. She hasn't taken sides. I really do love Didge. Abbie on the other hand is a bad influence. I haven't forgotten the 'Natasha needs to have a threesome' remark from that tape that night. I can just imagine her constantly setting Tash up with guys, pushing her into it. It's been haunting me for six fucking months. My eyes search for her again. I am still reeling from the info that Natasha hasn't slept with anyone else.

She's still mine.

"She's dancing," Bridget smiles.

I frown at her. "Huh?"

"You're looking for Tash?" she questions.

"No," I answer. Actually, if the girls are here, who is she dancing with?

Then I see her, she's laughing and talking up close to some guy in his ear. He has his arm around her, and I find myself clenching my jaw in anger. I look away in a rush. I need a drink, so I head straight to the bar as jealousy starts to pump through my veins. What am I doing? She shouldn't affect me this way. I order three shots and drink them in succession. I need to loosen the hell up. I get the rest of the drinks for everybody and head back to the group and there she is...with Cyril? I put my head down so I don't make a scene and strangle him on the spot. What's his name again? I troll my brain. Fuck he's so...geeky.

Cameron leans over to talk in my ear. "Who's the bozo?"

I shrug in annoyance.

Natasha walks over and grabs my arm affectionately. "Joshua, baby, you remember Simon?" She slurs into my ear.

I nod and put my hand out to shake his. I really want to break this fucker's fingers right now. Work friend, work friend, work friend, I remind myself. Cameron smirks as he goes up on his toes in cheek and puts his hand out to shake hands.

"Simon."

"Cameron." Cameron smiles. He and Adrian smile broadly at each other. Why do they love it when I sweat like this?

"Adrian." Adrian holds out his hand to shake the loser's hand. "Simon." He smiles.

Natasha walks over to me and slips her hand under my suit jacket and around my waist. She kisses my shoulder.

"Let's dance, baby." She grabs my hand and tries to pull me onto the dance floor.

I shake my head. "I don't want to dance."

She pulls a whiny face and I smile. She really is a very cute drunk.

She turns to geek boy. "Simon, will you dance with me, honey?" she slurs. She wouldn't.

He raises his eyebrows and smiles. "Of course, milady." He wraps his arm around her and they dance off through the crowd.

My eyes flick to Cameron who is smiling into his drink. "Don't look at me, she asked you first."

I swig my drink without tasting it. Bitch.

Natasha doesn't come back for over an hour and I find myself constantly looking for her. Where in the hell is she?

"Hi, I'm Elsa," a pretty brunette purrs. "And this is Carmen." She points to a stunning blonde who beams at us.

I smile as I turn to her. "Hello, I'm Joshua and this is Cameron and Adrian." They both turn to her and smile. From the corner of my eye, I see Natasha's yellow dress on the other side of the dance floor. My eyes flick over. She's in Simon's arms and dirty dancing. My face drops and Adrian turns to see what I am looking at.

He does a low whistle.

I immediately turn to face the dance floor and put my hands in my pockets as fury heats my blood. I run my tongue over my teeth in contempt. He's kidding himself. She's blind drunk...nice friend he is. He slowly runs his hand down her back and pulls her into him by the waist. She leans in to listen to something he says and throws her head back in laughter.

I stand rooted on the spot as fury courses through me. Turn around, turn around. Turn the fuck around. I can't, I can't make myself walk away. Natasha steps back, overbalances and nearly falls over. He helps her up and then leans in and kisses her neck. My eyes widen and I stand still as I watch. Her bodyguard walks over to them on the dance floor. He whispers something to her as he gently grabs her by the elbow. Thank God he's finally doing his job. Natasha turns and talks to him and then turns away from him in annoyance, Simon grabs her again and she giggles loudly. That's it, I snap. I storm over to them.

"What do you think you're doing?" I snap to the geek. "What does it look like?" he answers as he spins her

around and she laughs out loud.

"It looks like you are trying to get yourself murdered," I spit.

Natasha does an over exaggerated point at me. "Hey, murder on the dance floor. That's funny." She bursts into laughter and starts running her hands over her eyes in a pulp fiction move. I glare at her in return.

"Get lost, idiot. She's here with me," the loser replies as he twists her, so she has her back to me.

"I don't think so." I pull her from his grip.

"Joshua," she giggles as she falls onto my chest. I put my arm around her in a protective gesture.

My eyes flick to Ben who is now standing with her bodyguard against the wall. He nods in approval.

"We're leaving," I snap

"No, we are not, we are leaving when I say, and I say not

yet. I want another drink," she replies as she pulls from my grip and then stumbles toward the bar.

I narrow my eyes after her and follow her angrily to the bar.

"What will it be?" the male bartender smiles to her. She leans forward onto her elbows on the bar and smiles

cheekily at him. "What do you want it to be?" She giggles.

I grab her angrily by the arm. "I tell you what it's going to be. You're going home immediately. You are out of control." I jerk her toward me.

She screws up her face. "Fun cop." "Me?" I snap.

"Yes, you."

I narrow my eyes at her again.

"Shouldn't you be talking dirty to me about now?" she whispers as she looks at my lips and smiles affectionately at me.

Why does she have to have those perfect dimples when she smiles at me? How much can a man take? I need to find some resistance...and quickly. I can feel it slipping by the minute.

"Something about me being creamy and wet," she whispers. My eyes widen as she runs her hands down her perfect body and back up to settle on her hips. The way her neck is arched in the light I could just sink my teeth straight into it. I feel myself harden at the thought.

Bridget walks over to us. "Hey." I drop my eyes to somehow hide my devious thoughts.

I talk into my drink as I take a sip. "Didge, control Natasha or I am taking her home, and she's going to cop it." My eyes drop back to Natasha's perfect leg....they need to be around my ears, while I give her what she needs...hard.

Bridget smiles broadly at me. "Take her home Joshua, in fact I dare you to take her home."

I look at her sarcastically and Adrian walks over to us.

Natasha grabs him in an embrace. "Adrian, come and swim in the pool with me." He pulls back immediately.

"We are not going to the pool bar. No way in hell." The pool bar located outside is massive and is a full marble bar all around a huge swimming pool. People are in and out of it all night...very drunk people. The toilets are unisex in that part of the club, if you know what I mean.

"Natasha, you are not going swimming in that dress," I snap. "It will be totally see-through."

She smirks at Bridget. "He's very whiny tonight, isn't he? He really should just shut up and look pretty over there." She points her wine glass at me as she stumbles to the side again, her wine sloshing over her glass.

Bridget and Adrian laugh into their drinks as they both grab her arm to steady her.

"How about I put that smart mouth of yours to good use." My eyes hold hers.

She giggles into her drink. "Maybe you should."

"What have you girls been doing today anyway?" Adrian asks.

Natasha grabs his arm. "Oh my God, Adrian, you won't believe it. I hardly believe it myself."

Bridget waves at Natasha and shakes her head to signify silence, she puts her finger to her lips in a sshh signal. Natasha ignores her.

"We had massages today...with happy endings." She nods to accentuate her point.

I spit my drink out. "What?" I snap angrily Bridget and Adrian burst into laughter.

Fury rips through me. "Are you fucking kidding me?" I yell. She giggles into her glass. "Abbie organized it. It was awesome by the way. His name was Antonio."

Fucking Abbie. "You had sex with a masseur?" I yell. I'm furious, some dirty masseur had his hands all over her. My skin bristles with jealousy.

She screws up her face and pushes me in the chest. "No, just a massage, silly...but I might on my next visit. Who knows what could happen? I'm mixing it up." She wobbles her head at me and does a bicep curl. "It's actually pretty fun being bad you know." She giggles into her glass as she staggers sideways.

My eyes flick to Adrian and Bridget who are killing themselves laughing.

"I think Abbie actually had sex with her masseur," Bridget leans in and whispers in a very loud voice and the girls laugh again.

"Why am I not surprised?" Adrian says dryly.

"Scrubber," Natasha smirks.

"Internal?" I snap. I can't believe this shit.

"Huh?" She questions.

"Did he touch you internally?" I yell as my anger hits a new level.

She smiles cheekily and rolls her eyes dramatically.

"Not yet...but who knows what will happen on my next visit? As soon as I work out where a female VIP room is, I'm going there too. Aren't we Didge?" Bridget laughs and nods.

Right, that's it. I grab her arm. "We are going home now and you and your smartass mouth are going to fucking cop it."

She giggles as I start to drag her toward the door. "Joshua...I have to go and tell Simon I am leaving," she stammers.

I jerk her again. "The only person you need to worry about is me. Get that through that thick head of yours."

She giggles and goes to run away from me. I grab her and throw her over my shoulder and smack her hard on the ass.

"Behave," I snap.

"Make me," she squeals in laughter.

My eyes flick to Ben as I storm toward the door. "Car," I mouth.

He nods and smirks as he takes out his phone.

# CHAPTER 15

**Natasha**

I'M HOT, so hot I may vomit. Oh God, I feel bad. I blow out a deep breath and rub my face in disgust. I don't even remember getting home last night...how in the hell did I get home? I put my head back down on the pillow and close my eyes as my head starts to thump. I'm not getting out of bed today. I just feel too sick. A hand slides up my leg and onto my behind, my eyes widen, and I jump in shock. I roll over in a rush. I didn't know I was in bed with someone. Who in the hell am I in bed with?

To my utter relief it is my love.

Joshua is fast asleep and naked next to me...holy shit. I look down in a rush. I'm naked too. Shit. We had sex and I was too bloody drunk to even know about it. What an idiot. I need to do some immediate repair work. I hop out of bed as quietly as I can and tiptoe to the bathroom. My eyes widen at the mirror. Holy crap, I look like total shit. I quickly jump in the shower and start to wash myself double time as I dry-retch.

Why do I feel so sick? I don't even feel like I've had sex, not that I would remember what that feels like. I wash my hair, brush my teeth, remove my makeup and exit the shower in three minutes flat. Please let him still be asleep. I head back to the bedroom and thankfully he is. I take off my towel and hop back into bed with him. He feels so warm, so hard. I nuzzle into his chest and cuddle him as I pull the blankets back over us. Being so warm and in his arms again I feel myself relax and doze back into slumber.

I WAKE GENTLY to the feeling of gentle kisses trailing down over my shoulder. I smile while my eyes still stay closed.

"Morning," I whisper.

"Morning, Miss Marx," he whispers as he bends and kisses my neck.

Mmm, that feels good. His hand runs freely up and down my body as he leans on the other one for support.

My eyes open slowly, and I look at him.

"How did we get home last night?"

He smiles. "You were very drunk, so I brought you home and ended up staying with you."

I smile shyly. "Oh."

"We didn't have sex, don't worry," he whispers as he kisses my neck again.

Why in the hell would I worry? That is the last thing I would ever worry about. My head drops back to give him better access to me.

I frown. "We didn't?"

He shakes his head. "No, I didn't want you to hate me and accuse me of taking advantage of you."

I look at him sadly.

"I could never hate you Joshua, you know that." I bring my hand up to rest on his cheek.

His eyes meet mine and he nods and gives me a gentle kiss on the lips. "I could never hate you either," he whispers.

The close proximity of his body next to mine reminds me we are naked. "If we didn't have sex, why are we both naked?"

He smiles. "You undressed us both, did a dance for me, then fell asleep."

I bite my bottom lip in embarrassment. Why am I so ridiculous?

"Dance, oh jeez, that must have been entertaining."

He smirks. "It was actually."

"Did you take me while I slept? I know you like that," I whisper as I lean in and gently kiss his lips, my lips lingering over his.

He pulls me closer to him and I feel his erection up against my stomach.

He brushes my hair off my face. "I do love that, but I didn't," he breathes.

He kisses me, his tongue gently searching my mouth, his hand moving to the back of my head to hold me how he wants me.

A throb starts to pulse between my legs as I start to swell in anticipation.

"Did you want to?" I whisper.

"Yes." He kisses me gently again.

"I'm glad you didn't."

He pulls back and his eyes search mine. "You are."

I nod and bring both of my hands up to his face. "I've been waiting for you for fourteen months, Joshua, I want to be conscious when it finally happens between us."

He kisses me again, harder, more urgent and I feel my legs fall to the bed in silent invitation.

"You've been waiting for me," he speaks into my neck as he kisses it.

"Every day," I murmur as arousal starts to steal my ability to speak.

"Why?" He kisses down my body.

"Because I am still yours," I whisper nervously. "I still belong to you, baby."

He pulls back immediately and looks at me, his hand sliding down over his rippled abdomen to his thick length. He grips it and slowly starts to stroke himself while looking at me.

This man is so hot. "You are still mine?" he whispers as he strokes himself.

I nod as my eyes drop to his hard length in his hand up against his stomach. He's got that look in his eye, the one where he doesn't care, where he loses control. His jaw hangs slack as his strokes get stronger and I feel my arousal start to pump between my legs.

He cracks his neck. "On your back," he mouths.

I immediately fall to my back and he grabs my legs and rips them apart. His eyes drop to the wet flesh between my legs, and with his fingers he pulls me open to his gaze. Very slowly he pulls his two fingers through my wet sex and puts them in his mouth and sucks them, then he licks his lips as his gaze holds mine.

"You taste so fucking perfect," he whispers. Very slowly he kisses my inner thigh and runs his stubble up the inside of my two legs. I can't breathe as I focus on the ceiling to keep myself from jumping off the bed. I run my hand over the top of his buzz cut hair and over his strong shoulders. This man is divine.

"Do you know how perfect you smell to me?" he smirks into

my thigh. Oh jeez, that's going too far, I don't need to hear this shit. I put my hands over my face in embarrassment. Then he is on me, his tongue licking through my wet flesh, his strong arms lift my legs over his shoulders as I whimper. His hands hold my hips where he wants them. I lie in a daze somewhere between heaven and ecstasy as I watch his strong shoulders and head move between my legs. I have no control over this situation, he will take me how he wants. We both know that. He brings his fingers up and slowly inserts one into me, and we both groan in pleasure.

"Oh my fucking God, you're tight," he whispers into me.

I put my head back, he's right, I am ridiculously tight. This is going to hurt, and I can't wait.

He inserts another finger and I whimper as his tongue unleashes its power over my clitoris, and as my arousal climbs my legs start to close by themselves.

"Open," he snaps as he grabs my legs and pushes them back to the bed. "Keep your fucking legs open," he snaps. My heart rate escalates at his domination and I nod as I gasp for air.

He pulls back to watch me and really starts to work me with his two fingers. My back arches in pleasure and I groan out loud. His eyes are locked onto mine. Pure predatory arousal fills his face.

He is working me so hard that the bed is rocking, and I am grabbing his forearm as if I am going to try and stop him, but we both know I have long passed that point.

"Jo...Josh," I pant

"Come for me, beautiful girl, and then I will give you what you need." My body starts to convulse, and I shudder violently as an orgasm rips through me. He brings his face down into me and starts to lick me again. I jump as I try to get away from him. I'm just too sensitive.

He grabs my legs and rips me back down the bed to him, where he pries my legs back open. "Stop it. I need to taste the cream you're giving me, nothing tastes better...or more beautiful." His tongue dives deep into me and I hold his perspiration, clad shoulders as I gasp for air. I smile goofily at the ceiling as my hands hold the back of his head. He shouldn't be teaching technology to his students, he should be teaching them what to say and do in bed. Joshua Stanton is ridiculously hot in the sack. He kisses his way up to my stomach and breasts and then my lips where he kisses me deeply. I can taste my own arousal on his lips. My hand slides down over his rippled abdomen and gently take his engorged length in my hand. I can feel every hard vein pumping with blood. He pulls back as his eyes hold mine and his jaw goes slack as I stroke him up towards his chest and he groans in pleasure.

"Does that feel good, baby?" I whisper into his mouth.

He nods and kisses me again. "Yes," he whispers as he grabs my face in his two hands.

I slide down his body and take his nipple into my mouth and he grabs my hair in two handfuls on each side of my head.

"Do you want to blow in my mouth, baby?" I whisper into his chest.

"Fuck, yeah," he whispers as his grip tightens on my hair.

I move lower to where I am blessed with his perfect manhood. I run my tongue over the tip where I am rewarded with a gasp from him and a gush of pre-ejaculate into my mouth. He tastes so good. I take him in my mouth and start to suck heavily on the upstroke. He hisses in arousal and throws his head back in pleasure as his hands grip my hair in a painful pressure. I build a rhythm and start to take him as deep as I can. My body is aching to be filled. His panting and groans are a good indication that he is enjoying this as much as I am. He grips my hair and really starts to ride my open mouth. I love it when he does this, totally forgets what he is doing, his body's need for orgasm takes over and he rides my mouth so hard he might hurt me. The power he has over me and the hard grip on my hair have me panting, chasing my own orgasm. I feel him harden and quiver, I bare my teeth and he gasps as he comes in a rush into my mouth. My gag reflex kicks in and I have to stop myself from heaving. I giggle as I choke.

"Don't choke," he laughs as he runs his hands through my hair. I nod and kiss my way back up to his face. "I've missed you, my beautiful Lamborghini," I smile.

He smiles sadly at me and kisses me again.

"Don't," he whispers into my neck.

Huh...don't. Don't what?

My face drops. "What do you mean?" I ask.

"Tash, I don't want to talk." He continues kissing my neck and his fingers once again find that spot between my legs as they fall open against my will.

"What do you want to do if you don't want to talk?" I ask.

He pulls back and smiles sexily at me. "I think that's pretty obvious. I want to fuck."

I smile again. "Ok, fuck now, talk later," I whisper.

"Or not." He smiles as he rolls me onto my back and starts to slide the side of his engorged length through my dripping wet sex. Shit, he feels so good. His body has a sheen of perspiration all over it and his eyes are fixed, watching the parts of our bodies that are connecting.

I look him in the eyes. "Baby, I need you inside me," I whisper. "I can't take one more minute without you."

His eyes close in reverence and he nods as he starts to grip his length to feed himself into me.

The front door bangs shut, and we hear keys hit the bench.

My eyes widen in horror and I jump up in a rush and run to my door and shut it.

"Hello, love," Mum's voice echoes through the apartment. "Oh, my God. It's Mum, she has a key," I stammer as I jump around and search for my robe in a panic.

Joshua's eyes widen and he slaps his hand over his forehead in frustration, then he flops back on the bed onto his back.

"Perfect timing," he mutters under his breath.

I giggle, run over and kiss him on the lips. "Don't move a muscle." I point at him to accentuate my point. "I mean it, I will be five minutes. Lie there and think about what you are going to do to me."

He smirks as he bites his bottom lip. "No, I will lie here and think about what you are going to do to me."

I point at him again. "Yes, good idea. Do that." I smile broadly again at him and lean over him and kiss him tenderly. I bring my hand to his face. "Back in a minute."

"Hurry." He raises his eyebrows to accentuate his point. I smile and leave the room.

I walk out to the kitchen where I see Mum standing at the kitchen sink looking out the window. Her back is to me and she has the kettle on. I walk up behind her and cuddle her from behind.

"Hello, my beautiful Mum." I smile. Shit, I hope I don't smell like sex.

She turns and I see she is crying. My face falls. "What's wrong?" I ask.

She shrugs and gets a handkerchief from her bag on the counter.

"I just have to watch her die. This is my worst nightmare happening again and there isn't a damn thing I can do about it."

"Oh, Mum," I whisper as my eyes fill with tears. "I'm so

sorry."

She sobs. "Me too." I walk her over to the lounge and we take a seat.

"What has been going on this weekend, is she ok?" I ask as I grab her hand.

She nods. "I have just had to watch her say goodbye to all of her old dear friends. It's just so horrible, Natasha, everyone is crying and she is being so strong. I feel like I need to be strong for her, but I don't have the strength anymore." She sobs into me as I cuddle her.

"It's ok, Mum. You fall apart and let me be strong for you.

I'm strong enough for the both of us at the moment."

She cries into my arms. This situation is just so heart-breaking.

Why do people have to die?

For ten minutes I sit quietly as she sobs. I hate watching her like this, she is normally so strong, bulletproof. I remember when Dad died, I was like this and she was strong for me. It's my turn to do the same for her.

My bedroom door slowly opens. Oh shit, I had forgotten about Joshua. My eyes flick in his direction.

Mum looks up and sees him, and she stands in a rush. "Joshua, darling, I'm sorry. I didn't know you were here." Her eyes flick to me in a question and she smiles.

He gives us a lopsided smile. "Hi," he says gently.

I smile broadly up at him. He is wearing dark denim jeans and a white v neck t-shirt, his clothes from last night. His muscular physique is screaming to my body to get back to the bed. Even straight out of bed he looks totally beautiful, like he just stepped off a modelling shoot. His dark hair and skin are in stark contrast to his white shirt. He walks over to Mum and bends and gently kisses her cheek.

"You ok?" he whispers as he puts his hand on her shoulder.

My eyes drop to his muscular forearm, the visible veins run up his arm and disappear under his shirt sleeve. Just being in the vicinity of his super-fit body is arousing to mine.

She nods. "Sorry, I didn't mean to interrupt you kids. I will leave you to it."

Joshua shakes his head affectionately. "No, I was leaving anyway," he says quietly.

My face drops and I grab his hand. "No, don't go. Stay with me today."

He looks at me and smiles. "No, spend some time with your mum, I will catch you later."

I stand in a rush. Catch me later...when? When later? I nod reluctantly. "I will walk you out."

I follow him to the door, and he turns to my mum. "I will see you later at the hospital?"

Mum smiles and nods. "Yes, dear. It's lovely to see you here, Joshua." She smiles broadly and I shrivel with embarrassment, she knows exactly what we have been doing. Joshua smiles and dips his head, also embarrassed.

I walk him to the door and out onto the landing. "Sorry," I whisper as I rub my hand on his cheek.

He nods and looks at the ground. "It's ok," he says quietly. "Can I see you tonight?" I whisper.

He frowns at me. "Umm, probably not."

I frown. "Are you doing something?"

He shakes his head as he takes my hand and looks at the ground. "Tash...I don't want anything."

I frown again. "What do you mean?" I ask as panic starts to fill my veins.

"Natasha, I don't want to pick up where we left off...Last night... this morning, it was a mistake."

# CHAPTER 16

## Natasha

"No, DON'T SAY THAT." I grab him in an embrace.

"Tash, don't," he murmurs into my neck.

"Can I see you tonight? Please, baby, I need to explain a few things," I beg as I run my fingers through his hair.

He looks at the ground, "I don't think so."

I cut him off and pull his face back to look at me. "Stop thinking. We will go out for dinner, back to that Italian restaurant. The one you like, remember it?" I smile a hopeful smile at him. "We went there on our first date." I nod as I smile.

"Why?" he asks.

"Josh, I want to explain why I left you. You don't understand why, and I want you to know."

His eyes fill with hurt. "Yes, I do, I had the audacity to sleep with someone else while we were broken up. Remember?" he says dryly as his eyes penetrate mine. He's seeing if I bite.

Hmm. "Please Josh." I grab his hand. "Please!" I pull a whiny face like a little kid and bounce on the spot.

He smiles a resigned smile. "Okay, dinner only, tonight. I will pick you up at eight."

I stand up onto my toes and kiss him quickly. "Okay, thank you. I will look forward to it. Actually, are you sure you don't want to come back in with me now to save time later?" I point to the door with my thumb.

He widens his eyes at me. "No," he mouths at me as he smirks.

I smile as I hunch my shoulders. "Okay, eight. What do you want me to wear?" I bite my bottom lip in cheek.

His eyes hold mine as he raises a brow. "What do you want to wear?" he asks sexily.

"You," I whisper as I smile.

He shakes his head and smiles darkly. "Behave, Miss Marx, or your mother might get a show on the living room floor."

My eyes widen. "Oh right, shit, I forgot she was here." I kiss him quickly and rush back into the apartment to see my mother making tea.

I hunch my shoulders and bite my lip to hide my smile as I close the door behind me.

"And?" Mum smiles.

I flop onto the lounge and hold my heart. "Oh my God, Mum, he's so perfect it's scary."

She blows onto her coffee to cool it. "He's definitely gorgeous, I will give him that. Sorry to interrupt. I have put the key back on the counter, so I don't do it again."

I smile sadly at her. "You okay?" I ask.

She shrugs. "I will be. It just got to me, seeing all of Mum's friends saying goodbye to her."

"It would," I sigh. "It will be ok, Mum. She is going to be

with Grandpa when she dies, and Dad. Dad will be there to meet her." My eyes tear over.

She nods as her tears start to fall. "I miss your father, Natasha." She sobs as she drops her head into her hands.

I rub her back. "Me too, Mum, me too."

IT'S ten past eight and Joshua hasn't arrived. I'm starting to panic. I have been ready since seven. I stand at my front window looking up the street. Where are you, baby? Please come. Then I see the four-car procession pull around the corner and I practically jump for joy. He's here. I quickly pour myself a glass of wine to calm my nerves. This is it, our whole future rests on me and how I handle this tonight. I don't know why I thought he would just take me back, but I did. He's not going to. I just know it.

Knock, knock.

I smile as I open the door. "Use your key. You don't need to knock."

"Hi." He looks around nervously and I see him catch sight of the framed photos I have of him on my sideboard. He frowns. "You ready?"

I stand back from the door. "Come in." I gesture with my hand to the living room. "Would you like a glass of wine?" I ask. I need to drag this night out as long as I can.

He smiles and nods.

"Yes, please. How are you feeling?" He gestures to my drink.

I cringe with embarrassment as my cheeks turn red.

"Was I appalling last night?"

He laughs. "Yes, totally." He nods to accentuate his point.

I put my face in my hands.

"Can't you be a gentleman and tell me I wasn't that drunk?"

He laughs out loud. "No, I have never seen you so drunk. It was very entertaining. You even let me in on a few of your sordid secrets."

My eyes widen. "Like what?" I pour the wine into his glass as he holds it.

"Like the massage yesterday," he sneers.

My eyes flick up to meet his. Oh shit, me and my big mouth. Why in the hell would I tell him that? I'm mortified knowing it myself.

I close my eyes as shame rips through me. When I open them Joshua is glaring at me.

"Why in the hell would you let some sleazy masseur touch you?" he snaps.

"Why do you let cheap strippers and whores touch you?" I stammer.

He narrows his eyes. "That's different," he snaps.

I frown. "No, it's not. I know you went to the VIP room on Friday night. I think you said that you needed to get laid, to be exact."

He puts his hand on his hip. "Well, I didn't. So, stop it." "Joshua, you brought this up, not me."

"Did you orgasm?" he snaps.

I cringe again. "Ready to go?" I need to change the bloody subject, so I gesture to the door.

"No, we are not going anywhere until you tell me what that masseur did to you."

I start to twist my fingers in front of me in shame. "We went and had pedicures and manicures and waxing...what you like." I'm talking way too fast and nervously. "You know how you like me smooth." I smile and widen my eyes at him to try and be cute. It doesn't work and he continues to glare at me blankly.

"And?" he snaps.

"And Abbie has this massage place she goes to once a month and she made appointments for us. Didge and I thought it was just regular massage and then when we got there, I had this masseur and–"

"Antonio," he says deadpan.

Oh shit, I even told him his name. I need to wear a muzzle when I'm drunk in public in future, this is appalling.

"Yes, and anyway, you know the rest is history and yada, yada, end of story." I start to pull my fingers through my hair nervously.

"Elaborate on the yada, yada," he says dryly.

I screw up my face in shame. "I was naked and it was tantric and..."

"And?"

"And I was lying on my back with my legs on his chest and he did something to my hipbones and..." I throw my hand over my face in horror.

"And?" he snaps again.

"It made me orgasm."

He folds his arms angrily in front of him. "Did he ask you if you wanted sex?"

I nod my head. "Yes," I sigh as I cringe in embarrassment. "Why did you say no?"

I swallow the large lump in my throat. "Because you are the only man who gets to touch me there, Joshua, you know that," I whisper nervously.

His eyes hold mine. "Good answer. And for the record if you go back to that massage parlor you will meet a grizzly painful death, and so will he."

I smirk. "Okay."

"Do you understand me?" he says dryly as he raises both of his eyebrows. "I am not even joking, Natasha. I've been picturing strangling you both all day." I nod as I smile at him. He strokes my cheek with his hand and rubs his thumb over my lip tenderly. I lean into his touch. This is going better than I thought, he's jealous. Surely that's a good sign.

"Ready to go?" he smiles.

I nod and grab his hand. "Lead the way, Mr. Stanton."

Half an hour later, we are being shown to our seat in the back of my favorite Italian restaurant. Joshua pulls out my chair for me and I sit nervously. He has been painfully quiet on the car trip from home to here. I thought it was going well but now I am nervous again. What is going through that brain of his?

The waitress brings us over two menus. "Would you like to order any drinks?"

"Yes, I will have a bottle of the Barossa Valley shiraz, please." He raises his eyebrows at me in a question.

"Can I just have a Diet Coke, please?" I fold my hands in my lap nervously.

"Sure." She smiles and leaves us alone.

He sits silently as he runs the side of his pointer back and forth over his closed lips, his thinking pose. His eyes are fixed on me.

I open my menu and pass him his.

"What are you having?" I ask. He shrugs as he reads it. "Do you come here often?" he asks.

I nod and smile. "Yes, this is Abbie's and my favorite restaurant."

His eyes meet my face. "Who was that guy Abbie was with last night?" he asks.

"Arm...I mean Tristan. Her sort of boyfriend."

He frowns at me. "What does that mean? Sort of boyfriend?" He goes back to his thinking pose, finger over lip.

I shrug as I read my menu. "She is seeing him."

"Are they exclusive?"

Shit, a trick question. If I answer no, then she sounds like a slut and if I answer yes, then she cheated on him yesterday with the masseur.

I shrug and smile. "Not sure."

He narrows his eyes at me. "Not sure," he repeats.

I scratch my head in frustration. "No, I mean I think they have an open relationship."

He nods and our drinks arrive. He tastes the wine. "That's fine," he says quietly after tasting it.

"What's with the sudden interest in Abbs?"

He shrugs. "Just curious." His eyes lift to meet mine and he raises his eyebrows in defiance.

"Joshua, Abbie is a really great friend to me. I don't care how many men she sleeps with. It has nothing to do with me."

"I thought that too but after her little appointment for you yesterday I'm not so sure."

I put my head on its side in frustration. "You're still on that."

He frowns. "Yes, I'm still on that, it's not easy to forget," he snaps angrily.

"Ok, let me ask you this. How was the VIP Room on Friday night? Did you get laid like you wanted to?"

"No," he snaps.

"Why not?"

"Because I had you on my mind and they were a very poor substitute. That's why," he sneers angrily.

I smile broadly at him. The waitress comes back over to us. "Can I take your order?"

I smile and gesture to Joshua.

"I will have the soft shell chili crab for starter and spaghetti marinara for main," he says quietly.

"Mmm, that sounds good. I will have the same." I smile at him across the table and he frowns in question.

"What are you smiling at?" he asks as the waitress leaves us. I shrug and hold out my hand for him. He takes it gingerly.

"I'm just glad to be here with you, that's all."

"Tash, don't overthink this, it's just dinner."

I nod and put my head down as my cheeks heat. "Joshua, we need to talk."

"No, we don't, leave it," he sighs.

"I need you to know what was in my head last time you saw me," I whisper.

"I know what was in your head, Natasha."

"Have you been with Amelie since you went back to America?" I ask nervously.

He shakes his head. "No, I haven't." "Why not?" I ask.

"Because I don't have feelings that way for Amelie. I told you that." He shakes his head in frustration.

"You see, Josh, I wanted to give you the chance to explore if you did. I thought that you were with me out of guilt and deep down you really loved Amelie. I was setting you free so that you could choose who you wanted, unencumbered from past emotions."

He sits back angrily. "What a load of shit," he snaps.

"It's true. baby. Think about this from my angle. I pursued you last time, it was me who chased you, me who called you. I had to bribe you with sex to be monogamous with me, I kept telling you to stop thinking and just feel. And then I told you I loved you and you didn't say it back, not until you found out that I hadn't slept with anyone else. I know that you felt guilty that I had saved myself for you and you felt that you owed me. I had loved you unconditionally, Josh, from a distance for so long and I knew you had a connection with Amelie." I drop my head as tears threaten. "I felt it in the barn that day," I whisper.

"Natasha...I loved you," he whispers as he leans forward in his seat.

I smile at him through my tears. "Loved, as in past tense?" He shrugs sadly.

"And then you were with that girl and I still didn't get the hint and I fought harder to hold us together."

He frowns. "That stripper was to save you from making a mistake and having my children."

I smile through my tears again. "Joshua, having your children could never be a mistake for me. For anyone."

He sits back and runs his finger back and forth over his lip as he listens.

"Joshua, I was so in love with you that I couldn't see straight and then Dad died and I blamed myself. In some fucked-up way I thought that cutting you out of my life was my punishment for killing my father. But the reality is that it nearly killed me being away from you. I was sick, Josh. I died a little inside every day I was away from you."

He sits deathly still as he listens. "Me too," he whispers as he rearranges his knife and fork. I see his eyes flick around at the security scattered around the room. I had forgotten they were even here.

"Josh, remember at Willowvale that day I asked you why you weren't with Amelie?"

He nods. "Yes."

"Do you remember what you said to me?"

He shakes his head. "No."

"You told me that you were not with Amelie because you had never let it go there because you were in love with me."

He sits back in his seat as he thinks. "I needed to know that you were not with Amelie because you didn't want her, not because of me. It planted an ugly seed in my head, Josh, and I couldn't get it out. It festered until it became an infection and it poisoned me from the inside out."

He shakes his head. "It wasn't like that, Tash." He picks up my hand again across the table.

"Then when I was on death's frigging door your mother came to me and told me you were not handling things well either and I decided to come to you, and we had that lovely time in the hospital...remember?" My eyes search his.

He smiles sadly.

"Josh, we made love, I had missed you so desperately, I thought you were pleased to see me as well."

"I was," he whispers.

"I sat in the same room as Amelie and she knew that she had slept with you just three days before and you didn't tell me." I put my hands into my face as the raw emotion lingers in my psyche.

He sits forward in his seat. "Tash, I wanted to tell you. How do you tell someone you love that you had sex with someone else? The words wouldn't leave my mouth," he whispers.

I wipe a tear angrily from my face, why am I such a crybaby? "Josh, I would have understood if you went to a sex club or saw one of your stupid sluts. It wasn't the fact that you had sex with someone else. But you had feelings for Amelie, we both know that you did. You made love to me knowing that another woman was sitting in the waiting room meters away who was in love with you too. Her heart was breaking also, Joshua."

He drops his head in shame. "Tash, it didn't go down how you think it did. I was mortified. I stopped it halfway through. I will never forgive myself for doing that to us. But I needed you to forgive me, and at a time when I needed you to prove your words and love me unconditionally, you turned your back on me."

I shake my head. "No, baby, I was right there with you with a broken heart but I had to give you that choice and I knew that if you knew I was still in love with you, you would not have left. I never turned my back on you. I would never do that. I couldn't speak to you because I knew if I did, I would tell you that I loved you and that everything was going to be alright."

He sits back again and frowns as he thinks.

I grab his hand in desperation. "I am still in love with you, Joshua...more than anything I want us to work at getting back together." My eyes search his and he drops his head.

"Tash, I can't."

"Here we are." The entrees arrive, and we both sit back in a rush.

The waitress puts them on the table and leaves us alone. "Baby, no pressure. I just want us to spend some time

together, and see what happens." I smile as I put my hand on his forearm.

He puts a spoonful of his crab into his mouth.

"The only relationship I am interested in is a sexual one."

I pick up a lemon from the table. My eyes widen.

"What?" I whisper.

"I don't want a relationship with you, but I am happy to have some fun," he says, void of emotion.

Horror dawns. "You're happy to have some fun." I repeat with my lemon in midair. "Joshua, I'm not interested in that kind of relationship. I can get sex from anybody. I want love from you, not to be your fuck buddy," I whisper angrily.

He sits back and shrugs as he shovels in another mouthful of food.

Of all the nerve, I'm here laying my heart out on a platter and he's thinking about his frigging dick. What an asshole! He might just be wearing that soft shell crab in a minute.

"Take it or leave it," he snaps.

"Leave it," I reply angrily as I start to eat at double time. "And while you're pissing me off," I snap, "why didn't you

tell me about the idiot that is trying to kill you?" He narrows his eyes at me.

"Ok, while you're pissing me off what has happened to make you have three security guards now?" he snaps.

I glare at him. "Well, if you must know, it could be a simple robbery or it could be some lunatic murderer Coby Allender from jail whose accomplice maybe broke into my house and stole my vibrator and underwear." I stick my fork into my lemon so far that it squirts me in the eye. Fuck, I rub my eye as it starts to burn.

He chuckles at my misfortune. "Not funny," I snap as I rub my eye.

"So how do you know this lunatic has your vibrator?" He takes a bite off his fork.

I fake a smile. "Because he told everybody in jail and described it to me."

He sits back in a rush and rubs his face. "Does Max know about this?" he frowns.

"Yes," I answer as I start to eat again. I could be blinded tomorrow from that bloody lemon, my eye is burning like a flaming volcano.

I point my fork at him. "And while we are at it, you will be apologizing to Max tomorrow for being such a wanker the other night."

He throws his napkin onto the table. "I will be doing

nothing of the sort. He should have brought you to me in America. He works for me."

I roll my eyes. "Excuse me, Captain America, newsflash. He was helping me seeing he is my bodyguard. So do not start your shit with me. Apologize tomorrow."

"I see you're still on your medication," he says dryly.

I hold my head to the side. "What medication?" I snap. "Bitch pills." He smiles.

For some stupid reason I giggle. "Shut up. I can't believe you think I will be your booty call."

He smiles darkly at me. "I more than believe it. I will place money on it."

"You're hopeless on the punt," I snap as I shovel a forkful of food in my mouth.

He smiles broadly. "Actually, I am pretty good on the punt, if you must know." He wipes his mouth with a napkin.

I wave my fork in the air as I speak. "I am not being your booty call. If you want to leave the door open for us to repair our relationship, then that's great. If you want sex only, go back to the VIP Room," I sneer. Stick to your guns Tash, stick to your guns.

"Okay. Deal," he says dryly.

I frown at him. "What do you mean, Okay deal?"

He shrugs his shoulders. "Okay, point taken."

"Okay, point taken we are going to work on our relationship? Or Okay point taken you are going back to the VIP Room?" I frown.

"Point taken, I am going back to the VIP Room." His eyes penetrate mine.

My fury ignites and right between his eyes is looking like a good bull's eye target for my fork to be hurled at him.

I pick up my Diet Coke and start to scull it. I drink the whole thing and slam it back on the table.

He raises his eyebrows as he chews his food. "Thirsty?" "Yes," I snap. "Like a camel."

He smirks and keeps chewing. I need a comeback. Quick, think of a comeback.

"Okay fine then, if we are not going to try and work on our relationship I may as well go back to the massage parlor and take up some of the optional extras." I put some food in my mouth and smirk. Take that, asshole.

His knife and fork hit the plate with a clang.

"Is that a threat?" he sneers as he leans into the table.

I sit forward and fake a smile. "No, that's a promise."

"Listen here, you," he growls. "I will not be held at ransom over our fucked-up relationship. You left me, not the other way around, and now you think you can snap your fingers and I will run back to you happily. Snap out of it, this isn't the fucking 'Notebook', Natasha, there will be no happy ever after. I have been with several women since we broke up, so don't start your shit with me."

I sit back in shock and drop my head as tears fill my eyes. "Sorry, I shouldn't have said that," he whispers as he senses my hurt. "I didn't mean to say that."

I nod as the stupid tears start to fall. I keep my head down and don't make eye contact with him. He's been with several women since me, of course he has. I wipe my eyes angrily as hurt rips through me. He reaches over and picks up my hand. "I'm sorry, baby, I didn't mean to say that. It fucks with my head thinking of you in that massage parlor, don't say things like that."

I keep my head down, I can't even look at him. He's right, this relationship is totally fucked up, who was I kidding?

"It's ok," I whisper through my hurt.

"No, it's not. I'm sorry," he whispers.

I nod and slowly continue eating my food. What I would really like to do is drop my face in my plate like a pig and slurp everything down in one second flat.

I stay silent through the main while never making eye contact with him. He watches me intently.

He grabs my hand affectionately and rubs his thumb over the back of my fingers. "Tash, don't be upset, I didn't mean to say that. They mean nothing to me."

I nod again while looking down. If I don't stay strong now, we will never have a future together, I know that for sure.

"Tash, baby, talk to me. I can't stand it when you're upset like this."

I shake my head, I can't talk because if I do I will probably scream and lie on the floor in a two-year-old tantrum while trying to kick him.

"It's ok, Josh. I get it," I whisper as I wipe my mouth and fold my napkin while looking down.

"Get what?" he asks.

My eyes flick around to the bodyguards scattered around the room pretending not to look at us.

"I get why you don't want to be with me, it's ok." "What do you think you get?" he frowns.

I shrug. "Look, let's not drag this through the mud any further. It's not the '*Notebook*', right." I scratch the back of my neck in frustration. "Let's go home." I look around the restaurant to escape his gaze.

"But you haven't had dessert," he says quietly.

"I've lost my appetite. Can you take me home please?" I lean down and pick up my bag from under the table. I take out my phone and check it.

He sits still, watching me.

"I didn't mean to say that about the other girls, ok."

I nod and look down. "But you did, so let's just leave it there."

"What do you think you get?"

My eyes meet his. "I'm not a supermodel or gorgeous. I don't do coke or gangbangs. I'm smart and geeky and I hold making love as something sacred that happens between two people who are in love. I'm still in love with you and you are not in love with me. I have told you that I want to work on us and spend some time together and you are not interested. That's what I get."

His eyes hold mine. "But you are gorgeous."

I look down at my lap. "Obviously not enough, Josh. Let's go." I stand in a rush and gesture to my bodyguard toward the door. He nods and starts to exit the restaurant.

I stand quietly as I wait for Joshua to pay. He turns and smiles nervously at me.

"Let's go," he smiles as he puts his arm around me and ushers me out the door.

I don't speak on the car trip home and he is babbling, something about horses and then some project at work. Then he is onto Cameron and Wilson. I just sit still and stare out the window as I listen. He's unusually talkative and I am unusually quiet.

We get to my house and he parks the car. I turn to him. "Thank you, I will see you later." I get out of the car in a rush.

He gets out also. "I will walk you up."

"No, that's not necessary. I'm fine." I walk to my apartment in silence with him following me. What is he doing?

We get to my door and I open it and turn. "Thanks." I give him a small smile. "I will see you at the hospital sometime." He storms into my apartment. I roll my eyes and follow him in. Great, now he wants to fuck with my head even further. Of course he does, how stupid of me!

I put my keys on the counter and head to my kitchen. I put the kettle on.

"Tea, please," he calls from the lounge room.

What the hell is he playing at? I really want him to leave. Go back to the VIP Room, asshole.

Five minutes later I enter the lounge room with two cups of tea. "Here you are." I place the two cups on the coffee table and my eyes flick to him. He has taken his shoes off and is lying on the lounge watching television. Hmm, what now?

I kick my shoes off and sit on the opposite lounge and tuck my feet under my legs. I sip my tea and pretend to watch television.

"For the record, the reasons that you think I don't want you are the exact reasons I do want you," he says flatly.

I look down and sip my tea as I nod. Now he wants me, what the hell is going on here? I don't think he even knows.

"Why are you acting so weird? This isn't like you. You normally scream at me and fight with me. Why are you being so...controlled?" he asks.

I shrug as my eyes lift to meet his. "Because I'm not doing it again."

He frowns. "Doing what again?"

"I'm not begging you to be with me, forcing you to be monogamous, screaming like a teenager to get my own way."

He frowns.

"Josh, one of the reasons I needed time away from you is because I needed time to grow up. I was so crazily in love with you that in our previous relationship I acted like an immature child. I thought I could hold you with tantrums and constant fighting. I was sick with insecurity and jealous all the time, constantly questioning myself about whether you really loved me or not."

He frowns as he looks at me and listens.

"The reason I can't be your booty call is because I am desperately in love with you and I know I am not strong enough for you to walk out that door in the morning and not know if I am going to hear from you again or not. I already know I can't do that."

He drops his head as he thinks.

"Josh, I know I messed up here and I'm sorry. I should never have pushed you away both of the times that I did. The first time I was out of my head with grief and then, second time, I did it so we could have a real crack at a future together. You would have gotten so sick of the insecure jealous girlfriend constantly fighting with you over every stupid thing that you would have left me anyway in the long run. Joshua, any woman who comes into your world needs to be strong enough to take it on. I wasn't back then."

He drops his head as he thinks.

"Josh, I don't want you to be here because you think that's what I demand. I want to come home every night and know without a doubt that at around eight o'clock or whatever time it is I am going to hear your keys in the door. And you know why? Because you want to see me, you want me to be the last person you see every day. The first person you wake up to." I shrug and gesture to the bathroom. "You know how I feel now. Take some time to think about it. I have your money, I haven't spent a cent of it. Give me your account numbers so I can transfer it back. It's not your money I wanted Joshua...I wanted you. I will see you around. I'm going to take a shower."

I stand and rush into the bathroom where I run the water as

hot as I can stand it and get in. I stand under the scalding water and go back over the conversation. I think that actually came out pretty well. I have been practicing that speech for months. It took all of my might not to scream at him in the restaurant and tell him to fuck off, but I know that if we are to have a future together, I need to grow up. I want an adult relationship not a volatile teenage crush. After about fifteen minutes the bathroom door opens, and he walks in. "Can I stay tonight?" he asks as he very carefully looks at my face and not my body. "No sex," he whispers as he continues to look at my face.

I smirk and nod and turn my back on him, and he leaves the room.

I smile to myself and wash my legs. I wonder what the night will bring. No sex, this should be interesting.

# CHAPTER 17

## Natasha

SHIT, now I have done it. I feel like a mother who is punishing a child and then wants to renege on the punishment. How am I supposed to sleep with that beautiful man all night and not have sex? Who am I kidding? Once again, this isn't punishment for him. I'm punishing my stupid self. I take my time finishing up and drying myself and I leave the bathroom with a towel around my chest. I walk back into the kitchen and flick on the jug. Joshua's eyes follow me across the room. He throws his arm across the back of the lounge and ticks his jaw and cracks his neck as his eyes drop down my body. I swallow a golf ball-size lump in my throat.

I remind myself, short-term pain...long-term gain. Short term-pain...Long-term gain. What a stupid saying, who thinks up this shit? Probably some superhero workout idiot at 5 am in the morning. I'm in short-term pain alright, my ovaries are about to escape my body and crash tackle him on the lounge. I shake my head and continue to make my tea.

"Do you want another?" I ask, without lifting my eyes from my teacup.

He shakes his head again. "No, thanks." He bites his bottom lip and continues to watch the television. How odd, so he wants to stay but has said no sex and now he is watching television and is seemingly disinterested in talking to me. What's my plan of attack? Hmm, ok, get dressed.

I walk back into the bedroom and start ratting through my pajamas drawer looking for a matching pair. Honestly, why am I such a dag? I really should own a decent pair of matching sexy pajamas at my age. After much deliberation I decide on a white cotton nightgown. It's either that or mismatched boy-leg shorts and a crop top...and they just don't cut it in this *I need to be sexy without trying* environment.

Mum bought this nightie a couple of years ago and in all honesty, I have worn it a total of five times. It has a low round neck with shoestring straps and little white flowers embroidered around the bodice area. It is crisp white cotton and hangs just below my knees. Mental note to self, tomorrow buy some decent leisure wear. I spend a fortune on going out clothes, shoes and work clothes but I never buy anything to lounge around in... very stupid in this kind of situation. I pull my hair messily into a low knot bun and walk tentatively back into the lounge area.

Joshua's eyes snap straight to me and his eyes scan hungrily down my body. He cracks his neck gently as if trying not to. I smile on the inside. Bingo.

"What are we watching?" I ask as I sink onto the lounge.

He shrugs. "Not sure actually," he says softly.

I pick up my tea and take a sip as my eyes linger on the

beautiful man sprawled out on my lounge. He's wearing light blue super faded fitted jeans and a navy-blue V-neck t-shirt. His muscular forearms, that are raised above his head, are screaming at me at a deafening pitch and those bloody triceps ... the mind boggles.

His eyes lock on mine. "Where do you want me to sleep?"

I swallow nervously and I shrug. "Where do you want to sleep?" I ask quietly.

"With you," he replies gently.

Oh God, me too. I smile. "Ok, but I am not being your booty call remember." I raise a brow.

He smiles. "Maybe I can be yours." His eyes penetrate mine and he's giving me that come fuck me look he does so well.

I bite my lip to stifle my smile. Yes, that's exactly what I want, Joshua Stanton as my booty call. Be strong, Natasha, you can do this.

"Shall we go to bed then?" I ask nervously.

He smirks. "No, if I go to bed with you now, your feet are going to be around my ears in about seven minutes flat, especially in that little purity number you have going on." He runs his tongue over his bottom lip as his eyes drop down my body.

I smile again as I visualize him on top of me, my feet around his ears. Shit. I need sex.

I nod and walk into my bedroom and retrieve the quilt from my bed and two pillows. I walk out and put them onto the lounge next to him.

"We will watch television out here for a while then," I smile.

He frowns at me as I spread the quilt out and put the pillows up one end. I pull the covers back.

"Are you cuddling my back?" I ask.

He smirks. "I think I can do that."

I lie to the front of the lounge and lie on my side. "Get in behind me," I say.

"I thought you were never going to ask." He smiles as he stands and pulls his jeans down. I instantly look away. If I see he's aroused it's all over. I am only human after all. He leaves his t-shirt and tight trunk underpants on and crawls in behind me. He puts his bottom arm under my head and his top arm around my waist and kisses my temple.

"That's better," he whispers into my ear as goosebumps run over my body.

I smile at the feeling of him wrapped around me and his lips on my temple. This is more than better. This is heaven. I start to relax and listen to his regular breathing.

I hold my hand up and he takes it gently in his and we lie together in silence watching a stupid show on ice truckers.

AFTER A HEAVENLY COMFORTABLE silence of about half an hour, Joshua kisses my temple again and I smile into him.

"Josh," I whisper.

"Mmm," he answers sleepily.

"If I could be anywhere in the world tonight, doing anything I wanted..."

"Mmm," he answers.

"I would want to be here with you, doing just this." I feel him smile behind me.

"Really?" he replies.

"Really," I smile. He kisses my temple again.

"You can be quite endearing when you want to be, Miss Marx, and very easily pleased," he whispers.

I smile again and turn my face, so he kisses my cheek. "You

can shut up and look pretty now," I whisper. I feel him smile behind me as he kisses my temple again.

"Goodnight Josh," I smile.

"Goodnight Tash," he whispers.

*I struggle to break free. The sound of Joshua groaning as they hit him echoes through the dark wet tunnel. Three men are holding him while three others are taking turns hitting him.*

*"Stop it. You're going to fucking kill him. Please, let him go," I sob out loud. "Please, what do you want?"*

*They start to kick him, and I scream. "NO! You are going to kill him! Please stop it." I sob while I fight the two men holding me as I try desperately to break free. They throw me onto the ground and one of them kicks me in the stomach. I scream in pain and I hear Joshua go crazy again as he tries to break free.*

*"Let her go," he screams. "Kill me... just let her go. It's me you want."*

*They pick up a metal bar and hit him across the face. "Noooooooo!" I scream.*

*"We are not letting her go. Who will we take turns fucking with her gone? There are nine of us to please, you know."*

*Joshua goes crazy. "I'll fucking kill you when I get free," he screams. "I swear to God, if you touch her, you gutless pricks you're fucking dead."*

*I look to the corner where Ben's dead body is slumped in the corner.*

*I close my eyes, the pain too much to bear. They continually hit him until he slips into unconsciousness.*

*Dear God, no!*

*One of them hits me hard across the face and I fall to the ground. They gather around and one of them unzips his pants.*

*"Joshua!" I scream. "No!" I struggle again as I try to break free. "Joshua!" I scream.*

I am shaken awake. "Tash...baby, I'm here. It's ok."

My terrified eyes flick around the room as I sob and shake in fear. It was just a nightmare. Joshua pulls me into an embrace.

"You're safe, it's ok," he whispers. "Jesus. What were you dreaming about?"

I sob into his chest as he cuddles me, and my eyes flick around the room again. We are in my living room. My body shakes with fear, and perspiration dampens my skin. My chest racks with sobs, why am I still having this horrible nightmare? What does it mean?

"Tash, talk to me. What were you dreaming about?" he whispers into the top of my head as he holds me tightly.

I sob again. "The one where they kill you and rape me," I whisper.

He frowns. "The same dream you had in the hospital?" I nod and start to wipe the tears from my face.

"How often do you have this dream?" he asks, horrified. I shrug. "At least twice a week," I whisper.

He frowns again. "What? You are this scared at least twice a week on your own, in the middle of the night?"

I nod as I drop my head in shame. "I feel like I am going crazy," I whisper.

"Tash" He pulls me back down to lie with him. "It's ok. I'm not going to die, and no one is going to rape you...no one, except me maybe." He smiles as he kisses my forehead again.

I snuggle into his chest as my heartbeat starts to slow down. His t-shirt is wet from my tears. He idly starts to run his fingers through my hair as he thinks.

"When did these nightmares start?" he asks.

"Two days after Dad died," I reply sadly.

"It's not true, Tash. It's just a dream. Nobody is going to get you. You are safe."

I nod. "Josh, you are not safe, that crazy man is after you.

What if it's a premonition? What if they do get us? What if it's Dad trying to send me a message through my dream?"

He tutts in sympathy. "Stop thinking like that. We have so much security around us no one can touch us."

I nod and kiss his chest in a thankful gesture.

"What do you do to calm yourself when you are alone?" he asks.

I shrug, embarrassed.

"Huh?" he asks as he kisses my forehead again.

"I take a hot shower," I whisper.

"Come on then, up you get." He pushes me up from his chest and onto my feet. "Shower time."

I get up slowly, walk to the bathroom and hear him open my linen closet in the hall and get me out a towel. I turn the hot water on and wait for it to heat up.

He walks into the bathroom and over to me. I'm embarrassed. I feel like a little kid freaking out over a stupid dream. He slowly pulls my nightdress over my head, as his eyes don't leave mine. His hands run down my legs as he removes my panties, and he gently kisses my stomach on the way back up my body.

He opens the glass door to the shower and ushers me in. I stand under the hot water and feel myself start to relax. Why is hot water therapy so damn effective? I lean on the wall...my habit when trying to relax. Then I feel the door open and turn to see a naked Joshua getting in with me. My eyes drop down the length of his body...to his tattoo. My name branding his perfect body. I grab him in an affectionate embrace, unable to help myself.

"Turn around, Presh, and let me wash your back," he whispers into the top of my head.

I smile broadly up at him. He frowns. "What?"

"You called me, Presh," I whisper.

He smirks. "Did I?"

I nod and smile again as I turn away from him. His hands slowly rub soap all over my back and he washes me in deep massaging strokes, his hands rubbing deep into the muscles over the tops of my shoulders. Down my arms, back up over my shoulders. My eyes close at the contact. Hmm, this feels so good. He gently kisses the side of my ear and I smile into him.

"Thank you," I whisper. He stills. "For what?"

"For being here and looking after me. It means a lot."

He turns me and kisses me gently on the lips.

"Do you want to know a secret?" he asks.

I nod and smile.

"I don't want to be anywhere else either," he whispers. Our eyes meet and my heart melts. I love this man.

I pull his face down to meet mine and I kiss him. My open lips linger over his and my tongue slowly invites him in. We kiss again, more deeply, more passionately, and I feel his erection grow against my stomach. His hands move to hold my face and he kisses me urgently. My hands drop down his body to his hips and back up to the backs of his shoulders. His strength and the power of his body starts to take me to a place where I lose all coherent thought.

I pull back from him. "Let me wash you," I whisper.

His tongue runs over his bottom lip as his gaze holds mine. I turn him away from me and start to soap up his back. I swallow in awe, Joshua's body is perfect, never have I seen such a perfect male specimen. I can see every muscle in his back, his buttocks are rock hard and, Abbie's right, I could very well grate cheese on that stomach. He stands with his hands, above his head, resting on the top of the shower screen.

My hands run freely over his back and I am starting to feel my pulse between my legs, hear my heartbeat in my ears. I bend and wash his legs, over his buttocks and then I turn him around to face me. Water is beading all over him and his eyes are on my lips. My eyes drop to the perfect muscle between his legs. Rock hard and ready for action as it lies up against his stomach. God, he's so beautiful. I hold his eyes with mine as I re-soap my hands and drop my hands to between his legs. His breath catches as I take his lips in mine and stroke him upwards towards his face. He kisses me deeper and I stroke again, deeper this time, more urgent. He groans and takes hold of my face as his tongue takes possession of my mouth. My God, he's so hot. I start to fist him deeply and he groans as he watches me, his mouth hanging slack as he breathes heavily. His eyes close and I really let him have it, my hand stroking him hard and long, my tongue diving deeper with want. His arms are wrapped around me protectively and the hot water runs over our backs. His eyes start to close and I know he's close.

He lurches forward and grabs hold of my behind. "Tash," he whispers into my neck.

I put the palm of my hand over the end of his shaft and pull him hard into it with my other hand, signifying hitting the inside end of me.

"Tash," he whispers as he lurches forward, and I kiss him deeply again.

"Come for me, baby," I whisper.

His eyes roll back in his head and he groans from his stomach as he comes in a rush into my hand. I smile a triumphant smile into our kiss, that's it, that's it. I keep gently stroking him to empty him completely as he kisses me tenderly.

He rests his head into the crook of my neck as he breathes heavily, and I can feel his heart beating hard in his chest.

He lifts his head and looks at me and I smile. He kisses me again as he pushes the hair back from my face. His hands drop down my body. "Your turn," he whispers.

I shake my head and pull back from his grip as I continue kissing him.

"This isn't about turns, Josh," I murmur through the kisses. "What's it about?" he frowns.

"Love," I smile as I kiss him again. "This is about love." He smiles into my neck and cuddles me tightly.

"Remind me to comfort you from your nightmares more often," he murmurs into my neck.

I laugh and shake my head as I open the shower door. "Get to bed, sex maniac."

He smiles and smacks me hard on the ass as he brushes past me. "You know it, baby."


DEJA VU...WHY, oh why, is it coming back to haunt me? I wish I was having it about Joshua telling me he loved me. But no, I am having it because I woke alone this morning. No note, no kiss, no goodbye. Just a memory of some intermittent tenderness last night...or did I dream that too? I am sitting in the cafeteria at the hospital where I work, it's lunch time. My phone beeps a message and I look at the screen in hope. Jes, my heart drops.

**Hi Doc,**
**Can we have dinner tonight?**

I frown. I do not want to have dinner with you, Jes, I want to have dinner with Joshua. I type him a message.

**Sorry, I can't.**
**My gran is sick, and I am tied up at the moment.**
**I will call you in a few weeks.**

A reply bounces back.

**When?**
**I miss you.**
**I haven't seen you for two weeks.**

My stomach drops, he shouldn't be missing me. We are just friends. I smile and text him back.

**Call up short and slutty Barbie.**
**Take her for dinner**
**Unlike me, she will repay you with a blow job.**

I smile as I imagine him reading it. A message bounces back.

**Call me.**

I laugh and drink my coffee. He really is gorgeous. Jes and I have become friends and, unlike the relationship between Joshua and me, it is just so uncomplicated. I don't care if he sleeps with anyone else, I don't want to go out with him, but I have an underlying affection for him. It's strange. I have never had it before with any other male. Either I wanted them, or I didn't, but with Jes it's different. He makes me understand Abbie in a way I never have before. She has a deep affection for the men she dates but she is not in love with any of them, yet she cares for them and she has sex with them. Until I met

Jesten, I could never understand that, but now I think I do. He makes me laugh and he calls me every couple of days, either with a dirty joke or to arrange coffee or something and, if he doesn't call me, I do notice it ... but it doesn't bother me, weird.

Back to Mr. Stanton, did we have a moment last night or was that wishful thinking on my part? How did it go from him comforting me, to me jacking him off in the shower and then him being wrapped around me affectionately all night? He said before that he never stayed with me because he couldn't say goodbye to me. Was that the case this morning or was he just dying to chew his arm off to get out of there without waking me up? I rub my hands over my face in frustration. Joshua Stanton, you are a total mindfuck... welcome back!

## Joshua

It's 7.30 am and I have been back from the gym for an hour. I am showered and ready for work. I sit at my computer in my hotel room as I plug my phone into it. I didn't watch this yesterday because I didn't want to see it before I went out with Natasha last night. I didn't need further ammunition to weaken my resistance. On Saturday night, when we got back from the club and she was drunk, she made me film her while she danced for me. I press play.

Her laugh echoes through the computer monitor and I smile broadly.

"What are you doing with my phone?" I ask. The phone camera pans around the room randomly, ceiling, floor, wall, and then it comes onto me. I am sitting on her bed with my back up against the headboard, and I am fully dressed.

"Oh yes, ladies, Joshua Stanton is back on my bed and in the house. Are you jealous much?"

She laughs and then the camera goes up and down in a nod. I smile at her idiocy. "I know, I know. Let's make another movie," she giggles. "What shall we call it?" She walks around the end of the bed with the camera still on me and I raise my eyebrows in question. She trips over the end of the bed and drops the phone. "Oops, who put that bed there?" she giggles.

I can hear my loud laughter at her in the background. She laughs again and the camera goes in all directions again as she stands back up and focuses the camera back on me.

"What shall we call our new movie, baby?" she asks.

My heart stops at the sound of her calling me that, I can see it on my face as it falls. Maybe I should turn this movie off, it's just going to mess with my head even further. I bring my pointer up to my mouth and run it over my lips as I think and lean back on my chair.

"Natasha on her knees," I smile at the screen.

"Ohh yeah, that's a good one," she snaps. "What about Joshua just jizzed?"

I hear my laughter echo through the room and the camera goes all over the shop again as she laughs uncontrollably.

"I like that one too," I smile. "Give me the phone I want to film you."

I hold my hand out for the phone and she shakes the camera side to side in a no signal. "I am filming you. Oh, I know, why don't I do a dance for you?" She bursts into laughter again and I find myself smiling broadly at the computer screen. She's such a frigging idiot. I have never been with a woman that doesn't try to be cool in front of me and yet Natasha is a total fool in front of me all the time... and I love it.

"Oh my God, I know the song. Pass me my phone." She holds out her hand and I pass her phone to her from her handbag.

"Give me the camera," I hold out my hand and she passes me my phone and I start to film her.

She is wearing a short yellow dress and has her shoes off.

Her dark hair is messed up and sexy. She looks edible.

She holds her hand out in front of her to accentuate her point. "Oh my God, this is our new song because I am singing it to you...right?" She steps to the side as the alcohol steals her balance and she laughs as she fiddles with the phone. "Where the hell is this song?" she snaps, and I laugh out loud again. "Got it, are you ready?"

The camera goes up and down in a nod and I find myself smiling at the computer screen.

The door opens, I pause the film and my eyes flick to Cameron and Adrian as they walk into my room. "Do you mind?" I snap.

They both lean over my shoulder to see what I am watching. "Not a bit," Cameron smiles as he pulls up a chair.

Adrian narrows his eyes at the screen. "What is she doing?" he frowns.

I sit back in my chair. "Dancing," I smile.

Adrian smiles broadly. "She's so hot. Play the tape." He pulls up another chair on the other side of me. I slowly press play, it's a Rihanna song. 'Only girl in the world.'

Natasha grabs a hairbrush off her side table and starts to sing into it.

*La la la La la la*
*Want you to love me, like I'm a hot ride Be thinking of me, doing*
*what you like.*

287

She runs her hands up and down her body while she dances, and I immediately feel myself harden. My eyes close.

Adrian laughs out loud. "I love this girl." She starts to flick her hair around crazily.

We all sit still, riveted to the spot. She sings again.

*Like I'm the only one that you'll ever love Like I'm the only one who knows your heart.*

She points at me and leans in and kisses me slowly. The camera goes onto the side and then rests downwards on the bed. I swallow uncomfortably as both of the boys look at me.

"I thought nothing happened," Cameron says flatly.

I shrug my shoulders as my eyes go back to the screen. She jumps up on the bed in a rush and my laughter fills the room again.

"Listen to yourself laughing." Adrian smiles at me as he puts his hand on my shoulder in a reassuring gesture. I nod as my eyes stay riveted on the screen.

She stands above me on the bed, and she sings into the hairbrush while flicking her hair around crazily.

We all sit silent as she drops in a straddle over my body and slowly lifts her dress over her shoulders. She is wearing a yellow lace bra and G-string that match her dress. Her beautiful tanned body is on display. I immediately press the pause button.

"For my eyes only, boys," I snap as my eyes flick to them. "Please tell me you are going over there right now to tell her you want her back," Cameron sighs.

I shake my head sadly. "No, it's over between us. You can only come back so many times after being kicked to the curb."

Adrian frowns. "But you stayed there last night."

I nod and drop my head in shame. "Yeah, I was a total prick at dinner and made her cry and I just can't stand seeing her upset. I couldn't leave her."

Adrian's eyes hold mine. "Why do you think that you can't leave her when she's upset?"

I shrug as I link my hands on top of my head.

"I know why." Adrian smiles. "You're still in love with her."

With a heavy heart I sigh. "Natasha and I are finished, I can no longer trust her, end of story."

# CHAPTER 18

Adrian

8.30 AM and I sit in the small corner office at the job we start today at Broadtec. I have arrived early to prepare for the day ahead. It's a poky space with no view, a usual prerequisite of ours when working. I go for a quick walk around the office as I try to locate the kitchen or a coffee machine. This place is a nightmare, how am I supposed to be productive with no caffeine?

Six years ago, Joshua designed this company's software for them as one of his first jobs and he signed a contract stating he would be the one to upgrade the systems. Back then signing a contract for future work sounded like a smart choice. Little did he know that he would own a multimillion-dollar company today and that this job would be a massive pain in the ass. It has been on our diary for six months, but I couldn't get Joshua to come to Australia after the Natasha debacle. Now we are here for his grandmother and it seems like a good time to cross it off the list. It should take about six to eight weeks if all goes to plan. I start to go through my emails and my phone rings. I look at the screen and the name lights up.

Nicholas Anastas

Shit, what does he want? I haven't heard from him in six months, since I last avoided his calls. I stare at the ringing phone on my desk for a moment, I frown and press decline. I keep reading my emails as I scratch my head in frustration. I open one from Frank which reads:

---

*Hi Murph*
*This was in the company email inbox from a Mrs. Jones. Not sure what to make of it but I thought I should forward it on to you. The attachment is very interesting!*
*Keep me posted.*
*Frank*

---

Frank is one of my PAs in LA. I have three. He liaises with the public and social network platforms and then filters anything onto me that I need to address. The workload is just too great for me to handle alone and Joshua wants nothing to do with it. He has no desire to be the successful millionaire or dominate the world, but his brain has ensured that he does it effortlessly anyway. I deal with the staff, the clients, the workload and Joshua takes care of the tech side of things. He doesn't mix with the clients or make friendships outside of his close circle. It works well between us, that is except when he breaks up with his girlfriend and then goes AWOL for a month. That is a total nightmare for all concerned.

My phone rings again and I look at the screen.

Nicholas Anastas

I roll my eyes and push reject again. Take a hint. I blow out a breath as I click the email open. It reads

---

*'Contact me at mrs-jones@hotmail.com or the wife gets the lot.'*

---

Shit, my heart sinks. I click on the attachment.

It's jumbled and the camera is shaking around. I lean in to the screen to listen to the audio. I can barely hear it. It looks as though the camera is attached to something she is carrying. I can see two sets of legs, one obviously hers but the other? It can't be Joshua; he would never wear track pants around a woman. I press pause as I try to study the screen; is it even Stanton? I narrow my eyes and lean in close as I try to get my bearings. I pick up my phone and ring Ben.

"Hey," he answers.

"Hi, can you come up here please?" I ask.

"Sure, what's up?"

"I'm not sure," I answer as I sit back in my seat in concentration.

"See you in a minute," he sighs.

Ben and the security team have an office on the second floor. They moonlight as computer techs as a cover because the seven of them can't be in our office with us. It's just too small. We ensure Joshua has one guard with him at all times. Ben has come in early with me this morning to go over the security of the building. My phone beeps with a text and I pick it up and read it, Nicholas Anastas.

I hear you are in Sydney. I want to see you tonight.

Not now, asshole. I click off the message in annoyance. I press play again. They seem to go into a room, and I screw up my face in question. What the hell is this?

Ben walks in. "Hi. What's up?"

I sit back on my chair as I flick my pen around in annoyance. "Not sure. I think Stanton fucked up."

He crosses his arms in front of him as he rolls his eyes. "Play it," he snaps.

We watch the two sets of legs start to go upstairs. Ben leans in and turns up the volume so we can hear the sound.

"So, what did you say your name is?' Joshua's distinct voice is heard.

"What do you want it to be?" she replies, and I look at Ben deadpan and he smiles stupidly.

"Original," I say flatly.

As clear as day, we hear Joshua reply. "My bedroom is this way... Natasha."

Our eyes widen in shock. "Holy shit, who is this slut and how did she get past security with a fucking camera?" I stammer as I run my hand over my face in horror.

Ben changes his stance nervously as he crosses his arms. "I don't know, let me find out."

"She is threatening to send this shit to Natasha. Do you have any idea how postal Stanton is going to go when he sees this? He can kiss Natasha goodbye. Why would he even mention her name?" I can't believe this.

Ben shakes his head. "I don't know. Let me look into it today and we will tell him tomorrow. Contact her and see what she wants. Try and buy us some time."

"Christ," I snap, "I don't have time for this shit. What exactly do your moronic security team actually do? I expect you to check every female that comes into contact with him for cameras. It's common sense."

He swallows nervously. "Hmm, you would think." With that he walks out of the room.

I blow out a breath to try and calm myself. This is a disaster.

Joshua is going to hit the roof.

My phone beeps a message and I angrily snap it from the desk to check it. Nicholas Anastas.

You either ring me or I will be at your office at 1 pm.
Don't push me.

I frown at the screen. Don't push me...don't push me, cock head. I text back angrily.

What do you want?

He texts back immediately.

I want to know what happened between us.

I roll my eyes.

Nothing.

Stop looking for something that wasn't there.

He texts back.

That's bullshit and you know it.
See you at 1 pm.

I puff air into my cheeks in frustration.

Joshua walks into the office and smiles as he puts his briefcase on his desk. Then he stands still and puts his hands on his hips as his eyes scan the room. "This office fucking sucks," he says dryly.

I glare at him in annoyance. "Shut up. I'm not in the mood," I snap.

His eyes flick to me and he smirks. "What's up your ass?"

"Nothing," I snap

He laughs. "Maybe, that's the problem." He picks up a pen and throws it at me.

I narrow my eyes at him.

Knock, knock. We both turn to the door and see two men in suits and a very attractive woman.

"Hello. We have just come to welcome you. I'm Paul and this is Alex and Tatiana."

We both stand and shake hands with them and smile cordially. "Tatiana and Alex here will be in the office next to yours and will help you in any way they can." Paul says, "Hopefully this reprogramming will run as smoothly as possible."

Joshua frowns at the woman and she smiles broadly at him. "Oh my god," Tatiana puts her hand on her chest. "It's you," she purrs.

He frowns again. "Have we met before?" he asks.

She laughs and nods. "Yes, we met at a wedding last year. We were seated next to each other. Remember?"

He smiles and nods. "That's right, I do. Yes, of course."

My eyes flick between them as she blushes. Oh God, give me a break.

"We will be in the office next door if you need anything." Alex smiles and they leave the room.

Joshua turns and smirks and raises his eyebrows. "Interesting morning, huh." He smiles.

I sit back down in my seat. "You have no idea," I sigh.


**Natasha**

I walk into the hospital and head straight upstairs to the palliative care unit. I have a bad feeling today. I just hope Gran is ok.

I run into Mum in the hallway. "Is everything okay?" I ask nervously.

She smiles warmly as she kisses me on the cheek. "Yes, she is doing really well. She has had us laughing all day."

I put my hand on my chest. "Oh, thank goodness, I've been a bit nervy," I sigh.

Mum smiles sympathetically as she walks past me down the hall. Bridget, Cameron and Will are sitting together on the seats. Bridget is seated opposite the boys and has her legs resting on Cameron's legs who is oblivious and on his phone. She and Will are deep in conversation.

"Hi," I smile as I put my bag on the seat next to them.

"Oh hi," Bridget smiles. "Loving that Kate Middleton dress." She raises her eyebrows at me. I smile. I love this dress too. It's cream and fitted and hangs just below the knee. It's very simple but beautifully cut and it hangs really nicely. I am in matching cream high-heel shoes. My hair is in a loose, low ponytail and I have my glasses on and minimal make up. I stand and stretch my back. I've been on my computer all day and it's as tight as anything.

"You been at work?" Cameron asks, his eyes not rising from his phone.

"Ahuh," I answer flatly. "You guys been in yet?" I ask as my eyes flick around, and I put my hands on my hips.

"Not yet," Bridget answers. "She has a line up in front of us."

She gestures to a group of oldies sitting in the other waiting room.

"Mmm, okay. I might go and get a coffee then," I sigh. I pick up my bag and head back downstairs to the cafeteria.

I walk down to the cafeteria in a daydream as my security trails behind me. How is it I don't even notice them with me anymore? Max has taken a week off to go away with his girls. I think Joshua has just pissed him off too much to be around, something he has denied of course. As I head down the hall to the cafeteria, I see two of Joshua's bodyguards waiting outside, leaning up against the wall, and I get a rush of adrenaline. He's here. I try to hold my idiocy to a minimum and not jump in the air. I enter the cafeteria as casually as I can, and my eyes scan the space. I see him. Joshua is sitting at the table closest to the door and his broad back is facing me. He is on the phone and has a notepad in front of him and is writing some-thing down. I walk over behind him to say hello when my eyes glance at the notepad and I read the name Coby Allender written on it. He speaks down the phone unaware that I am here.

"I want a list of past offences and the evidence being presented at the upcoming trial."

He listens for a minute. "No, when is the trial?" He listens again. "I see." He listens again. "Tell me, do the police think he is guilty?" My eyes widen, who is he talking too? I walk past him and straight to the counter.

Fishface looks at me. "What will it be?" she asks flatly. God this woman is a bitch.

"Skim cap." I raise my eyebrows at her as if to say, yes you, you are a bitch, and I know it.

She nods and takes my money and I turn to see Joshua scribbling on his paper. His eyes flick up and connect with mine, and he smiles sexily. I literally swoon. He only has to look at me and I melt into his eyes. I smile and turn back to the counter and I watch him in the reflection of the fridge door in front of me. He keeps writing and talking, then he hangs up and rips the top piece of paper off the notepad, folds it and puts it in his inside suit pocket. He takes a sip of his coffee and sits still staring at me, then he gently cracks his neck and I smile. Some things will never grow old. I take my coffee and walk over to him.

"Hi," I smile.

"Hello," he smiles back.

What I really want to do is slam my hand on the table and scream where the hell where you when I woke up this morning, asshole, but I have to remind myself that this new improved version of myself is non drama queenish, and boy does it suck.

"Did you have a nice day?" I smile as I take a sip of my coffee. He nods. "Yes, we started a new job today, so I was busy."

I frown. "New job?" I question.

He smiles. "Just a little six week one."

"Oh," I nod as disappointment runs through me.

"You?" he asks.

I shrug. "It was ordinary, nothing exciting."

He smirks as he sips his coffee. "We are heading back upstairs." His eyes linger on mine.

I nod and smile and he rises from his seat and follows me out. We walk into the crowded lift and stand silently next to each other. He is so tall and big, his body oozes power in that dark charcoal three-piece suit. I can feel the electricity coming from him as my body weakens with want. I wonder if any of the other women in the lift can feel the heat oozing from this fine specimen. As I watch the numbers above the door light up, I silently make a pact with myself. I am not mentioning last night or asking him when I am seeing him again. I need to be strong, even if it kills me, and it probably will because he is acting like he doesn't have a care in the world and I could quite easily strangle him with a smile on my face. Calm, calm, calm...keep fucking calm. We walk to the lounge seating area and we sit opposite each other.

"Have you been in yet?" I ask the others.

"No," they all reply flatly without looking up.

Joshua takes out his phone and starts to read and scroll through it. I sit with my legs crossed trying to look everywhere but at him. Bridget and the boys are deep in conversation about Adrian.

"So, is he seeing him tonight?" Abbie frowns.

Cameron nods and throws his hands behind his head. "Yep," he answers as he leans back in his chair.

I frown. "Huh, who is he seeing tonight?" I ask.

"Nicholas Anastas," Bridget replies.

"How did that come about?" I frown.

"He texted him this morning demanding to see him," Cameron says as he raises his eyebrows.

"How hot. I love it when a man demands to see you. Now that's romance." My eyes flick to Joshua who doesn't even hear me and is smirking at his phone. Hmm...take a hint, bastard.

Joshua laughs and bites his bottom lip to stifle his smile as he watches something on his phone and his eyes flick to me. I frown in question. What is he looking at?

My phone beeps a message. I pull it out of my bag.

It's a text from Joshua. I smirk and open it, it's a movie. I frown as I hit play, and my eyes narrow at the screen. I smile as I see the camera wobble around and I see Joshua sitting on my bed smiling at me. I press pause and retrieve my earphones from my bag and plug them in so I can hear what is going on.

My eyes flick to Joshua as I put the earphones in, and he smiles broadly at me. Jeez, what's so funny? I press play again and sit still as I listen to my drunken voice. Oh my God.

"I know, let me do a dance for you," I slur.

The camera goes to me. Holy shit, I look like a train wreck, my eyes widen in horror and I feel myself flush. I look up and Joshua has just taken a picture of my face. I fake a smile. "Very funny," I mouth. He laughs and looks back down with his arms folded in front of him. I continue to watch the nightmare unfolding in front of me. Oh no, what am I doing now?

I hold my hand up to my mouth as I watch myself start to spin on the spot. I feel myself blush as I see what I look like. What in the hell kind of sexy dancing is that? Oh shit...it gets worse. I start to do high kicks in the air like a cheerleader on crack. I smile in embarrassment as I hold my hand over my face. This is woeful, no wonder the poor bastard ran this morning. He has been forced to watch this tape, damn technology. My eyes stay glued to the screen again as I take off my clothes and straddle Joshua. I lean in and kiss him, and his hand reaches out from behind the camera and he feels my breast and then his hand runs under the rim of my underpants.

I watch myself bend and kiss him and then say the words, "I love you, Joshua." The film goes off. I sit and stare at the phone in horror, do I laugh, or do I cry? Here I am trying to channel

Kate Middleton when I am actually channeling Absolutely Fabulous and so much for playing hard to get...I told him I loved him. I look back up to see that Joshua and the others have gone in to see Gran.

I walk in slowly and stand behind the group with my heart still racing. Everybody sits around Gran's bed and makes idle conversation with her. She seems happy and is laughing. Joshua turns to see me and stands to give me his chair and I smile and take it thankfully. We stay with Gran for over an hour and then gradually one by one say goodbye. This is the part I hate. I have to wait for him to say something about seeing me, what if he doesn't? We walk to the lifts together and shuffle in. I stand at the back next to Joshua and the others all stand in front of us jabbering about something. Joshua links his pinky finger with mine, and I find myself smiling at the floor. The lift gets to the bottom and the doors open and everybody exits. Joshua pulls me back into the lift by the finger and pushes the button. The door closes.

We stand still, held together by the smallest part of our body. He bites his lip as he looks at me. "What are you doing tonight?" he asks quietly.

"Nothing," I reply as my eyes search his.

"I'm thirty, seventy wanting to see you tonight," he breathes.

I frown. "Thirty, seventy," I repeat.

A whisper of a smile crosses his face as his eyes penetrate mine. "Thirty percent of my brain wants to see you and seventy percent of my brain tells me it's a mistake."

I smile as I bite my bottom lip. "Can I change the odds with a closing argument?"

"Perhaps," he whispers as he raises a brow.

"What if I said I was going to make you coffee and dessert?"

He shrugs. "Thirty-five, sixty-five."

I smile as my eyes hold his, our pinky fingers still linked. "We could spoon on my lounge again and you could kiss my neck as you cuddle me."

"Seventy, thirty." He raises his eyebrows.

I bite my lip and smile. I like this game. "We could take a shower," I whisper. "You could wash me, I'm feeling very dirty."

His eyes darken. "Ninety, ten, your way."

I smirk. "I could wear my white nightie again and you can run your hands all over me as I tell you how much I missed you all day," I breathe.

He smiles broadly as his eyes twinkle. "Were you on the debating team?" he asks as he cocks his head to one side.

I smile mischievously as I bite my bottom lip, feeling very proud of myself.

"You give a very good closing argument, Miss Marx." He raises a brow.

I smile as I pull back from his grip. "Yes, and it was the white nightie that won me arguments back then too."

"I don't doubt it. See you in twenty." He releases me and hits the lift button, and the doors open.

I RACE HOME like a lunatic to try and smuggle in my new clothes that I bought in my lunch break before he gets here. I drop the groceries in the kitchen and throw the clothes into my wardrobe still in their bags. I run around and make my bed like a maniac. I thought I would have had time to come home to straighten the house up before I went to the hospital tonight, but I got snowed under at work. I rush to the kitchen to wash up my breakfast dishes. It sure doesn't pay to be slobby. I am just finishing the last dishes when I hear the key in the door. I smile, what a lovely sound that is.

Joshua walks in and smiles warmly at me. "Hi," he says quietly as he puts his keys on my side table.

I smile shyly. "Hi" Why does he make me feel so nervous?

He walks into the kitchen and over to me where he cuddles me from behind, kissing my neck. I put my hand up and on his cheek.

"How are you?" he asks softly.

I close my eyes in comfort. "Better now that you're here," I whisper.

"Hmm," he sighs.

He pulls back and picks up the plastic bag of groceries on the floor. "Do you want these put away?" he asks.

I nod and smile. "Yes, please." I continue wiping up.

He puts a few things in the fridge and then he asks. "Why do you have this? Do you like protein now?" He frowns as he holds up a large jar of protein powder.

I shrug self-consciously. "I just thought you might like to stay for breakfast tomorrow...I mean, that's if you're not busy." I look down at the floor in embarrassment. Do I sound as desperate as I feel?

He pulls my face up to his as he smirks. "Did you now?" He kisses me gently on the lips and I feel myself melt.

He takes out his phone and texts someone and then walks around and flicks the kettle on. "Would you like a cup of tea?" he asks.

"Yes, please." I smile. This is going well, so domestic. I sit on the lounge and flick the television on. I curl up on the single lounge that I always sit on.

He fusses around in the kitchen for a moment and he comes in carrying two cups of tea. "Why are you sitting over there?" he frowns as he sits on the double lounge.

I smile again. Let me rephrase that, this is going really well.

Maybe he didn't mean a word he said in the restaurant last night. I stand and move over to the sofa and sit next to him, he pulls my feet onto his lap and he kicks off his shoes and takes a sip of his tea.

"Do you like your new job?" he asks as he blows on his tea. I shrug. "It's ok, I suppose."

He frowns and his eyes flick to me. "Just ok?"

I hunch my shoulders. "Yeah, Gran got sick just after I started so I haven't really been in a good place at work. I don't know, I don't feel like I have made a difference yet."

He smiles sadly. "Oh," he whispers. "Is that why you do your job, to make a difference?"

I raise my eyebrows. "Yes, I suppose."

"Why did you stop working at the sexual clinic?"

I drop my head. "I just saw me and you in too many of my clients and it was messing with my head too much."

He frowns. "Me and you? What do you mean?"

I blow out a breath, how did we get onto this deep subject? Do I say this out loud? "Umm...I saw men everyday who were deeply in love with their wives but regularly slept with other women and I saw women everyday whose husbands had been unfaithful, and they have never recovered from it and had absolutely no self-esteem." I scratch the back of my head uncomfortably and my eyes meet his. "It was just too close to home," I whisper.

He drops his head as he thinks. "Do you think that that is what happened between us?"

I shrug. "I know it's not how it happened and that there were crazy circumstances but..." I shrug, unable to articulate what I want to say.

"Tash, if I had thought we even had 0.5% of getting back together I would never have left your side." He reaches over and grabs my hand and I squeeze it affectionately. "You know that don't you?" he whispers as his eyes meet mine.

I smile as my eyes tear up and I am lost for words, so I try to change the subject. "Tell me about this job you are doing."

"Um, I did their programs years ago and stupidly signed a contract for the upgrade so while we are here, we are getting it out of the way. It should take about six weeks or so."

I nod. "So, who is doing it with you?" I ask

"Four techs and Murph."

I smile. "What does Murph actually do?"

He shrugs. "Nothing, just manage things. I don't like to go anywhere without him." He smiles shyly. "I don't really like dealing with all of the management shit. I just want to be on my computer and not deal with anything or anyone else."

I smile. "You are lucky to have him."

He nods. "Yeah, I know. Cam and Murph are good value." I smile broadly. "What about me? Am I good value?"

"You, my dear precious girl, are exceptional value." He smiles as he picks up my foot and kisses the top of it and my heart fills with joy. Exceptional value, who would have thought? My God, Joshua Stanton... do you know your value?

# CHAPTER 19

**Natasha**

WE LIE in my bed contented and satisfied. That was close, how I held him off from sex I will never know. If he had pushed for it, I would have caved. I told him that we were not being intimate, but the reality is I crave for it from him, ache for it. I don't have it in me to not let him touch me and he is heaven under my hands. When I am here and in the moment with this man, nothing else matters. This is where I am supposed to be, with my love in my bed. Joshua has his head on my chest, my arms are wrapped around him as I gently run my fingers over his back, his hand is on my stomach and he intermittently kisses my chest as he lies close. Something is going on between us, I can feel it. There is a tenderness that I haven't felt from him since my father died and ,God, I've missed it. I'm exhausted, I need to go to sleep. I kiss the top of his head gently. "Baby," I ask. "Hmm," he replies.

"Can you be here when I wake up, please?" I ask. I can't help myself.

"Yeah, okay." He kisses my chest again and snuggles his head into my breast and breathes a deep contented sigh.

I am just drifting off. "Tash," he whispers.

"Mmm," I answer.

"You didn't give me your closing argument yet."

I smile broadly and kiss his head again. "Joshua," I whisper. "Yes," he answers.

"I missed you today," I whisper.

I can feel him smile into my chest and I smile into the darkness. "Do you want to know something else I did today, Josh?" I whisper as I kiss the top of his head again and rub my hand over his short hair.

"What?" he answers.

"I loved you today." I feel him smile and he kisses my breast as he links our hands together.

"You really should be on the debating team, Tash, you do give a great closing argument," he sighs.

I smile broadly and after a few minutes of silence in the darkness I hear him speak.

"Goodnight, Tash," he whispers.

"Goodnight, Josh.

I WAKE to the sound of someone quietly knocking on the front door. Joshua answers it. "Thanks man. I will be leaving here in about an hour."

"Ok, Max is downstairs. What do you want me to tell him?" a male voice replies.

"I want to speak to him so I will be down a little earlier." "Okay thanks." The door closes.

Joshua walks back into my room with an overnight bag and a suitcase. He puts it on the chair at the end of my bed. He opens the drapes, and I am blinded by the blazing light. "Are you making me breakfast?" He grabs my foot out from the bottom of my blanket and starts to twist my toes.

I frown as I rip my foot from his grip. "Mmm," I groan. "Up." He smiles as he runs his stubble up my neck.

"Mmm," I groan again. Why does he have to be so damn perky in the mornings?

"I mean it, you wanted me here in the morning. I am here, so get up." He slaps my behind.

Oh God...so annoying. I lean up onto my elbows. "What time is it?" I frown.

"I have usually been in the gym for two hours by this time, lazybones." He smiles.

"That's great, coffee and eggs on toast," I mutter as I flop back onto the bed.

He smirks and exits the room. I lie and try to wake up as I hear him fussing in the kitchen. Five minutes later he comes back in with a cup of coffee.

"Here you are." He passes me the coffee.

"Thank you." I smile. He leans in and tucks a piece of hair behind my ear.

"I have to work for the next four nights."

I frown. "Huh?"

"The company's computers we are doing the upgrade for need to be worked on after hours for the first week. I start at five and then will be working all night on them."

I frown as I take a sip of my coffee. "That's annoying," I mutter.

"Tell me about it. I want you to stay at your mother's while I am working," he says matter of factly as he stands and takes his suit out of its bag.

I screw up my face. "Huh. What for?"

"I just do."

"I'm just not," I reply.

"Yes, you will be. Don't start your shit," he snaps.

I drink my coffee again. Here it comes, I forgot about this side of his personality. Hmm, funnily enough I haven't missed it at all.

"I live here on my own, Joshua. I think I am safe."

He shrugs. "I don't care what you think, you are not staying here alone. End of story." He turns and walks back out of the room. I lie in bed as I fume. What the hell is this about? He is acting all boyfriendy when he has specifically told me that he doesn't want to get back together. I would love to throw that in his face, but I don't want to push him and get the wrong answer. He's so damn confusing.

I walk into the kitchen where he is making me breakfast. This domestic version of Joshua Stanton is simply delicious, and I smile broadly.

He raises his eyebrows in question. "Yes," he murmurs.

"A girl could get used to this."

"Could she now?" he smirks as he puts my breakfast on the counter.

I cuddle him from behind. "Yes, she could." He turns to make his protein shake.

I sit at my breakfast counter. "Thank you," I smile.

He smirks and takes a sip of his shake. "So, will you go home with your mother tonight straight from the hospital?" he asks.

I take a bite of my food and shake my head. "No, I told you I am staying here."

He raises his eyebrows. "And I told you that you are not."

I chew my food and swallow so I can speak. "You are not the boss of me, Joshua. You can't tell me what to do."

He drinks his shake as he glares at me. "Seeing as I had my hands on the back of your head and my cock in your mouth for half of the night, I am the boss of you and you will do what I say." I glare at him, of all the nerve. The words booty call rattles around in my empty head. "Maybe tonight when that cock is in my mouth, I just might bite it off," I snap.

He smiles broadly. "Try it, see what happens to you." He takes a drink of his shake. "And you won't be here tonight, you will be at your mother's."

I can't help it and my face mirrors his stupid smile. "Stop it." I shake my head.

"You stop it. I don't want you here alone because I don't want anything to happen to you while I am at work."

I frown. "Josh, I have been here on my own for eight months since you left. Nothing is going to happen to me. Max takes care of me and if I get too scared, he sleeps in the spare room."

He folds his arms in front of him as he stares at me. "Really?"

I raise my eyebrows. "Really, and if you are going to make me have a bodyguard it is Max or nothing, the choice is yours."

"No, I think I am going to swap Max with Ben," he says in his best matter of fact voice.

I narrow my eyes. "Don't you dare. I am not hanging around with Ben. No way in hell."

"Well, do as you're told," he snaps. He then walks into the bathroom and runs the shower.

I sit still at my kitchen counter and look at my eggs on toast as my blood starts to boil. All I want to do is yell you are not my boyfriend so shut up. But I need to keep calm and play the game, I want to win him back at all costs...this is going to be a damn tough assignment.

## Adrian

### The night before

I walk up the street towards the restaurant I am meeting Nicholas in. How did I let him ambush me like this? My security is trailing behind me and I am painfully aware of their presence. I'm proud to be gay but when I have people watching me on a date, or a brush off in this case, I feel uncomfortable. I guess everyone who has security trailing them everywhere feels like this. Joshua hates it probably more than me. Apparently at his dinner date with Tash the other night she cried at the table and he was mortified that they had security witnessing the whole nightmare. I hope they catch this maniac soon. We could all do with some much-needed privacy. I blow out a breath in a nervous gesture. Nicholas keeps telling me there was something there between us on the last date and he wasn't wrong... there was too much there. Too much sexual energy, too much intelligence and humor, too much yearning for intimacy and I know it can only end badly. He lives in France for heaven's sake. I'm nipping it in the bud before it turns sour, as relationships always do for me. What I don't like though is the way he has called me out on it. He obviously doesn't get the brush off very often. Today when he rang me, he was furious and told me if I don't go out to dinner with him alone tonight, he will come into the office and ambush me in front of whoever is there and he doesn't give a fuck who hears what he has to say, those exact words.

I get out my phone to check the number of the street the

restaurant is on. We are going to O'Shea's, an oyster bar and restaurant. It's just up here. I stop out the front and peer in through the window and turn to my two security guards who are four or five meters behind me. After the graffiti in our office back home a month ago, with the words Joshua Stanton and Adrian Murphy Next written in blood on our office wall, Ben has been security crazy. Joshua and I are being guarded to a ridiculous degree. The police don't know whose blood the writing was in, but it's messed with all of our heads. If you are crazy enough to use your own blood to graffiti some- one's office it's a nightmare. If it wasn't his blood...that's worse.

"Just wait out here, please. I will be fine," I ask the body-guards. Their eyes flick to each other and they nod. "Ok, no worries." I open the large heavy doors and enter the restaurant tentatively as I look around. Nicholas stands up next to a table at the rear of the restaurant and waves. I smile and make my way over to him.

God, what am I doing here? I nervously walk over. He is dressed in a grey suit, white shirt and grey tie, and his tall stature dominates the space around him. His longish dark hair hangs just above his collar and has a curl to it and he is wearing a long five o'clock shadow. His piercing dark eyes penetrate mine. He brings the term Greek god into a new stratosphere. Fuck!

He smiles warmly and holds out his hand to shake mine. I smile, take it and am immediately jolted by a strong charge of sexual energy. *Oh, he'd be good alright.* I feel myself harden, and my eyes drop immediately to try and hide my arousal.

He smirks and keeping hold of my hand, he lifts it up and tenderly kisses the back of it.

"Hello," he smiles with my hand still in his.

"Hello," I smile as I nervously pull my hand from his grip.

The intensity of this guy is off the hook.

He holds out his hand to the table. "Take a seat," he smiles.

I sit at the table for two towards the back of the restaurant. It is adorned with six flickering candles at all different heights. The crowd is eclectic, and the music is earthy. The restaurant is quite dark and the candles on all of the tables add to the ambience.

"Would you like to order some drinks?" the waitress asks.

My eyes flick to Nicholas whose eyes are firmly on me. He smiles affectionately and I blow out a breath and read the drink menu. Right.

"I'll have a Martini, please." I look at Nicholas.

'I'll have the same." He smiles at the waitress and then back at me.

She leaves us alone. I don't think I have ever been so nervous, why does he make me feel like this?

"I don't like being ambushed into dates with people," I say dryly as I pretend to read the menu.

He nods. "I don't like having to ambush you to see me either."

"So why do it then?"

He smiles. "Because I wanted to see you and I knew it was the only way I could get you here."

"Ok, you have seen me, what now?" I raise my eyebrows in question as I look at him blankly.

He smiles broadly. "Are you always such a charming

date?" I smile in embarrassment. "No, you are getting the deluxe package." He smiles and picks up the menu.

"I see. How have you been?" he asks.

"Okay. You?"

"I'm good. Our last meeting has left me a little confused though." His eyes search mine.

I frown. Let's just get right into it then. "Why?" I ask trying to feign nonchalance.

"Because I had the best night I had had in years and then you walked me out to the car remember."

I look down nervously as my heart rate picks up. "Yes, I remember." I rearrange the napkin on the table.

"You kissed me." His gaze penetrates mine. My eyes rise to meet his. "Yes," I whisper.

"It was insane." He bites his bottom lip as he looks at me. "Off the charts. I know you felt it too."

My eyes flick around the room in uncomfortable tension. "Look, I'm sorry, I shouldn't have kissed you. I..." I shrug my shoulders as words escape me.

He smiles sexily. "Don't apologize, I'm not complaining." My eyes meet his. "What are you doing then?"

"Here you are." The waitress puts our two drinks on the table.

"Thank you," I smile. My eyes flick back to the ridiculously hot, intelligent man across the table from me.

"I want to know why you never returned any of my calls," he asks.

I look around the restaurant in annoyance. I don't need this shit. "I'm sorry if you don't get brushed off often but I am not after anything and I don't fuck around so..." I shake my head as I try to articulate my thoughts. "What's the point? You live in France remember. Besides it was six months ago, why are you bringing this up now?" He puts his hand across the table and grabs mine, and I swallow as I look at our entwined hands.

"I'm bringing this up because the thought of you has been haunting me for six months and I want to know have ever thought of me?"

My eyes meet his. "Maybe," I answer quietly.

"It's a yes or no answer," he says dryly.

"Yes," I reply as I look at him again.

He squeezes my hand. "What have you thought?"

I swallow nervously and shrug my shoulders. "I wondered what would have happened if I called you."

He smiles a broad smile at me and raises his eyebrows. "You did?" he whispers. "So, what did you think would have happened between us?"

I shrug. "It probably wouldn't have gone anywhere to be honest. I'm not into the whole casual sex thing and I'm guessing someone who looks like you is." I smile.

He licks his lips as he smirks. "To be honest most men do throw themselves at my feet and I feel nothing, not interested at all and then you come along with your masculinity, intelligence and don't give a fuck attitude and throw me completely off balance and yet you want nothing to do with me. It's...frustrating."

I laugh. "Is that how I come across? Masculine, intelligent and don't give a fuck?"

He takes a sip of his drink and nods. It is then I notice that he is still holding my hand across the table. I immediately pull out of his grasp.

He smiles and looks at his outstretched arm on the table and pulls it back slowly. "You are different to most men I have met, Adrian."

I raise an eyebrow. "How so?"

"You're very masculine and yet have an inner gentle quality. You're intensely sexual and yet you don't sleep around, even though you are one of the best-looking men I have ever met. Your two best friends are straight and yet you are entirely comfortable being gay. You're very intelligent and portray strength as you run the company and look after your two best friends, but it makes me wonder. When all is done and dusted, who looks after you, Adrian? Who satisfies you sexually...emotionally? Who loves you when you come home from work each night?" His eyes darken and drop to my lips.

I sit back affronted and look at him in horror. Who says that on a first date?

"That's very deep." I stammer. "You got all that info on me from dinner six months ago?"

He smiles into his drink. "Perks to being a psychologist."

I smile as I drain my glass. "My best friend is in love with a psychologist and he reckons it's the biggest mind fuck in history."

"Is that Joshua?" I nod and smile. "Is he back with Natasha?" he asks.

"No, but hopefully they will work it out."

"You have an affection for Natasha?"

I smile. "I adore her. Joshua's life is crazy, super rich, and yet Natasha is this beautiful pure soul who has loved him since they were kids. They are first cousins and have fought this attraction since they were teenagers. I don't know two people more in love."

He raises his eyebrows. "Wow." He smiles as our meal arrives. "Have you ever been in love Adrian?"

I swallow nervously. "I thought I was once."

He smiles wistfully and takes a mouthful of food. "Do tell."

I shrug my shoulders. "It's quite pathetic when I say it out loud really. I entered my first relationship when I was fifteen and we were together six years. We were madly in love and I wanted to come out, but he didn't. I couldn't live my life pretending I was someone that I wasn't, that he was just my roommate. My parents knew about us so I thought it would be ok but, in the end, it wasn't, he freaked out and ran. He even hooked up with a girl to prove to the world he was straight. I will never forget the night he came to me crying, to tell me that she was pregnant and that he was going to marry her." My gut twists at the memory and I take a large gulp of my drink. "And now I have the honor of every time he gets drunk, him calling me and telling me how much he loves me and misses me and that he made the biggest mistake of his life and yet he can do nothing about it because he is now a father of three." I look around the room in annoyance that he got me to say that out loud. "So, when you ask me have I ever been in love, I tell you if that's love I want nothing to do with it ever again."

He looks at me affectionately and grabs my hand over the table again and I squeeze it in a thankful gesture. I can't believe I just told him that, I have never told anyone other than Josh and Cam.

"I see." He nods.

"You?" I ask. Trying to take the spotlight off myself.

He nods and takes a sip of his drink. "I was married," he says quietly.

Oh shit, that's right. My stomach drops.

"What happened?" I ask quietly, already knowing the horrible answer.

"He died eight years ago in a snow skiing accident," he says sadly.

I squeeze his hand again. "I'm sorry," I whisper. "What does that feel like? To love somebody so intensely that you want to marry them?" I ask as I smile.

He shrugs. "Scary I suppose." He smiles broadly as he puts his elbow on the table and leans on his hand. "You will find out one day. I wouldn't write yourself off just yet. How old are you anyway?" He frowns.

I smile. "How old are you?" I ask.

"Probably too old for you," he answers.

I smile. "Without a question." He smirks. "I'm forty-two."

"You are old," I smile. "I'm twenty-seven."

He smiles warmly at me. "Let's forget about age and pasts and futures and just enjoy some time getting to know each other while we are both in Sydney. What do you say?"

"I don't normally hang around with hot middle-aged men." I smile.

"I don't usually hang around with blond Americans either so we are even." He smiles at me with a rather beautiful twinkle in his eye.

*What the hell am I doing?*


## Natasha

I walk down the street toward the café near the hospital that I work at and my phone rings.

"What time is your lunch break? I'm coming to have lunch with you."

I smile. It's Jesten.

"Jes, I'm on lunch now."

"See you in ten. I'm around the corner." He hangs up. Shit, now I've done it.

I wait in the meeting spot near the café and he walks around the corner, smiling broadly. He laughs and pulls me into an embrace and picks me up and spins me around.

"Hey, hot Doc." He holds me at arm's length and looks me up and down. "You are especially smoking today." He winks.

I laugh and he pulls me into an embrace, and we walk down the street with his arm casually draped around me. Why do I feel so comfortable with him?

"Why have you been ditching me?" he asks.

"I haven't. I've just been really busy that's all," I sigh.

We eat lunch in comfortable silence, and I am painfully aware of the security trailing us. I have had lunch with Jes heaps of times over the last couple of months and yet now I'm freaking out that someone is going to tell Joshua.

"Have you been going out much?" I ask.

He nods as he shovels in his food. "Yeah. You?"

I shake my head. "Not really. I have just been hanging at the hospital every chance I get."

"I've been training a bit. I'm fighting again next week."

I roll my eyes. "Please don't talk to me about your ridiculous sport. It's embarrassing that you would think I would be remotely interested."

He smiles broadly as he shovels in another mouthful of food. "My trainer rang me today to tell me that your ex-boyfriend is back in the country and that today he registered to fight."

I stop with my fork midair. "What?" I stammer as my eyes widen. "He is the only person who has beaten me so far and I have gotten a lot better since then." I look at him, mortified.

He fake punches his fist. "Can't wait to take the idiot out."
Holy fuck...can't be. I grab his arm. "You can't fight him,
Jesten, he will kill you."

He narrows his eyes. "Thanks for your confidence but I'm
thinking I might kill him instead."

My eyes widen in horror. "Jesten, I mean it, you have no idea
how crazy he can get. When you told me to think of you when I
had sex with him, he went insane." I swallow nervously.

He smirks. "Can't wait to bait him again." Oh. My. God.

"So, did you?" he smiles. I frown at him. "Huh?"

"Did you think of me when you had sex?"

"You're deluded." I shake my head. "No. Definitely not." He
fake punches his fist again as he smiles.

If I tell Jesten that I am trying to get back together with Josh,
he will go crazy and try to kill him and if I don't tell him he is
going to try and kill him anyway. Who am I kidding? Joshua
will kill him first in either situation. I put my head in my hands
as I try to think of a solution to this dilemma. Shit, shit, shit.
This is a frigging nightmare.

My phone beeps a text and I look at the screen. Joshua. I
smile broadly.

**What are you doing?**

My stomach drops and I look around nervously. Shit, is that
a trick question? Have the bodyguards told him I am having
lunch with a man and told on me. I swallow nervously and text
back.

**Having lunch with a friend.**
**What are you doing?**

I nervously wait for a reply.

"Have you heard from him?" Jesten asks.

I glance back at my phone as I wait for his text. "Huh who?" I mumble.

"Your ex-boyfriend."

My eyes snap up from my phone to look at Jes. Shit, another trick question. If I tell him before the fight that I have been seeing Joshua it will only make him angrier.

"Umm, you know, not really." Why am I such a terrible liar?

He frowns at me. "What does that mean?"

My phone beeps a text and my eyes flick to the screen. Joshua.

**Just thinking about how hot you were last night.**

My face nearly splits open with glee. "Huh?" he asks again.

I frown, oh shut up, you're annoying me. I want to be sexting Joshua right now.

"Jes, I don't go out with anyone who cage fights. End of story." I stand.

"I need to get back to work," I say nervously.

"I'll walk you back." He gestures to the door and follows me out of the restaurant.

My eyes flick to the bodyguard who is with Max, who is he? And what is he thinking? Is he a snitch?

We get back to work and Jesten grabs me affectionately in an embrace. I stand rigid and evasive as I feel the glare of others on my back.

"Tash, I want to take you on a date," he whispers into the top of my head.

Huh? What the hell? I pull back. "Jesten, you want to sleep with me, and I am not that kind of girl."

He smiles. "Can't you be that kind of girl for one night? We would be so good together."

"Seriously, Jes, go out with someone else. I am not interested in you that way." With that I break out of his grip and punch him playfully in the stomach. I turn and walk into the hospital and immediately take out my phone. Right, back to more important things. I sit in the foyer as I think what to text back. I narrow my eyes as I look at the ceiling deep in thought. Joshua is telling me that he wants sex only but after the tenderness last night I now know that's just not true. And the whole wanting me to stay at Mum's to keep me safe thing is his way of over-the-top caring, so he has blown the not-caring act out the window as well.

Do I want to push him for some kind of communication with me about our relationship or should I just play along and not scare him off? I know he cares for me and I don't feel anything but affection when I am with him. Let's just see what happens. I smile and text back.

**It was you who was hot Mr. Stanton.
Is this a disguised booty call?**

I bite my lip and wait.

**Totally**

I smile again and text.

**I'm thirty, seventy wanting to see you tonight
What's your closing argument?**

I smile as I wait for a reply.

**Meeting just started.**

**Got to go.**

I smile at my phone. He's calling me later. This is going very well indeed.

## Joshua

It's 11 pm and I am in Tatiana's office doing a backup of the hard drives for the company's computer systems before we close them down. Adrian and Alex are in the office next door and the offices are dead silent and deserted. Why did I agree to do this shit job? The security guards are outside and I have allocated extra staff to watch over Tash at her mother's house. I haven't had a minute alone to call her back yet.

Tatiana has been fawning over me all day. Why does she have to be so damn attractive? It's very... distracting. I narrow my eyes at the screen when I see in my peripheral vision her stretch out next to me. She's wearing a skintight black secretary number that's low cut with the biggest cleavage I have seen, and I know she has a suspender belt on underneath it. Adrian pointed it out earlier when he was making fun of her. "Would you mind if I stretched out on this desk and had a little nap?" she purrs.

I keep my eyes on the screen. "Not at all." Void of emotion.

She's been giving me double-meaning phrases all day.

This is sexual innuendo at its best.

"So, are you still with your girlfriend?" she asks.

"Wife actually," I murmur as I keep typing, my eyes not leaving the screen.

"Hmm," she replies. "You don't seem like the marrying

type." I raise my eyebrows, just fuck off and let me finish this job.

"Why do you say that?"

She fakes a laugh. "Don't you remember how you were dancing with me at the wedding? That was no married man dance."

I roll my eyes. "I was trying to make my wife jealous actually."

"Hmm. Does she get jealous very often?" she purrs again.

My eyes flick to her and she is practically lying across the desk and she has unbuttoned her two top buttons. Fuck.

I look back at the screen nervously. I need to get out of here. "You know I never understand why someone would want to get married and tie themselves to one person when there is so much pleasure to have in other beds."

I swallow. "Really," I answer flatly. I'm not having this conversation with her.

"You know, I was wondering," she runs her hand up my arm, "seeing as we are going to be working all crazy hours while we do this upgrade, if we should try to get to know each other more intimately...if you know what I mean?" She slowly licks her lips and leans over me.

"No one will ever know."

# CHAPTER 20

## Natasha

I SIT BACK on the lounge at Mum's and look at my watch for what must be the hundredth time today. 11.15 pm. Joshua didn't call me back like he said he would. He's probably just been busy. That's the logic talking, but my stupid mind is back in overdrive, and I can't help but wonder if he knew I was having lunch with Jes and was just texting me to distract me and now he is not ringing me to punish me. He told me he only wanted sex and I said I wouldn't be his booty call and yet I have been nearly just that. What the fuck am I doing? Am I imagining the chemistry between us, is it still even there? Is it wishful thinking? Why do I do this to myself? The new improved non-drama-queenish version of myself is not supposed to think like this. I rub my eyes in frustration and fatigue. I'm tired from all my prick-teasing antics last night.

"Do you want another cuppa, love?" Mum asks as she stands and stretches.

I nod and smile. "Yes, and then I'm off to bed." I look at my watch. 11.25 pm, hmm.

"Are you waiting for something?" she frowns. "You keep looking at your watch."

I roll my eyes shamefully and blow out a breath. "Hmm, yeah, Josh said he was going to call me, and he hasn't so...I don't know." I shrug my shoulders. "Who knows what's going on, Mum, it's like frigging *Dynasty* around here."

She smiles warmly. "He called me this morning." "Huh? Who? Josh?" I frown.

She nods and looks wide eyed at me and walks into the kitchen.

"Why did he call you and not me?" I ask as I put my hands on my hips in annoyance and follow her.

"He wanted to make sure you could stay here." She starts to make the tea and pours the water into the cups.

I screw up my face. "Oh, what next? He's a control freak," I snap.

"Why in the hell does he think it is ok to call my mother and ask if she can babysit me? I'm not a child?"

She takes her tea and walks back into the lounge room. I reluctantly follow her.

"What did he say anyway?" I ask as I frown. This is bullshit, mindfuck Stanton at his best.

"He told me that he has stayed at your house for the last couple of nights with you."

My eyes widen. "He did?" I whisper.

"And he told me that he couldn't stay with you for the next few nights because he had to work so would it be ok if you stayed with me."

I screw up my face again. "He's lost the plot," I snap.

"I am safe at home. Why does he think someone is going to get me? He's becoming paranoid," I huff.

She smiles again. "He's not worried about someone getting you, love. He didn't want you home alone in case you had a nightmare. He couldn't stand the thought of you being home alone and scared."

My mouth drops open as I am rendered speechless. "What?" I whisper.

I bite my lip to stifle the huge grin that is threatening to split my face open. "He said that?" I ask.

She nods and sips her tea.

I put my hand up to my mouth and think. "He still loves me, he wouldn't even think of that if he didn't love me."

"That's what I was thinking, love." She raises her eyebrows. "I didn't know that," I whisper through my smile.

"Why don't you call him now? I'm sure he has just been tied up at work and time has gotten away from him. Ask him to come over when he finishes if you want."

I smile and stand. "Thanks Mum." I give her a kiss on the cheek. "I will."


## Joshua

I sit back in my seat, affronted, and run my pointer over my lips as I think. "No one will ever know, you say."

She smiles and leans over me further. "It's a crime for a man as virile as you to only satisfy one woman. Nature didn't intend it to be that way. That is why he gave men like you a roving eye and uncontrollable lust. One woman would never be able to satisfy a man like you, Joshua, we both know that."

I run my tongue over my top teeth. "You think I have a roving eye?" I ask.

She nods slowly as she smiles. "The way you danced with me at the wedding, the way you looked at me this morning in this dress. I can tell that you want me and my body." She slowly runs her finger down her clavicle and over her breast.

I frown as I think. Is that how I come across, as having a roving eye?

"You're an attractive woman, a man would have to be dead not to notice you," I say flatly as I turn back to my computer screen.

"You normally do more than notice though, don't you Joshua?"

I stop dead in my tracks, how does she know that? It turns my stomach to think she has only known me since I have been with Natasha and yet she has nailed me in one. Have I given Natasha a reason to be insecure? My mind flicks back to the wedding and how I handled my jealousy that night.

She leans over me and gently kisses the side of my face. "No one will know," she whispers in my ear as she runs her hand down the side of my face.

I grab her hand midair. "I will know," I sneer as my eyes lock on hers.

"It's natural, Joshua, just go with it," she purrs.

I frown at her. "I'm not the man you think I am, get out of this office or I am walking right now."

She pulls back. "Joshua, don't be like that. I am just being honest."

I glare at her. "While we are being honest, I don't cheat on my wife. I am not that man anymore. Get out of my sight," I shake my head in frustration.

She stands angrily. "We'll see, you will be begging for sex any day now."

Adrian comes to the door. "Is everything ok in here?" He looks around and frowns at the tension in the room.

I start to retype. "Adrian, can you please escort this trollop out of the office. I won't be needing any further assistance from her." My eyes flick to him.

He smiles broadly at me. "I'd love to." He gives me a wink. I sit in the quiet of the office and drink my coffee alone as

I wait for the hard drive systems to back up half an hour later. My mind keeps rerunning over the conversation with Tatiana. 'One woman would never be able to satisfy you, you have a roving eye. The way that you looked at me this morning, the way you danced with me at the wedding'. Is she right? Am I such an ingrained player that I don't even know when I am doing it anymore? My mind goes to Natasha, have I made her feel insecure? That was never my intention, she had me completely.

Up until half an hour ago I blamed her totally for our break-up and now...I'm completely confused. I think back to the conversation in the car at Willowvale that I had with Natasha about Amelie. I hardly remember what was said and yet Tash knows the conversation word for word. Did I really say that I wasn't with Amelie because of her? I thought it was obvious to everyone that I didn't want Amelie...but then even Amelie thought I wanted her, so of course Tash would think that too. I put my head in my hands as I try to think this through. The other night at dinner I watched Natasha cry and tell me that she loved me and yet I told her I only wanted sex from her. Of course, she doubts me, I doubt myself. Why in the hell would I do that to her and then go home and cuddle her all night, in fact every night since? I put my head into my hands on the desk. I'm confused. I can't be brought to my knees by her again. I break into a cold sweat just thinking of how dark those days were.

But then when I'm with her...she's so perfect...we are perfect. She radiates this inner honesty, but I don't know if that is because I am so blinded by my feelings for her that I only see what I want to see. How could someone so gentle and loving break me three times and not care...but then... have I caused her to feel insecure and hurt?

Have I brought this hurt on myself?

Why in the hell did I let myself sleep with Amelie and then not tell Tash about it? And the money, was Amelie telling the truth about Natasha bringing up money in their argument?

I sit back in my chair and put the heels of my hands into my eye sockets.

"You ok in here?" Adrian stands at the door and smiles warmly.

I nod. "Can I ask you something Murph?"

"Sure." He walks in and takes a seat next to me.

"Do you think I give off the vibe that I'm on the market?" He smiles. "Yes, definitely."

I frown. "If I was going out with you, would you be insecure?" He smiles and raises his eyebrows.

"Most definitely."

I sit back in frustration and bite on my thumbnail.

"Do you think that I honestly love Natasha?"

He smiles as he puts his hand on my shoulder. "Without a doubt. What's going on?"

"Tatiana said that I give off a vibe that I'm a player and she knows that I could never be loyal to one woman. Do you believe that?"

He smiles warmly. "Josh, men play around till they meet

the right person. Don't beat yourself up because you have had fun for the last seven years. Why are you bringing this up now?"

"I just don't understand why." I shrug, unable to articulate what I want to say.

"Why Tash pushes you away?" he asks, and I nod.

"Joshua, you are one of the most eligible bachelors in the world, good looking, built like a gorilla, rich as hell. And for someone like Natasha who is so quintessentially Australian and so down to earth, it would be hard to take all that on. I actually don't know how I would handle it either. I think she does an amazing job at handling your life by refusing to give into it and it's a learning curve for her as well, I think. It's the man you are from now on that counts. You always say you want to be a loyal husband."

I look at my computer screen and nod.

He pats me on the shoulder. "Tonight, you did just that." He smiles broadly.

I give him a sad smile and huff. "And I'm not even fucking married."

He laughs out loud and I shake my head in disbelief.

My phone rings and I look at the screen, Presh. I smile.

"Hi Tash," I answer. Adrian smiles and pats me on the shoulder as he leaves the room.

"Hi baby," she breathes down the phone.

"I didn't get to call you yet," I smile into the silence of the office.

"That's okay. Are you busy? Shall I let you go?" she breathes down the phone.

"No, all good. Are you at your Mum's?" I ask.

"Ahuh." The phone goes silent. "Thank you for worrying about me," she whispers.

My heart melts. "That's okay." She can be so damn beautiful when she wants to be.

"What time are you finishing?" she asks. I look at my watch. "About three I think."

"Do you want to come over to Mum's when you finish work and stay here with me? Mum said it would be ok."

I frown. "Tash, I...don't think." She cuts me off.

"It's just, I really wanted you to be the first person I see tomorrow."

I melt again. "You won't be awake then," I whisper as I smile. "Text me when you are on your way and I will open the door for you. I just want to see you."

I melt again. Adorable. "Okay, I will text you when I'm close." "Okay, I love you." I can hear that she's smiling, she hangs up.

I blow out a breath and sit back in my seat. I put my hands behind my head as I think.

Decision time.

What's it going to be Stan...Yes or No?


Natasha

Beep, beep. My phone beeps a text. I roll over sleepily and pick up my phone from the side table.

**Are you awake?**

I smile sleepily and reply.

**Yes**

It bounces back again.

**I'm ten minutes away.**

I smile and text back.

**K**

I smile and lie down then start to doze. Another text comes through.

**I'm at the door.**
**It's locked.**

Oops! I fell back asleep. I jump up and go to the front door and open it in a rush. And there he stands. Tall, dark and extremely handsome. I smile broadly and go to cuddle him.

He looks around at the guards. "Tash, not here. Inside." He pushes me back in the house. I smile bashfully. I am wearing grey satin boxer shorts and a white tank top, and my hair is all over the place. He is in a dark suit and never has he looked more beautiful. Gently he tucks a piece of my hair behind my ear and tenderly leans down and kisses me. He's so much taller when I have no shoes on. He runs his fingers down my cheek and wipes them over my lips as he seems to study my face, his face is serious and pensive.

I smile. "You're very intense tonight, Mr. Stanton," I whisper as I run my hands over the back of his hair.

He smiles down at me. "Am I?"

I nod and kiss him again. The kiss ends, and we stand silently, resting our cheeks together intimately as we embrace. What's going on here? This is new.

"Thanks for coming," I smile into the quietness. "Are you

hungry? I can make you something," I whisper as I pull him into the kitchen by the hand.

He follows me in and stands resting his behind against the counter in the corner of the kitchen.

I start to fuss around in the pantry. "Do you want some toast? A cup of tea?" I ask.

He smiles and nods. "Yes, please." He looks around the house. "I haven't been here for a long time," he says quietly.

I smile and nod. I don't want to bring up the last time he was here. It was horrific.

He stays silent and I know he has remembered that awful day also. I silently make his snack while he watches me, and I hand him the plate.

"Thanks" he smirks.

"You're welcome," I breathe.

"Show me your room," he whispers.

I nod like a nervous fourteen-year-old about to show her boyfriend her room for the first time. "This way." I take his hand and lead him down the hall to my bedroom. Why does it feel more intense in this house than it does in mine? I'm nervous.

I get to the door and gesture with my arm into the doorway. "Here it is," I stammer.

He can sense my nerves and smiles as he walks in and looks around. "Has it changed since you moved out?"

I shake my head nervously. "No, this is how I left it." I close the door behind us.

He sits in the chair in the corner and smiles again as his eyes scan the room.

"Hmm, it's nice. Your presence is very strong in here," he whispers.

I smile meekly. I know why I am nervous. This is the first

time Joshua has been here as my boyfriend...booty call, whatever the hell I am. "My presence? That's very deep," I stammer.

He puts his toast and tea on the side table and sits on my bed and rubs the mattress in a circle. He pats it for me to sit next to him and I do.

"Is this the bed you slept on?" he asks. I smile and nod.

"Did you ever think of me when you were lying in it?" he whispers as his eyes darken and drop to my lips.

"Yes," I whisper.

"Did you ever touch yourself while you thought of me?"

I drop my head and he puts his finger under my chin and brings my face back up to his as his eyes search mine.

"Yes," I whisper again as I twist my hands nervously in front of me.

"Did you ever think you would have me sleep in this bed with you?" he smirks sexily as he runs his hand down my clavicle and cups my breast.

"No," I whisper.

"How are we going to celebrate our strength in this bed tonight?" he whispers as he leans in and kisses me softly and his lips linger over mine.

He's right, this is a momentous night. I would lie here and cry myself to sleep every night wishing that he wasn't my cousin, wishing that we could be here together, wishing that I had my parents' support. And here we are eight long years later, he is not biologically my cousin although my stomach twists with the hurt that knowledge brings. We are here together, and my mother is one hundred percent behind us. I make an internal decision; I love this man and I do want to celebrate my strength...with him.

I kiss him gently. "I want you to make love to me in this bed tonight, Josh. I want more than anything to be able to celebrate our strength together." My hand drops to his face and I kiss him gently again.

"Tash," he whispers. His lips take mine and the emotion behind it rips my heart wide open. That's it, I'm gone.

I smile as my eyes fill with tears. "I love you," I whisper. "Make love to me, baby. I need you."

He kisses me again, more urgently, more intensely. His tongue gently licks my lips as his hands hold my face, and my insides start to liquefy. He stands and, with his eyes not leaving mine, he starts to undress slowly, and my heart starts to thump in my chest.

"What about your toast?" I ask nervously.

His eyes flick to the side table and his vegemite toast on the plate. "Fuck the toast."

I giggle. "Sshh," he snaps. "You mother is upstairs."

I giggle again as I hold my hand over my mouth to stop myself from making noise.

He strips naked and turns to face me, his eyes still on mine. My eyes drop to the perfect man in front of me, my name firmly branding his beautiful body. His dark skin and rippled abdomen call to my libido on a level I will never understand, but it's his heart that I love. The fact that he comes wrapped in such beautiful sexy packaging is just a bonus, the icing on the cake. I would love him the same even if he was a broke skinny surfer like he was when we fell in love.

He walks over to my door and flicks the lock, then returns and turns on my lamp on the bedside table.

"I want to see your face as I fill you, precious girl." He kisses me again and I practically melt into his arms. My body starts to weaken with arousal. I need this. I can feel the pulse throbbing between my legs.

He very slowly, while not breaking eye contact, pulls my

shirt over my head. His eyes drop to my breasts, to my erect nipples. Slowly, so slowly, he drops his hands to my behind and very gently slides my boxer shorts down my legs. He hisses as he sucks on my nipple. His hand drops to between my legs where he parts me and starts to slowly circle my clitoris with perfect pressure.

"There's my girl. You're so wet baby," he whispers into my chest.

I nod, unable to talk, with my hand on his forearm. Every time with this man is like the first time, the very first time he touched me. That panting excitement when I feel like I can't breathe from his touch...without his touch, like I'm seventeen and a virgin, new to the joy of love making. I can feel the want in his hands, and it brings me to my knees I can't move, I am frozen on the spot. My head drops back and my eyes close in anticipation, and goosebumps run over my body as he starts to gently bite me. This is what he does so well, pushes me with that little bit of pain until I'm desperate for him to actually hurt me. For him to take me without abandon, to take his pleasure from my body and damn the consequences.

"Lie down, Presh," he whispers.

I look at the bed and nod nervously, why am I so damn nervous?

"It's okay, baby, I won't hurt you," he whispers as he senses my fear.

I slowly take a seat on the bed and he turns and switches off the light and crawls over the bed and lies down. His hand strokes over my hair and he smiles at me.

"Why are you nervous?" he asks quietly.

I shrug, embarrassed. "I don't know," I whisper.

He pulls me down to lie next to him. "I'll make sure you're ready, Presh, I won't hurt you. You know that." He gently licks my neck, my eyes close, and his chest hair gently dusts across my skin.

I nod as the stupid tears fill my eyes. "I'm not scared of you hurting me physically, Josh," I whisper.

He pulls back and looks at me affectionately and his eyes twinkle. "Do you have any idea how perfect you are?"

I smile through my tears and his eyes hold mine. "You're not the only one here who is frightened, Tash."

He bends and kisses me gently and I stupidly sob. Why the hell am I crying? What's the matter with me? *Stop it.*

His lips gently take mine as I melt into his touch, my legs fall to the mattress in silent invitation and his hands roam up and down my body gently. I know he is desperately trying to curb his arousal. His hands find that spot between my legs again and he groans into my neck as he feels how wet I am.

"You feel so good. I can't wait to be inside you," he whispers. "I need this so badly." My eyes close in pleasure.

His fingers part me as his open mouth moves from my neck to my jaw to my mouth. I can't even kiss him back as my arousal starts to heavily thump. I lie with my mouth open, panting... waiting. His open mouth moves down my body and I shake my head.

"No, baby. I want you up here with me." I try to stop him moving down as I grab a hold of him. I need him to kiss me through this.

"Tash, you need to orgasm first a couple of times or I won't be able to get in. It has to be this way, Presh," he whispers.

I kiss him again and he moves lower between the sheets and into the darkness under the blankets. I smile at the ceiling with my hands on the back of his head. In a normal sex romp with Joshua Stanton there are no blankets because he flips me around so much that they don't stay on the bed. There is definitely no silence as I am usually screaming in ecstasy and the bed is hitting the wall with such force it could be used for demolition, and there is no darkness, it is usually blazing light because he wants to look at my body as he takes me.

I lie still as I feel his silent gaze on me and feel his breath on my inner thighs. His fingers slowly part me and I feel him gently blow on my open weeping flesh. God, I need this. With his open hands holding my legs apart at my upper thigh I start to quiver with need. His tongue goes to work and gradually I feel my body start to meet him as his hands pull me onto his face. He's in me completely, tongue, stubble and face, and he's loving it. Oh...oh...dear God, I shudder as my body lurches off the bed in orgasm.

"Sshh," he whispers as he grabs my hand affectionately.

There it is, the gentle gesture that is my breaking point.

He immediately pushes two fingers into me, and I bring my knees up and, my feet flat to the mattress, I try to calm myself and lie back as I try to control my breathing. His tongue unleashes on my clitoris this time and he works me with his two fingers, in and out...in and out...in and out, oh shit. Then he adds another finger and I flinch at the tight pinching sensation. He stops.

"Did I hurt you?" he asks into me.

"No, it's ok. It's a good burn," I whisper as I rub my hand over the back of his head in a reassuring gesture.

He keeps working me and the bed starts to move, and he stops. "Sshh, stop breathing so heavy." He whispers.

"I can't believe you are telling me to be quiet, you are usually making me scream," I whisper.

"Sshh," he says again.

"Stop shushing me," I whisper as I smile at the ceiling.

Then he lets me have it, three fingers and the best oral sex you have ever felt. He works me so hard that I am moving up and down in my bed. Without realizing it, my feet have lifted, and I lie with my legs in the air. My hands are firmly on the back of his head, he groans into me and I gently convulse into another orgasm, then, before I realize what has happened, he has lifted my legs and pushed into me in one movement. God... he's big. He breathes heavily into my shoulder as he stays still and deep to let me acclimatize to the hard intrusion. Holy... mother of God, this man is divine. He kisses me and I run my hands over his broad muscular shoulders. How have I lived without this?

He starts to pant as he tries to control himself. He kisses me again, more urgent and I know he has to move.

"I'm okay," I whisper. "It's okay, baby."

He nods and slowly pulls out. Ohh, it burns. I close my eyes as I try to deal with the full sensation. He stays still again.

"Are you okay?" he asks in a nearly unrecognizable husky voice.

I nod. "I'm good, go." I bring my hips up to meet his and put my hands on his behind.

He groans into my ear as he takes the lobe between his teeth. The dull pain of his bite combined with his breath on my neck and the burning hot fire between my legs has me starting to really move underneath him. I need more, I need it harder.

"Sshh, gentle baby," he whispers as he tries to calm me. "We have to be quiet."

"I can't be quiet. Fuck me," I whisper.

He smiles into my neck. "There's my beautiful slut, I've missed her." He kisses me again and starts to move. "Baby, I won't last, it's been too long," he whispers, but I am way past worrying about his orgasm because mine is here already. I cry out and lurch forward as the orgasm rips through me. He quickly puts his hand over my mouth and I giggle into it. He closes his eyes and with one, two, three strong pumps his orgasm gently takes him over. Never have you seen anything so beautiful as Joshua Stanton orgasm. His eyes close and he shudders, his mouth opens slightly as he gasps for air.

We lie together panting. I can feel his heart beating in his chest heavily along with mine. We start to kiss passionately and the depth of feeling I have for this man once again moves me to tears.

He wipes my tear away with his thumb as he kisses me gently.

He rolls onto his back and drapes my body over his as he holds my hand. Our heartbeats are still going at a hectic pace. We both lie staring at the ceiling as we try and catch our breath.

"Tash," he whispers.

"Yes," I answer.

"Am I seeing this right? Do the glow in the dark stars on the ceiling spell Joshua?"

I giggle in embarrassment. "Maybe," I whisper. "Everyone wants their name up in lights, right?"

He laughs. "You're an idiot," he whispers as he kisses my forehead. I sigh happily as I kiss his broad chest and start to relax.

"I fucking adore you," he whispers, and I smile into his neck. Who would have thought at five in the morning on a Tuesday in my mother's house under the veil of silence I would once again hear those much needed magical words from the beautiful Joshua Stanton?

# CHAPTER 21

**Natasha**

I WAKE to the sound of talking in the kitchen. I frown and look around. I pull myself out of bed, put my pajamas back on and head out, and there I see it. My heart warms at the sight of Joshua sitting at the kitchen counter on a stool in his complete suit talking to Mum who is making bacon and eggs. "How many eggs?" she asks

"Two please," he answers, as he casually flicks through the paper.

"This is my favorite start to the day ever," I smile as I hunch my shoulders in excitement and clap my hands in front of me.

Joshua and Mum both frown at me in question.

"Having breakfast with my two favorite people of course," I smile as I walk around to Joshua and put my arm over his shoulder and around his neck. His eyes flick to Mum.

"It's okay," I say.

He subtly shakes his head at me to signal silence, this is shy Joshua at his adorable best.

Mum has her back to us, and Joshua reaches over and grabs my hand as he gives me a wink.

"What are you doing today?" I ask.

He raises his brows. "I'm going to go for a surf and then train at the gym, go to the hospital and then Adrian and Ben want to see me about a few things and then I suppose it's back to work tonight."

I nod and smile at Mum as she hands me a cup of coffee. "Why do you need to train?" Shit, that bloody fight. I knew it.

"Tash, I train every day, you know that."

"How long do you train for?" I ask as I take another bite of toast.

He shrugs. "Couple of hours I suppose." Hmm, that's why he always looks like he's been photoshopped.

"Are you still going to the gym?" he asks as he smirks.

Of all the nerve! I widen my eyes at him. "Of course." Not really, I can never be bothered, but I will from now on. Mental note, get to the gym today, you lazy bitch.

Mum puts our bacon and eggs onto the countertop. "Here you are, I'm going to get ready to go to the hospital. Enjoy." She smiles and rubs Joshua's arm as she walks past us.

Joshua's horrified face drops to his breakfast and I giggle. "Don't you like bacon and eggs?" I ask.

He smiles. "Yes, of course." He picks up his knife and fork and starts to pick at it.

I smile with my cutlery in my hands. "When was the last time you had a breakfast like that?"

He shrugs. "Probably five years ago."

I frown. "Why?"

"I don't like feeling like shit and how I train and what I eat determines that." I smile and nod. Shit, I had better find some hard-core motivation somewhere and soon.

"Can you stay here again tonight?" he asks.

I frown. "Josh, I am ok at home. I have been having these nightmares all along and even if I were here, I wouldn't wake Mum up anyway."

His face drops. "Can you just humor me please?"

I smile and rub my hand up his leg as I remind myself, he is only being over the top caring. "Okay," I sigh.

"Can you humor me?" I ask.

"On what?"

"Can you not cage fight anymore?" I need to stop him from fighting Jesten, and if it's the last thing that I do. It can only end badly. He rolls his eyes as he finishes his mouthful. "Tash, we are on day one." He holds his pointer up to accentuate his point. "Can you not start your shit, please? We have had this conversation before, and I am not giving up something that I love just because you perceive it as dangerous." I smile goofily.

"What?" he asks.

"Are we on day one?"

He smirks and raises an eyebrow. "Yes." I smile.

"So was yesterday negative one?"

He shakes his head as he breaks into a smile.

"No, yesterday was zero."

I nod. "Right, so where were we a month ago?"

His eyes hold mine. "In the black hole. Now eat your breakfast." I smile and shovel in a mouthful of food...loving day one!


## Joshua

I walk into Ben's room. "What do you want to see me about?" I ask. His nervous eyes flick to me. "I'll call Murph."

"What's going on?" I ask.

"Murph, Stan's here. Okay, see you soon." He flips his phone shut.

I bet Max has resigned and they are telling me together. Good, I want him gone.

Adrian walks through the door with his laptop and smiles at me nervously. "Hi Stan," he murmurs.

Adrian turns on his computer and then flicks the jug on while it boots up.

"Take a seat," he says quietly.

"What for? Aren't we going to the gym?" I ask.

"We've got a problem." He opens an email and I read the words:

---

*'Contact me on mrsjones@hotmail.com or the wife gets the lot.'*

---

Wife? I frown at the screen. "Who sent this?" I ask. Adrian shrugs.

"It was sent to the work email in LA."

"Play," I sigh.

He presses play and my stomach clenches. It is a vision of me and a woman. I can tell by the legs. I frown as I try to remember when this was. I sit back in my seat and run my pointer over my lip as I think. "When was this?" I ask.

Adrian's nervous eyes flick to me. "Here in Australia." "What?" I frown.

He points to the screen. "Here, see, it's the house in Bondi. It's the girl who told us the other night Natasha's email, remember?"

My eyes widen in horror. I sit shellshocked as I watch myself get a drink and then walk up the stairs with her.

"What was your name again?" I ask.

"What do you want it to be?" she replies.

"My bedroom is this way...Natasha," I answer.

I stand in a rush. "Are you fucking kidding me?" I scream at Ben as I point to the computer monitor. "Why wasn't she searched for cameras? I thought she was lying the other night."

He frowns uncomfortably. "I'm not sure," he answers.

I start to pace as I run my hands through my head.

"Who's the wife she refers to?" I ask, horrified.

"I'm guessing Natasha." Adrian winces.

"What?" I scream. "Is this a joke? Why do I have security if they don't check girls for cameras?"

Ben drops his head.

"Have you been in contact with her?" I ask Adrian. He nods solemnly.

"And?" I yell.

"She says she has film of the first night you were together ...three hours of footage."

"What?" I punch the chair in anger.

Adrian and Ben jump at the bang. I start to pace again with my hands on top of my head.

"What does she want?" I snap.

"Five million dollars," Adrian whispers.

"What?" I scream. They both stand silent and still.

"How long have you known about this?" I ask.

"Two days." Adrian frowns. "We were trying to sort it before we told you."

"What? Trying to sort out why my security is so shit?" I glare at Ben.

"Joshua, calm down, blaming someone is not going to help the situation," Adrian says quietly.

"Oh really, what am I paying for? Tell me that. What is the rule of my fucking house?" I ask Ben.

He drops his head. "All women are checked for cameras."
"So why wasn't she?"

He shrugs. "She was but we think it was hidden in her bag."

"Oh this is perfect," I yell. "Fucking perfect." I drop to the bed and put my head into my hands as I try to think. What if Natasha gets that footage and is forced to watch me have sex with another woman? She'll lose it...who wouldn't?

I stand and walk over to the window as I look to the street below. She's got me. I have no choice. "Pay the money," I say flatly.

"What?" Adrian gasps. "Joshua, no, she could drag this out for more and more. We need to go to the police."

I turn in a rush. "If you think for one minute, I am having Natasha watch me have sex with someone else you can think again. I will not put her through this and if I have to kill this stupid bitch to shut her up then I will."

"Stop it, you're talking crazy," Adrian snaps.

I turn to Ben. "Get those fucking tapes back at all cost. Do what has to be done," I snap and leave the room.


Natasha

I look nervously at myself in the closet door mirror. I look like Frankenstein's version of a medic: half hooker, half nurse. We are going with Adrian to a fancy dress ball for Nicholas Anastas's charity tonight. Joshua hates fancy dress balls with a passion, but I have promised to wear a naughty nurse outfit to sweeten the deal. I have a skintight white short nurse's tunic on that has a zipper down the length of the front of it with a little pointy collar. The girls are standing to attention in the bustiest bra I could find, I have on high sheer-white stockings that come above my knee with a little red satin bow at the top and I am wearing white patent sky high stiletto shoes that are without a doubt the most uncomfortable shoes known to man.

I need to bring Mr. Stanton out of his shell at all costs. All this softly, softly quiet business at my mother's house this week is about to drive me insane. I love the gentle love making but now I just need to be taken hard. My hair is out and teased in a Bridget Bardot do and I have the full cat makeup on. Let's do this. I walk into the living room and the girls both turn to look at me. Bridget is taking a large scull of her drink and chokes as her eyes find me.

"Holy shit," she snaps. "Are you trying to give him a heart attack?"

I smile and nod as Abbie hands me my wine. Abbie's eyes scan up and down as she nods. "Now that's what I'm talking about," she coos.

She points her wine glass at Bridget. "Why didn't you get us outfits like that? We look like shit."

Bridget looks down at herself. "I think we look ok." She shrugs her shoulders.

"We look like men," Abbie snaps. "This outfit is totally sexless." I giggle as I look at the two of them dressed in their doctor's coats and pants. It's a government services fancy dress ball, you have to dress in something from a service.

"I didn't see you at the fancy dress shop, you ungrateful witch. I got the best that was there," Bridget frowns.

I laugh out loud. "I like the outfits, Didge, they are very..." I smirk as I try and think of the right analogy. "Medicinal."

"Medicinal," Abbie snaps. "That will do me. I don't want to look medicinal. I want to look hot."

Bridget rolls her eyes. "Blah, blah. Abbie, you would look hot in a garbage bag. Who are you kidding?" I smile, thank frigging God I picked my own outfit.

We arrive at the function hall an hour later, and our driver pulls into the round circular drop off area. This is a Government Services Fancy Dress Ball, a fundraiser for mental health. It was organized by Nicholas Anastas for his combined charities and this is the fifth year he has held this event. In front of the function center is a wide sandstone staircase that winds up to the huge double doors into the venue. There are four people lined up on each side of the door on the landing at the top of the stairs welcoming the guests as they walk into the ballroom. Nicholas is the last on the right. He is wearing a full white navy uniform and hat.

"Holy shit, he's hot," Abbie purrs as her eyes find him.

"I know, that's him."

"Who?" she questions as she frowns.

"He's the guy who Adrian has been seeing, Nicholas Anastas," I whisper as we walk up the steps towards the welcoming group.

"You're joking, that's him?" she snaps. "He's totally straight, no way he's batting for the other team," she whispers angrily.

"Would you think that Adrian was gay if you didn't know him?" Bridget whispers.

Abbie frowns. "Maybe."

"I wouldn't," Bridget smirks.

We get to the top of the stairs and Nicholas's dark eyes find me, he smiles warmly and immediately walks over to us. "Natasha, my dear, thank you for coming." He kisses my cheek, oh dear, he really is quite...

"Hello." I smile nervously and am suddenly painfully aware that I look like something from the Rocky Horror Picture show. "These are my two friends, Bridget and Abbie." I hold my hand up to them awkwardly.

He smiles and shakes their hands, and the girls exchange looks. "Are the boys here yet?" I ask. He smiles. "Not yet." He gives me a wink and then moves on to greet the next person in the line behind us.

'He's divine," Bridget murmurs in amazement.

"I know," I reply as we enter the opulent ballroom. Our eyes immediately look around the space.

"I could turn him," Abbie smiles.

"Wow," Bridget whispers as she rolls her eyes at Abbie. "Yeah, into a pumpkin." She giggles.

"Jeez, this is an extravagant affair," I murmur as I look around. "But do they make a good margarita?" Abbie whispers.

Bridget smiles. "I will get us some, back in a minute."

The decorations have a distinct disco feel. There are mirrored balls and colored lights circling around the room. The crowd is eclectic, and it seems funny with everyone dressed in a uniform, like weird. Bridget finally returns from the bar with a round of margaritas when I see it. The four hottest men in history entering the room. It's as if the room stands still in awe. I know I am. Ben, Cam and Adrian are in front and then, at the back, always at the back, is Joshua. Dear God, it's every Magic Mike fantasy that I ever had. They are wearing the same outfits. White tight tanks, green army cargo pants, green army cap and dog chains.

"Shit," Abbie purrs.

I smile deviously. "I know, right?" I whisper.

"Army," Bridget whispers.

"And you know what that stands for?" Abbie murmurs as her eyes scan up and down the four gorgeous men.

I take a sip of my drink and smile. "Code for fuck me," I whisper as my mind gives me a visual of being taken by that god.

"If you don't tap Ben tonight, you're an idiot," Abbie says to Bridget as her eyes follow them.

"Hmm, maybe?" Bridget whispers.

My eyes scan up and down Joshua's muscular body as he walks effortlessly through the crowd across the room. I can see every muscle in his arms and shoulders through the shirt that leaves nothing to the imagination, his dark skin and ripped muscles are screaming at me...to every woman who is present. His dark hair and chiseled jaw line only accentuate his large red lips. My God, he's beautiful, how is it possible that one human being can be so virile...so blatantly sexual. His eyes search the room until they meet mine and he stops dead and smirks sexily at me as his eyes drop hungrily down my body. I feel the burn from his gaze as his eyes go back up to my face. He ticks his jaw and cracks his neck hard. There it is...the jackpot

...more valuable than winning the lottery to any female with a

pulse. My heart rate picks up speed in anticipation. He walks through the crowd on a mission and he grabs me roughly around the waist and jerks me toward him. Oh shit.

"If you have any intention of walking for two days, precious girl, I suggest you go home and change," he whispers huskily.

I bite my lip to hide my smile, bingo.

His dilated eyes drop to my lips and I lick them slowly as anticipation runs through me. He jerks me to him again, he's just so...ridiculously hot.

I feel myself weaken to his strength and a burst of arousal breaks the dam.

"Well?" he snaps.

I run my hand slowly down his face and kiss him slowly as my tongue rims his lips.

"I'll forgo walking for a week if you give me what I want," I whisper.

He cracks his neck hard again and kisses me roughly, all suction, all domination. "Natasha, I mean it, when you look like that, I can't be held responsible for how rough I take you. You are playing with fire and are going to fucking cop it."

Mmm, that's sounds good. I smile sexily as I run my fingertip up the back of his neck.

"I hope so, Mr. Stanton, you can't have a party if you don't send out an invitation," I whisper into his ear as I lick it.

He bends and kisses me as he grabs the back of my hair and I feel his hardness pressing onto me. Oh shit, I could orgasm right here, doing just this. His tongue ploughs through my mouth and previews me a glimpse of what I am going to get tonight and, quite frankly, I don't care if I can't walk for a month. I need this...so damn hard.

"We are going home very soon," he snaps and pulls out of my grip and walks to the bar.

I stumble back and turn and as I pull out of my arousal fog, I see Cameron, Adrian, Abbie and Bridget's eyes firmly on me. Oh shit, I forgot they were here listening.

"Oh my God, can we come and watch you guys have sex?" Abbie giggles into her drink. "He should be put in a cage." I bite my bottom lip to stifle my smile.

"You got that right," I answer as I look around nervously. How does he make me forget where I am like that?

"Adrian, did you see Nicholas in that naval uniform?" I grab his arm.

"I know," he smirks.

"He's a damn fine specimen," Bridget tutts. "He is, isn't he?" I answer.

Joshua returns from the bar with Ben and our eyes meet across the group. Once again, his eyes drop down my body and he cracks his neck as he takes a sip of his beer from the bottle. The group continues to talk around us, but I am lost, lost to the need of the man across the circle from me. I can feel it from here. He can't even act unaroused as I can see the large erection in his pants. He really should be in a cage... because he's the one who's going to fucking cop it...and he's not walking tomorrow either. We both stand staring at each other as we drink our drinks in silence. I have never been more aroused in public. I walk over and run my hand down his face as I kiss him gently.

"Let's dance," I whisper.

He swallows as his eyes drop to my cleavage. "I need to be alone with you," he growls.

My breath catches. "Me too, baby. Patience." I smile as I run my hand over his chest and lean into him.

"Fuck, Tash, we need to go home now. I need you," he whispers as he closes his eyes as if in pain.

"Sshh, patience, big boy. You can have whatever you want when we get home."

His eyes widen and he holds his head on the side in question. "Anything I want?" he repeats in a whisper.

I bite my lip to stifle my smile as my eyes drop to his perfect body and I nod. "Anything you want," I whisper again. The words he first teased me with about his need in a wife come back to me and I raise an eyebrow in a teasing gesture.

He swallows the lump in his throat and cracks his neck hard as he pulls me into him by my behind. "Be careful what you wish for, precious, I don't have it in me to be gentle tonight." I feel my heart flutter as I bring my hand to the back of his head as he buries it into my shoulder. He once again rubs his engorged length into me as he growls into my neck.

"Will you two fucking cool it? We are at a charity ball, for Christ's sake," Cameron snaps as he looks around, embarrassed.

Joshua and I jump back from each other as we realize what we must look like. Jeez, what the hell am I doing?

"Fuck off," Joshua snaps to Cameron as his eyes flick around in annoyance. "I will do what I like."

Cameron frowns. "Go and do it against the wall then, we have to stand here while you two make a porno in front of our eyes." Bridget clinks her glass with Cameron and Adrian and Abbie laugh.

I drop my head as I giggle in embarrassment and Joshua smiles and pulls me onto the dance floor.

"Dance with me, my beautiful slut, before I fuck you into next week," he purrs.

I laugh out loud. "You are a born romantic, Stanton."

He smiles broadly. "Sshh, don't tell anyone." He spins me around until we are at the back of the dance floor and we pick up exactly where we left off. Erection in my stomach, hand at the back of my head, tongue in my mouth and me desperately needing a change of underwear.

# CHAPTER 22

Adrian

I STAND with Cameron on the side of the dance floor. We watch Joshua spin Natasha around as they both laugh. No one else is in the room for them.

I smile broadly. "Have you even seen him dance with a girl before?" I ask Cameron as I drink my drink.

"Nope" Cameron shakes his head as his eyes stay glued to the two of them.

"Me neither." I smile. "He's like a different person with her."

Cameron frowns. "If I ever get that pussy whipped, please get me castrated."

I laugh into my drink. "Me too." Cameron shakes his head in disgust.

"What?" I ask.

He shakes his head and takes a swig of his beer. "How is this going to go when that silly bitch sends this email to

Natasha, huh? What then? It will be Armageddon once more."

My stomach drops as I run my hand through my hair. "I know. I am trying to get him to tell Natasha before that happens," I mutter.

Cameron shakes his head in disgust. "Just pay the money and be done with it."

I frown. "You can't be that stupid! She will just keep coming back for more money and Natasha will finally find out," I snap angrily.

"Can you imagine if Natasha sees that tape of him with her? She'll lose it."

"There's a sex tape?" Abbie snaps from behind us. Fuck!

My horrified eyes meet Cameron's.

"What are you talking about?" Cameron snaps.

"Who's blackmailing Joshua?" she asks as she puts her hand on her hip. "Has he been fucking around again?" she sneers angrily.

I shake my head as I try to think quickly on my feet. What in the hell did she just hear?

Cameron's eyes flick to me. "No, of course not!" he snaps angrily. "Stop eavesdropping."

"You tell me right now or I am going to tell Natasha." Her angry eyes move between the both of us.

Cameron's nervous eyes flick to Natasha and Joshua who are now kissing on the dance floor. "I don't know what you are talking about," he snaps.

"I'm not stupid and I won't tell Tash. I mean it, tell me!" Cameron's eyes meet mine. "It was before he was with

Natasha."

Abbie narrows her eyes. "Where?" she snaps.

I swallow the lump in my throat. "Here in Australia," I whisper quietly.

She narrows her eyes. "Go on," she sneers.

"Joshua was with a girl before he was with Natasha at the wedding," Cameron says nervously as I take a drink.

"Yes, TC the prostitute," she says.

Cameron frowns. "TC? What does that mean?"

She pulls a disgusted face. "Tunnel cunt."

I spit my drink out and Cameron bursts out laughing. "That about sums it up actually." He laughs.

"Anyway, she had a camera in her bag and now wants five million dollars or she is going to send the tape to Natasha at work," Cameron sighs.

Abbie narrows her eyes as she puts her hands on top of her head in frustration. "She's such a bitch," she snaps.

I frown. "You know her?"

She nods. "Unfortunately, yes, she does this shit often, blackmails men to get what she wants. She's sleeping with my roommate." My horrified eyes meet Cameron's.

"You know where she lives?' I stammer.

"No, but I can find out. If she thinks she's doing this to Natasha she has another think coming. That bitch is going down. Leave this to me and don't you dare pay her one cent and don't tell Joshua I know."

Cameron's eyes flick to me. Shit, now we have done it.

Abbie storms off through the crowd.

"That's going to backfire," Cameron snaps.

"Tell me about it," I stammer as I feel a hand snake around my waist from behind. Nicholas leans into my ear. "Hello," he smiles.

I smile warmly over my shoulder. "Hello."

Cameron's eyes light up. "Hello, Nick, nice to see you."

They shake hands. I put my hand out and he smiles at me and then leans in and kisses my cheek. 'I don't think so," he whispers into my ear.

I swallow uncomfortably and step back as my eyes drop to the perfect specimen before me, tall and dark in full naval whites. I feel myself harden.

His eyes drop down my body as he takes a sip of his drink and he licks his bottom lip seductively. "I like your outfit," he smirks.

I smile nervously as my eyes flick to Cameron who smiles into his drink. "Thanks." My heart rate just picked up by thirty beats per second. Why does he make me feel like this?

"Are you having a good time?" he asks.

"Amazing," Cameron answers. "How many years have you been doing this event?"

He and Cameron start to talk but I can't concentrate on the conversation. Every one of my senses is standing to attention. I have never had such a physical reaction to any person before and it's very unsettling. He's taller than me and lean but it's his intelligence and confidence that arrests me and holds me captive. I'm so nervous I feel like I can't breathe.

Nicholas's eyes flick intermittently to me as he talks to Cameron. What's he thinking? I really should be joining in the conversation, but I can't even talk. This is ridiculous. As he continues to talk to Cameron, he puts his hand out and gently runs it up and down my arm. Cameron's eyes meet mine as he smirks at me. Fuck, Nicholas is a confident bastard.

His hand finds the bottom of my arm and he links our hands. "Can I steal you for a moment?" he asks.

Cameron smiles. "I'm going to the bar. He's all yours." He walks off.

He smiles broadly at me. "All mine, hey?" His eyes drop to my lips. "I like the sound of that."

I swallow nervously.

"Come, I want to show you something." He pulls me by the hand through the crowd and I reluctantly follow. I can feel the gaze of people on my back as we get to a door which he opens. As he ushers me into a staircase and starts to walk up it, the door opens behind me and my two security guards walk in. Nicholas turns to them annoyed. "Can we have some privacy please?" he asks me with a raised eyebrow.

I frown. "Umm" I turn to the boys and wince. "Where are you going?" one of my guards asks him. "To the roof," he answers flatly, obviously annoyed.

"We will search the roof and then you can go," the guard replies as I swallow uncomfortably again.

They head up the stairs to the roof and Nicholas and I stand still on the steps.

"Is this normal?" he snaps as he fiddles with my fingers in his hand.

I nod. "Yes, unfortunately," I reply quietly.

He shakes his head in frustration. "I think you are safe here."

"Maybe I'm in more danger now than ever," I breathe as my eyes search his.

He smirks sexily at the double meaning. "Maybe you are." He runs his hand over my chest and goosebumps cover my flesh as his touch puts me on fire. His dark eyes hold mine.

"Clear," we hear from the top of the stairs and the moment is broken. I pull my eyes from his gaze. He grabs my hand again and we walk up the stairs where we arrive to a rooftop terrace with a garden. Fairy lights hang strung in a zigzag across the top from poles and large timber benches scatter the space. "This is nice." I smile as I look around.

He smiles warmly as he runs his hand down my face. "Like you."

I smile. "I'm really not that nice."

"I beg to differ." He leans in closer to me.

"Why did you bring me up here?" I ask.

He smiles. "I'm hoping you're going to kiss me again."

I smirk. "Oh, really."

"Yes, really." He bites his lip to stifle his smile.

"I told you I don't fuck around Nicholas," I whisper.

"I don't want a man who fucks around. I want someone to make love to me when he feels enough emotion to do so."

My heart stops.

"And I want that person to be you, Adrian," he whispers. "You do?"

"I do," he whispers as his eyes drop to my lips.

I can't help it. I don't have any willpower left. I lean in and grab the back of his neck and pull him into me as I kiss him gently. His lips are soft and hard and...fucking perfect.

## Natasha

An hour later I am dancing with the girls and I feel Joshua's heat before I see him. My love has come to dance with me. The girls dance off through the crowd as Joshua's strong hands envelope my waist from behind, and he kisses me slowly over my shoulder. As our bodies move together I can feel his hardness behind me, his breath in my ear, his hands close to obscene as they run over my hipbones and up to my breasts and down my arms.

Joshua bends his knees as he pushes his erection into my

back and starts to slowly suck on my neck as his hands slide up and down the sides of my body. My eyes close as my head drops back to his shoulder and I gently sigh.

"I'm taking you home, beautiful slut," he whispers into my ear as he bites it.

"Mmm," I reply with my eyes still closed.

"Now or I am going to take you on the dance floor."

My dilated eyes meet his. "Take me here. I want you to fuck me here," I whisper.

He turns me and pulls me close to him as he growls into my neck. "Do you have any idea what I am going to do to you tonight?" His tongue plunges into my mouth and I whimper as I hold off an orgasm. "How hard you are going to cop it?" he growls.

"Mmm," I groan as I rub my groin into him. "I need it hard, baby, give it to me as hard as you can," I whisper as I run my tongue through his open mouth.

"I need to fuck until we are both raw."

My eyes close. "I'm aching for you to fill me," I purr as I feel a distinct throb between my legs.

"That's it, we are leaving." He turns and pulls me off the dance floor by the hand and back over to the others. He signals to the bodyguards to get the cars; I stand still on the spot as I try to catch my breath. Cameron hands us both drinks and Joshua regrettably takes his and I smile. "Thank you," I mouth. Everybody is talking around us but Joshua and I stand staring at each other, off in our own little world. My eyes drop down the beautiful man in front of me. White tight tank stretched over his rippled torso, green camouflage army pants that are bulging at the groin, green cap, dog chains and big black boots, dark sensual eyes. One could not even imagine having this as a sight to look at, dream about...let alone love. I've died and gone to heaven.

"Will you just go?" Abbie snaps into my ear. I frown at her in question.

"If I have to watch Joshua give you that come fuck me look one more time, I'm going to cry tears of blood. I can't handle it, he's too fucking hot! Tie him up."

I giggle. "I know," I whisper as I bite my lip.

He stands still with his legs wide, watching me as he drinks his beer. This is arousal, deep-seated...dangerously high arousal. He isn't even talking to the boys and I know exactly how he feels. We are on a one-way track to orgasm, and nothing else matters. Everything else outside the two of us is trivial. He gets the signal from Ben and grabs my hand and kisses the back of it. "We are leaving," he says to Cameron and the others.

I smirk at Abbie and wink as she mouths the word "Bitch." I wave at the group as Joshua drags me out of the hall.

Joshua ushers me into the limo and immediately pushes the security screen up. He climbs in behind me and sits patiently as he waits for the screen to go up. I sit like a child waiting for my next instruction as I try to catch my breath. The screen goes up, he pulls me over and straddles my legs around him as he hitches up my dress. His hard erection digs into my softest part that is now dripping wet.

He groans as he runs his hands through my hair. "I want you. I have never wanted anything so much." His tongue ploughs through my mouth as he grinds his hips into me and rocks me onto him. One hand is on my breast kneading it and the other is guiding my hip to rub me over his erection...back and forth...back and forth.

"Baby," I sigh, "I'm going to come." I whisper into his mouth as I quiver, trying to hold it.

"Come, you're going to need all the lube you can get tonight, precious." For ten minutes he grinds me hard onto him. I am in a squatting position and my feet are on the seat, and my underpants are dripping wet. Back and forth...back and forth...back and forth...until I can hold it no longer and the dam breaks and I burst into orgasm. I cry out and he kisses me as I pant into his mouth. What must we look like? He in full army kit and me dressed like a nurse from a brothel dry humping each other in a car like a pair of horny teenagers.

We continue kissing and I can feel his arousal amping up by the minute as he is getting rougher and rougher with me. "I need that beautiful tight cunt around my cock now," he growls, his breathing labored as he grinds my body over his. The car stops and he puts his head back against the head rest to calm himself as he pants while watching me. Boy, if the look he is giving me has anything to do with it, I really am going to cop it. I think I might need that cage now after all. He waits for a minute and then opens the door slowly and we gingerly climb out. The bodyguards all look away and I wonder what they must think of our behavior on the dance floor tonight. How do I keep forgetting they are watching everything we do? Joshua takes my hand, and we walk up to my apartment in silence. We get to my apartment and the guards do their mandatory security check. Joshua smiles lovingly at me and kisses the back of my hand and I melt. He's perfect...absolutely perfect.

"It's clear. We will be outside sir."

Joshua's eyes flick to me. "Downstairs will be fine thanks. I will call you if I need you."

They nod and head down in the lift.

I smirk at him. "Why do they have to wait downstairs?"

He raises an eyebrow as he leads me into my apartment. "I don't want my staff listening to my girl scream all night, that's why." He throws me onto the lounge, sits next to me and immediately unzips his pants. Jeez, let's get straight to it then...what the hell. He grabs his wallet and pulls out a condom and opens it and rolls it on.

I frown. "What are you doing?" I ask.

"Getting ready to fuck my girl," he whispers darkly as he rolls it down his length.

"Why are you putting a condom on?"

He smirks sexily as he strokes himself. "Because I have plans for you in a minute and I am not eating my semen."

My eyes widen. "Oh," I whisper.

"Yes, oh," he smiles. He lifts me and pulls me over his lap to straddle him and starts to rub me over him again as he kisses me deeply. His pants are open, and he is free.

"I haven't had sex with a condom since I was seventeen," I say quietly.

He pulls back and he looks at me tenderly.

I give him a bashful smile. I'm embarrassed I just said that out loud. I just cemented how inexperienced I am. He kisses me again more urgently and rips my underpants off and throws them on the floor and then he lifts me over him.

"Josh...I can't take you like this straight up. You know that," I whisper as I start to panic.

"Shut up and fuck me," he snaps, and he slams me down onto him with his hands on my shoulders. I cry out from the shock of the overwhelming fullness and my head throws back. Shit...okay, I am...He lifts me and slams me back down and my legs open further as I feel myself moisten and open for him as he slides in as far as he can go.

My eyes widen and his eyes darken. "That's it, baby, take me...feels good doesn't it?" he grinds out, his mouth is open and slack as his eyes drop to my lips.

He grabs my waist and waits for me to adjust to the overwhelming sensation as he pants, trying to control himself from moving. My heart is racing out of control. This is what I need, for him to take me uninhibited without concern for being gentle, being quiet or being committed. I kiss him roughly and mouth the words, "Fuck me." His eyes roll back in his head and he really starts to move me as his hands grab my shoulders for leverage from behind. He's so hard, so deep...and so damn hot. He's completely taking me over and there is not a damn thing I can do about it. I close my eyes as I try to deal with the intense punishing rhythm.

"Your beautiful cunt is so tight around my cock. Can you feel it?" he growls as his hips work at a piston pace.

"You feel so good. Fill me, harder, faster," I cry.

He seems to lose control as he stands suddenly, lifts me and pushes me against the wall. His hips are now pumping into me at such a fast pace all I can do is hang on. Oh God, my head is against the wall and he is taking me hard, ripping into me as his body starts to drip with sweat. He drops his head to my shoulder and groans from his stomach as he jerks in orgasm while he breathes heavily into my neck. We stay still, lost in the moment. The connection between us is so intense I can hardly breathe. I tenderly pull his face back to mine and kiss him gently as once again the emotion I feel for this man nearly brings me to tears.

"I love you," I whisper through glassy eyes.

His haunted eyes meet mine and I frown. What was that look?

Why did he look at me like that?

"Baby, what's wrong?" I whisper as I gasp for breath.

He shakes his head and drops it to my shoulder again as he

appears to try and compose himself. What the hell is going on here?

"Nothing's wrong, Presh, that's what's wrong," he says sadly.

I frown as I try to understand the meaning of that statement.

He gently pulls out of me, eases my feet to the ground and he kisses me again.

Trying to erase the last twenty seconds, I smile. "Shower?" He smiles broadly. "Are you feeling dirty, my beautiful slut?" I smile shyly.

"As a matter of fact, Mr. Stanton, I am."

I SLOWLY WAKE to the sound of heavy breathing. Joshua is out cold next to me. Having sex for hours will do that to a man. He must be exhausted. I know I am. I sleepily trudge to the bathroom and return to the bed and lie down. Joshua throws his arm over my stomach and he leans over and kisses me while his eyes stay closed.

"Morning, beautiful," he sighs sleepily.

I lean in and kiss his cheek. "Morning," I smile.

He rolls to his side and winces, still with his eyes closed. "Shit... you must be sore."

I giggle. "Yes, some sex fiend took his liberties from my body all night."

With his eyes still closed, he smiles, grabs my behind and pulls me into him. "Yeah, well, you did put out the invitation to the party with that outfit."

I giggle again and he kisses the top of my head. "What time is it?" he asks.

I shrug. "About nine I think."

"Hmm," he groans. "I have to get up."

"Why?" I frown. "It's Saturday. Can't we stay in bed all day?"

He opens his eyes for the first time and smiles. "I wish. I have to train."

I really am over this work out shit. "You don't have to train. I am making you breakfast, then I'm taking a shower with you and then when I want to go back to bed for a nap you can go to the gym." I smile sweetly.

He smirks. "Not happening, I'm going in twenty minutes." He hops up slowly and walks to the shower.

I lie on my back. "Take note, I just put out an invitation and I got a decline," I yell.

He calls back from the bathroom. "Not a decline, just a rain check." I roll my eyes, same shit.

I make my way to the kitchen and start to make my coffee. I need to ask him about that comment last night. It's weighing heavily on my mind. Joshua walks through my apartment with a towel around his waist and opens up the front door. A bag is sitting outside waiting for him. Who put it there and why do I keep forgetting about those bloody bodyguards lurking around my apartment?

He scoops it up and saunters back to my room as he smirks at me. Hmm what did he say again? I narrow my eyes as I try to think of the exact wording, *nothing is wrong that's what's wrong.* What in the hell does that mean? Does he want something to be wrong between us, haven't we had enough wrong? I'm ready for right. I make him a protein shake, put some toast in the toaster and pour our coffee while deep in thought. How am I going to handle this? I can demand an explanation, or I can try and work it out in time. Maybe he didn't mean it. Five minutes later he walks out in a pale blue tank and black sports shorts and sneakers. I hand him his shake.

He raises his eyebrows and smiles broadly. "Good service." He gives me a wink as he takes a sip.

I turn and start to butter the toast and he sits on the stool at the counter.

"What did you mean by that comment last night, Josh?" I ask as I turn. Oh great, just blurt it out why don't you, so much for not saying anything. Idiot.

"What comment?"

"Nothing is wrong, that's what is wrong," I ask as I raise an eyebrow.

"Tash, don't, I'm not in the mood for this shit today." He shakes his head in frustration.

I frown. "What does that mean?"

"It means I don't want to talk about it, it was nothing."

I give him a small smile as unease starts to fill me. He's giving me mixed signals again.

We sit in silence for a while. "What are you doing today?" he asks.

I shrug. "Nothing really, grocery shopping and laundry. I am going to the hospital this afternoon."

He nods as he drinks his shake.

"Do you want me to invite Cam and Adrian over with the girls for dinner? I can cook,"

I ask as I give him a hopeful smile.

He shakes his head. "No," he replies flatly. "Oh." My face drops.

He smirks sexily at me. "I want you," he tucks my hair behind my ear, "to cook me dinner and then put that edible white nightdress on and spoon on the lounge with me while we watch the game in peace. I want you to myself."

I smile broadly as relief fills me. "You do?"

He stands and kisses me gently as he brushes his fingers

down my face. "I do. I will meet you at the hospital about four then?" he asks softly.

"Ok, sounds good." I give him a weak smile but as he disappears, I stare at the closed door he has just exited through.

What's going on with me? Why do I once again feel insecure?


I sit in the car in the hospital parking lot waiting for Bridget to arrive. I didn't want to risk being alone with Margaret. I'm such a wimp. I know I have to tell him...but when is the right time? I don't even know what's going on between us, without adding paternity into the mix. Joshua's car procession comes around the corner and I smile. I watch in slow motion as he gets out of the car and walks around and leans on the hood as he speaks. His body language is tense, who is he talking to? He seems stressed as he hangs up. He then immediately dials a number as he stands legs wide and one hand on his hip. My eyes flick to the security behind me and I see one of them answer the phone. Joshua has just rung them, he is keeping tabs on me. He does know I went to lunch with Jesten...shit, shit, shit. His eyes scan the car park until they find my car and he smiles and makes his way to my car as I slowly get out of it. "Miss Marx." He smiles as he kisses me gently on the cheek.

I smile nervously as my eyes flick to the ten men surrounding us. "Hi," I answer quietly.

"What are you doing out here?" he asks as we turn and start walking into the hospital, the guards dropping behind us as he takes my hand in his.

"I was waiting for Bridget," I answer.

Cameron has been waiting there. "Hey Tash," he smiles. "Hi Cam."

We walk silently into the hospital, hand in hand, and then into the lift where the security drop behind.

"You guys are coming out tonight, yeah?" Cameron asks. "No," Joshua answers flatly.

"We're staying at home." He picks my hand up that he is holding and kisses the back of it again and I find myself melting at his feet. Maybe I am just imagining the mixed signals thing?

Cameron screws up his face. "Oh God, how boring staying home on a Saturday night."

"I suppose it depends on who you are staying home with. Staying home with Natasha is anything but boring." Joshua smirks and I smile like a little kid, this man really is divine.

"I'm going out with Abbie and Didge then," Cameron says flatly.

"I think Didge has a date," I answer.

Cameron raises both of his eyebrows at Joshua as he smirks. "Looks like it's just me and Abbie then."

Joshua shakes his head. "No," he says flatly. I giggle.

Cameron screws up his face. "What do you mean no?" he asks affronted as he puts his hands on his hips.

"I've told you not to touch her," Joshua snaps as the lift door opens and he pulls me through the door by the hand.

"I will do what I want," Cameron smirks. "To who I want. And she will fucking love it just quietly."

I smile and Joshua rolls his eyes as he drops my hand like a hot potato. Huh? I look up to see why he has just dropped my hand and I see his mother standing at the end of the hall looking down at us as we approach. He obviously still hasn't bloody told her about us.

I walk to the lounge area and take a seat opposite Joshua and Bridget comes up in a rush.

"Oh, guys, they just put a sign up in reception. There has

been a car accident and they need someone with blood type AB, at the children's ward immediately. Does anyone know of anyone with that blood type? Apparently, it's rare."

My eyes snap up to Joshua and I stare at him, shit. My eyes nervously glance over to Cameron. He narrows his eyes in return as he folds his arms and leans back onto the wall. Holy fuck, that's Joshua's blood type...should I say something? No, let Cameron say something. For ten minutes I sit silently next to Joshua, praying for him to remember his blood type. How can someone so smart not even remember his blood type? What am I going to do? If I don't tell him a child could die and I already know that less than two per cent of the population have this type of blood, the chances of finding some immediately are slim to none. Why isn't Cameron saying something? Maybe he doesn't know? No, he knows alright. Shit.

I sit and listen to Bridget and Joshua talking about some hotel in France that they have both gone to, but my mind is in overdrive.

Time is ticking and I am starting to sweat. I start to fidget in my chair and try to work out what to do. My eyes flick to Cameron who is sitting as calm as anything, watching me. What's he watching?

I have no choice. I have to say something. "Joshua, I think that is your blood type, baby," I whisper to him.

He frowns at me. "What?" he asks.

I swallow the nervous lump in my throat. "The child that needs blood has the same rare blood as you."

Joshua frowns and looks at Cameron who is staring at me blank faced...oh crap.

"She's right, it is your blood type. We had better go to the children's ward."

Joshua shrugs and stands immediately, and Cameron

stands. "I'll come with you." His eyes flick to me. "Natasha, come with us."

Oh shit, no way am I going. "No, I will wait for you here."

Cameron narrows his eyes at me. "I insist." He fakes a smile at me and holds out his hand. I swallow again and look at his outstretched hand. Now I've done it. I stand and follow the two boys down the corridor in silence. We get to the children's ward. "Hello, I'm a doctor, and my brother here has blood type AB,

I understand you need a donation."

The nurse puts her hand on her chest in relief. "Oh, thank God, yes please come this way." She ushers Joshua away down the hall.

Cameron turns to me. "What do you know, Natasha, and I want the fucking truth."

# CHAPTER 23

**Natasha**

Cameron's fierce eyes meet mine. "Well?"

I swallow uncomfortably, *holy mother of God*.

"What do you mean, Cameron?" I ask as I step back from him defensively.

"I mean...how do you know Joshua's blood type?" he snaps.

I frown at him. "I looked on his chart in the hospital. How did you think I knew? What's this about?"

He narrows his eyes at me and steps back as he seems to regain his composure. "Nothing... I'm just having a weird day." He runs his hands through his hair in frustration as he shakes his head.

"Cameron, if something is wrong involving Joshua I would like to know about it," I question.

He studies my face as he assesses me. "Like I said, nothing is wrong. I'm going back to the room to see Gran. I will see you up there." With that he leaves the room in a rush.

Hmm, ok, I rub my eyes in frustration. Shit, that was close.

I'm starting to perspire from nerves. Cameron is onto something and I need to find out just exactly what that is and what the hell I am going to do about it.

## Joshua

I sit in the hospital room as the nurses prepare to take the blood, my mind in a rush. Max just called me to let me know that Coby Allender has been googling Natasha from his computer in jail...what does that mean? Who is this nut job and what does he want? His trial is on Wednesday and the word is that the police don't have enough evidence to prove he committed the murders, but they know he did it. More than likely, he will get an innocent verdict in court. Is Natasha in danger if he gets out? Max seems to think that she is. My stomach churns. This is another total mess that I don't have time for.

Natasha walks into the consultation room and smiles at me warmly. That's all it takes to make me weak...and calm. Her beautiful smile complete with those dimples.

"Are you ok?" she whispers as she gently kisses my cheek and runs her hand over my hair.

"I am now," I smile. Why does she make me so needy? I take her hand in mine.

"How did you know I had this type of blood?" I ask.

"I saw it on your chart in the hospital in LA." She kisses me again.

I nod and she sits quietly in the chair in the corner of the room. "Is the child going to be ok?" she asks.

I nod. "I think so, they take the blood and screen it and then give it to him."

The nurse walks back in the room and starts to prepare to take the blood and we both sit silently watching her. My eyes linger on my beautiful girl who is deep in concentration watching the nurse. She pulls her glasses from her bag so she can see what is going on and I smile at her.

"What?" she mouths as she smirks.

I shake my head. I've never known a woman who is so damn sexy in glasses. Her intelligence is a huge trigger to my libido.

Ten minutes later we have finished and are walking back to the room, and we stop off to get a coffee from the cafeteria. The fawning of the girls behind the counter is actually getting embarrassing. It's ok when Cam is here because he loves to flirt but I just find it downright embarrassing when he's not there.

"Hello, Joshua," one of the girls coos.

I smile and nod as I dip my head. "Hello," I reply. They all giggle.

Natasha looks at me deadpan. "How does she know your name?" She raises an eyebrow as she folds her arms in front of her.

I smirk. "Because she puts it on my coffee every day," I answer. Natasha screws up her face at me. "I bet she does." She puts a finger in her mouth to symbolize she's going to be sick and I give her a wink. I love it when she gets jealous.

"Must be that penis in my pants," I smirk as I raise my eyebrow in jest.

"Hmm, you mean the one I am just about to cut off as an optional extra," she whispers as she looks around in annoyance.

"Or suck," I whisper back as I lean in and kiss her cheek. "No. Not happening, no sucking tonight, Stanton," she smirks as she takes a seat.

"We'll see," I smile.

We wait for our coffee in silence, her phone is on the table and beeps a message at the same time she goes to get the coffees from the counter. I read it, it's from someone called Jes.

I'm at the gym and haven't seen you for forever.
I'm coming over to yours tonight.

She comes back and sits down with our coffees. "Jes messaged you and she's coming over tonight," I remark as I take my coffee from her hand.

"Huh?" She frowns as she looks at her phone.

"Your friend Jes texted."

She snatches the phone from the table as she sits and reads the message. "Huh, so she is, fancy that." She takes a large gulp of her coffee and then spits it onto the table.

"Fucking fish face makes the coffee too fucking hot," she snaps as she grabs a napkin and wipes her mouth.

I laugh out loud. "Fish face, who is fish face?"

"The idiot behind the counter who looks like a fish," she stammers with the napkin over her face as she looks around in embarrassment.

I can't help it, I laugh out loud again.

"My tongue has third degree burns from that bitch," she stammers. "Surely you don't have to ask for coffee to be at a drinkable temperature, now do you?"

I shrug. "Mine's fine."

"Yes, well you're good looking with a penis. We already know that," she mutters as she wipes the table.

"What time is your friend coming over?" I ask. "Do I know her?"

Her eyes meet mine. "No, not really. I'm going to text her and tell her not to come. I want you to myself."

She starts to text and I feel a contentment sweep over me as I lean back in my chair and drink my coffee. Bridget walks in and over to us.

"Don't get the coffee unless you want a tongue transplant," Natasha snaps as she keeps texting.

Bridget laughs. "Mmm, fish face to the rescue again hey."

I raise my eyebrows as I smirk again. "You call her fish face as well?" I ask.

"With those silicone lips that title is well deserved," Bridget mutters as she searches for her wallet in her handbag.

"Who are you texting?" Bridget asks Natasha.

"Umm, you know Jes, my girlfriend from work." Bridget frowns.

"No."

"Don't worry then," Natasha snaps as she puts her phone onto the table. She glares at Bridget.

"For God's sake, go and tell her the coffee is too hot if it's that much of an issue," Bridget sighs.

My phone rings. It's Murph and I answer. "Hello."

"We got a problem."

I frown. "We do?" I ask as I sit in my chair.

"Hooker says she is sending the email tonight to Natasha if you don't ring her immediately."

My eyes flick to the girls who are deep in discussion and I stand and walk over to the window.

"What do you mean?" I answer angrily. "I don't want to

speak to her." I look back towards the girls to ensure they can't hear what is being said.

"Yes, I know," he answers quietly.

"I thought you said you were handling this," I whisper angrily as my blood pressure rises.

"Look, I think we should go to the police," he says flatly.

I frown and look out the window and into the parking lot below. "It will be too late then. I'm warning you, Adrian, if Natasha sees this tape someone is going to die," I whisper angrily as I look around again.

He stays silent as he thinks.

"Well, what do you want to do then?" he asks.

I try to think of a solution. "Hack Natasha's email and crash the system to give me time to think."

"I don't know how to do that."

"Get someone else to fucking do it then," I snap as my angry eyes glare at Ben who is standing at the back of the cafeteria. He frowns in question.

"I think the less people who know about this the better. You had better come back here and do it yourself," Adrian asserts.

I roll my eyes in frustration. "Fine. See you soon." I hang up angrily and turn to see Tash and Didge still deep in discussion. What in the hell am I going to say about where I am going? I have just told her I want to stay home alone with her tonight.

Ben walks over to me. "Is everything ok?" he asks.

I glare at him. "No, everything is not ok," I whisper. "Because of your staff's incompetence the hooker is sending the email to Natasha tonight." I rub my forehead in frustration.

His eyes widen.

"Ben, I will say this once, if Natasha sees the tape someone's head is going to roll."

He shakes his head in frustration. "Josh, I don't know what to say. I don't know how this has happened."

"Do I need to remind you?" I snap angrily and walk back to the girls. I take a seat back at the table and my eyes linger on Natasha's beautiful face with my heart pounding in my chest. Maybe I should just tell her.

Natasha smiles and takes my hand over the table and I feel myself melt a little.

"How's your tongue?" I smirk.

"Burnt to oblivion," she replies flatly.

I smile. I can't tell her. Who am I kidding? I need to find out her email addresses so I can hack the systems. How in the hell am I going to do that? This is abysmal.

I need to speak to Cameron. He'll think of something, he always does. "I'm going to go back upstairs. I will meet you up there," I say as I squeeze Natasha's hand across the table, and she smiles.

"Okay, see you up there," she replies.

I stand and leave the cafeteria. I need to find Cameron... and fast.


Natasha

I watch Joshua leave the cafeteria followed by his security team. "Oh my God, Bridget, this is a disaster," I stammer as I grab her arm over the table.

She frowns. "What is?"

"Jesten, that's who. He texted me, and Josh read the text and now I have lied to Joshua and he thinks Jes is a girl."

She rolls her eyes as she drinks her coffee. "Just tell Jes you are back with Josh, easy."

"I'm going to eventually, but they are fighting each other next week in the stupid cage fighting shit and Jesten will bait Joshua even more if he knows that we are back together and we both know Joshua will kill Jesten even harder if he knows we are friends now," I stammer, exasperated. She screws up her face in disgust.

"I'm too tired for this shit and you can't kill someone harder. If they are dead, they are dead."

I put my head into my hands on the table. "Why hasn't he texted back? What if he just turns up at my house?" I whisper, mortified.

She smiles broadly at me. "That would actually be funny though, wouldn't it?"

I glare at her. "No, not at all."

"Imagine if Joshua answers the door, like in a towel and it's Jesten, what do you think would happen?" She smiles.

I put my hand over my mouth as the horrific scene unfolds in my head.

I take my phone back out of my bag and text Jesten again.

**Matter of urgency.**
**I'm at work all weekend.**
**I will call you on Monday.**

My heart rate has picked up and I am starting to sweat. "Why isn't he texting me back, so I know he got the message, the idiot," I snap

"Because he thinks you are at work. Chill out, for Pete's sake." Bridget rolls her eyes at me. "I think Abbie is breaking up with Tristan tonight."

My face falls. "Why? They have been getting on so well."

Bridget shrugs. "She thinks she isn't ready to settle down and Tristan is the kind of guy you marry and have kids with."

"Shit," I whisper. "That's shitty, poor Tristan."

"She's an idiot, someone else will snap him up and she'll lose him." She sighs.

I shrug. "Who knows, I think if you are meant to be you will always find a way back to each other." I smile.

Bridget narrows her eyes at me. "That's romantic bullshit and you know it."

"Josh and I have always found our way back to each other." I shrug.

"Hey, on that note has he told you he loves you yet?" Bridget questions with a raised brow.

I sip my coffee. "No, it's a noticeably absent comment in our conversations."

She nods as she sips her coffee. "But you've told him."

"Yes, every day," I mutter.

"Hmm," she says flatly.

"Look it's only been a week and I am not pushing for the sentence because I already know he has feelings for me. I can feel it."

"I hope you're not being deluded and he's using you for sex," she sighs.

I drink the last of my coffee. That thought has crossed my mind more than once. "Me too."

We make our way back upstairs and see Joshua and Cameron sitting in the lounge area, both scrolling through their phones. Josh's eyes flick up and he pats the chair next to him. I smile and take it. I watch Cameron to try and see if there is any indication that he knows about Joshua's paternity. What am I going to do about this? That was close downstairs. If Cameron is onto this and I think he is then it will only be a matter of time before Joshua finds out. My stomach drops at the thought that his mother may very well implicate me in this mess.

"Tash, I have a friend who is after an internship at your hospital. She wants to know if you would pass on her resume. Can I email it to you?" Cameron asks.

Huh, umm. "Yes of course," I mutter, distracted.

"What's your email address for work?" he asks. Joshua doesn't look up and keeps scrolling through his phone.

I shuffle through my bag and dig out my purse to retrieve a business card. "I don't even know it, it's on here." I pass Cameron the card and he takes it and puts it in his wallet.

"Thanks." He smiles. "Josh, what time are we training at the gym?" he asks.

"Straight after here," Joshua answers.

I frown. "I thought you trained this morning?"

He smiles and puts his hand affectionately on my leg. "I did, Presh, but I am doing a bit tonight with Cam and Murph. I won't be long."

I roll my eyes. "Aren't you over the gym? Doesn't it get boring?"

He smiles warmly at me. "I won't be long." He stands. "I will see you soon." He bends and gently kisses my cheek.

"Okay," I sigh. This may be good anyway because I can try to sort out frigging Jesten. Bridget smirks at me and I narrow my eyes at her. "What?" I mouth.

"You and your flaming vagina." She giggles.

"Come on, as soon as we see Gran you are going to help me find Jesten."

She screws up her face at me. "No, I'm not."

I nod. "Oh yes, you bloody are."

· · ·

It's eight o'clock on a Saturday night and my boyfriend is supposedly at the gym when I know he was there for three hours this morning. Where is he and what is he doing? He said he was going to be quick and I thought he would be here about six. I sit with my coffee on my lap on the lounge. Is Cameron currently telling him about his suspicion regarding Joshua's paternity...what does Cameron know? My eyes close at the thought of the horrible conversation that one day my beautiful Lamborghini is going to have. It will come out eventually, the truth always has a way of coming out. Bridget and I didn't find Jes tonight but it looks like Joshua isn't going to be here anyway so I don't know why I was so worried.

My phone beeps with a text. Lambo.

**Hi Tash,**
**I have been caught up helping Adrian with some computer stuff.**
**Go out with Cameron and Abbie if you want.**
**I'm sorry**

I frown in frustration. What, so he's not coming over now? I pick up my phone and immediately dial his number. He answers first ring. "Hi sweetheart," he says softly. My stomach drops. He only calls me sweetheart when something is wrong, past experience has shown me that.

"Hi, what's going on?" I ask.

He stays silent. 'I'm just doing some computer stuff with Adrian. I said I would do it for him, it's been a lot harder than we thought and we can't get it right. I'm sorry."

I bite my lip as I listen. "So, you don't want to see me tonight?"

"No, I never said that. I want to see you tonight. This is pissing me off actually. But I may be another hour or so and I thought you may want to go out rather than wait for me."

I sit back in the chair in frustration. "No, I don't want to go out, I want to see you." I sigh, disappointed.

"How much?" He smiles down the phone.

I smile in return. "I really, really want to see you and I am not going out so just come over when you have finished."

"Ok, baby, I will be as quick as I can." His spirits seem to have lifted.

"I love you," I whisper.

He hesitates. "Bye, Presh." He hangs up the phone.


I'M SHOWERED and in the requested white nightie on my lounge under a blanket at 10.15 pm when I hear the key in the door. I pretend to be asleep and I hear Joshua put his keys on the side table. He walks over and kneels in front of me. He kisses my cheek tenderly.

"Hello, my beautiful girl," he whispers.

I open my eyes and smile shyly at him. I can't even pretend to be mad when he greets me like that.

"Are you ok?" I whisper.

He gives me a sad smile. "I am now that I have come home to you." He brushes the hair back from my forehead.

I take his hand and kiss the back of it. "Your body is here, Joshua...but has your heart come home to me?" My eyes frost over with tears.

He kisses me softly on the lips. "My heart has never left you, it's been with you for more than eight years, Presh. I'm a shell when I'm not with you."

My eyes hold his as he rubs the backs of his fingers down

my face. My beautiful gentle Josh is here. I kiss him tenderly. He doesn't let his guard down with me very often and I have to take advantage.

"Where were you tonight, baby?" I ask.

He frowns. "I told you, sweetheart, doing computer stuff with Adrian. I'm sorry I took so long. Right now, I don't want to talk about anything or anyone, I want to spend the night with my girl and not have to think."

I frown as I play with my blanket. "Did you fix the problem?"

"I think so," he replies quietly.

He kneels up and rests his head on my stomach and I run my hand over the top of his head, and he blows out a deep breath.

"Right now, I need to go to my place of clarity and then I need to go to my place of Zen," he whispers into my stomach.

"What's your place of clarity?" I ask softly.

He kisses me gently again. "My place of clarity is when nothing else matters but me and you and the tenderness we have with each other."

"When do you get the clarity, Joshua?" I love him in this mood because he tells me the truth without thinking. The glass force field he puts around himself is temporarily disabled.

"The only time I have clarity is when I'm tasting you, with my head between your legs and your hands on my head, your hand in my hand. The way you taste, your scent, your love...is the only time I forget all the shit in my life."

I frown. "Joshua, that's oral sex."

He pulls back and smiles softly. "I haven't told you this before, Tash, but I don't do that to other women."

"What do you mean?" I ask softly.

He shrugs, embarrassed. "When we first broke up when we

were young I did it a few times and I didn't like it. It was too intimate, too...different to what we had. So, I stopped doing it altogether." He takes my hand in his and gently kisses the inside of my wrist. I melt into his eyes, to his touch.

"But you love to do that, Joshua, it's who you are. I don't understand."

He shakes his head and smiles. "No, Tash, that's not who I am. It's who we are, when you are with me like that, I know I am getting you ready so that I don't hurt you. I'm preparing your body to take mine. It's like..." he pauses as he thinks of the wording. "It's like you are a part of me, like your body is an extension of mine. Like I can't live without your taste in my mouth, I can't get close enough to you...and then when you climax." He lets out a contented sigh.

He kisses me gently and runs his tongue through my open mouth. God, I love this Joshua, why can't this part of his personality be here all the time. My arousal starts to pump heavily between my legs.

"That's how I feel about sex, Josh, making love is something just so beautiful between us that the thought of having mere sex with someone else repulses me. I would rather go without the meaningless act," I whisper.

He kisses me again and it is the most beautiful passionate kiss that he has ever gifted me with. The emotion behind it brings tears to my eyes.

"I love you," I whisper.

He smiles shyly and scoops me off the lounge and carries me to bed. "Give me some clarity, my precious girl."

I giggle in anticipation. He gently lays me on the bed and stands and slowly removes his clothing while not breaking eye contact. His large physical strength is palpable. Natasha, the name is etched down his side, how can one man hold so much power over my body? My legs drop open to the mattress. I couldn't close them if I tried. His eyes drop to my open sex and he licks his lips and cracks his neck. My nipples harden under his gaze and he reaches out and runs his hand down the length of my body.

"I fucking adore you," he whispers.

I smile as I pull him down to me. "I need some of that clarity, baby," I whisper. He smiles deviously as he disappears down my body. He spreads me wide to his gaze with his thumbs and I hold my breath. I always hold my breath as he looks at me but now that I know that he doesn't do this to anybody else it has just amplified the whole beautiful experience.

"You're so fucking perfect," he whispers. His hot tongue slices through my weeping flesh and I whimper as my body bows off the bed.

He stills me. "Sshh baby, let me enjoy you," he whispers.

I nod as I close my eyes and try to stop myself from bursting into orgasm, as I start to quiver with need.

His tongue starts to lick me in deep long strokes and my hands fall to the back of his head. This is what I love...where everything makes sense, where nothing makes sense and he's right...perfect clarity.

I start to pant as his mouth takes what it needs from my open body and I convulse into an orgasm. He closes his eyes and groans into me, and I grab the back of his head in reaction.

"Stop," I stammer, "stop it." I'm too sensitive.

"Never," he growls into me, "I will never stop." He seemingly loses control and picks up my legs and puts them over his shoulders as he really lets his tongue loose. I'm going insane and he gently bites my clitoris and stretches me out to his mouth. Dear God...he's so damn good at this. My body starts to move by itself and I have lost the art of being submissive. I want this, I want his tongue on me...inside of me. I am moving up and down the mattress as he inserts two fingers and I lurch forward as I climax again. He keeps my legs over his shoulders and leans forward and plunges his large length into me deeply. He stays deep and still, his eyes close as he tries to calm himself and when they reopen, I shudder in anticipation, beautiful gentle Joshua has gone and Mr. Stanton is on top of me. His mouth hangs slack and his eyes are dark with arousal as he holds himself off my body with straightened arms, his open mouth starts to run the length of my neck and he starts to ride me...hard. Long punishing strokes where I know he will take me how he wants, as deep as he wants to, and I can do nothing but hold on and pant.

Joshua Stanton was born to fuck, not to make gentle love, although he does that perfectly, he was designed to take a woman and rip the orgasm from her body and damn the consequences or anyone who tries to stop him. It's when he's like this, when he has no control and he can't stop, that he's at his unstoppable best.

Tonight, I am the luckiest girl in the world.

# CHAPTER 24

**Natasha**

I sit and stare at the computer monitor in horror. What in the hell is wrong with my emails? Where have they all gone? It's Monday 11.00 am, and I am at work. Joshua and I didn't spend the day together yesterday, but he ended up coming over last night. I didn't ask him where he was on Saturday night, although the question is weighing heavily on my mind. All of these questions between us and yet I feel that he is cemented to me and that he's in love with me...without actually saying the words. He didn't let me go all night and when he thought I was asleep I could feel him gently kissing my shoulder from behind in the darkness. He now sleeps all night with a hand somewhere on me, as if he is only reassured when we are touching. What's going through that pea brain of his? At the moment though I have more pressing issues, I'm trying to pull a client file from my emails that was sent to me last week. Where the frigging hell is it?

All of my emails seem to have disappeared and my send and receive isn't working.

Emma, my colleague, walks into my office. "Natasha, I have just forwarded you an email that came to my inbox by mistake." I frown as I flag a problem with our computer tech team.

"Thanks, what is it?" I ask.

"Not sure, an email addressed to me but the subject line says please forward to Natasha Marx."

My eyes look up from my computer. That's odd. "What does it say?" I ask.

She shrugs. "I don't know. Check it out. It should be in your inbox."

I roll my eyes. "My computer is totally shit and I can't access anything. Can I open it on yours?"

"Yeah, sure." I move back from my desk and she leans over me and opens her email on my computer. "I have to go. I have an appointment. Do you want to have lunch?"

"Yeah, ok, if I can find this file I will. Otherwise, I'm in big trouble," I mutter as I open the email addressed to me. Emma leaves the room.

I frown as I look at the email. Is it from Josh? No, the sender says blocked...weird? I click on the attachment. It's a rolling picture and then it goes black. Huh? I sit forward and play it again...it doesn't make sense. I play it again...I can't make out anything. Josh must have sent me something. I smile and dial his number.

"Hi Presh," he answers.

I smile. "Hi baby, can you send the email again? I can't make out the picture."

He stays silent.

"Did you hear me? I can't open the attachment." I sigh as I doodle on my notepad.

"Ahh...Yeah, okay. What email did I send it to?" he replies.

I frown. "It went to my work friend's email by mistake and she gave it to me."

He stays silent.

"So anyway, just resend it, okay." I repeat as I start ratting through my filing cabinet. "My email system has totally stuffed up and I'm in trouble if I can't access this next client file," I murmur.

He stays silent for a moment as he listens. "Do you want to have lunch today?" he sighs.

I smile. "Definitely, hey did you see if I left my phone at home this morning? I can't find it anywhere," I ask.

"No, I didn't notice," he replies. "What time is your break?"
"One thirty."

"I will call you when I get to the hospital," he says quietly.
"Okay, see you then."


## Adrian

Joshua and Ben walk in front of me as we search for a good coffee and two guards trail behind. It's 3.00 pm. Joshua is in a filthy mood. He went to the hospital to have lunch with Tash and he was going to tell her about the tape. This woman has other email addresses, and he knows it is only a matter of time before Natasha finds out, so he wanted to tell her first. Apparently her friend joined them for lunch though and they weren't alone so he couldn't do it. He's not happy. Joshua's phone rings.

"You found your phone, Presh," he smiles as he answers it.

He listens and then stops dead. I nearly run into the back of him. "Where's Natasha?" he snaps. I frown at Ben in question. Joshua holds his hand over the phone. "The hooker has

Natasha's phone. Get her guards on the line," he snaps to Ben. Ben shakes his head and immediately dials a number as Joshua continues to speak. He's furious. "It's ok. Max is looking at her right now. She's safe," Ben sighs as he holds the phone to his ear. Thank God.

"You have ten fucking minutes," Joshua snaps. He hangs up.

His eyes flick to us. "We are meeting her, and I am going to finish this once and for all. I've had about as much shit from this bitch as I am going to take."

We stand in the hall, waiting for the lift to take us to the fourth floor in the Novotel hotel. Joshua has his hands in his pockets and is looking at the floor. He's furious. I am nervous as hell. What if this woman has bouncers up there waiting for us?

"Just stay quiet, everybody," Ben says flatly. "Let me do the talking."

Joshua's angry eyes meet mine and he walks into the lift.

*Knock, knock.* Ben knocks on the door, and it opens in a rush.

The blonde opens the door and smiles sexily at us. Joshua glares at her.

"Come in." She gestures into the room.

We walk in and say nothing. There is no one else in the room and it is empty except for a bed.

"What do you want?" Joshua snaps.

My eyes flick to Ben. I knew he wouldn't keep quiet.

She fakes a laugh. "I don't want to be spoken to like that, Joshua, or is it baby?"

Joshua narrows his eyes at her.

She crosses her arms in front of her. "It's so pathetic how she looks at you like you're a god. I was watching her run her hand up your leg at lunch today. She thinks you are perfect; how very wrong she is."

He runs his tongue over his top front teeth in contempt.

"I didn't come her to listen to your dribble. What do you want?" he snaps.

Ben holds his hand up to Joshua to signify silence.

She frowns at Ben's hand. "This is between Joshua and me, goon, keep going and you can wait outside."

Ben puts his hands on his hips and smiles slyly at her as he shakes his head in a threatening way.

Her eyes flick back to Joshua. "I told you I want five million dollars, or I will give the tape to the boring wife."

Joshua turns his back on her, and I roll my eyes. "There is no way in hell you are getting five million dollars. You have got to be kidding. We are going to the police," I snap.

She smiles and looks at Joshua. "This isn't up to you, it's up to Joshua. He's the one that is going to break the stupid bitch's heart."

Joshua turns and grabs her by the throat and slams her head up against the wall.

"Joshua," I stammer. "Stop it."

He smacks the back of her head against the wall again as he squeezes her neck hard. Ben stops me from grabbing him...Jesus.

"You know what happens to dirty whores like you?" he sneers.

"They make a lot of money," she gasps through her stranglehold.

"You're going to end up in a body bag. I mean it, do not push me. You have no idea who you are dealing with. If you go near Natasha again, I will fucking kill you!" He slams her head again. "Do you fucking understand me?" he screams into her face I stand still and shocked, my eyes wide. I've never seen Joshua like this.

She breaks free from his grip and grabs her neck as she chokes. "Don't touch me," she stammers as she holds her throat.

He smiles at her like the devil himself.

Shit, this situation is totally out of control. "Joshua, calm down. Stop it," I yell.

"Start talking, stupid," he screams.

"Five million," she coughs.

He shakes his head. "One million today in cash and I want my men to go with you and take your computers and phone and all copies on the spot."

She frowns. "You can't take my computers and phone."

He raises an eyebrow. "I can take anything I fucking want."

"I want five."

He shakes his head. "This is my first and final offer. One million, take it or leave it."

She hesitates as she thinks, and we all stay silent. "I will show her," she stammers.

Joshua smirks. "And then I will kill you...the choice is yours." Her eyes flick to Ben who right at this moment I think might actually kill her...fuck this is crazy shit. They are even scaring me, and I know neither of them is capable of this violence. My heart starts to race as fear grips me.

"I want cash," she looks at Joshua nervously.

"I can have it in thirty minutes," Joshua sneers.

"What's it going to be?" Joshua yells.

She's scared it's obvious. I'm fucking scared and I am friends with these two.

"You go and get the money, Joshua, and Peter and I will escort little miss here to get the computers and extra copies," Ben says flatly.

Joshua's eyes meet mine. "Search her house," I snap at Ben.

He nods and grabs her by the arm and pulls her toward the door.

"One hour," she sneers. "One hour back here with my money." Joshua glares at her and I start to panic again. I think he's losing control.

## Natasha

Weeknights are meant to be relaxing and calm, but I have never been so anxious. I was a regular person. I had a normal life... that is until Joshua Stanton came back into it. Now it seems I jump from one nightmarish situation to the next. Totally unrelated stupid things that are making my head spin. I feel like I am in an out-of-control plane and I don't know if the landing is going to be ok or if I am going to crash and burn.

Cancer, serial killers, hit men, bodyguards, paternity...Jesten, Joshua's feeling about me. I just want some damn peace...with a boyfriend who I know loves me. Why can't I be in love with a normal man...a boring, weedy, slightly overweight man? My stomach clenches as nerves fill my system and I look at my watch for the fiftieth time tonight. Why haven't they contacted me yet?

It's Tuesday night and I'm waiting for the call from Bridget and Abbie to let me know that the fight between Jesten and Joshua is over...and that Jesten is still alive. Nine pm, it's got to be on soon. I got home from the hospital at seven and have been waiting ever since. I put my head into my hands as I sit on the toilet. This is a nightmare. How am I supposed to be calm when I know what is going on in the Luna Park Convention Centre just across town? My phone rings, it's Abbie.

"Hello," I answer. "Hi, it's Abbie."

"I know who it is, what's happening?" I snap.

"Right, so Joshua is fighting Jesten. I just saw it on the draw." "Shit." I was hoping that they wouldn't be put against each

other. "Are they fighting right now?" I ask.

"No, not yet, I will call you when it starts."

"Ok," I hang up.

I walk into the kitchen and pour myself a vodka with soda and go out onto my balcony and light a cigarette. Desperate times call for desperate measures. I need to calm my nerves. I'm a walking basket case.

I pace up and down my balcony for another forty minutes with my stomach in my throat. What if Joshua actually hurts Jesten? What if Jesten hurts Joshua? No, that won't happen, Joshua is too strong. Maybe I should have gone. Shit, this is total bullshit. I dial the number again.

"Hello," Abbie answers.

"What's happening?"

"I think they are next," she replies.

"Oh shit." My heart starts to thump.

"Hey, did you know that Bridget likes Ben?" she asks.

I frown. "Who told you that?"

"Cameron and Murph."

"Huh?"

"Apparently they call each other all the time."

I screw my face up as I hold my hand in the air. "What?"

"I know that's what I said and now she is sitting with him and they are giggling and flirting and shit."

I shake my head as I listen to this story. "Are you serious?" "Totally, oh here they come. I will call you back," she yells over the noisy crowd. Oh my God, oh my God. I pace through my apartment with my hands on my head.

Twenty minutes later my phone rings. I snatch it from the table. "Hello."

"Okay, so."

My eyes widen. "So what?"

"Um, so they really hate each other."

My horrified face drops. "What happened?"

"So, the fight was okay. Josh won."

"Yes," I answer nervously.

"But then it got out of hand again and they kept fighting after the bell."

I bring my hand to my face as my eyes widen. "Yes."

"And I think Joshua has done something to his arm and then he knocked Jesten out."

"What!" I shriek. "What do you mean?"

"Joshua hit Jesten so hard he fell to the ground and then he didn't get up."

My eyes widen in horror. "Is he dead?"

She laughs. "No, I don't think so. No, definitely not, he's alive."

"Where is Joshua?"

"He is in the dressing room and Cameron is with him." "Okay I'm going," I hang up and immediately dial

Cameron's phone."

"Hi Tash." He answers first ring.

"Is Joshua ok?"

"He's fine."

"Is the guy he fought alright?" I close my eyes as I wait for the answer.

"Yeah, I just went and checked on him, he just hit the ground hard and knocked himself out. He will be ok."

"Can I speak to Joshua?"

"He's in the shower. I will drop him at your house on our way home."

Hmm. "Okay, see you then." I hang up, dry-retch again and get into a scalding hot shower, the only place lately where I seem to be calm.

Two hours later, I am sitting on my lounge drinking tea while trying my hardest not to get fuming mad. Where are they? Have they gone out? The key turns in my door and Joshua walks in, his arm in a sling. Cameron is behind him.

I glare at him while biting my tongue. Don't say it, don't say it.

Don't fucking say it.

"You're an idiot," I blurt out. Shit, I said it.

"Hello," he says deadpan as he walks into the kitchen and throws his keys onto the kitchen counter.

Cameron silently shakes his head at me to signify silence. I roll my eyes. This is the testosterone bullshit again.

I stand in an outrage. "What have you done to your arm? You need to go to the hospital."

He opens a beer and takes a swing.

I roll my eyes. "Cameron, what is wrong with his arm?"

"He will be fine in the morning. I will leave you two love-birds to it." He raises his eyebrows at me and smiles cheekily in jest at me being stuck with him. He slaps Joshua on the back as he leaves the apartment.

"I'm going to bed," I sigh. He nods. "See you in there."

I lie in bed as I hear him fuss around in the kitchen and make toast and tea, seemingly unaffected.

I am so tired I feel like I actually had the fight tonight, this man and this life with him is messing with my head and is utterly exhausting.

THE SOUND of pills getting popped from their packets greets me when I hop out of the shower in the morning and I walk into the kitchen to investigate. I slept like a baby and don't even remember Joshua coming to bed last night. My eyes cover his body and I gasp in shock. Joshua's face is a mess, he has a fat lip, a black eye, his ribs are bruised, his hand is the size of a watermelon and he's taking painkillers. I can't even be sympathetic; this is beyond ridiculous.

"What are you taking?" I ask.

"Just anti-inflammatories," he murmurs.

I scowl and head back to my bedroom to get dressed for work. What an idiot.

He follows me and gets back into bed and pulls the covers over himself.

I frown at him as I put my hand on my hip.

"What are you doing?" I ask.

"Going back to bed, what does it look like?" he murmurs.

Now he wants to stay in bed. "Are you not working today?" I ask.

"Mmm, later," he groans.

I can't help it, compassion gets the better of me.

"Are you alright?" I ask as I bend and rub his forehead and gently kiss it.

He nods but doesn't say anything.

"Are you going to go to the hospital and see about that broken hand?"

He nods again, still silent.

"Would you like it if I did this to myself and my body?" I ask.

"No," he answers quietly.

"Then you understand why it drives me insane that you do this for fun."

He nods again.

"I'm going to work. I will see you later." I bend and kiss him gently on the cheek and he lies still. He must be really sore, he isn't even joking about naughty nurses.

"Bye, babe," he whispers croakily and then rolls over and closes his eyes.

Hmm, figures, I beg him to stay in bed with me all weekend and now on a Wednesday because it suits him, he is staying at home in bed, so typical.


It's official, operation slim down is damn boring. "What will it be?" the cashier asks me.

I smile as I look at the coffee list on the blackboard on the far wall. "Damn it, I'm going to be naughty. Can I have a caramel latte with one sugar and a cinnamon roll, please?"

It's Friday, I've finished work for the day and have called over to see the girls I worked with at SSAC. I'm not meeting them for another half an hour, so I called in here to fill in the time. I haven't been to this coffee shop before as it's out of the way. I sit at the bar bench and read a magazine as I wait for my order. "Order for Natasha," the cashier calls. I take my order and am on my way out of the café when I catch sight of Joshua sitting in the corner of the café with Adrian and...that bitch from the wedding. Is he kidding? How is he still in contact with her? My blood boils and I march over.

"Hello," I stammer.

Joshua looks up and his eyes widen in shock. "Tash...baby." He stands immediately. "Join us." He pulls out a chair.

I fake a smile. "Adrian." My eyes shoot to Dolly Parton and she smiles broadly. I glare at Joshua who of course is looking his sensational best. Why does he have to be so fucking good look-ing? I fall into the seat uncomfortably.

"This is Tatiana." Joshua introduces her way too quickly.

"We've met." I smile a little too sweetly at him as I am reminded of why I called her Tittiana on our first meeting. His face drops. He was hoping I didn't remember who she was...bastard.

"Tatiana works with us on this new job we are doing," he stammers nervously.

Oh, this is just great. "Really?" I smile. "How nice." My eyes flick to Adrian and he smiles knowingly.

"Yes, what a coincidence. I didn't know she worked for this company. Did I Adrian?" Joshua is talking at double speed. Busted, asshole.

"Right." I drop my head as fury starts to pump. We have discussed his work on numerous occasions, and he hasn't mentioned this once. He puts his hand on my lap and grabs my hand. I smile sweetly.

You are one sneaky son of a bitch.

"So lovely to finally meet you, Natasha," Tatiana purrs. "I've heard all about the woman who has finally tamed Joshua."

Ha. What a joke! "I bet you have," I purr.

I fake a smile at her as my eyes flick to Joshua who has started to perspire. Adrian smiles broadly and winks at me. He's loving this.

"So, how long have you been married?" she asks. My eyes drop to her enormous breasts. Good grief, does anyone at all look at her face, she must wear a back brace under her clothing.

Huh, my eyes widen. Joshua squeezes my hand as I try to rip it from his gorilla grip.

"We are not married," I snap. I hold out my hand. "I don't see a ring on this finger...do you?"

She frowns at Joshua. "But I thought you said?" He coughs uncomfortably.

"I bet you have," I smile sarcastically. "Joshua's stories get a little exaggerated sometimes and then on other times he totally leaves things out altogether, don't you, honey?" I raise my eyebrows.

Joshua sculls his coffee to escape my glare.

"I have to get going, lovely to see you again." I smile at her as I stand.

Joshua stands. "I'll walk you out."

"Not necessary," I smile. "See you later." I storm out of the café with him hot on my heels.

"Seriously, Josh, go back inside," I sigh. "Natasha," he snaps. "What was that about?"

I smile sweetly as I boil with anger on the inside, what an asshole. How could he not tell me about working with her? Act calm. Act calm, act fucking calm. I frown. "What are you talking about, Joshua?"

"Where are you going?" he asks as he grabs my hand.

"Out with my friends. I told you."

He rolls his lips as he contemplates saying something. "What is it you want to say, Joshua?" I raise a brow in question.

"I didn't tell you I worked with her because I knew you would lose your shit." His eyes stay firmly on mine.

I smile. "Always thinking of me." I pull from his grip.

"How thoughtful you are, no, my shit is completely togeth-er," I sneer.

He narrows his eyes at me. "I'll be over around eight?" he replies as he leans in and kisses my cheek.

"I look forward to it," I reply. I walk back to my car with a red glow shooting from my ears. He has got to be joking.

———

MY PHONE DANCES silently around the table.

"Are you not even going to answer it?" Bridget frowns. "No." I screw up my face as I drink the last of my margarita. "I'm off him, he can go to Hell." We are at the Cargo Bar.

I've ditched Joshua. I didn't even tell him I was going out. This

is the fifth time my phone has rung in fifteen minutes.

"Who is this chick anyway?" Abbie asks. "You could take her."

I nod. "Totally, but if he thinks I'm going to be a mushroom and kept in the dark for the rest of my life he can think again. Our whole relationship is oneway traffic. His fucking way and I'm over it." The girls both nod as they listen.

"I told him I wouldn't be his booty call and yet I am." I take a drink. "I constantly open up to him and tell him I love him like a pathetic schoolgirl and yet he says nothing back. Every damn night he turns up at eight o'clock and it is just assumed that we will have awesome sex all night."

Abbie glances at Bridget. "Yeah, sounds totally shit." Bridget laughs into her drink and I giggle. "It is."

They both shake their heads at me. "So, let's get this straight, you are annoyed because he comes around to your house every night and gives you awesome sex without complications?" Abbie frowns.

I nod. "Basically."

"God, I wish, where do I find a man like this?" Abbie sighs. Bridget giggles and clinks glasses with her. The group of young guys we know are here and bound over to the table. "Let's dance." They start to groove on the spot. The girls both stand and move to the dance floor and I stay seated. "I'm not dancing," I sigh.

"Yeah, me neither," replies the young one with the curly brown hair.

"Where have you been? You haven't been here for weeks," he asks. I nod. "I know," I frown. "My gran got sick, so we have had some stuff on."

"Oh shit," he replies. "Is she ok?"

"No, she has cancer," I sigh.

"Sorry," he mutters.

"I met a girl," he blurts out to change the subject. My eyes widen. "Really? Tell me." I smile.

"She's blonde and beautiful." I smile.

"She's away at the moment with her parents." He shrugs. "How did you meet?" I sip my drink, this guy is so cute. "At work," he replies.

My skin prickles. I feel him before I see him. My eyes flick around the space and sure enough there he is. Tall, dark, handsome and extremely infuriating. Shit. I turn around in a rush and swallow the lump in my throat. Bloody snitchy bodyguards. Joshua is talking to my bodyguard against the wall.

He walks over to the table. "What do you think you are doing?" he snaps.

I swallow uncomfortably.

"What are you doing here?" I ask.

"Answer the question," he replies.

I narrow my eyes. "Talking to this wonderful man actually." The boy next to me widens his eyes in fear and I bite my lip to stifle my smile, poor bastard.

Joshua's furious eyes hold mine. "Leave," he snaps to my companion.

He nods immediately and goes to stand up. I grab his arm. "Sit back down. You are not going anywhere," I reply.

"You have five seconds," Joshua growls. The poor boy's eyes are the size of saucers as his eyes flick between Joshua and me. Joshua is scaring even me.

"Cut it out Joshua," I snap. "You leave."

"Five...four," Joshua starts to count in a cool calculated voice and the boy practically jumps and runs. Joshua stands with his legs wide and his hands in his suit pockets, fury dripping from his every pore as he ticks his jaw. His tall body leans down to me. "What the fuck are you doing here?" he sneers.

I swallow the fear in my throat. I don't think I have ever seen him so angry.

I drain my glass. "What does it look like? Drinking," I stammer. He narrows his eyes at me. "I have been at your house worried and I find you are in a bar drinking with other men and ignoring my calls."

I twirl my hair uncomfortably. "I don't feel like seeing you tonight," I reply.

He grabs my arm. "You want to fight, precious? Say when."

I pull my arm from his grip. "Stop it. You're acting crazy." My eyes flick around to the bodyguards who are all purposely looking away.

"You haven't seen fucking crazy yet," he whispers so coldly that I get a shiver down my spine.

I snap my eyes away from his glare. "Stop carrying on," he angrily whispers.

"Who's carrying on, Joshua? I'm in a bar trying to enjoy myself and you turn up here like Fabio. Go away, please."

"Get your ass in that limo now," he growls. Of all the nerve, I screw up my face. "No."

"Now," he screams.

Fuck, he's losing it, I look around nervously.

"I said no," I reply calmly as I try to rein in my thumping heart.

"Go." He raises a brow. "You can leave here with dignity by your own free will or you can kick and scream while I drag you. Either way you will be in my car in two minutes." His cold eyes hold mine. I stand. "You are an asshole," I snap as I storm past him out the door.

I wait at the limo as he walks out with the guards. "Can you let the girls know I am leaving?" I ask one of Joshua's guards. He nods and goes back into the club. Joshua opens the car door for me, and I glare at him as I hop in. I feel like a naughty child in trouble with my parents. He gets in behind me and pushes the security button. It goes up slowly.

I sit silently, looking out the window, as we weave through the traffic. I can feel the anger oozing from him.

He leans over and pulls my face to his. "I will say this once and once only. Do not ever fucking stand me up again."

Fear grips me. "Stop it."

"You will do as I ask and show me respect. Do you fucking hear me?" he yells.

I pull my face from his grip. "And what respect do I get in return, Joshua?" I reply coldly. "Bumping into you having coffee with a woman, is that the respect I deserve?"

"I work with her," he yells.

"And last time I saw you with her you were dry-humping her at a wedding you were attending with me. Don't give me demands on respect, asshole, because you give me none."

"I don't want her!" he screams.

"What the fuck do you want, Joshua? You don't even know."

"You know nothing about me," he snaps as the car pulls up at my house.

"I know I don't, because you tell me nothing," I yell as I jump out in a rush. He gets out after me. "Go home." I yell. I need to get away from him immediately. I can't handle these mind games anymore. I'm going insane. He slams the car door hard and storms after me into the building and the guards all look away. We stand in silence in the lift. I hate having security, what must they think? He opens the door and I storm inside. He slams the door behind me.

"Go home," I yell.

"I am home," he yells.

I turn to him angrily. "If you are home why is there a glass force field around you?"

His chest rises and falls in anger.

"I can't break through it, I try and try and your heart is so closed up that you won't let me in at all...and I can't fucking handle this ambivalence anymore. You don't even know what you want!"

"I want you," he whispers as his eyes hold mine.

I shake my head angrily. "Well, start acting like it. I can't deal with walking on eggshells anymore, Joshua. Make your decision. I have done my time for leaving you, my punishment is over. Let me in!" I cry.

He grabs me roughly and brings his lips to mine. "I want you," he whispers as his tongue gently swipes through my lips.

My eyes close as my hand comes around to the back of his head.

"Prove it," I whisper into his mouth.

His dark eyes drop to my short red dress and he grabs the front seam and effortlessly rips it apart. I gasp at the violence of the act. I stand before him in my underwear, vulnerable and half naked.

"Don't you ever tell me I don't want you," he growls. "It's a damn need. A fucking obsession." He grips my hair in his hands. "I don't know how to control it, it controls me. I have a need to be so deep inside you that's it's all I can think about."

He bites my neck hard and I cry out in pain as he rips my underpants off, turns me and bends me over the dining table in one motion. His fingers plough through my weeping flesh from behind and my eyes close in reverence. He brings his body over mine as his fingers pump in and out of me. This is what I need, to be taken so hard that I can't remember any of the shit that goes on between us. He lifts my right leg onto the table to fully open me to his onslaught and I cry out as I am gripped with the sharp sting of his possession. He lines his throbbing length up and pushes into me as he growls, and I sigh in relief. His hands splay onto my shoulders as he rips my body back onto his. Back...forward...back he pulls me roughly. I feel him harden and I know he's close, the front of my leg is hitting the table so hard I know I will be bruised tomorrow, and I don't give a damn. Bring it on...I need this.

"I want you." He rips into me. "I need you." He growls as again he slams me back onto his length. I drop my head to the table to try and deal with the punishing rhythm.

"Come Natasha," he yells. "Make me come...Squeeze my cock with that beautiful tight cunt of yours."

And I fall, so deep into ecstasy...where I have never been

before that my voice is stolen as my body contracts and I cry out silently. One...two...three pumps and I feel the telling jerk as his body empties itself into mine. We fall onto the table in a heap as we both gasp for air. His lips rest on the back of my neck and I smile as he kisses the side of my face.

I don't know what just happened between us, but I think I found a crack in the glass.

————

MY EYES open sleepily to the faint sound of my phone ringing and then I hear Joshua's phone ringing. We both sit up immediately. Dear God, what's happened? I pick up my phone and see Mum's name and the time, 4 am, and my stomach tightens. Oh no.

Joshua answers his phone and walks into the living room and I sit on my bed.

"Hi Mum," I whisper through the lump in my throat.

"She's gone, beautiful girl," she sighs through her tears.

Pain lances through me.

"Where are you?" I whisper as my eyes close.

"I'm at the hospital, love."

"I'm on my way." I hang up as the tears start to fall.

Joshua walks back into the room and his haunted eyes meet mine. I burst into full blown sobs as he sits next to me on the bed and I fall into his arms.

"I'm sorry, baby," he whispers into the top of my head. "I'm sorry too, Josh."

I sob out loud as the pain of the finality of the situation hits home.

My beautiful gran has gone, and I will never see her again and it's just not fair.

. . .

DEATH, what is it? What does it mean? And where do you go after you leave this life? It can't be the end...can it? Is heaven wishful thinking? These questions have been running through my head and in my thoughts since Dad's death and have once again been magnified.

I sit in the church in a daze. It's been a week since Gran died and today, we bury her. Bridget and I are on either side of Mum. She is inconsolable and sobbing uncontrollably.

I have cried more with this death than I did with Dad's. I haven't stopped actually. Where do the tears all come from?

When Dad died, I was in shock and couldn't comprehend what had happened, but this time I know exactly what is going on. There are no drugs, no antidepressants and no guilt but still way too much hurt. I sit and stare at the pastor through the blurry tears that fill my eyes. I have no notion of what he is talking about, my eyes are fixed on the coffin and the picture of Gran, sitting on the top surrounded by flowers. She looks happy...kind...loved.

I start to feel that pain in my throat that I get when I am trying to hold in hysteria, and I look around the filled church. Mum, Robert, Margaret and Didge and I are in the front row and behind us are the Stanton boys. Joshua is sitting directly behind me and every now and then I feel his reassuring hand on my shoulder. Just having him here eases my pain. The service ends and I watch in horror as the Stanton boys, who are all in tears, rise and move to carry the coffin out to the hearse. The black suits, the black cars, the black day, it's too much, and I put my head in my hands and weep.

I can't handle any blacker, I need some light.

. . .

IT'S Saturday and I am lying on my lounge feeling sorry for myself. Joshua has been fussing around me and desperately trying to cheer me up since the funeral. I know I should get up and do something, but I honestly just don't have any energy or motivation. Bridget scammed some cheap tickets to Hawaii through her work so Abbie and she are taking Mum there tomorrow night for some much-needed respite for ten days. Mum deserves a break and I know she needs it. She hasn't been away since she lost Dad. Joshua wanted me to go with them, but I only just started my new job, and I didn't want to call in sick.

Deep down though, the real reason is I didn't want to leave Joshua. The reason he is in Australia is no longer here and he will no doubt be returning to America any time soon. I would have been a head case being away and not knowing if he will be here when I got home. He still hasn't said anything about me returning with him and whether in fact we have a future together. I'm not asking. Something changed the other night...I think for the better. I finally cracked the glass force field. For the first time he showed me emotion and even though it was anger...it was there and it was real. The Tatiana thing is stupidly playing on my mind. I know he didn't tell me so I wouldn't worry but the fact is he didn't tell me, and I feel like I'm going crazy with all this over analyzing. The puzzle isn't fitting together.

"Can I get you something to eat, Presh?" Joshua leans over me and kisses my face gently as he rearranges the blanket he has put over me.

I take his hand and smile at him. "Thank you."

"For what?"

"For being here, it means a lot." I smile. "Are you okay?" I ask.

He smiles sadly and shrugs. "What do you want to eat? You have hardly eaten in a week." he sighs.

"A Big Mac," I reply flatly.

He frowns, horrified. "From McDonald's." I smile and nod.

His eyes widen. "I don't want you putting that shit in your body, Natasha."

I narrow my eyes. "Don't make me choose, Joshua. The Big Mac will win every time."

His mouth drops open in jest. "You would choose a Big Mac over me?"

I smile. "Every time."

He smirks, stands and takes his phone out and rings Ben. "Can you go down and get Natasha McDonald's, please." He listens. "Yes, that's what I said, McDonald's." He frowns and his eyes flick to me.

"What do you want?"

I smile. He's actually doing it. "I will have a large Big Mac meal with Coke and an apple pie, extra salt on the fries."

He looks at me, mortified. "Are you serious?"

I smile and nod. He frowns, seemingly embarrassed. "A large Big Mac meal and an apple pie. Thanks." He hangs up the phone.

He sits on the lounge and pulls my feet over his legs. "The guys are all going out tonight to the Ivy. Do you want to go?" he asks.

I screw up my nose. "Not particularly. You go if you want." "I'm not leaving you here alone. I will just stay home." He flicks the channel on the television with the remote.

I frown. "Do you feel like going?"

He shrugs. "Not really but sitting around here being depressed isn't enticing either."

He's right. I have been acting like a sad sack of shit. "Okay, fine, we'll go." I give him a small smile.

He smirks, picks up my foot and kisses the top of it. "Let's go to bed."

"No way Stanton, today I'm getting my orgasm from my Big Mac."

The GIRLS and I stand at the bottom bar in the Ivy at 11.00 pm. I'm wearing a black strapless pant suit with a thick gold belt and gold high heel sandals. My hair is in a full high ponytail. Joshua told me I look like a Charlie's Angel tonight. Happy with that description just quietly, I'm glad he dragged me out. My phone beeps a message.

**They are playing our song.**
**Talk dirty to me.**

I smile and bite my bottom lip. Right, he wants to play. "What are you smiling at?" Abbie frowns.

I smirk. "Joshua wants me to talk dirty to him."

Bridget giggles and takes my phone off me. "What will we write?" She bites her lip as she thinks.

I take a sip of my margarita as I narrow my eyes. "Hmm, I need something to drive him wild, like really filthy." I roll my lips together as I think.

"What does he write to you when he's talking dirty?" Abbie frowns in question.

I giggle into my drink. "I can't repeat it. Joshua Stanton is the king of dirty talk."

"Of course, he is," Abbie snaps. "Is there anything he's not good at? Please tell me he turns into Shrek at midnight."

I nod as I finish my drink. "He's shit at two things actually, committing and telling me he loves me."

Bridget laughs as she comes up with an idea. "I know... how about...Do me doggie?"

I burst out laughing as I frown. "Do me doggie? What the hell Bridget?"

Abbie laughs. "That's totally shit, do not text that." She points at Bridget. "You want to turn him on, not turn him off. Don't ever bring up dogs in the promise of passion."

Bridget frowns. "I think that's good. I would text that," she stammers.

Abbie and I laugh again and clink our glasses. "Do not talk dirty to any men Bridget...please." I giggle.

Abbie laughs as something catches her eye from across the room and she frowns.

"Back in a minute," she snaps as she takes off through the crowded club.

"I need to go to the bathroom, Didge." I frown.

"Ok, I will get another round of drinks. Meet you back here," she replies.

"Ok."

FIVE MINUTES LATER, I am in the cubicle in the bathroom and I hear the door bang open from the club.

"You got a hide showing your face around here." I frown, that's Abbie's voice.

"I will go where I want." A girl's voice replies. "And get your hands off me."

I bite my lip and quickly pull my pant suit up. Oh shit, army guy must have stuffed up with this girl. I better just stay in here in case Abbie needs me to try and pretend to be tough. Oh God,

I hope not. I'm such a chicken. My heart starts to race in a panic. "I know about the blackmail, TC," Abbie snaps.

"What does TC mean?" she yells.

My eyes widen. Shit, it's TC, she must be blackmailing James. I bite my fingernail as I listen.

"Tunnel Cunt!" Abbie yells.

I find myself smiling in the cubicle with my hand over my mouth. Abbie is so tough.

The door opens. "Get the fuck out before I kick your ass," Abbie screams.

"I'm calling a bouncer, bitch," I hear someone yell as they leave through the door again.

Bloody hell, Abbie is losing her shit. She's telling off innocent people now.

I stay still riveted on the spot.

"Cameron told me you are blackmailing Joshua for millions of dollars so that you don't send a movie of him and you to Natasha. It was before he was even with her. It has nothing to do with her."

My eyes widen in horror...WHAT!?

"I swear to God, if you hurt my friend, you are dead meat," Abbie screams.

"You're all psychopaths. He threatened to kill me!"

"I'm going to fucking kill you too," Abbie screams. "And my way will be much more painful, bitch!"

"Owww. Let me go!" TC screams.

I put my hands over my mouth in a panic. What will I do? What will I do? They are having a cat fight.

The door opens again and I hear a bouncer's voice. "Out, girls," he snaps.

The girls both leave in a rush. "Kick her out. She's causing trouble," TC screams.

"Fuck off, idiot," I hear Abbie yell as the music floats through the open door.

The door bangs shut and then silence.

I stand from the toilet as the adrenaline starts to pump.

What in the hell was that?

Joshua is being blackmailed and he hasn't even told me, but he told Abbie and Abbie didn't tell me? I am furious, I have never been so mad in my entire life. I leave the bathroom and storm through the club to the staircase and I take them two at a time. When I get to the top I look around and I see Abbie still arguing with TC up against the wall and Ben is standing over them with his hand around TC's arm obviously about to throw her out. Joshua, Cameron and Adrian are about three meters away glaring at them. Joshua's nervous eyes find me through the crowd, and he starts to walk toward me in a rush.

"Let's go, baby," he murmurs way too fast.

I grab his drink for him en route to the girls and storm over to them and throw it straight in TC's face.

It's as if the whole club stops silent. The boys' horrified eyes widen and everyone collectively holds their breath.

I slap her hard across the face. "I know about the tape, you dirty whore!" I scream.

Her eyes widen as she steps back from me, she can tell I'm a donkey on the edge. "I am going straight to the police and you will be charged," I yell.

She laughs in my face and further infuriates me. The guards all wrestle her and lead her out.

I turn to Joshua as contempt drips from my every pore. My eyes hold his.

"Natasha," he gasps.

I hold my hand up to him in a defensive manner. "Don't," I yell.

I am way too mad to listen to his crap. All three boys look like they have seen a ghost and are silent and wide-eyed.

My eyes flick around, and embarrassment fills me. Everybody here knows what is going on but me, he has made a fool of me once again.

"Natasha," Abbie grabs my arm.

I pull it from her grip. "Stay the hell away from me," I yell.

# CHAPTER 25

**Natasha**

I STORM up the stairs and push through the crowd until I get to the door.

"Some creepy guys are following me. Keep them here till I get a cab, will you?" I ask the bouncers.

"Sure thing," the huge bouncer replies as he crosses his arms in a definite tough guy gesture looking for a challenge.

I exit the club and run straight out onto the road. As I lift my hand for a cab, I turn and see my three bodyguards in a scuffle with the bouncers as they try to get out of the doors and follow me. A cab pulls up and I immediately jump in.

"Where to, love?" the driver turns to me and smiles warmly. My eyes flick to the door of the Ivy. "Umm, Rose Bay, please."

I am furious, how dare he keep another secret from me? He obviously doesn't give a damn about my feelings. My phone rings and the name Lambo lights up the screen.

Should I answer it? I tap my tooth as I think. Shit. "Hello," I snap.

"Get your fucking ass back here now!" Joshua growls.

My blood boils...is he serious?

"You have got to be kidding," I snap. "Why didn't you tell me about this?"

"Because I knew you would be a drama queen."

"Drama queen?" I yell.

"Well, seeing as you are on your way home without your guards and you have just jeopardized your career by assaulting a lunatic, yes I would say you are a drama queen. Get your ass back here now!" he screams and then he hangs up.

I start to hear my pulse in my ears and put my hands over my mouth. Shit, he's right. If that lunatic presses assault charges my career is screwed. What an idiot. He's right, I am a drama queen. I close my eyes in disbelief at the turn of events. Why is my first instinct to run? I sit in silence as I stare out the window. Should I go back?

I can't believe this shit, bloody TC. Abbie said she was trouble. My phone rings and I jump and look at the screen. Bridget.

"Hello," I answer.

"Tash, what the hell is going on? Abbie and Cameron are having a screaming match and Joshua just told Ben off when he told him he couldn't catch you. Where in the hell are you?'

I shake my head in anger. "Did you know that TC is bribing Joshua for millions of dollars?"

"What?" she stammers.

"She has video footage of her and Joshua having sex before we got together and Abbie the bitch knew and didn't tell me."

"What the hell?" she whispers. "That's why she and Cam must be fighting. Cameron must have told her, and she let the cat out of the bag."

"What's Joshua doing?" I ask.

"Looking super pissed off with his hands on his hips and talking to the guards."

"Sorry to bail. I just can't believe he didn't tell me," I sigh. "You can't blame the poor bastard. Look how you reacted."

Regret hits my stomach and I blow out a breath. Why didn't I stay and talk to him like an adult?

"I know," I sigh. "I can't come back, I'm too embarrassed. I feel like an idiot."

"Do you want me to come home with you?" she asks

"No, you stay with the others and call me tomorrow," I sigh. "Ok, chick, love you." She hangs up.

The cab pulls up out the front of my apartment ten minutes later and Max is waiting out on the footpath. He opens the door for me and ushers me out.

"You know better than to run off like that," he sighs.

"Get lost, Max, don't lecture me unless you want a black eye," I snap as I storm toward my apartment.

He smirks as he pulls out his phone. "Hi Josh, I have her... no, she's fine." His eyes flick to me. "Do you want to speak to her?" He turns his back to me, and I frown. "Okay." He answers and he hangs up.

"Why didn't you put me on the phone?" I ask.

"Um, he didn't want to speak to you," he answers nervously.

"What?" I snap as I narrow my eyes. Oh, that's it, I storm toward my apartment with renewed vigor. He didn't want to speak to me...well, I didn't want to speak to him, asshole. I get into my apartment and ring Bridget straight away.

"Hi," she answers.

"Joshua just didn't want to speak to me, when he's the asshole," I snap.

"Hmm," she answers.

"He is the one keeping secrets and now I'm the one not being spoken to. He can kiss my ass!" I scream.

"Okay," she murmurs.

"What does okay mean?" I scream.

"Okay, I think you are acting crazy. It was before he even was with you. You just lost your grandmother so of course he wanted to protect you."

"But do you see my point?" I scream.

"Stop yelling. Yes, I see your point," she snaps. "Just don't worry about it till tomorrow, I don't think Joshua is."

I frown. "Why do you say that?" I ask.

"He has just come back from the bar with a tray of tequilas," she whispers.

"Oh really," I fume.

"Yes, really, and since I have been on the phone, he has drunk three of them."

"Oh really," I fume again.

"I will stay with him and the boys and call you tomorrow," she replies flatly.

My stomach drops. "Okay, don't let him out of your sight," I snap.

"Alright," she snaps. "Calm down." She hangs up.

I strip off and head straight to my therapy of choice, a steaming hot shower where I sink to the floor and wallow in self-pity.


"Shhh, shhh." I wake as I hear laughter echoing through my apartment.

I look at my bedside clock. 4.45 am, frigging idiot. Then I hear Bridget's laugh and then Cameron's voice. Oh great, they have all come back here. I feel a wave of relief hit me. I have been over-analyzing my drama queen behavior all night and Bridget is right, I should have stayed and talked to him. With the relief that he is here I snuggle back into my pillow to try to go back to sleep. My door opens and I hear them all laughing. I smile to myself while I pretend to be asleep. What are the idiots doing? I look in the mirror doors and Joshua is hanging by one arm from the door frame holding something out and Bridget and Cameron are hysterical with laughter behind him, pushing each other into the room as if I am a monster.

"It's not working," Joshua laughs.

"Hold it out to her," Bridget giggles.

"I'm just going to throw it at her head," Joshua whispers loudly. Bridget burst out laughing. "I'm telling you, once she gets that McDonald's she will forget she ever had the shits."

Oh my God, they have McDonald's and are trying to hold it out to me to be funny. I find myself smiling into my pillow, trying to act asleep.

I feel something small hit my head and Cameron and Joshua burst out laughing again as Bridget shushes them.

I feel something hit me again and then again while they kill themselves laughing. Cameron is on the floor on his hands and knees trying to compose himself.

"We are so funny." He laughs as he slaps his hand onto the carpet.

What the hell? I put my hand to my head in question. Oh my God, they are throwing fries at my head.

"What the fuck?" I yell.

The light turns on and Joshua bounds onto the bed and Cameron throws his whole packet of fries over the two of us.

"Cameron," I scream.

Joshua smiles cheekily as he lies next to me on the bed

propped up on an elbow. He picks up a fry from the bed and eats it.

"I bought you a Big Mac as a peace offering." He holds out his hand and in it is a mangled Big Mac with half the wrapper missing.

I frown at his hand. "I'm good," I mutter.

"It's really good, I had three," he slurs.

I can't help it. I smile. "You had three Big Macs?" I ask. He does an over exaggerated nod, boy he really is drunk.

"Oh Hell," Bridget whines. "The room is spinning. I don't feel so good," she slurs.

"How much have you idiots drunk?" I ask.

"Way too much," Joshua sighs as he closes his eyes and throws the back of his forearm over his eyes.

"Joshua, put the food in the trash before you go to sleep," I snap.

He shakes his head. "No," he says flatly.

"Just save it for breakfast," Cameron answers as he walks into my living room and flops onto the lounge.

Joshua immediately starts to drift off and Bridget goes to the bathroom.

"I'm going to throw up," she moans.

I stand in annoyance and go to my linen closet and grab a blanket and throw it over Cam on the lounge and grab a bag and start picking up the fools' fries that are scattered throughout my bed. Joshua is out cold, asleep on his back, and Bridget is in the bathroom throwing up.

I walk down the hall to her. "Are you ok Didge?" I ask.

"No, call me an ambulance," she mutters from her seat on the floor.

I smile. "Come on into my spare bed." I try pull her up. "No, just leave me here. I'm fine."

"Are you sure, baby?" I wipe her forehead.

"Mmm." She puts her head onto her arms over her knees.

I hate that spinning room feeling. I leave the lights on for Didge and go back to bed and I screw my face up in disgust as I enter my room. Joshua smells like he has been tipping the tequila all over himself...and he's been smoking, he stinks.

I smile as I drift off to sleep, at least he's here. Drunk as a skunk and incoherent...but here, nonetheless.


I'M hot and crowded on my bed, and it is still very dark. Those expensive drapes are without a doubt the best thing I have ever purchased. I feel Joshua's large erection in my back as I lie on my side and I can tell by his breathing he is still asleep. Bloody hell, he's always up for it...conscious or not. I wriggle away from him. I'm exhausted and need to sleep some more. Fifteen minutes later, I feel Joshua's hand grab my hipbone and bring my body back down to meet his.

"Mmm," I grumble as I try to move away from him. He's got to be kidding. I am way too tired. "Don't," I mumble again.

He kisses my neck from behind and grinds his erection into my behind as he grabs my hip...when did he take his clothes off?

"Don't ever say 'don't' to me," he whispers as he kisses the back of my neck again and pulls me harder back onto him.

My eyelids are still too heavy to open and I smirk. "Joshua, I'm off you, remember?"

I can feel him smile into my neck. "I'm off you too. Fuck now, fight later."

I smirk. "Shut up and go back to sleep."

"No, I need sex now. I don't wait." He bites my neck from behind and I flinch and giggle.

"Eww. Stop it," Bridget snaps.

My eyes fly open, shit, Bridget is in bed with us. I flick my arm out and sure enough she is lying on the other side of the bed in the darkness with her back to us.

"Bridget, I didn't know you were here. What are you doing in my bed?" I giggle as I elbow Joshua in the ribs swiftly.

"Being repulsed by bad porn apparently," she murmurs flatly into the darkness.

I giggle into my pillow and Joshua reaches over the top of me and roughly ruffles Bridget's hair.

"Stop it," she snaps as she shoos him away.

"Didge, leave now, your sister is about to get nailed." Joshua and I laugh, he's teasing her.

"For fuck's sake. You are gross!" she yells.

"Cameron, get in here, your brother is being an animal," Bridget yells into the living room with her husky, I've had too many tequilas, voice as she flicks on the lamp.

I laugh again and Joshua pretends to try and jump on top of me to further infuriate Bridget. I squeal in laughter.

Cameron sleepily walks through the door in his boxer shorts as he rubs his hands through his hair.

"What's going on?" he asks.

"Joshua is saying he is going to nail Natasha."

He stretches and raises his eyebrows as his eyes flick to us. "Sounds fair," he mutters as he walks in and flops across the bottom of our bed.

Joshua immediately tries to kick him off. "That means get out, you two." He grabs me again in an over-exaggerated cuddle and I laugh.

"Stop it," I whisper as he bites me again.

I screw up my face. "How much did you drink last night? You were so drunk."

Joshua kisses my shoulder and closes his eyes again as he ignores my question.

"It was all Stan's fault, oh my God, how many trays of tequila did we drink?" Cameron stammers.

Joshua shrugs as he keeps his eyes closed. "It was Didge," he murmurs.

"Liar." She sighs with her back still to us.

TEN MINUTES LATER, nothing has changed, Cameron is across the bottom of my bed snoring with his back to us and Bridget is asleep next to us with her back to me and Joshua is right behind me, grinding me into next week.

Mmm, he does feel really...really good.

"I need you, my precious girl," he whispers into my ear as he brings me by the hipbone back down onto his erection.

I turn my head towards him and smile into the side of his face. "Stop," I whisper as my hand brushes through his stubble. "I can't," he whispers as his tongue starts to lick my neck in a long deep stroke. Each stroke of his tongue is deeper...longer and I know he is doing it on purpose to simulate going down on me. My eyes close as I lie still. This is wrong. I am supposed to be angry with him so why is my body starting to pump with arousal. Joshua's hips are moving by themselves and I know I won't be able to hold him off...and I don't want to.

"Go take a shower, baby, and I will meet you in there," I whisper.

He smiles into my neck. "Hmm," he whispers as his fingers swipe over my clitoris.

I pull away. I am so not having sex in the same room as Bridget and Cameron, even if they are asleep.

"Shower," I repeat.

He nods and kisses the side of my face and gets out of bed slowly so as not to wake the others.

"Hurry up," he whispers, then he bends and bites me on the behind and leaves the room. I roll over and smile into my pillow.

Ten minutes later, I must have drifted back off because I wake to Joshua lifting me out of bed in a towel and carrying me like a bride to the bathroom. The shower is still going, and the room is steamy.

"You fell asleep," he whispers darkly as he puts me down on the bathroom floor.

I rub my eyes sleepily. "Hmm," I groan.

"You're going to pay for that," he smirks as he lifts my night-gown over my head. He smells like soap and toothpaste. He sits on a towel he has put onto the side of the bath and pulls my legs to either side of his. His eyes are riveted to between my legs and he bends and inhales me deeply, and my eyes close in reverence. He is so damn hot. He inserts three fingers into me brutally and I flinch at the tight sensation.

"I need to be rough," he whispers into my stomach.

My lips become wet and swollen. He arranges me to straddle him as he holds his thick length up and then pulls me down onto it by the hipbone hard.

"Ahh," I whisper as the sharp sting burns me.

"Did that hurt, Presh?" he whispers darkly as he watches me. I nod nervously as my eyes drop to his lips.

"I'm going to hurt you some more, baby, I'm in the mood for pain." He pulls me up and slams me down onto him and my legs start to open by themselves. "Bring your legs up to the side of the bath, I need you in a squatting position," he whispers into my chest as he bites me.

"Josh, it will be too deep," I whisper half-frightened.

"Not possible, I can never be too deep. Do it," he snaps in a whisper. "Your body was built to take me like this."

I slowly bring my legs up and he breathes heavily into my neck and really starts to pump into me as he holds my shoulders from behind.

"Fuck, you feel good!" His eyes watch my lips.

My head drops back in pleasure, he's so damn good at this "Do you feel how deep I am inside you?" he breathlessly

sighs as his body pumps mine.

"Yes," I whimper. Oh God, I'm going to come already."

"Feel how the muscles deep inside you contract around my cock as I pull out," he huskily breathes. My eyes close at the sound of his velvety aroused voice.

He picks up the pace and really starts to slam me onto him.

...God, he wasn't joking when he said he needed it rough. This is hard core if ever I saw it.

"Mmm, I could just fuck you all day, my precious girl," he whispers as the sweat starts to bead on his brow. Our bodies are sliding with the perspiration covering our bodies. My eyes drop to every muscle that I see in his upper body as his arms lift me up and down onto him.

My knees are up around his shoulders and he bites my neck hard and, that is it, I scream into his shoulder as he rips the orgasm from me, and my body lurches forward from the overwhelming power. He then sees that as his green light and he really lets me have it, up and down, up and down, so hard that I don't think I can handle it any longer.

"Josh," I whisper, "I can't....keep..."

"Shut up and fuck me," he whispers darkly as he bites me hard again, and his brutal hits into my flesh and starts to liquefy my insides. One, two, three hard pumps and he lurches forward as he comes in a rush and I feel the heat of his semen burn me from the inside out. I drop my head to his shoulder as we both struggle for breath. I smile into his body as his aggression turns gentle and he starts to gently shower my face with soft kisses. How can one person go from being a sex crazed animal one minute to being gentle and tender in the next? I lean into him as exhaustion hits me once more. My vagina is throbbing with over-use and he is still deep inside me. We sit in silence as the steam continues to fill the bathroom.

"I'm angry with you," he whispers into the top of my head.

I pull back and look at his face.

"You're angry with me?" I frown.

He nods and lifts me to ease himself out of me and puts me onto the ground.

"Why didn't you tell me about that girl and the sex tape?" I frown. He glares at me and brushes past to get into the shower.

"Because I knew you would overreact." He pumps the soap dispenser and starts to wash himself double time.

I stand naked outside the shower and put my hand on my hip. Is he kidding?

"Overreact," I repeat. He is unfucking believable.

He glares at me and nods in defiance. "That's what I said, didn't I?" I throw him a filthy look.

"Hurry up. I want to get in," I snap.

He moves to the side and I brush past him angrily.

He washes his hair and I start to wash myself and then he gets out angrily and starts to dry himself.

"You haven't seen me overreact yet, Joshua."

He rolls his eyes and fakes a smile. He is bloody kidding himself. "Listen, asshole," I snap. "You do not get to keep secrets from me with no consequences. I've had all the deceit from you that I am going to take."

He lurches at me like the devil himself. "And I have had

enough of trying to protect you only to be treated like an asshole. It was before we were together, so it has nothing to do with you."

"What?" I scream. "Nothing to do with me, are you kidding? What the hell are you talking about, you idiot, it has everything to do with me."

"This isn't about you or me Natasha," he screams.

I screw up my face. "What the hell are you talking about now? You've totally lost it."

"Do you think I want my children to be able to google me having sex with a prostitute in twenty years?"

I stand still. Shit, he's right. If this gets on the internet, he's totally screwed.

"But, of course, it's about you, Natasha...everything is about you!" He wraps the towel around his waist angrily and leaves the bathroom.

My God, he's an asshole. I turn the shower off, wrap a towel around me and storm out dripping wet after him. I find him in my bedroom rummaging through the closet for something to wear. Cameron and Bridget are in the same positions we left them in on my bed fast asleep.

"What the hell is that supposed to mean?" I scream.

"It means you were supposed to stand by my side last night and unite with me but of course you would blame me and leave."

"Why do you say that?" I scream. He has got to be kidding. I am not taking the blame for his keeping secrets. What a prick.

"Because it's what you do best!" he screams.

"Shut the hell up, you two," Cameron sighs.

"You shut up," I yell in reply to Cameron. "Get out of my room, I want to get dressed."

"Oh God, what happened to the bad porno?" Bridget groans. "At least that was quiet."

Joshua glares at her as he grabs some of his underpants from a drawer in my closet.

"It turned bad, really fucking bad!" he yells.

"Shut up, you idiot!" I scream. "You haven't seen really bad yet!" I spray my underarms with deodorant angrily.

"Oh God, go away," Bridget groans as she pulls the pillow over her head.

Joshua pulls up his underpants and shorts.

"Cameron, we're leaving. Get up."

Cameron is still lying over the bottom of my bed with the back of his forearm slung over his face. "Oh God," he murmurs. "Now, fucker!" Joshua screams. He hits him on the back of the arm as he storms out into the lounge room.

Red steam is shooting from my ears, he is kidding himself. I have done nothing wrong and I will not apologize for leaving the club last night. He fucking deserved it. I follow him, still in my towel. He is at the sink having a glass of water.

I storm into the kitchen. "You are kidding yourself, Joshua Stanton. I will not take the blame for leaving the club last night. I was embarrassed that everyone knew what was going on but me again."

He narrows his eyes at me as he finishes his drink. "What the hell is that supposed to mean?"

"Remember last time you made a fool of me was in the hospital when you were fucking Amelie," I yell.

He throws his glass into the sink and it smashes. He holds up one finger at me. "It was one time, there was no fucking!"

"Same thing!" I scream.

He narrows his eyes at me. "Actually, you are right, you left me then too. Just fuck off now and be done with it." He grabs his keys and leaves the apartment without his shirt on.

I can feel my heartbeat in my ears, I am just so damn angry.

Cameron staggers out of the bedroom. "Shit, I still feel drunk," he croaks to Bridget who is laughing behind him. He turns and kisses her on the cheek. "Have a great trip."

Oh shit, my heart drops. Bridget and Abbie and Mum are going away tonight for two weeks, I had forgotten. I hate this day already.

It's seven o'clock and I have just returned from taking the girls to the airport, I am in the lift and my headache is thumping. Max is by my side. I'm trying desperately to not be stressed and to hold off this migraine, but it's getting worse. I check my phone for the hundredth time. I haven't heard from Joshua all day. Is this how it is going to be with us from now on, both harboring grudges and resentment for past mistakes? Drama after drama.

He's right, I should have stayed with him last night in a united front, but I was just so shocked. He didn't ask for this stupid bitch to do this to him but on the other hand surely, he must understand that I need honesty in a relationship more than anything. He should have told me, but then who am I to talk? I'm the ultimate deceiver. The secret I am keeping from him is a lot worse than a blackmail case. This is such a mess. I'm as bad as his mother. He's holding me to ransom with punishment for leaving him in the past. If only he knew that I have only ever left him for him. I would never go of my own accord, nothing is more important to me than my relationship with him.

"Are you staying in all night?" Max asks.

I give him a sad smile and nod. "Yes," I whisper. I haven't told Max that I had a fight with Joshua, but I am thinking he already knows. He was here when Joshua left this morning, furious and shirtless.

"You have a headache?" he asks gently.

My eyes flick to him. "Yes, how did you know?"

He smiles sympathetically. "Your hands are shaking, that only happens when you are getting a migraine."

I look at the ground as my eyes fill with tears and I nod.

Why does my bodyguard know me better than anyone else? "Do you want me to call the doctor?" he asks. I shake my head.

"Have you heard from him?"

I look back at the ground and shake my head again. "No." He nods and stays silent as the lift doors open.

I slowly make my way into my apartment and Max smiles. "I will be out here if you need me, ok?"

I nod and close the door quickly behind me. I don't have it in me for someone to be nice to me at the moment. I may crack under the pressure. Why didn't I just go to Hawaii with the girls? I walk to the kitchen and instantly go to the medicine cabinet. I need something that will knock me out and stop me thinking. I can't deal with this damn headache today. I finally find some Mersyndol and take three and then drink a large glass of milk to fill my stomach.

I shower and dress and crawl onto the lounge under a blanket.

I wake to the feel of my hair being swiped back from my forehead and my blanket being rearranged over me.

"What's wrong?" Joshua asks.

"Nothing, just a headache. I'm okay," I whisper as I pull the blanket up to my chin in a defensive manner.

He stands over me and puts his hands on his hips. "You don't look ok, you look like shit," he murmurs.

I look up at him and smirk. "You look worse, but thanks for the compliment."

He flops onto the lounge next to me and throws his feet onto my coffee table. For ten minutes he sits next to me and I can feel the anger radiating out of him. In the end it gets the better of me and I can no longer keep my mouth shut.

"Did you come over here to ignore me, Joshua?" I ask. He bites his thumbnail and shakes his head.

I roll my eyes and pull my blanket back up around my face. "Whatever," I murmur.

For another half an hour I sit with him fuming next to me and my head feels like it is about to explode. "What is it Joshua? Why did you come here if you are furious?"

He jumps up in a rush. "I'm not mad with you," he yells, and my eyes close from the echoing sound.

I frown. "Who are you mad with?" I reply.

"Myself mostly."

I frown again. "Why?" The pain in my head becomes so intense that my eyes tear up and it starts to throb. I can't handle this conversation now.

"Because I can't stay away from you!" he yells. I sit up and frown at him.

"Every goddamn day at three o'clock I start to watch my clock counting the hours until I see you and it makes me sick."

My eyes fill with tears as my head starts to really thump. "It makes you sick missing me?" I ask, mortified.

"I shouldn't miss you. I should hate you, I shouldn't feel the way I do about you!"

The pain in my head becomes too much to bear. "But I love you," I whisper as the stupid tears roll onto my cheeks.

"Natasha!" he screams. "Are you listening to me at all?"

My head throbs and my tears fall. I don't have the strength to deal with him now. I stand slowly. "Joshua, I am unwell. I can't argue with you tonight. I need to go to bed," I whisper in a strained voice.

He frowns as his face falls. "Are you ok?"

I shake my head. "No, I am not. I have a terrible headache. Can we talk about this tomorrow? I need some peace and quiet, Josh, please give me some."

# CHAPTER 26

Joshua

I WAKE to the sound of smashing glass. I sit up in a rush and flick the lamp on. Natasha isn't in bed and I immediately jump up and run out into the living room.

"Natasha," I call in a panic.

"In here, baby, I'm okay," she calls from the bathroom. Relief hits me, thank God. I go to the bathroom and find that she is anything but okay. She is on the floor on her knees throwing up and her hands are shaking heavily as she tries to hold herself up.

I drop to my knees next to her. "What's the matter?" I ask as I brush her hair back from her perspiration-clad forehead.

"Migraine," she whispers. "Can you get me my phone, please?"

I nod and run from the room. I don't know anything about migraines. "Where is it?" I call in a panic from the bedroom.

"In the closet in my handbag," she replies.

I run into the closet and flick on the light as my eyes dart around the small space. I'm getting her a new closet on Monday. This is ridiculous. Shit, there are about ten handbags all hanging from a shelf. "Which one?" I call but she doesn't answer. "Natasha, which bag?" She doesn't answer again, and I sprint back to the bathroom to find her throwing up again.

"What do you want me to do?" I ask.

She continues to throw up violently and I run my hands nervously through my hair.

"Max," she whispers.

I screw up my face. "Huh?"

"Call Max," she groans.

My eyes widen as she throws up again, she's going to die any minute. I sprint to the bedroom and grab my phone off the bedside and dial Max's number.

"Hello," he answers.

"Max, get up here, Natasha has a migraine and I don't know what to do."

"I will call her doctor," he answers calmly.

"Do you have the number?" I snap.

"Yes, this happens a lot."

My eyes widen in horror, a lot...what does that mean? "Okay." I hang up.

I run back to the bathroom to find Natasha holding her head and crying as her hands shake violently. What the hell is going on? I fall to the floor next to her and cut my hand on a piece of broken glass on the floor. "Shit," I snap.

"I broke a glass. I'm sorry," she whispers.

"Tash, you're scaring me. What's happening?" I pull her onto my lap and hold her head as she cries.

"The doctor will be here soon," she sobs in a calming voice as if sensing my fear. What if she is having an aneurysm?

"It's ok, I'm ok," she whispers as she comforts me. "I'm ok, baby, go and unlock the door."

I nod and ease her down onto the ground beside me and unlock the door. Max is waiting outside.

"Where is she?" he asks.

"In the bathroom," I answer as I run back up the hall towards her.

Max goes to the kitchen and gets a large dish from the cupboard and goes and puts it in the bedroom before coming into the bathroom.

"You should put some clothes on." He nods.

I look down at myself. Shit, I'm naked, I hadn't even realized. I nod and head to the bedroom and throw on some clothes.

Max walks into the room carrying Natasha and he puts her into bed.

"It's okay, honey, the doctor will be here soon, and he will give you a sedative and everything will be ok," he says gently as he lays her down.

She nods as she holds her head and I stand still, riveted on the spot in shock. This has happened a lot, I can tell by Max's calm reaction. Why in the hell do I not know about this?

A guard walks into the apartment with a doctor behind him. "In here," I yell.

The middle-aged woman smiles and immediately opens her briefcase and starts to check Natasha and I stand still at the end of the bed.

"It's been a while since you had one of these," the doctor murmurs as she takes her blood pressure.

"Yes, five weeks," Max replies.

I narrow my eyes at Max. "How often does this happen?" I ask.

He shrugs. "When she is stressed."

Guilt fills my stomach, this is my fault. Max's eyes dare me to say something and I feel anger rise in my stomach.

"You can go, Max," I say flatly to him.

He rolls his lips as his eyes flick to Natasha. "I will stay with her if you need to go out," he replies.

"That won't be necessary. I will be staying and looking after her. Thank you." I can't hide my annoyance that he knows more about my girl than I do.

He nods and leaves the room.

I sit on the chair in the corner of the room and watch silently as the doctor checks her over.

"Natasha, dear, I am going to give you a sedative now. Do you want me to call someone to look after you?"

I stand. "I will be staying to care for her."

Natasha holds out her shaky hand as she smiles weakly and I take it in mine. The doctor smiles at our interaction.

"This is a sedative that I am giving her. She will be out for around eighteen hours."

I frown as I listen. "It's ok, she has had this many times before. It is the only way we can get the migraine to stop. It's quite common."

I nod and watch the doctor give her an injection.

"Here is my card, call me if you need anything," the doctor says and then she leaves us alone.

"Is your hand ok?" Natasha whispers.

A lump in my throat forms, here she is half dying and she is worried about a nick on my hand.

"Yes, sweetheart, I'm ok," I lie down next to her and put my cheek to hers.

"I'm sorry," I whisper. "I didn't mean to upset you."

"Don't be stupid, it's not your fault. I'm sorry you have to stay here with me," she whispers.

I bend and kiss her forehead.

"Josh, I need to go to the bathroom."

I nod, help her up and lead her to the bathroom and wait silently while she goes.

"Is your head ok?" I ask as I brush her hair back.

"I'm ok, you know me, the ultimate drama queen. Nothing in halves," she smiles, and I find myself returning her smile. I really do love this woman.

"Come on, back to bed." I help her back up the hall and she changes clothes and slowly hops into bed. The clock reads 4.45 am. I lay next to her and hold her close as she drifts off into unconsciousness.

It's 12 pm, Tash is fast asleep like an angel next to me in bed and I am on my laptop googling migraines and their treatment. Apparently, she was having them every couple of weeks after her father died. Not as bad as this though, according to Max. The only time she had one this bad was when I came to her after we broke up and she turned me away. That one went for four days and they sedated her twice in a row. I needed sedating myself at that time. My eyes flick to the beautiful woman lying next to me.

I wish I could just get over this shit and forget the past. I just can't...I'm trying. I am so in love with her and it's fucking with my head, scared to live with her, petrified to live without her. I can't stand this hold she has over me. She rolls and I notice her pajamas are slightly soiled, what's that? My eyes widen. Shit, she has her period. My eyes dart around the room in a panic. I don't know anything about this shit. Hang on, it's early, it's not due for another week, maybe she's hemorrhaging.

I run to the lounge room to retrieve my phone and ring Cameron.

"Hey," he answers.

"Cameron, you need to get over here immediately.

Natasha is unconscious and hemorrhaging." "What the fuck?" he snaps.

"No, not like that. I mean she has a migraine and the doctor knocked her out and I am looking after her and now she is bleeding."

"From where?" he snaps again.

I shake my head in frustration. "From you know where." "Where?"

"Where girls bleed from."

"Oh Jesus," he groans. "She has her period, Stan, that's all."

"What do I do?" I shriek.

"She will have some stuff in her bathroom. All girls do, just follow the directions on the pack."

My eyes widen as I walk to the bathroom and start rattling through her cupboards and drawers.

"What does it look like?" I ask Cameron.

"What does what look like?" he snaps.

"Whatever this girl shit is!"

He laughs down the phone. "You're such a dumb fuck. Do you want me to come over and sort her out?"

My eyes widen in horror. "No, I do not. I can look after my girlfriend just fine thank you." He is not laying a finger on her.

"Whatever." He sighs. "Call me if you need help."

He hangs up.

I rat through the cupboards and find one pad, no packet. Oh, this is just great.

I walk back to the closet with the pad and start looking for more things. Surely, she has more packets somewhere. I look through her handbags and find a few tampons. I hold one up to look at it and narrow my eyes...hmm. This is weird shit.

After cleaning Tash up, I go back to the closet to start searching for more packets. How many will I need? Why isn't she more organized? This is so typical Natasha. In the bottom of her closet I find a couple of shoeboxes stacked on top of each other and I open the top one. I frown. It's full of books. Small leatherbound books. I open one. It's a diary. I rat through the other boxes, these are all diaries and she has kept every single one. Twelve, there are twelve diaries here. My eyes widen at my find, but I have more pressing issues at the moment...like where do I get more pads? I am going to have to go to the shop myself. She wouldn't want me to send my staff. Where do you even buy this stuff? I take out my phone and call Cameron again.

"Hey," he answers.

"Where do I get this stuff?" I ask in a rush.

"Huh, what stuff?"

"Girl's stuff, you idiot, what do you think I mean?" He laughs.

"The pharmacy, fuckwit."

I nod. "Hmm, makes sense. Right." I hang up and call

Max. "Max, I have to go out for ten minutes. Can you come and sit in the living room and watch Tash for me?"

"Yeah, sure. I will be right up."

FIFTEEN MINUTES LATER, I am in a pharmacy, walking up and down the aisles looking for the relevant section. My guards are waiting out the front on my instruction. I finally find what I am looking for and my eyes flick over the shelves, hmm. What size? I frown as I look at the large selection of tampons and I rub my chin: mini, regular, super...mini... she would be mini...she's definitely not super. I grab a basket and ten packets of mini tampons. Now pads. My eyes flick over the packets, wings...wings...what the fuck is that? Night-time, what's the difference between day and night? I frown and rub my head in frustration. Maternity, I thought women didn't get their period when they are pregnant. Seriously, I should have listened in school at those sex education classes. I end up grabbing one of each packet and head to the cashier with my hands and basket full.

There are two young girls on the counter and their eyes flick to each other as I unload my shopping basket. This is embarrassing.

The girl on the checkout smiles. "How many girlfriends do you have?"

I smile in embarrassment. "Just one."

The both smile broadly at me and I squirm uncomfortably. "Overkill?" I smirk.

"Slightly," says one of the girls. I smile in return and rub my forehead.

"That will be $192.00, thanks." The checkout girl smiles. Shit, this stuff is expensive. I nod nervously, pay and head back to the car with my five bags of supplies. Even checkout chicks are now putting shit on me, what next?

I walk into the apartment to find Max sitting on the lounge and I walk past him and carry the bags into the bedroom, Tash is still asleep. I bend and kiss her forehead softly and return to the lounge room.

"Thank you," I nod to Max. "Did she wake up at all?"

He shakes his head. "No."

I walk into the kitchen and flick the jug on. I would kill for a decent coffee right now.

"Can I talk to you?" Max asks.

I raise my eyebrows at him. "What is it?"

"I just wanted to explain why I helped Natasha leave LA." I stare at him deadpan and raise my eyebrows.

"I couldn't let her be alone in LA, she had no money, and she was so vulnerable. I had watched her go through absolute hell since her father died."

Fury erupts in my stomach. "And what do you think I had been through? I was in the hospital for a drug overdose."

"You slept with Amelie and she was distraught," he replies.

I narrow my eyes at him. "I know what fucking happened," I yell. "You can go," I snap. "I'm not explaining myself to you. You have no idea what is going on between Natasha and me, so cut the bullshit!"

He stands. "Are you going to fire me?"

"If it wasn't for Natasha you would have been out on your ass long before this and you know that."

"I don't want animosity between us. I want to stay guarding Natasha and I want us to get along," he replies.

I roll my eyes and put my hands on my hips as my angry eyes meet his. "At this moment the only thing I am worried about is Natasha waking up. I want her to be safe from that psycho Coby Allender and if you do your job and keep her safe, we will get along just fine. Other than that, I want nothing to do with you."

He stands slowly.

"Loyalty is earned, Max," I snap. He nods and drops his head.

"I appreciate you being loyal to Natasha, but let's leave it at that," I say flatly.

He nods and leaves the apartment silently.

I go back in to check on Tash. She is lying on her back with the blankets pulled up around her face. I smile—so perfect. I gently lie next to her and kiss her cheek.

"Are you ok, Presh?" I whisper. No reply.


It's four o'clock. I have been lying next to Tash in my boxer shorts for most of the day watching television. My eyes constantly flick to her...over her. I'm worried she has a brain tumor. This migraine thing is not normal for a healthy woman. I have been looking after her feminine needs all day and the intimacy of the act is turning me inside out. I crave this level of attachment to her, from her. I notice the walk-in closet light is on and I get up to turn it off. My eyes flick to the shoe boxes in the bottom of the wardrobe, her diaries. I walk over and pick up the boxes and go back and lie in bed. I open the first one: 2002, she was thirteen. I read a few pages and smile, adorable and so childlike.

I flick through the next few books. They are so candid.

She talks about everything from school to being grounded. She thinks she's a geek and complains about being too smart.

I smile broadly. I rat back through the box and find the one I am after: 2006. I pause before I open it, should I do this? Do I want to know what's in her head? I close it and put it back in the box. No...I don't. I get up and make myself a protein shake and sit at the kitchen counter while I think. Maybe I will just read the first one, the one where she and I first made love. I go back to the bedroom with renewed vigor and open the diary. I flick through till I get to the date I am after.

*28/12/2006*

*Dear Diary*

*We swam today all day. I'm missing Bridget. I spent the day with Joshua and I'm sunburnt. Joshua is trying to teach me how to surf. I don't really want to learn but it means I can spend time with him. He makes me happy, he makes me laugh.*

I smile, I remember that day.

*31/12/2006*

*Dear Diary*

*I spent the day with Joshua again. Something is wrong with me. I am having bad thoughts about him. I sit here on my deck chair and he is opposite me as we all sit around the campfire. He is drinking hot chocolate. I want to move my chair next to him. I can't stop thinking about him, I think I like him. He makes me feel butterflies in my stomach. It's New Year's Eve and all I want is for him to kiss me at 12 o'clock. He keeps looking at me and I don't know if I'm imagining it. I think I am going crazy. He's my cousin.*

I smile and turn the page.

*2/1/2007*

*Joshua has not talked to me all day. I think he knows that I like him. God, I'm such an idiot. I want to go home, I'm embarrassed. I miss Bridget. She would know what to do.*

**I remember that day, I was confused and purposely kept my distance. I turn the page.**

*3/1/2007*

*OMG, big news. I asked Joshua when we were in the water at the beach why he wasn't talking to me and he told me because he wanted to kiss me, and he was having bad thoughts. I couldn't help it. I smiled and he splashed me and then tried to drown me.*

**I smirk to myself, did I really try to drown her?**

*4/1/2007*

*At the beach today I was sunbaking, and Joshua was lying next to me. He asked me why I smiled yesterday, and I didn't know what to say. I should have lied but I couldn't. I told him that I have been having bad thoughts too. He held my hand as we sunbaked. I loved today.*

**I smile broadly. I remember all of this. It was exactly the same for me.**

*5/1/2007*

*Today was the best day of my life. Joshua and I spent the day surfing and then tonight when we were washing up with Cameron in the kitchen Joshua kept looking at me differently. The last couple of days he has started doing this cracking the neck thing when his eyes drop down my body. It's fucking hot. What does it mean? Cameron went back to the others and Joshua grabbed my face and rubbed his thumb over my lips. He kissed me, just gently. He told me that he wanted to know how I tasted and that he couldn't help it. I grabbed him and kissed him properly. Like tongue kissed...kissed. He backed away and told me to go to bed because he shouldn't be doing this. I told him I think about him when I go to bed. He closed his eyes and told me to stop but then he kissed me again. It was the best kiss ever. He's so beautiful.*

.   .   .

447

*6/1/2007*

*Joshua came to wake me up this morning, he came into my tent and told me he has been thinking about me all night and hadn't slept. I couldn't help it, I made him lie next to me and we kissed for over an hour. I have never felt so...happy. He makes me feel special.*

My eyes flick to the perfect woman lying beside me and I put my hand on her leg. "That's because you are special, precious girl," I whisper as I lean and kiss her again and inhale her scent.

*6/1/2007*

*I'm being bad, I can't help it. I asked Joshua to come to me tonight when everyone has gone to bed. He said no. I'm an idiot. I am forcing myself onto him. I will not embarrass myself tomorrow. I will stay away from Joshua, and if it kills me.*

My face drops; is that how she felt...because that's how I felt.

*7/1/2007*

*Joshua came to me last night. I woke up and he was in bed with me. It was perfect and...he was hard. We made out all night.*

*I have never felt like this. The clothes stayed on, but I wanted them off. I wish I was more experienced, so I knew how to please him.*

I frown as I read the last line, is she kidding? She was my every fucking wet dream come true, hot, smart, beautiful... innocent. How could she have thought that she didn't please me? I put the book to the side and lie down next to her. I shouldn't be reading this, but I can't help myself. I lean over her and kiss her gently on the lips.

"Presh...wake up, baby. I want to see if you are ok."

No response. I pick the book back up and continue reading.

*10/1/2007*

*I love him.*

*I love him and I can't have him. We laugh all day and make out all night. He is perfect, my every dream.*

**My face drops.**

14/1/2006

*Things have turned physical between us. Last night we were both completely naked together. Joshua is so patient and gentle with me...he is teaching me how to orgasm. I love him so much. I need him in my life.*

16/1/2007

*He wore me down.*

*I couldn't help it. Joshua has been trying to go down on me all week and I haven't wanted him to. I'm embarrassed. Tonight, he took over and wouldn't listen to me. OMG. HE IS AMAZING. I took him in my mouth too but he wouldn't come in my mouth. He tasted perfect. I never thought sex would be as beautiful as this.*

**I smile broadly, this is exactly how I remember everything. I wouldn't come in her mouth because I didn't want her first head job to be traumatizing. My face drops as I realize that thought. I loved her even then.**

18/1/2007

*I want it to be Joshua. I want to give my virginity to him so he will always know that I love him. I don't know how to ask him, he may not want to sleep with his cousin. WHY ARE WE RELATED?*

**I close my eyes in pain, why are we related?**

19/1/2007

*Joshua and I made love last night. It was beautiful and it fucking hurt. I am no longer a virgin. I told him I loved him, but he didn't say it back...it hurt my feelings.*

**I put the book down and rub my face with both hands. I knew I fucking hurt her. I can still remember the feeling of**

her hanging on to me so tightly. Christ, why the fuck am I reading this shit? It's messing with my head. She always tells me she loves me and I never fucking say it back. What's wrong with me?

*23/1/2007*

*Joshua and I cannot get enough of each other. We sneak away every chance we get. We can't stop, I will never get enough of him. We are now making love at least four times a night, it doesn't hurt anymore...it feels good...amazing. I'm addicted to his touch...to his love. We only have two more weeks together. Joshua told me he has never been in love before, but he thinks he loves me. I hope he does!*

**I smile and keep reading**

*23/1/2007*

*Joshua makes me laugh. We get each other's jokes when no one else understands what we are talking about. Even without the sex he is my perfect man, tall, athletic, smart. He looks at me this way when he thinks I'm not watching, and he cracks his neck. It's the hottest thing I have ever see...it means he is getting hard. Ready for me, my new favorite thing is going down on him. I love watching him come apart...so hot.*

I rearrange the erection in my boxer shorts. Reading that she loved going down on me even back then is a major turn on. I can remember how much she used to love it...it's burned into my brain. My eyes flick to her half-naked body sprawled out on the bed. Ohh, you're going to cop it, baby girl, when you wake up. Hard, I need it hard. I stroke myself to try and stop the need. I bend and kiss her stomach gently and my cock hardens further. God, I want her.

I hear the front door open. "Hey, it's me," Cameron calls from the lounge room.

I jump nervously and throw the diaries back into the box and kick it under the bed. I bend and kiss her thigh and quickly wrap a towel around myself to hide my erection. I head out to see him.

"Is she still out?" Cameron asks as he hands me a coffee. "Thanks." I take it and nod.

"What's with the boner?" he smirks.

I look down to the obvious erection through the towel and I shrug.

"She's unconscious," Cameron says flatly.

I smirk and nod as I sip my coffee. "I know." My eyes meet his.

He shakes his head and rolls his eyes as he walks up the hall to Natasha's bedroom. He stands at the door as he takes a stethoscope from his pocket. I quickly scoot past him and pull the blankets up over her. It is just getting dark, so I flick on the side lamp.

He smirks at me. "You know I'm a doctor, right?"

I nod. "Yeah, I know. I also know you're a sex maniac." He rolls his eyes.

I smile and bend to kiss Tash on the side of the face again as I gently take a seat beside her with my coffee.

He picks up her hand and starts to take her pulse. "What time will she wake up?" I ask.

He shrugs. "Between twelve and sixteen hours after she was sedated."

"Do you think she has a brain tumor?" I ask. He smiles as his eyes stay on her face.

"No."

"Do you think she has brain cancer?"

He shakes his head again. "No." He widens his eyes at me.

I watch him silently as he pulls up her shirt and listens to her chest.

"How are you going with the period thing?" He smiles.

"Fine," I snap as I take a sip of my coffee.

He smiles broadly.

"What?"

"This domestic version of Stan is very entertaining." I fake a smile.

"Hilarious."

He picks his coffee up from the side table and takes a seat on the end of the bed.

"What happened? Why did she get this migraine?"

I shrug. "Probably because I am an idiot who keeps stressing her out." I sigh.

"Did you tell her you didn't trust her?" I shake my head. "No."

"Did you argue?" he asks.

"No, she was calm, and I argued. Tell me, Cam, do you think Natasha loves me?" I sigh.

He smiles. "I hope so." My face drops.

"Of course, she does, idiot." He frowns. "Why would you even say that?"

I shrug and take a drink of my coffee. "She keeps leaving me." He shakes his head. "Josh...she has had her own reasons. She has never cheated on you. Hell, she hasn't even slept with anyone else." He frowns.

I run my hands through my hair in frustration. "What are you worried about?" he sighs.

"That she is going to leave me again, and that I won't cope," I mumble.

"Josh. Get over it. Every man on the planet gets fucked around at some point. Why are you carrying on?" he whispers angrily.

I shrug as my eyes flick to Tash.

"You call her the drama queen. I reckon you're being the drama queen. Of course she was pissed the other night and left. You were filmed with a stripper. I'm pissed off with you myself for being so stupid," he snaps. I pick up her hand and kiss the back of it.

"I'm still in love with her," I whisper as my eyes linger on her beautiful face.

Cameron rolls his eyes. "Tell me something I don't know."


## Adrian

I wake to the sound of the shower running and I smile as I roll over and look at the ceiling. I haven't felt this happy for a very long time. After spending every night with Nicholas for the last month we have finally become intimate over the weekend. It's Monday morning and he hasn't left my side since Friday. Satisfaction is running heavily through my veins, both emotionally and physically. The shower turns off and ten minutes later I hear Nicholas out in the kitchen. It's weird he didn't wake me up like he has every other day. I rise and walk out. He is dressed in his suit and is sitting on the lounge putting socks on.

I saunter into the kitchen and flick the coffee machine on.

"Good morning, I smile.

He looks up from what he is doing, and his haunted eyes meet mine. I frown in question.

"Put some clothes on," he whispers.

I frown again and put my hand on my hip. "Excuse me," I mutter. He's got to be kidding, we have been naked the whole weekend.

He drops his head again and fiddles with his socks.

"What's up?" I ask as I lean on the counter. Something is obviously the matter.

He stands. "I'm in love with you," he whispers.

I smile. "Well, that's good because I am in love with you," I reply.

He drops his head. "Don't," he whispers. I frown.

"What do you mean don't?" I reply.

"Adrian, you can't love me."

"Why not?" I snap.

His haunted eyes meet mine again. "Because I am married." I frown. "No, you are widowed."

He shakes his head frantically. "You don't understand. I feel guilty for feeling like this about you when my husband is dead. I swore I would never love again and here I am playing happy family with you."

I narrow my eyes at him. "A game you insisted on," I snap.

"I haven't slept all night. I should not have done this to you. I thought that I was ready, but I don't think I will ever be ready." Hurt pierces my heart and I hold his gaze.

"Do you think he wouldn't want you to be happy? You deserve to be happy, Nicholas, you have lost enough."

"He deserved to live and to have his husband to be loyal to him till the very end," he whispers. "This isn't about me...or you. This is about Pierre and his memory."

Nausea rolls in my stomach. "Get out," I snap as I storm to my bedroom and sit on the side of my bed. Five minutes later I hear him pick up his keys and the door quietly shut behind him.

Tears fill my eyes. "I loved you too, Nicholas, I loved you too," I whisper.

## Joshua

It's 12.30 am and I sit in the chair next to Natasha's bed watching her in silence. She should have woken up by now. I am giving it half an hour and then I am calling Cameron. This is bullshit, something is wrong. I read the diaries. Every sordid detail of the way I have treated her is right there on paper in black and white from her perspective. How can she still love me after everything I have put her through? I smile, she loves me...even after all that, she still loves me. I haven't found the most recent diary. I looked everywhere but she has obviously hidden it. My stomach is twisted with guilt, she knows more about my past with other women than I thought. I have been blaming her for our demise when I should have been listening to her reasoning. It makes sense when I see it from her point of view, as twisted as that is. I am going to make it up to her, and if it's the last thing that I do. I have never loved her more.

# CHAPTER 27

**Natasha**

"She's not awake, you need to get over here. Something is wrong."

My heavy eyelids flutter as Joshua's voice echoes through the apartment from the living room, the bedroom is dark and lit only by the side lamp.

"She should have been awake four hours ago." He goes silent as he listens.

"I mean it, get your ass over here now, Cameron." He goes silent as he listens again. "Or maybe I should take her straight to the hospital." He listens. "Hang on, I will check." He walks back into the room and I sleepily open my eyes.

"Hey, baby," I whisper.

He closes his eyes in relief and puts his hand on his chest. "She's awake, call you later." He hangs up.

He sits gently on the side of the bed. "Are you ok?" He brushes the hair from my forehead.

"Sorry," I whisper in a throaty voice.

He frowns. "What for, Presh?" He bends and kisses my cheek gently and I smile.

"You had to stay with me. I hate these stupid headaches," I mumble.

He smiles broadly and pulls me into an embrace. "You scared the shit out of me. I thought you were going to die."

I smile again. Hmm, beautiful Josh is here. "I need to go to the bathroom," I whisper.

He helps me out of bed, and I walk gingerly to the bathroom as he holds my hand.

"It's ok. I can walk by myself," I whisper.

He frowns. "Natasha, you have just been unconscious for eighteen hours. I am helping you."

"I need a shower," I sigh as I lean against the vanity. Joshua runs the shower and then turns and smiles warmly at me.

I frown. "What?" I ask.

He bends and kisses me again on the forehead.

"Josh, I need to go to the toilet. Can you go out?" I whisper.

He is still leaning over me. "No."

I frown. "Josh, give me some privacy, please."

"Presh, I have been looking after your needs for the last eighteen hours. We have no secrets anymore."

My eyes widen in horror. "What?"

"You have your period and I have been looking after you." He kisses my face again as he pulls me into an embrace.

"Oh, my fuck." I put my head into my hands in embarrassment. What must he have seen? I am mortified.

"Why are you doing that? It was the most intimate thing I have ever done. I loved every minute of it." He kisses the side of my face again.

"Oh Josh, just get out!" I snap. This is horrifying.

"Presh." He smiles as he kisses my neck.

"Out now!"

He stands, seemingly disappointed, and leaves the now steamy bathroom. I pull my pants down and look down and smile. I have two pads on, one on top of the other. I giggle to myself. What an idiot, what is that going to do?

He knocks on the door. "Yes," I answer.

He slowly opens the door and passes me a packet of tampons.

I smirk and snatch them from him, and he smiles. I look at the packet and frown.

"What are these?" I ask

He widens his eyes. "Tampons," he says flatly.

"What size are these?" I smirk.

"Your size," he answers, affronted.

"Did you go to the shop and buy these?" Oh my God, now I have seen it all.

He nods.

I bite my bottom lip to stifle the huge grin on my face. "You went to the shop to buy me tampons?"

"So," he snaps, "isn't that what guys do for their girlfriends?" I smile and hold my hand up to him and he takes it gently.

"Thank you," I whisper.

He bends and kisses me again as he relaxes.

"For the record though, mini tampons are for thirteen-year-old girls. My size is super."

He frowns. "There is no way in hell you have a supersized vagina."

I giggle again. "Get out, idiot."

He shakes his head and strips off as he gets into the shower.

"I told you, no more secrets." He turns his back to me and starts to soap up.

I finish up, brush my teeth and get into the shower with him.

He turns and pulls me into an embrace and cuddles me tightly as he covers my face with kisses. "Don't scare me like that again, Presh, I thought you were going to die," he whispers into the top of my head.

I lean into his chest and smile. The hot water running over us is soothing and I feel myself relax.

"I'm sorry," he says quietly.

"Josh, I get the migraines all the time. It wasn't your fault." "I don't deserve you," he whispers.

I frown and pull back to look at his face. "Why do you say that?"

He shrugs. "I just don't." His eyes search mine.

"I love you," he whispers as the water falls over him.

I raise my eyebrows. "You love me because I have my period?" I wipe my hand down the side of his face gently. "Every woman in the world has periods, Joshua."

He kisses me gently on the lips and his lips linger on mine. "I'm not in love with every woman in the world. Only you," he whispers.

Ok, he's lost it. I went to sleep, and he hated that he missed me, and now I wake up to this.

"I love you too," I whisper gently as I frown.

He kisses me as he holds my face. His tongue gently swiping through my lips, then dives deeper and my mouth opens in invitation. One of his hands finds my behind and the other gently cups my breast.

"I've missed you," he whispers as he kisses me again.

The intensity of my man gets to me and I find a lump forming in my throat.

"I was only asleep for a day, Josh," I smile into his kiss.

He shakes his head in between kisses. "I mean, since we were kids. I've missed you every fucking day since we were kids. I love you more now than I did then. I was just too scared to tell you."

I pull back from his lips and smile through my shock. "What?" I whisper.

"Forgive me, baby. I am so sorry." His eyes glaze over.

What the hell? "Josh, what's wrong?" I ask. He's starting to worry me now.

"Has something happened while I was asleep?"

He shakes his head and smiles sadly. "Nothing could ever be wrong as long as we are together."

He kisses me softly and the feeling behind it nearly brings me to tears. "I love you," he whispers again. Our kissing turns desperate. I can feel his arousal pump hard against my stomach as my sex begins to throb with want. I take him in my hand and stroke him upwards, and he closes his eyes in pleasure. Before I can move, he pushes me up against the wall and starts to kiss me deeply. His tongue dives into my mouth as his hips grind into mine. Instinctively I lift one leg around his waist, and he groans in pleasure. When I feel this emotional about him, I need to be physical. His fingers find that spot between my legs and his eyes roll back in his head in pleasure. He must remember that I have my period and he pulls back from me in a rush.

"I'm sorry." He shakes his head in disgust.

"What for?" I smile as I take him in my hand again.

"You are not well and here I am half raping you. Come, get out." He kisses me quickly and exits the shower.

I stand still as he wraps a towel around his waist and holds one out for me. I smile as I step into it and he wraps me in an embrace with the towel and kisses my forehead again.

"You need to eat, precious girl. I will cook you something." He smiles.

I needed that intimacy, but he is right, I do feel weak.

Half an hour later I am sitting at the kitchen counter watching Joshua cook me bacon, eggs, toast and tea. I have a robe on, and Joshua is in his boxer shorts. His broad back and tight ass are on full display, and he looks damn edible. I sit and watch him silently, my mind in overdrive.

He smiles softly and walks over and kisses my forehead gently and then cups my cheek and studies my face.

"What is it?" I ask.

He frowns. "What's what?"

"Why are you acting like this?" I ask quietly.

"I can be nice to my girlfriend, can't I?" He goes back to his place in the kitchen.

I frown. "See there lies a problem just there. You don't call me your girlfriend. I call you my boyfriend, but you don't use that term."

He flips the eggs as he puts his hand on his hip. "That's bullshit. I call you my girlfriend and I call you my wife sometimes actually." He passes me my cup of tea and I smirk as I take a sip. "And I can tell you I love you...can't I?" He raises an eyebrow in question.

I smile. "Yes, but why now when last time we saw each other you were telling me that you hate the hold I have over you and that you don't want to miss me."

He turns back to the hot plates. "I was just worried that's all and I thought you were going to die, and it scared me."

I nod as I take another sip. "And?" I ask.

He turns and looks at the egg flip he is holding as he contemplates saying something. "And I read your diaries." His eyes meet mine.

My eyes widen. "You read my diaries?" I whisper, mortified. He nods. "Joshua. They are private, how dare you!" I stand in a rush and he comes over and grabs me in an embrace.

"Tash, I couldn't help it. I found them when I was looking for pads and shit and then I was just going to read the one where we had sex the first time and then I couldn't stop."

I pull out of his grip. "And that's why you told me you love me, because you read my diaries?"

He shakes his head in a panic. "No, I told you I love you because I do and before I read the diaries I didn't believe that you actually loved me. I thought you just thought you did."

"I told you I fucking did!" I scream. "For once it would be nice if you believed what I said!" He is unbelievable, what the hell have I written in those bloody diaries?

He grabs me again. "Baby, stop fighting me. I love you. It doesn't matter anymore. All of this bullshit that goes on between us doesn't matter one bit."

I don't have the energy to struggle as he wraps his arms around me, and we stand still in an embrace.

"What matters is the two of us being together and me making you happy. I am not going back to America."

I pull back and frown at him. "Why not?"

"Because I am not leaving you again."

I smile stupidly. "You're not?"

He smirks as he shakes his head. "No, I am not." He bends and kisses me gently.

"And you are going to stop being a drama queen and leaving me every minute."

I smile. "I am?"

He nods and kisses me. "You are."

"And you're not going to America?" I repeat as I rub my hands over his broad shoulders. Hope blooms in my stomach.

"No, Presh, I'm not." He bends and tenderly swipes his tongue through my lips. "Now eat your breakfast because you are going to need your strength."

"Why will I need my strength?" I ask.

He smirks as his eyes drop down my body and he gently cracks his neck. "Because I have the worst case of blue balls known to man and as soon as you are well enough you are going to cop it...both barrels."

I giggle as he sits me back onto the stool and he serves up my breakfast.

He bites his toast as he leans over the bench onto his elbows. "You do know I am going to kill Christopher next time I see him, right?" he remarks casually.

My eyes widen and my fork stops midair.

He takes a bite of his toast then smirks and raises an eyebrow in a silent dare to say something.

I swallow the lump in my throat. "Why?" I whisper. He raises an eyebrow again. "You know why."

Oh shit, what the hell have I written in those bloody diaries?

So much for privacy.


**Joshua**

It's been a big day. I told the boys today that I am moving to Australia, and they took it better than expected. I know Murph's upset...I'm upset. I love LA...but I need Tash in my life, and I want to protect her from the paparazzi at all costs. They don't follow me here in Australia as much as in LA.

Cam was fine, he was always coming home to Australia but what does that mean for Adrian? I wish the thing with

Nicholas had worked out and then we could have all moved here together.

We have been home for a few hours. Natasha insisted we go to the police station and press charges against this lunatic. She demanded more money today, claiming she had another disk. I have to admit I do feel relieved having done it. It was appalling making the statement, but the policemen were understanding, I can't imagine the horror of my love watching me have sex with a prostitute. She will never look at me the same again if she sees that tape. My heart drops. I'm just so sick of all this drama, what does it feel like to have a normal private life without worry?

I continue reading emails on my laptop and rub my chin as I think. I am sitting up in bed and Natasha has just finished in the shower. My mind wanders to my horse stud, what am I going to do with the move? Natasha walks into the bedroom in a pale pink pair of underpants and a shoestring strap top to match. Her thick dark hair is in a loose braid that hangs down her back and her dark skin is in contrast to the pale pink. She looks edible.

My cock twitches and I run my tongue over my bottom lip as want starts to fill me.

I watch her walk around to my side of the bed and retrieve her diary from the second drawer. I inhale as she bends next to me...mmm she smells like soap. I start to feel my pulse between my legs. I put my hand on her thigh as she bends and run it up to her behind.

"You smell good," I smile as I inhale. I kiss her upper thigh.

"Of course," she smiles. "I always smell good."

I watch her walk back around to her side of the bed and sit with her back up against the headboard. She sits and thinks for a minute and then starts to write in her diary. I smile to myself. She writes in front of me now. I mean what's to hide, I have read them all. The fact that she writes in a diary is so nerdy but so damn cute at the same time. I try to concentrate on my email. Fuck, she smells good. I shake my head as I try to concentrate. I lean over, kiss her shoulder and lick her upper arm. She smiles and kisses the top of my head in return. I try to re-engage with my email. I can see her in my peripheral vision writing and feel her body calling to mine. A wave of arousal runs through me, she needs to be filled. I bend and take her nipple into my mouth through her singlet, her shoulders fall back to give me access and she sighs softly. I nuzzle my head deeper into her chest and inhale her scent. This is home...where I belong...with the woman I belong to.

I smile into her chest as the realization hits me and she runs her hand gently over the top of my head. I kiss my way down her body and slowly lift her top to get access to her skin. God, she smells good. I move lower and bite her through the fabric of her underpants and once again nuzzle into her as I inhale and close my eyes in pleasure. Hmm, my arousal starts to pump heavily between my legs, and I crack my neck to relieve the tight pressure. I slide her panties down her legs and off, and our eyes meet. This is my favorite thing in the world...her taste...her smell...her love is right here between us when I do this. Nothing feels better than to give her this pleasure, to give myself this pleasure. This is the one place I lose myself and there is nothing on this earth but me...and her...my precious girl. I part her with my fingers and look at her pink opening between fingers, our eyes meet again, and her breath catches, and she runs her hand tenderly down my cheek and swipes her fingers gently across my lips. I kiss her fingertips and then slowly lower and lick her deeply. She groans and writhes under me, deeper I lick as my eyes close in pleasure and I rub my hips into the bed beneath me to relieve the pressure in my thumping cock. Fuck, she tastes so good. My head starts to take on its own side to side action as I lose myself and start to get to a place where I cannot pull back. I couldn't stop if I tried.

My hands are under her legs and around on her hipbones. I could orgasm by just running my hands over her hipbones. When I have my hands on her hip bones I am usually inside her and pulling her onto me, they are a massive trigger. I run my tongue deep into her again and again and she writhes under me in pleasure. I gently take her clitoris between my teeth and pull back in a stretching motion and she groans loudly. My cock is really thumping now, and I grind it hard into the mattress for relief. I need to be inside her, and I need to watch. I slowly part her again and push a finger into her. We both groan and I start to feel my pulse in my ears as my cock starts to seep pre-ejaculate. She's so tight, so fucking hot and unimaginably perfect. My eyes close. I add another finger and circle my tongue over her clitoris as I start to pump my fingers in and out of her. Her soft sighs call to my body on a level that I will never understand, the need in me to be inside of her...to hold her is incomprehensible, yet the only thing that makes sense in this messed up world.

"Josh," she whispers as her body lifts off the bed to meet my face.

I smile into her, this is what I love. When she needs to be filled so badly that she starts to beg me for it.

"Josh, please, baby." She runs her hands over my head as

her legs drop all the way to the mattress. My eyes close in pleasure as I inhale deeply.

I keep pumping her hard so that the bed starts to move, and she starts to really writhe.

"Josh. Now!" she demands.

"I need to watch, Presh," I whisper as I sit up. I remove my boxers and sit towards the side of the bed. "Face the mirror my beautiful girl." She frowns and then sits in front of me, her back to my front. I arrange her body to lie back over mine and spread her legs wide to hook over my legs.

"Watch," I whisper. Her breath catches as she looks into the mirror and sees her beautiful pink vagina spread out in front of our eyes. My cock lies hard beneath her opening. I can see it weeping from here. I bring my hand over her shoulder and down to her beautiful wet opening and slowly start to run my fingers through her dripping flesh. Her eyes stay riveted on the mirror. My eyes are locked on the beautiful woman lying open for me in the mirror, her breasts rise and fall as she gasps for breath, the shadowing on her stomach, the pink coloring of her opening. The second opening... I want to be in there. I need to fuck that beautiful ass so badly. She's not ready for me there yet, I have to remind myself that every time I take her. I can't wait for the day when she is. I bring my finger up from her and put it into her mouth, she sucks it as her eyes close.

"Touch yourself," I whisper.

Her scared eyes meet mine in the mirror and I smile as I kiss her. "It's ok, Presh, it's just you and me here. You can be yourself with me. You know I love to watch you, baby, and we need to start doing things my way," I whisper as I bite her neck. "You want to please me, don't you?"

I kiss her deeply over her shoulder and she shakes her head nervously.

"I want you to put your fingers into that beautiful tight cunt of yours," I whisper into her neck as I watch her in the mirror. Her breath catches and she brings her hand around and starts to run them through her lips. I can smell her arousal and I crack my neck hard.

"In," I whisper, "put them in." My cock starts to thump with need. I watch as her index finger disappears into her body and my breath catches as her eyes close. "Two," I whisper. Her eyes hold mine as she adds another finger and I nearly come on the spot. My cock starts to throb with such velocity that I can hardly sit still. "In and out," I breathe as I run my hands over her body and start to squeeze her nipples. She starts to pulse her fingers in and out as her eyes close. The visual runs through my head of me taking her anally in this position as she does this, and it makes me clench to stop myself from orgasming.

I have never been with a hotter woman; she is on fire. She reaches down and picks up my penis and feeds it into her. Both of our eyes are locked onto the mirror as my cock slowly disappears into her body, she moans softly, and I bite my lip hard to stop myself from coming. I can't control it anymore. I pick up her legs and hold them back as I start to lift off the bed to give her what we so desperately both need. Her head drops back to my shoulder as I pound into her as hard as I can. She starts to hold herself off the bed on straightened arms so I can grab her hips and really piston into her. The sight of her open as my penis pounds into her body and the feeling of her deep internal muscles contracting around my cock tips me over the edge and I cry out.

"Keep fucking going," she moans, chasing her own orgasm and I give her everything I have until she screams out and falls back onto my chest and we both fall to the mattress.

Her tongue swipes through my open lips. I will never tire of the perfect intimacy between us.

"I love you," I breathe.

She giggles into my neck. "You are the Lamborghini of all Lamborghinis and I love you."

I smile as I gently pull out, we both lie silent and try to catch our breath as we look at each other and I smile broadly.

"What?" she whispers shyly. "You like to watch too." I smile.

She bites her lip as she giggles. "You are a bad influence on me, Mr. Stanton."

I lean in and kiss her passionately. I love this woman. We lie in each other's arms for another ten minutes.

"I'm having a shower," Tash whispers as she kisses me again quickly on the lips. "I smell like semen."

I smile and rub my hand over her ass. "I like you smelling like my semen."

"Shower," she repeats.

"Hmm," I sigh as I put the back of my forearm over my eyes. "Meet you in there, Presh." She stands and I roll and grab her ass. "Seconds?" I raise a brow in question.

"Hmm, later." She smiles as she jumps up and leaves the room, I hear the shower turn on and I lie in the silence for a moment as my heart rate slows. God, she's incredible. I have never had sex like I have with her. We are so compatible. I start to doze in a hazy state of contentment.

"Joshua, get in here," she yells, and I smile with my eyes closed. Demanding thing. I swing my legs to get out of bed and accidentally knock her diary off the bedside table and onto the floor. I yawn as I bend and pick it up. This is the new one that I haven't read. I open a random page and smile as I start to read.

"Joshua!" she calls.

*Joshua told me last night that he only wants to have sex and has no intention of picking up where we left off. I'm gutted, in tears as I write this, I thought everything was going to turn out alright between us. It's becoming more apparent every day that he doesn't feel the same as I do. Maybe he never has?*

Guilt hits me in the stomach. The night in the restaurant, I remember it well. Why am I such a selfish prick? I shake my head in disgust at myself.

"Josh I'm washing myself," she calls, and I smile again as I continue reading.

*I think the girls might be right when they say I will one day regret not sleeping with anyone else. I wish I could release myself from Joshua's grip...for just one night. I want to feel another man's hands on me...inside of me.*

Pain lances through my chest. What?

*I already know I will never be able to betray him like that. I belong to him and I guess it is something that I will die wondering about. How does it feel to have sex with someone you don't love? To have no emotional connection. No pain when they leave. I want it so badly, but I love Joshua more. I will stay loyal to him forever, even if he doesn't want me. The sick thing is even if we get back together deep down, I know I will always wish I had done it when I had the chance. Damned if I do, damned if I don't.*

I snap the diary shut in a rush and put my hand over my mouth as nausea fills my stomach. She craves another man's touch. I drop my head into my hands as I sit on the side of the bed, and a lump forms in my throat. I had no idea she felt like this…I just assumed. After every sacrifice she has made for me over the years she still craves another man's touch and no matter how hard I try that is something I cannot give her.

## Natasha

I look out the window as we turn into the hospital. It's Monday morning and Joshua is dropping me off at work. We have a security car in front and one behind us. I bite my bottom lip as I study him.

"Is something wrong?" I ask as I reach over and run my hand up the back of his neck.

He frowns and his eyes flick to me. "No, why do you say that?"

I shrug. "You're just quiet."

He smiles softly as he reaches over, picks up my hand and kisses the back of it. "I will be happy when this psycho doesn't get off today."

I nod uncomfortably. "Me too, do you think he will?" Coby Allender's bail hearing is going to court today. Max is going to watch in the public gallery.

He shakes his head in frustration and shrugs his shoulders. "Hope so."

I continue to watch him, that's not it. "Are you sure that's all it is? You have been quiet all weekend and you have hardly eaten a thing since Friday."

He frowns at me as he chews his thumbnail. "Natasha, a serial killer who has possibly stolen your vibrator and a sexual blackmail case against me is a reason to worry, don't you think?" he snaps.

I nod sympathetically. "Yes, you're right. Sorry." We pull into the drop off area and my guard gets out of the car behind us.

"Don't leave the hospital, okay?" He runs his hand up my thigh.

I smile softly as I nod. "Okay," I whisper.

"Take the guard with you if you leave your office." I smile again.

"What?" he frowns.

"You're very cute when you get all over-protective." I smile. "I mean it, do as you're told. This is serious." He frowns.

"Yes, boss," I whisper as I lean in to kiss him. "Will you call me when you hear from Max?"

"If the murderer gets off, I am coming to get you straight away," he snaps.

"Oh God, Joshua, now you're being a drama queen." I run my hand through his stubble. "I love you," I whisper.

His face drops and his eyes search mine. "I love you too," he whispers as he forces a smile.

I narrow my eyes at him. "Why do you look at me like that when I tell you I love you?" I ask.

He frowns. "Like what?"

I shrug my shoulders. "Nothing. I will see you when you pick me up."

He nods. "See you then."

"Do you want to go out for dinner?" I ask hopefully. "No," he answers.

"Why?"

"You know why, it's like sitting in a goldfish bowl with all the security surrounding us. I don't enjoy going out at the moment."

"Are you going to let us be prisoners in my apartment for the rest of our lives?" I sigh.

"You think I like this shit?" he snaps.

"Whatever," I sigh. "See you tonight." I exit the car in a rush, and he waits until I walk into the building. God, he's so bloody wound up at the moment.

Eight o'clock that night we are sprawled on my lounge watching television as I eat chocolate ice cream. My feet are on Joshua's lap and he is deep in thought. I can tell by the way he is running the side of his pointer finger back and forth over his lips, his elbow resting on the side rest.

"What are you thinking about?" I ask.

He looks towards me as I pull him from his thoughts. "Just how I would do anything to make you happy." He picks up my foot and kisses the top of it and smirks at me.

I smile and guilt runs through me. He is trying so hard, but I know deep down he is devastated about leaving his life in LA and Willowvale. When I put the pieces together I realized that he has not been himself since he told the boys he is moving here.

"Josh...I've been thinking about it." I bite my lip as I contemplate whether I am doing the right thing.

He raises an eyebrow in question.

"You know I love you too much to let you sacrifice for me." His face drops. "What do you mean?"

"I know you don't want to leave LA," I answer.

He rolls his lips as he thinks. "You have sacrificed enough for me over the years, Presh...it's my turn."

I smile sadly. "I don't want you to ever sacrifice to be with me, Joshua."

He smiles and kisses my foot again. His eyes hold mine. "I will move to LA," I blurt out.

He frowns.

"But...I want Mum and the girls to have unlimited plane tickets to visit me."

He frowns. "Tash, you love Sydney."

I smile. "No, Josh. I love you and if that means moving to the moon to be with you, then so be it." I shovel a large spoon of ice cream into my mouth.

He swallows and turns back to the television, seemingly deep in thought.

"Why do you want to move to LA?" he asks.

"Because you have been miserable since you decided to move here, and I want you to be happy."

He narrows his eyes and turns back to the television and scratches his head in frustration.

"We will move to LA on one condition." His eyes bore into mine. "What's the condition?" I frown.

"I want you to sleep with someone else."

# CHAPTER 28

**Natasha**

I SIT UP ION A RUSH. "What the hell are you talking about?" I snap.

"I want you to sleep with someone else."

I screw up my face. "Have you gone crazy?"

"I know you want to."

I shake my head in disgust. "No, I don't, that's ridiculous."

"I read it in your diary."

My mouth drops open in shock. Dear God, what have I written?

"Those diaries are private, Joshua."

"But in black and white, nonetheless." His eyes dare me to deny it.

"I don't want to sleep with someone else. That's ridiculous. How could you think such a thing?"

"Why would you write something like that if you didn't mean it?"

I shake my head in disgust and get up in a rush. "I was venting. I don't even remember writing that. You don't take it literally." I'm outraged, how dare he use this against me?

"I do," he snaps.

"Oh right, so we are going to break up...is this your pathetic excuse to cause trouble with us again? Haven't we had enough shit?" I scream as frustration pumps through my veins.

"No, quite the opposite. I am going to leave you for a week, and you are going to," he shakes his head at his inability to say it out loud, "do it."

He closes his eyes as if in pain. "And then we will leave for LA and start our life together. With no regrets."

"You are an idiot if you think I could possibly sleep with someone else," I scream. "Do you even know me at all?"

"You are going to!" He screams back. "I haven't slept since Friday knowing this is how you feel."

"What?" I shake my head in disbelief as my heart drops. "This is what you have been stressed about," I whisper gently as empathy for my beautiful man fills me.

He fakes a smile. "Reading that your girlfriend wants another man's hands on her...inside of her...will do that to a man." He drops his head in sadness.

My heart drops as I rush and wrap my arms around him. "Baby, I didn't mean it. I don't want to. I would never do that to you."

"I know you wouldn't and that's why I'm giving you permission." He pulls me into an embrace. "It will have no effect on our relationship or my love for you. I know you love me. I'm asking you to do this for me."

I shake my head into his chest as tears fill my eyes. I feel so guilty for making him feel like this.

"Josh, you are all I could ever want. Stop talking, please. I don't even want to talk about this."

"Tash, when I leave here in the morning I am not coming back for a week and you have a hall-pass to sleep with one man." He pulls my face up to meet his and he wipes my tears. "Just fucking one."

"I'm not doing it," I stammer.

"Natasha, listen to me. I know I could never settle down with you if I had never slept around. Curiosity would have got the better of me in the end. I can't expect of you what I couldn't do myself. I have thought hard and long about this and I know it's the right thing to do."

"I'm not doing it."

"Natasha...it's once, it is between us and nobody will ever know. I appreciate you will be discreet and not tell the girls."

I step back in shock, he's serious. "Do you want to sleep with someone else? Is that why you are doing this?" I scream. "Do you want a hall pass?"

He smiles sadly and shakes his head. "Tash, I will not leave my hotel for the week. You have my word. I don't want anyone else."

"This isn't you. You would never allow this!" I scream.

"I don't want to be the man that you think I am!" He throws his arms up in the air in anger. "Who am I, Natasha?" He screams so loud that he makes me jump.

I frown as confusion grips me.

"The rich, dominant, cage-fighting male who controls his woman!" he yells in frustration. "Is that all I am?"

The tears start to overflow my eyes. "Baby," I whisper gently as I reach for him. "I love that man. I don't want you to change, Josh, not ever."

"I don't want to be the man who deprives you and controls you," he whispers as his eyes search mine. "I want to be the man, who gives you everything that you want, the man who loves you unconditionally." His eyes cloud over, and I feel the tears start to run freely down my cheeks.

"You do...you are all I could ever want." I shake my head in frustration. "How could you even think that what we have is insignificant?"

He shakes his head. "You are misunderstanding me, Presh." He tucks my hair behind my ear gently and wipes a tear away from my cheek. "I know you love me," he says gently. "This is my way of proving to you and myself that I am worthy of your love. That our love is indestructible. That sex is sex and love is love and that you know without a doubt the difference between the two."

"Josh, I know."

He gives me a small smile. "My mind is made up. I have thought long and hard about this. Tomorrow I leave you for a week, and I will never ask a question about what you do in this week...I don't want to know." He hangs his head. "But I will assume that you will do as I ask." His eyes bore into mine and with renewed purpose he gets up in a rush and goes to the shower to cut the conversation short.

I slump into the lounge chair as my heart pounds heavily in my chest. Now I have heard it all. Joshua Stanton is the biggest mindfuck in the history of the human world. Sleep with someone else, who is he kidding, as if!

"TURKEY, swiss cheese and cranberry on rye, please, with a skim cap, no sugar," I mutter flatly to the cashier in the hospital cafeteria as I look into the glass refrigeration cabinet. I'm flat, oh so flat. It is Tuesday lunchtime, and I haven't spoken to Joshua since he left me yesterday morning in what was the worst goodbye you could possibly imagine. Since the time he told me that he wanted me to be with someone else he wouldn't touch me, he would only cuddle me and even pulled away from kissing me. His way of distancing himself from me...and sending me quietly insane. The sick thing is that if I am completely honest with myself...and I don't want to be...what he said actually rings true and I feel sick to my stomach. I have regretted not sleeping with someone else and knowing the difference firsthand between love and sex...and if I knew one hundred percent that I wouldn't hurt him and it would have no consequence on our relationship, I would do it in a heartbeat.

I EAT my lunch in silence as I look out the window, deep in thought about the conversation we had, a cloud of dread hanging heavily over my head. He said that he could never have settled down if he hadn't slept around and that he couldn't ask me to do what he wouldn't be able to do himself. How many women has he slept with over the years? In ten years' time will I look back and regret not doing this when I already know I regret it now. Why do I feel like this? I'm so confused. But on the flip side I am so proud of myself that I have only been with someone I love...but then that was never my intention. I never set out to do that, it just happened that way. I put my fingers to my temples as I think. I wish I could talk to the girls about this but I promised Joshua it is just between us and I know he is not telling the boys about it either. He is protecting my privacy, my decision. I don't think I have ever loved him more than I do now, to know that he would sacrifice what he wants to give me a choice is overwhelming. My eyes tear up at the thought. True unconditional love is what he is offering...and deep down that is all I have ever wanted...truly craved.

So why when I am so in love with Joshua does my mind keep going back to Jesten?

# CHAPTER 29

Joshua

I TAKE a sip of my Cointreau and a drag of my cigarette as I sit and watch the red dot on my screen flash on the map. She's leaving work. I run the side of my pointer finger back and forth over my lips as I think, my eyes riveted to the screen. I am in my darkened hotel room feeling very unbalanced. I bugged Natasha's phone and handbag weeks ago when I found out about Coby Allender. I need to know she is safe and that I can find her if something were to happen. Coby Allender didn't get off, his case has been adjourned for five weeks and it is a huge relief. Until yesterday I hadn't turned it on but now, I find I can't turn it off. I am putting myself through torture by watching what she is doing, but I need to know. A knock sounds at the door and I close my eyes in frustration. Go away.

It knocks again. I am not in the mood.

"I know you're in there," Cameron's voice rings out. I

shake my head in frustration as I minimize the screen and answer the door.

"What?" I sigh as I open the door.

"What are you doing?" Cameron snaps as he barges past me into the room, followed closely by Murph and Ben.

"What does it look like, idiot?" I snap.

Cameron and Murph throw each other a look. "Well, seeing you are drinking and smoking in your room alone and it's..." he looks at his watch, "3.00 pm on a Tuesday, I'm thinking something is up."

Adrian flops onto the bed and Ben opens the curtains and the sliding door.

"Do you mind?" I snap.

"Not at all," he answers.

"What's going on with Tash?" Adrian asks.

"Nothing."

"Is that the problem?"

I screw up my face. "What are you talking about?'

"Ben said you didn't stay there last night, are you fighting?"

I throw Ben a dirty look. "No," I snap. "Keep your nose out of my business, the three of you!"

"Why have you taken all of our guards off Natasha and replaced them with stand-in ones?" Cameron asks.

I narrow my eyes. "Get out, Natasha has a right to privacy you know. I could use some myself at the moment. Leave us alone."

"Max has stayed with Natasha." My eyes flick to Ben in a question.

"He refused to leave her," he replies.

I nod in relief. I took my guards off Tash and replaced them to give her some room to breathe, but I have been worried ever since. At least I know she is safe with Max watching over her.

"Turn that music down, for God's sake," Adrian sighs.

"I like this song," I reply as I light another cigarette. "What is it?"

"Arctic Monkeys, 'Do I wanna know'" I reply.

"Yeah, on repeat I'm not so sure," he sighs.

"Get out then."

"Get dressed. We are going to the gym," Ben snaps.

I blow out a deep breath. "Ok, I will be out in ten." They leave the room and I flick the screen back up and I watch the red dot move through the streets. She's in the car on her way home. I minimize the screen again in disgust at myself.

"Snap out of it, Stanton."


IT's nine o'clock and we have just returned from the gym and dinner. I'm missing Natasha. I just want to see her, hold her. How on Earth did I get so dependent on one person? I turn on my computer and wait for it to boot up as I sit and tap my fingers on the desk and blow out a deep breath. After what seems like an eternity the screen comes up and I watch the red dot flash on my screen. I narrow my eyes as I look at the address across the bottom of the screen: 117 Macquarie Street, Sydney. Where is she? What is she doing?

My heart starts to race as I type the address into the 'Find' toolbar.

Sydney InterContinental Hotel flashes up and my stomach twists. Oh my god, she's in a hotel. There is only one reason she would be there.

She's with someone.

I grab my head in my hands as pain lances through my

chest and I stand so suddenly that my chair falls to the ground. This is what I wanted her to do, she is doing as I asked. I pick up a glass on my desk and throw it against the wall. It smashes through the room. I find myself in a rage as I punch the computer monitor as hard as I can, and it smashes as it falls from the desk. I pace as I start to lose it, the door slowly opens, and I turn my haunted eyes to see Ben standing quietly in the doorway. By the look on his face I know he knows. He has spoken to Max and he knows where Natasha is. His eyes scan the room, he sees the glass and the broken computer screen and the tears running down my face.

"Mate," he says softly in his heavy South African accent. "What have you done?"

"Get out!" I scream.

"What have you made her do?" he repeats softly.

"Get out!" I scream again. I need to get away from him and I walk into the bathroom. I look into the mirror at myself. I make myself sick. I asked her to do this and yet I am gutted that she actually is doing it. What was I thinking? I break into full-blown sobs as pain cuts through my chest like a knife. I punch the mirror and it smashes into a thousand pieces. I hear Ben make a call.

"Hello, Steve, this is Ben. We will meet you in the gym in thirty minutes. Yes." He goes silent as he listens. "Organize some of your best. Stanton needs to fight."


## Natasha

"So, let me give you this brochure and then we can go through your other options." I listen as the genetic counsellor speaks to one of the clients I am seeing. She has just discovered that she carries the breast cancer gene and is considering a mastectomy. My mind is anywhere but in this room. A heavy lead ball sits in the pit of my stomach. It's Thursday and Joshua won't return my calls. What if he was lying? What if it was a test and I failed? I close my eyes in pain. What was I thinking?

A knock sounds at the door and I stand to answer it. Our receptionist is there.

"Hi Tash," she whispers. "Sorry to bother you but Bridget is on the phone and she said it is a matter of life or death."

I frown as I take the phone from her and put my finger up to the two women in my office, signifying to them I would be one minute. The counsellor smiles and nods and I step just outside the office.

"Hello," I whisper as I look around.

Bridget's panicked voice screams down the phone. "Oh my fuck, Natasha. You need to get over here. We broke into TC's house and then she came home, and we hid in the bedroom and then she left again but she put the deadlock on and now we are trapped in the apartment and we can't get out."

My eyes widen in horror. "What the hell? Who?" "Abbie and I, we were looking for the second disk."

I look at the people around me and duck my head to escape their glare.

"What do you mean you are in her house?" I whisper angrily.

"Get over here now or we are going to jump four stories off the fucking balcony."

"What's the address?" I snap as I feel the stress perspiration start to heat my armpits. "You idiots. We are going to get arrested." Oh my God.

"Get Ben or Max or somebody. The address is 72 Pacific Street, Potts Point."

I walk over to the reception desk and write down the address on the back of a card.

"Ok, I got it." I hang up and knock on the door quietly.

"Sorry, I have an emergency and have to leave urgently." The women both frown. "Is everything ok?" the counsellor asks as she raises her eyebrows.

I smile nervously as I nod too quickly. "Ahuh," I murmur. "It will be." As soon as I kill my two idiot friends. I grab my bag and leave.

I exit my office in a rush and start to run toward the lifts as I dial Max's number. He answers first ring.

"Where are you?" I snap.

"In the carpark. What's wrong?"

"Abbie and Bridget are locked in TC's apartment."

"What?"

"That's what I said. The idiots are locked in her apartment."

"Oh my God. I have to call Ben. Meet me out front."

I run out to the front doors and I find Max on the phone to Ben.

He shakes his head in frustration and hands the phone over to me.

"What's going on?" Ben snaps down the phone.

"I don't know. Bridget called me and said that she and Abbie had broken into TC's apartment looking for the disk."

"How did they know where she lived?"

I shake my head in frustration. "I have no idea. Actually, Abbie's roommate sees her sometimes so she must have asked him."

"Then what happened?"

"She came home, and they hid in the bedroom."

"Fuck," he snaps.

"I know and then she left again but she put the deadlock on

and now they are locked in the apartment and they can't get out."

"Did they find the disk?"

I widen my eyes and hold my hand in the air in frustration. "I didn't bloody ask."

"You stay there. You and Joshua can't be involved. We will handle this. Put Max back on." I hand the phone back to Max.

"Okay." He nods and takes the address from me. "Okay." His eyes meet mine. "I will get her to call him in a minute." He hangs up.

My heart is beating crazily. Breaking and entering, if they get caught...oh my God...this is a criminal offence. What were they thinking?

"Joshua wants you to call him in a minute," Max says dryly, then he texts the address to Ben.

I smile. He wants me to call him, thank God. Relief fills me. "Go back inside. You will only have one guard so do not leave your office."

"But I told them I was leaving for the day," I stammer. "Change your plans. I don't have time to take you home

first." I roll my eyes.

"Can't I come?"

"No, go back inside."

I head back inside and to the cafeteria. I order a coffee and take a seat. My stomach is in knots and I dial Joshua's number. He answers first ring.

"Hi Tash."

My heart swells and tears fill my eyes at the sound of his voice. "Baby," I whisper.

"Are you ok?" he asks.

"No," I sob, "I miss you." He stays silent.

"This is ridiculous, we can't be apart for this long," I stammer.

"I will see you again on Monday, Natasha. I said a week."

"Josh, no. It's only Thursday. I can't wait that long. I feel sick being without you."

"So, you are okay?"

"Just," I murmur. "I love you," I whisper. He stays silent as I hear him inhale deeply.

"Josh, what's wrong?" Panic sets in, why didn't he say it back?

"Nothing. I will see you Monday night, okay?"

My face drops. "Do you love me?" I whisper.

"Don't ask stupid questions," he sighs.

I smile. "I miss you."

"Bye, Presh." He hangs up.

Relief fills me, he called me Presh. It's ok, it's all going to be okay.


## Joshua

It's eight o'clock and I am at a Thai restaurant with the boys discussing the two stooges' breaking and entering today. We are at at table set up in the back corner. Ben had to break the locks to get them out. They were so lucky that they didn't get caught. On the upside, they found a whole case of disks and another laptop. Ben is going to go through them tonight and then destroy them. I wonder how many other poor bastards' films are in that box?

"I still cannot believe they broke into her apartment." Adrian shakes his head in shock.

"I know," Cameron splutters. "Ballsy."

Ben shakes his head. "It would have been imbecile Abbie's idea. She is a bad influence on Bridget."

I smirk at Ben.

"What?" he says dryly as he raises an eyebrow.

"You have a soft spot for Didge, just admit it." I pick my teeth with a toothpick as I lean back with my arm slung across the back of the chairs. He rolls his eyes. "She's a cool chick, that's all."

Cameron shakes his head and glares at him. "I told you not to touch her unless you plan on marrying her."

Ben hold his hands up in defense. "Nobody's touching anybody. Calm down."

I smile as I raise my hand for the bill.

"And nobody is getting married," he snaps. "So, stop worrying."

"Good," Cameron snaps. "I would hate to have to kick your ass."

Ben laughs.

"I would love to see that," Adrian smiles. "Ben would kill you with a smile on his face and his hands tied behind his back." I smile as I listen to the meaningless banter and my mind wanders to Tash. Hearing her tell me she loved me today has somehow made me relax. That and the fact I am so physically exhausted from fighting every motherfucker in Australia over the last two days. Ben knows me well. He knew I needed to kick some serious ass to stay sane, and that is just what I have done. I actually feel sorry for the poor bastards I fought on Tuesday night, I totally lost my shit.

"Let's go out." Cameron stretches as he cranes his neck to eye off one of the waitresses walking past.

"Yeah, ok," Murph replies. "I could do with a drink." Ben's eyes flick to me.

"I'm going to go and see Tash. You go, Ben. There are enough guards over there."

He smiles at me and gives me a wink. "I will drop you off there first."

I smirk. "Ok."


## Natasha

I lie on my lounge half asleep. It's nine o'clock. I am wearing my white nightgown. After a week of not sleeping, I have finally relaxed after speaking to my beautiful Joshua today. He called me Presh. It's going to be ok. I wish he was here. A knock sounds at my door and I smile, thank God he's here. He's forgotten his key. I bound to the door and open it in a rush.

My eyes widen at the sight of Jesten, not my beautiful man as I had hoped.

My face drops. "Hi Jes," I whisper. "What are you doing here?" This is uncomfortable.

"Can I come in?" His nervous eyes lock on mine.

I scratch my head in discomfort. "Umm." I look around nervously for an excuse for him not to enter. Good manners overtake my common sense and I stand back and hold my arm out. "Sure."

He walks in and stands next to my dining table. This is awkward.

"What are you doing here?" I ask gently, even though I already know the answer.

"I know you explained the situation with your boyfriend." "I did." I cut him off. "Loud and clear."

He nods nervously and his eyes search mine. "I want to know if you will reconsider and perhaps, we could..." He hesitates.

"Could what?" I snap.

"Try to make a go of it. Me and you." He grabs my hands. I frown. "Jes, don't."

"Tash, I care about you and when I rang you on Monday night and you told me you got back with your boyfriend I was gutted, and it has made me realize I have real feelings for you." I shake my head.

"Jess, don't. I'm in love with him, it will only ever be him."

He narrows his eyes. "Does this idiot have any idea how lucky he is?" he says softly.

I smile sadly and shrug. "I hope so or else I am making a huge mistake. If there was going to be someone else Jes...it would be you." I gently run my hand down his cheek, and he turns and kisses the inside of my palm.

"We could be good together," he says softly.

"I know," I whisper. "But it's not going to happen, I'm sorry." He steps forward and pulls me into an embrace and cuddles me, his lips dust my temple. "There is a chemistry between us, can you feel it?" he whispers into my forehead.

My eyes widen as I feel his arousal against my body. I do feel the chemistry. It has never been in question. "Jes, don't," I whisper into his neck. He puts his finger under my chin and pulls it up to meet his face, and he kisses me gently. "Jes," I whisper. He kisses me again, running his tongue through my lips more urgently and my hands rise to the back of his neck.

The key turns in the door and I jump back from Jesten in a rush. Holy shit.

Joshua opens the door and does a double take between Jesten and me. His eyes drop down my body to my nightgown.

"What the fuck are you doing here?" he growls at Jesten. My eyes widen in horror. OH. MY. GOD.

"You," Jesten snaps. "This is your boyfriend?" he screams at me.

Joshua storms into the apartment and punches Jesten straight in the face and he drops to the ground and I scream.

"Joshua! What the hell?" Holy shit!

He picks him up off the floor and they start to punch each other and Joshua throws him across the table and the vase of flowers smashes everywhere.

"I swear to God I am going to tear you from limb to limb!" Joshua screams.

I have never seen Joshua so crazy. He's going ballistic and throwing Jesten around like a rag doll. I think he's going to kill him.

"This is the fucking guy?" Joshua screams at me.

I shake my head as I burst into tears. He thinks I slept with Jesten. I can't believe I even contemplated it. What in the hell is the matter with me?

"You know I hate him. How could you?" Joshua is so mad that he looks like the incredible hulk and is scaring even me.

"No, no, no." I shake my head violently. What the hell have I done?

"She loved every minute of it," Jesten baits. My eyes widen in horror. Not now Jesten, you are going to get yourself killed.

Joshua punches him violently again three times in succession. "Joshua!" I scream. "Stop it!"

Jesten fights back and kicks Joshua in the stomach and they roll until the lounge tips over. Oh shit, this is really bad. I run to the front door and open it in a rush.

"Get in here," I scream to the guards who are all standing around listening, obviously letting Joshua kill Jesten on purpose.

"Max," I scream as I turn to see Joshua throw Jesten over his shoulder. "Joshua no. Stop it!" Oh my God, he's going to kill him. "I will get a knife and cut your fucking throat," Joshua screams as he smashes Jesten's head on the ground.

Ok, he's getting unstable and the stupid bodyguards are just standing around watching. I run down the hall and bang on Max's door. Max opens the door in a rush. His eyes widen when he sees me. "What's wrong?" A smash comes from the apartment and he frowns and runs past me into my apartment.

"Jesus," he yells. "What are you idiots doing? Stop this immediately."

The guards finally step in and break them up and start to drag Jesten from the apartment.

"I'm not leaving her here with this psychopath," Jesten yells at Max.

Max's nervous eyes flick to me and I think he agrees with Jesten. "I'm ok. He won't hurt me," I whisper.

"Tash, come with me," Jesten pleads.

My terrified eyes meet Joshua's. "It's ok, Josh, calm down, baby." I walk slowly over to him as he sucks precious air into his lungs. He's furious. He thinks I slept with Jesten. I slowly slide my hand up his perspiration clad arm as his dark eyes meet mine.

"Sshhh," I whisper to try and calm him. "Goodbye, Jesten," I snap, "Max show him out."

The guards leave the room, and I am left with my broken wild animal.

"Sshhh, it's ok, baby," I whisper. "He's gone."

# CHAPTER 30

**Natasha**

MAX STANDS in the doorway watching us. Joshua has his hands on his head and is breathing heavily, his eyes are downcast and unable to meet mine. I stand in front of him, my heart breaking. This looks bad, I am in my nightdress, it's nine o'clock at night and Jesten was here. Could he tell when he opened the door that I had just pulled from Jesten's grip? I would have lost it too had I walked in on this. I will never forgive Jesten for saying I loved it, what a trouble making asshole.

My eyes flick to Max who is still standing at the door, ensuring my safety no doubt. The worry is written all over his face.

"It's ok, Max, can you give us some privacy, please?" I murmur as my eyes stay planted on Joshua's broken face.

"Are you sure?" he questions.

"Fucking get out!" Joshua screams as he loses control once again.

I nod nervously to Max and mouth the words, "Go."

Max holds my glare and lifts an eyebrow in silent question. I give him a nod and he leaves silently.

Joshua is still gasping for breath.

"Baby," I whisper as I grab his face between my hands gently. "I swear on my mother's life I did not sleep with him." His eyes still look at the ground.

"Joshua, I went to the hotel the other night to make you think I had done it, I knew the guards would tell you, but I didn't have any intention of going through with it. It's only you, Joshua, it's only ever been you."

His angry eyes meet mine.

I shake my head nervously as tears of guilt fill my eyes. His glare holds mine. "How long?'

I frown, not understanding the question. "What do you mean?"

"How long have you wanted him?"

My eyes widen in shock as I understand the question. "I haven't wanted him, we are friends," I whisper, mortified.

Joshua raises an eyebrow in disgust. "Do not insult my fucking intelligence!" he yells, making me jump.

I swallow the lump of fear in my throat and drop my head. "Nothing has ever happened," I whisper.

"When he told you to think of him while we had sex, is that what you have been doing all along?"

My mouth drops open in horror. "Oh my God, no, how could you think such a thing? I have only gotten to know him in the last six months and we are just friends."

"A friend you are attracted to."

I nod softly. "Yes," I whisper as shame rips through my stomach and the tears fall onto my cheeks.

"He said you loved it." He runs his tongue over his front teeth in contempt as his eyes bore holes through me.

"I know and I am never speaking to him again for lying to you like that. He's baiting you, Joshua, and you took it hook, line and sinker. Nothing has ever happened between us, I promise," I cry.

He pulls out of my grip and storms to the shower and I run after him like a lost lamb.

"Don't be angry at me," I plead.

He undresses in silence and steps into the shower.

"You are the one who wanted me to do this and I couldn't do it!" I yell.

He turns his back on me in anger.

I start to slowly undress and step in with him.

"Josh, he turned up here tonight to ask me on a date. I said no and he was just leaving when you arrived."

He turns and his haunted eyes meet mine as the water runs over our heads.

"Baby." The pain in his eyes rips my heart wide open. I rub my hand through his stubble and go onto my tiptoes to gently kiss his lips. "I love you so much."

He drops his head to my shoulder, and I can feel his hurt. I know how it feels to have dark suspicions, it hurts.

We stand for a long time in an embrace, both lost in our own thoughts, with the water running over us. Eventually he lifts my chin up to meet his face, and his lips gently take mine.

I nod softly. "I get it, Josh...I finally get it. What you have been telling me all along. Sex is sex and love is love."

He kisses me tenderly again and his tongue swipes through my open mouth.

"For the first time I understand why you slept with Amelie," I sob loudly as tears rack my chest.

He pulls back and frowns.

"I understand when I wouldn't forgive you how much that must have hurt."

"It damn near killed me," he whispers as he drops his head to my shoulder.

I shake my head as the raw burn of pain sears my heart. I can't imagine the pain of sleeping with someone different and living with that guilt forever. Of losing the one that you really do love for a lifetime in the name of fifteen minutes of sex.

I pull his face back to mine. "Joshua, I love you desperately. Our life together starts tonight, right now." I smile and nod. "We are going to live in LA." I kiss him gently. "We are going to be so happy." I smile into his kiss as I feel his resistance melt. "We are too strong to be broken...we have proven that...time and again."

He kisses me more firmly as our passion starts to reignite. "Take me," I whisper into his mouth. "Show me how much I mean to you." My eyes drop to the large erection hanging heavily between his legs. I can see every wide vein on it pumping with arousal, waiting to give my body what it needs, to finally fill me totally.

He groans and slams me into the wall as his hand grips me painfully on the behind. His mouth drops to my neck and he bites me aggressively, and goosebumps scatter over my flesh. This is when we are at our best, our bodies so in sync with each other's that we couldn't stop this animal attraction even if we tried. This is love in its deepest form. He lifts me aggressively and holds me with my legs around his waist and he slams into me. His mouth hangs slack as his hooded eyes watch me struggle to take his thick large length. I can feel his heart beating through his chest as he struggles to hold himself still to let me adjust.

I cry out as his flesh rips through me and heats my blood, and my head drops back against the tiles in both pleasure and pain as my eyes close.

With our lips locked he lifts my body up and down onto his, slowly at first to let me acclimatize, and then with each stroke more deeply, each with more feeling than the last until I am screaming as he plunges deeply into me with his powerful body. My arms grip his ripped shoulders as I struggle for breath, my eyes close as I feel every muscle inside me contract against his brutal length. He bites my bottom lip and pulls it back in an aggressive yet unbridled passionate gesture that makes me lose my mind even more.

I have never loved this man more. He sacrificed his own needs to give me mine and even though in the end I didn't want what was offered, he gave me a choice. I will forever be grateful for what he has shown me about intimacy this week.

His love truly is unconditional, and I finally understand the Amelie thing. My heart breaks a little knowing what I have put him through. His hands come around my back and over my shoulders as he rips me down onto his body with such force that I start to lose my breath. His eyes close as he rides the wave of pleasure that has started to envelope us. My body convulses as I scream and lurch forward and he does the same. He grabs the wall behind me to balance us as his orgasm steals his balance. He shudders heavily as his body empties and I feel his hot semen burn deep inside my body. I sigh into his shoulder as he lets my legs slowly drop to the floor. He grabs my face and rips it to his.

"Do you get it? Tell me you get it! Do you finally understand how much I fucking love you?" he snaps.

My eyes tear over and I nod gratefully. "For the first time... Joshua, I can honestly say...yes."

. . .

I WAKE to the gentle dusting of kisses across my face, and he gently tucks my hair behind my ear. I smile with my eyes still closed. It is blazing light, we must have forgotten to shut the drapes last night. Beautiful gentle Josh is here, I can feel his presence and I haven't even opened my eyes yet. I slowly bring my hand around the back of his head and pull him into me.

"Good morning," I whisper into the top of his head as I kiss it.

"Are you ok?" he whispers into my chest.

"Mmm," I reply with my eyes still closed, but to be honest I just don't know. I have a serious throb between my legs and for once it's not from arousal. Rough sex for hours on end will do that to a girl.

I begin to get up. I need to go to the bathroom.

"Stay here with me, Presh. You are not leaving my side today." He smiles as he kisses me gently again.

"Josh, I need to go to the bathroom. I will be right back." I kiss him gently as I rise from the bed. His eyes scan down my body and he frowns.

"What?" I ask as I look down at myself.

He reaches up and runs his fingers over the four bruises on my right hipbone.

I frown. "What are those bruises from?"

His face drops at the realization. "My fingers."

I turn and look at myself in the mirror as I put my hair behind my shoulders, and I smirk. "I have the same four bruises on my left shoulder too."

His eyes widen in horror.

"That was some hold you had on me from behind when I was on my knees. No wonder I'm sore."

He looks down at the bed. "I'm sorry. I lost my head." My eyes hold his. "What was that? Round three?"

He swallows and nods, daring me with his eyes to say something.

"That wasn't sex, Joshua." "What was it?" he whispers.

"That was a claiming. You were showing me who my body belongs to."

He raises an eyebrow in silent disapproval. "And was the message understood?" he says coldly.

A frisson of unease runs through me and I nod. "Loud and clear, Mr. Stanton...loud and clear."


"So, did you give your notice?" Joshua asks as he drinks his protein shake while sitting on the counter as I cook.

"Aha." I pour the vegetables into the wok off the chopping board.

"One week?" he asks.

"No, I told you I have to give two."

"We are leaving in a week," he snaps.

I roll my eyes. "Listen." I point the wooden spoon at him. "I am moving to the other side of the world and I have things to tie up. I can't just leave in seven days."

"Like what?"

I raise my eyebrows. "Like my mother, like my apartment, like the two best friends I am leaving behind."

He swigs his drink angrily.

"I was thinking we might move to Willowvale when we get home," he replies.

I turn and frown. "What? Out in the country...with the horses?" Is he kidding?

He nods matter of factly and swigs more protein. I shake my

head. "No."

He frowns. "What do you mean no?" I widen my eyes at him. "No, I am not moving to the country. I want to live near Adrian, and I want to party...in LA."

He narrows his eyes at me. "Party?" he questions, affronted.

I nod. "Aha, I'm only twenty-five, Joshua. I can think of nothing worse than being locked up on a farm while you ride around on frigging horses like Captain America."

"Captain America doesn't ride a horse," he mutters. I roll my eyes in response. "I'm sure he did," I snap.

"We are moving to LA, you are buying me a new house and then when we are old and have two..." I hold up two of my fingers to accentuate my point, "two children, I will move to Willowvale...and not a moment before."

He narrows his eyes again. "Listen here...you will leave when I damn well say and if you think you are moving to LA to run amok you have another thing coming. I won't stand for it. And we are having six children!"

I walk over to him and smile as I rub my hand over his penis through his suit pants. He closes his eyes and leans back to give me access.

"You know, Joshua baby," I whisper as I smile into his neck.

"Hmm," he smiles.

"I can be very persuasive when I want to be." I smile and lick my lips as I unzip his suit pants. He lies back onto the counter on his elbows, and his eyes watch my mouth intently.

"Hmm," he sighs.

I slowly slide his pants down and give him one long lick up the length of his shaft. "You see, I know I have something that you need, and I'm prepared to bargain with it to get my own way," I whisper as I smile and lick him again.

He smirks. "Bitch," he whispers.

There is a knock at the door and Joshua jumps up in a start. "Piss off," he snaps.

I smile as I lick my lips and head for the door as Joshua straightens himself up in the kitchen.

I open the door in a rush to see Ben talking to two men in the hallway.

They turn to me and hand me a business card. I smile in question. "Hello."

Ben looks at me uncomfortably. "Natasha, these are police officers. They need to talk to you and Joshua."

I frown. "Is something wrong?"

They look at each other and then at me. "Can we come in, please?"

I frown and Joshua walks up behind me and puts his hand out to shake theirs. "Joshua Stanton."

"Can we come in Mr. Stanton?" the officer asks.

He opens the door and holds out his arm. "Of course."

The officers walk in and Ben follows them. They all sit on the lounge.

"What's this about?" he asks as they take a seat.

One of the officers hands Joshua a photo and he looks at it and frowns.

"Is this the woman who has been blackmailing you?" the officer asks.

Joshua's eyes drop to the photo. "Yes," he answers. "I've been through this." He passes the photo to me. Stupid bitch's face is staring at me in a mug shot. It looks as though it is a few years old. She is a brunette. My stomach rolls. God, I hate that dirty whore.

Shit! Abbie and Bridget are busted, their names should officially be changed to Dumb and Dumber. Who breaks into a house and then gets locked in there? I rub my forehead as nerves start to pump through me. If he asks me outright did they do it, what will I say? I can't rat out my two best friends. Joshua must be able to sense my nerves and grabs my hand reassuringly. Ben stands to the side uncomfortably.

"Have you found her?" Ben asks.

"I'm afraid we have."

I swallow uncomfortably. Oh shit, here it comes. Did your two stupid friends break into her house? I drop my eyes. I can't lie for shit.

"She was found dead this morning," the officer says. The room falls silent. Oh my God.

"Why are you telling me this?" Joshua snaps.

"You are, of course, a suspect, both of you." He gestures to me. My eyes widen in horror.

"We have been to her place and we have ten sets of different fingerprints from her apartment and we are analyzing them now."

My stomach drops again. Oh my God, the girls' fingerprints are all over that place.

My horrified eyes meet Ben's and he subtly shakes his head in a knowing gesture to tell me to hold it together.

"I'm sure she was blackmailing about ten different men," Joshua snaps.

"She was and you are not the only man or wife in question.

We are actually more interested in you, Ben."

Joshua's face drops. "Why are you interested in Ben?"

"He is a person of interest."

"What? That's ridiculous!" Joshua snaps as he stands in a rush. "We have been doing a little research on you, Ben. Ex special forces."

"Yes," Ben answers flatly.

"How much does Mr. Stanton pay you per annum?" Ben's eyes flick to Joshua. Shit, what is going on here?

"That's none of your business. Get out. I will not allow you to speak to him without a lawyer. How dare you insinuate he had anything to do with this?" Joshua snaps as he dials a number on his phone.

"Murph, get over here." He hangs up. My eyes widen as I sit riveted to the spot.

"Two million dollars a year, Ben, what kind of security do you get for that?" the policeman sneers. Shit, Ben gets paid two million dollars a year? That's a lot of money.

"That is none of your business!" Joshua snaps. "Of course, he gets paid well, I am a billionaire, and he is my chief of security. Do you think I would pay him peanuts?"

"I imagine two million dollars would buy you some hard-core loyalty."

Ben shakes his head calmly. "Check the security footage. I have been in this building and at Joshua's workplace at all times. I have nothing to hide."

"Did you hire a hitman, Mr. Stanton? You could definitely afford it." Joshua screws up his face.

"No, I did not hire a hitman," he snaps.

"She probably overdosed."

The officer shakes his head. "No, she was found in the dockyard hog tied with a gunshot wound to the back of the head."

My eyes widen even further. Crap...this is bad. Oh my God, what if the girls are implicated in this?

"Leave, please," Joshua snaps. "My staff and I have nothing to do with this and unless you are going to arrest us or let us have a lawyer present, we have nothing further to say."

They exchange glances and pass a business card to Joshua. "If you think of anything please let us know."

"I will," Joshua sighs as he stands. Ben leaves with the officers to show them out.

The door closes behind them and I turn to Joshua in a rush. "Oh my God, what if the girls are implicated in this?"

Joshua looks at me grimly. "Why did they break in there anyway?" he snaps. "What were they thinking?" He shakes his head. "What are they, Starsky and Hutch now?"

I put my hands over my face. "Oh my God, oh my God, oh my God."

"Calm down." He takes out his phone and dials a number. "Where are you?" he snaps. "Hurry up." He hangs up and

storms to the kitchen and flicks the jug. "This is a fucking disaster."

"I know, right, their names should be Dumb and Dumber." I shake my head with my hands on my temples.

He smirks. "That's a fitting title."

I glare at him. "Well deserved," I snap.

I go to my bag and start rattling through it.

"What are you looking for?" he asks.

"My phone."

"It's here on the counter."

I quickly dial Abbie's number. "Hi, Abbs." "Hi chick." She says cheerfully.

"You need to get over here immediately." "I'm at work, what's up?"

"TC has just been found dead and your and Bridget's fingerprints are all over her place."

She goes silent. "Did you hear me?" "Shit," she whispers. "On my way."

## Adrian

I sit at my desk, deep in thought. This whole blackmail thing is totally out of control and now the stupid girls have gotten involved, it could bring us all undone. I have to ask the question, it's been playing on my mind. Yet, do I really want to know the answer? Ben and Joshua walk in and take a seat at the desk.

"What's up?" Joshua asks.

"You know I love you guys, right?" I sigh. Joshua frowns in a question.

"I have to ask this. Did you two have anything to do with that hooker's death?"

Ben and Joshua look at each other and then back at me. "No," they both reply.

My eyes hold theirs. "Did you think about it?" They look at each other again.

"Maybe," Joshua replies.

I put my hand over my mouth and close my eyes. I knew it. "We would never have actually done it," Ben replies. "It was just a thought."

"Have you two gone totally insane? Why would you even think that?"

Joshua shrugs. "I told you I would do anything to keep the tape from Natasha."

I shake my head. "Ben, will you please start thinking for Joshua because where Natasha is concerned, he does not have one brain cell."

They both smile. "We have clearance to leave Australia. It came through this morning," Ben replies. "I know you don't want this, Joshua, but Abbie and Bridget will have to come back to LA with us until they catch who did this."

506

Joshua shakes his head in frustration. "They will not be fingerprinted here."

Ben shakes his head. "And what if they are and convicted of murder when they were only trying to help you out? How will you feel then?"

"Idiots," Joshua snaps.

I smile broadly. "What's wrong, Stan? Are the girls going to crash the slumber party you have planned?"

He narrows his eyes. "They are actually," he murmurs.

"What if they won't go?" I ask.

"I'm not giving them a choice," Ben replies. "This isn't a joke, this is serious now. They have put us all under a cloud."

Joshua shakes his head in disgust. "Let them know."

## Natasha

Joshua lies on my bed as I pack the last of my wardrobe. "Why are you bothering packing everything anyway? Just buy new things when you get there."

I look at him deadpan. "Is that what you do?"

He shrugs. "I have a full wardrobe at Willowvale and one for LA. That way I don't need to pack when I go."

"So, will I wear my jodhpurs in LA?" I ask a little too sweetly as I bat my eyelids.

"You do know that you are learning to ride," he replies matter of factly.

I raise my eyebrows. "Pff, as if." I continue folding. "I hate horses...and vets. I really hate vets with a passion." I widen my eyes to accentuate my point.

He quickly scrambles to change the subject. "I'm glad your mother is coming over in a month."

My heart drops. "I'm more worried about Mum more than

ever. At least before she had Bridget and Abbie to keep her company but now that they are coming, she will be left here alone." I keep folding the clothes and putting them in the suitcase.

He smiles sadly. "She can come too. I told you that."

"She won't. I've been trying to persuade her all week." I sigh. I blow out a breath and walk back into the closet.

"Hurry up. I'm hungry," Joshua calls.

I stick my head out of the closet. "Well, go and make us dinner, dick." Who is he kidding...*hurry up. I'm hungry.*

"I meant so we can go out for dinner. There is no food in the house."

I stick my head back out of the closet. "Joshua, we leave tomorrow. I am not going out for dinner tonight."

He shakes his head. "Looks like you are done to me."

I smile. "No, can you go and get my diaries from the shoebox and put them in this bag." I put a large tote on my bed and open my bedside table drawer as Joshua walks into the wardrobe. My heart stops as my eyes look into the drawer.

"Joshua," I call. "Yeah," he answers.

"Have you packed my things?"

"No," he replies. "What things?"

"Can you come here, baby?"

My heart starts to thump through my chest as I am gripped by fear and my eyes dart around the room. "Someone has been in here."

He frowns and walks over to see what I am looking at in the drawer.

My pink vibrator sits in an empty drawer, but my underwear is gone.

"Oh my God, he's been here. He has been in here."

Joshua frowns again at the drawer. "Are you sure it was ever gone?"

"Where is my underwear Joshua?" I yell as I grab my head in a panic. I run from the room to get my phone.

"Who are you calling?" Joshua snaps as he senses my panic. "Max," I spit out.

He takes his phone out and rings Ben.

"Can you get up here, please? We have a situation."

# CHAPTER 31

**Natasha**

I SIT on the plane next to Adrian on the flight into Phuket. Joshua has insisted we come here for a week on the way to LA. Apparently this is one of the only places on Earth that he can relax, and I can't wait to see it. I watch him silently as he plays cards with Abbie and Cameron. He didn't sleep last night. He, Max and Ben were up watching security tapes all night. My apartment was broken into yesterday by someone. I never imagined it, who would want to do this? It doesn't make sense. The motive for scaring the hell out of me is still unknown, and Joshua was frantic. I have never been so glad to get on a plane as I was today.

TC's murder, Coby Allender, the serial killer, Margaret Stanton and her ultimate betrayal, I can't wait to get the hell out of here. Joshua's uninhibited laughter echoes through the cabin, and I smile broadly at their interactions. He changed out of his suit two hours into the flight and since then the real beautiful Josh has come to visit. What must it be like to be him and under so much scrutiny all the time? What is comforting though is the fact that he is finally being himself around the girls. I suppose he realizes they are going to be around more than he previously thought and has finally let his guard down. Bridget is up the back of the plane talking to Ben and the other guards and Adrian has come down to sit with me. Abbie is getting her ass kicked at poker.

"They're cheating." Adrian smiles. I frown. "Who?"

"Joshua has been teaching Cam to count cards." He smirks. My mouth drops open. "Joshua knows how to count cards?" He raises his eyebrows and smiles. "Ahuh."

I narrow my eyes. "What must it be like to be that intelligent, Adrian?" I sigh.

He smiles sadly. "I imagine lonely, Cinderella."

My face drops. "Lonely?" I question.

"Joshua's insides don't match his outsides."

"What do you mean?" I ask.

"Look at him." He gestures and my eyes flick to my beautiful man, laughing freely as he plays, and I smile broadly.

"He looks like a movie star, so people expect him to be stupid, so then a lot of people annoy him because of their lack of intelligence. The people who are like him on the inside are computer geeks who have hardly any life experience because they have been on their computers or gaming for most of their life." He sighs. "He's between two worlds and that's why the paparazzi have so much interest in him. He doesn't fit the bill, he's not normal." He smiles.

I frown. "Is that why he spends so much time with you and Cam?"

He smiles. "Yes, I think so." He shrugs. "Cam is his brother and I am so close that I'm like his brother; he feels comfortable with us. He can be himself."

I smile as my eyes flick to Joshua again. "Did you think we were going to make it, Adrian?" I ask.

He smiles and takes my hand in his. "I hoped so, that's a big fucking tattoo."

A giggle bubbles up and I sigh, I am one lucky bitch. "Tell me about where we are going. Why does he love it so much?" Excitement starts to fill me at the life we are going to live together, and the future we have.

He smiles and puts his head back into the seat rest.

"Joshua owns four adjoining properties on the cliff of Kamala Beach in Phuket."

I lean back and he fiddles with my fingers that he still has in his hand.

"Joshua is himself there, no cameras, no girls, no bodyguards. Just Josh."

I raise my eyebrows. "No girls?"

He shakes his head. "I usually stay with Joshua in Kamala and Cameron and Ben each get their own house."

I smile wistfully. "Why do neither of you hook up there?" He shrugs. "We just don't. I don't know why. Cameron and Ben have a thing for Thai girls and that's why they get their own houses. Joshua and I just relax. We read, drink cocktails, go to the beach and swim. I don't know, it's just the way it has always been. We spend a lot of time there."

"How much time?" I ask.

He shrugs. "Up to eight weeks a year."

I frown. "Really? That's a lot of time."

"I think if Joshua could have his horses there that is where he would live permanently."

I smile as I listen.

"Are you ok?" I ask as I kiss the back of his hand.

He smiles sadly. "Not sure really, I thought Nicholas was different. I'm hurt."

My face drops. "I think he's still different, Adrian. It can't be easy to lose a husband. It is a natural progression to moving on, the guilt thing."

He nods. "He pursued me, Tash, and then when he found that there was really love between us, he told me he's guilty for feeling like this when his husband is dead." He shakes his head. "I should have known that the story wasn't going to end happily.

In fact, I did know and that is why I resisted him for so long." He sighs and I kiss the back of his hand again sympathetically.

"I'm sure it will work out. Look at Joshua and me, we have been to hell and back. Love always wins in the end, Adrian, I honestly believe that."

He widens his eyes at me in jest. "Yes, but your name is Cinderella, and you are living in a fairy tale with Prince Charming." He laughs.

"Prince Lamborghini you mean." I giggle and he laughs out loud.

"Prepare for landing." The voice sounds over the intercom.

Joshua leans over the back of our seats and I turn. How long has he been listening to our conversation? He gives me a wink and I know he has overheard what has been said.

Adrian stands and goes back to his seat and Joshua slumps back into the seat next to me.

He bends over and does up my seatbelt. "Are you ready to start our new life together, my precious girl?" he says gently.

My heart melts. "I am," I whisper.

"Do you know how adored you are?" he whispers as he bends and kisses me gently on the lips and I swoon at his feet.

"I do," I smile into his kiss.

"Do you know how loved you are, Joshua Stanton?" I breathe into his lips.

"I do," he replies softly.

He pulls back and looks at me and the emotion in his eyes brings goosebumps to my skin. I don't remember the plane landing. I just remember two hands on my cheeks and the beautiful intimate kissing from my beautiful Lamborghini.


FINALLY, I can relax.

We walk out onto the pool deck in Ben's and Adrian's house where breakfast is being served and I laugh as I see everyone. They all cheer at our arrival. It's been a massive week here in Thailand. My whole life has changed.

"You all look like shit." I giggle.

"Shut up," Bridget sighs.

Adrian lifts his head from his hands. "Where did you two disappear to last night?" he asks.

"We went to celebrate alone." Joshua smiles as he picks up my hand and kisses the back of it. My cheeks heat, celebrate we did.

"Where's Cameron?" I ask.

"In the kitchen," Ben replies.

Joshua and I walk into the house and into the kitchen to see Cam.

He is on the phone and his anxiety is obvious. Joshua frowns as he listens. Cameron hangs up the phone and drops his head into his hands.

I frown at Joshua in question. He shrugs. "What's up, mate?" Joshua asks quietly.

Cameron's haunted eyes meet his.

"The blood tests came back," he whispers.

"And?" Joshua replies.

"I'm not a Stanton," Cameron whispers.

*Continue reading for a sneak peek into the next book on Natasha & Joshua's story, Stanton Completely...*

# STANTON COMPLETELY EXCERPT

## AVAILABLE NOW

**Natasha**

**Seven days earlier**

*LIGHT BULB MOMENTS*

In what state does the subconscious mind need to be for one to be able to experience an awakening like this?

Is it the conscious mind? Does it need to be openly receptive to the information it had before? And why now? Why does this make sense only now? Why does it seem *so* real that it can't possibly be true?

I knew Joshua Stanton was wealthy. The houses, the lifestyle, the security.

Why the hell am I sitting here dumbstruck, peering out of the car like a child in a chocolate factory movie?

My name is Natasha Marx, I have thirty million dollars in my bank account.

I am in love with a billionaire.
And my life will never be the same.

The car slowly pulls into the driveway and tall black metal gates block the entrance. We are at the Kamala house in Thailand. The driver enters a code into the pin pad, and I watch them slowly open. My stomach drops at the sight of the huge stone fence surrounding the property and Joshua picks up my hand and kisses it as he smirks at my bewildered face.

"This is it? This is your house?" I ask. "Yes." He smiles softly.

Holy crap. The large lawn is at street level, but I can see it drops off to a cliff at the back of the property, and cobblestones line the driveway which winds its way through the tropical oasis. I can't see what's ahead and I crane my neck as excitement fills me. We drive past a waterfall, through the gardens to a circular bay.

"This is your house?" I repeat again as I frown. The main house is in front of us with driveways to the other houses on the property veering off to the side.

He leans over and kisses me gently as if sensing my inner freak-out mode. The car comes to a stop and parks in the covered area and other cars pull in behind us. My eyes explore the opulence surrounding me.

"Holy shit!" Abbie yells and I smile as I nod my head in agreement.

"Is this a house?" Bridget gasps. My God, I did not expect this. I expected a holiday shack on the hill, this is over the top frigging...I don't even know what...ridiculously extravagant money. Five men in traditional Thai dress come out of the house to the left, stand in a line and then simultaneously put their hands together, as if to pray, and bow.

"*Sawatdee Krap*" Joshua smiles as he and the boys bow their heads in reply. Oh shit, I didn't know about the bowing head and my eyes flick around to the others and I quickly bow my head to try not to be rude.

"*Sawatdee Krap*, Joshua," they all say and then burst into conversation.

Joshua and Cameron instantly reply in fluent Thai. Joshua then turns and pulls me by the hand to the front of the men.

"This is Natasha." He smiles as he picks up my hand and kisses it. They all smile and laugh at something he has said and then bow their head at me again. What...he can speak Thai? Oh jeez, I'm so punching above my weight here. Joshua smiles warmly. "Boys, can you show the girls to their house?" He grabs my hand and pulls me up the steps towards the house through two oversized carved timber doors.

"Oh my God!" I hear the girls scream excitedly as they disappear up the path to go next door and I shake my head in disbelief as Joshua pulls me into the house.

"Joshua," I whisper as I stop dead in my tracks.

"Welcome to our home, my precious girl." He bends and kisses me gently.

I'm overwhelmed, this is bullshit. High carved timber cathedral ceilings adorn the large room, the walls are rendered in a cream color, and dark timber floors are throughout. A wall of glass looks out to sea over the massive infinity pool and the backyards of the four properties are fenced individually for privacy. An island in the middle of the pool has a circular cabana, a thatched roof and lounge chairs are surrounding a fire pit. My eyes flick to Joshua. This is a visual sensation if ever I saw one.

"Are you serious?" I raise my eyebrows in question.

"Do you like it?" he asks.

I frown. "Ahuh," I whisper as I put my hands on top of my

head. I walk through the room and around to the left to an extravagant kitchen with every luxury appliance known to man. In front of it is a sixteen-seat dining table.

"How have you been happy to stay stuck in my tiny dump for the last month?" I frown. "This kitchen and dining area is the size of my whole apartment." I shake my head in disbelief.

He pulls me into an embrace. "I love your apartment. I feel more at home there than I do in my own home," he whispers into my forehead. "Money doesn't make you happy, Natasha, I know that firsthand."

We continue up the hall and through another set of double doors and my stomach drops. Dear God. A huge all white bedroom with a massive four poster bed in the center, fine white mosquito netting adorning it, and with yet another glass wall looking out to sea.

I burst out laughing. "This is the fucking bedroom?" I gasp. "Are you serious?"

He smiles broadly. "Look around while I go and get our bags." He leaves and I walk over to the window and put my hand on the glass as I stare out to sea. This place is unbelievable. Over to the left is another set of doors. I investigate and my eyes widen again. A white marble bathroom with a ridiculously large white stone bath sits in the center with a triple shower to the right. Bloody hell, Joshua Stanton, you are a mind fuck. I walk back out to the bedroom and run my hand up the beautiful thick timber of the post on the bed and stare up at the delicate netting. This is the most beautiful place I have ever been in. Stupid crazy rich. My eyes roam over to the bedside table and my heart stops...tears instantly fill my eyes. One lone white photo frame sits on the side table, a photo of Joshua and me. A selfie that he took of us on the beach one day all those years ago. We look so young. I am laughing at the camera and he is kissing my cheek. We look so happy...so in love. I have never seen this photo before, and I instantly pick it up as a lump of emotion forms in my throat. I turn to see Joshua standing in the doorway watching me silently.

"I love you," I whisper.

He nods as his eyes search mine.

"I'm so sorry," I whisper. How could I have put him through all this nonsense?

He nods again, unwilling to speak. "I'm here now." I smile softly.

He nods again.

"I'm not leaving again, I promise you," I whisper.

He drops the bags and rushes to me, burying his head into my shoulder and I smile. I've died and gone to heaven. I am in the most beautiful place on earth with the most beautiful man on earth. And he loves me, he's always loved me.

"The wait is going to be worth it, baby." I smile into the top of his head. "I am going to make you so happy." I start to shower his forehead with kisses.

He pulls back to look at me with darkened eyes. "Good." He smirks.

I smile broadly. "Good?' I question.

He smiles and nods again. "Because I am about ten minutes away from blowing in your mouth, my beautiful slut."

I laugh out loud and run into the bathroom. "You will have to catch me first," I squeal.

"One-way ticket," he growls as he runs into the bathroom and tackles me so that I fall onto the huge mat on the floor.

"You're going to pound town."

The flicker of the flames shadows my face as I stare into the fire. It's 10 pm and we are sitting outside on the lounge chairs surrounding the fire pit. Joshua showed me around this afternoon. This place is beyond heavenly. We went to the beach for a swim and his chef has just cooked us an amazing dinner. The others have headed off out on the town for a night of partying. I could think of nothing worse. How times change, I smile to myself. I am seated on one end of the long sofa with my feet up on the ottoman and Joshua has his head on my lap and is fast asleep. He's exhausted. He didn't sleep last night because of the break-in at my apartment.

I run my fingers continually over the top of his head and down his arm as I sit deep in thought watching the flames flicker. Who broke into my apartment? And what was the significance of my vibrator? I know I should believe that it's Coby Allender, but I don't. I think that was just a stupid coincidence that he mentioned it. It has something to do with Joshua, but what? My mind goes back to when it was taken, when was that? I rub my forehead as I think. It was when he came back to Australia and we were breaking up, not long after the hit on him. What was that hit about anyway? Was it an attempted hit or just a scare tactic? Somebody is trying to scare us. You don't steal a vibrator in a robbery and then return it unless you are specifically trying to scare the shit out of someone. It worked. I had the first nightmare I have had in weeks last night.

I run my hands over the top of Joshua's head as he sleeps on my lap. He's different here. The security has been dismissed. Max is staying in the last house on the block with the other guards and he has chosen not to go out tonight, although Joshua wouldn't have cared if he had wanted to. It's weird having all this privacy. My mind goes to Margaret and the horrible secret I am keeping. What a nightmare that situation is. Now that I know how Joshua has felt about me all along, I am riddled with guilt. He doesn't deserve to be deceived by the two people he cares about the most. I'm as bad as Margaret and I make myself sick. I've made the decision to tell him as soon as we get back to LA. It's going to be hard, but I have to do it because this guilt is eating me alive.

Joshua stirs, slowly wakes and sleepily smiles up at me. The honesty in his eyes cuts through me like a knife.

"Time for bed?" I smile softly.

He nods as he slowly stands. "Bedtime, Presh," he murmurs huskily as he grabs my hand and leads me to our bedroom. "I will be asleep before I hit the pillow," he sighs.

"Same," I murmur, but my mind is far from a restful sleep. I'm preoccupied with betrayal and paternity and vibrator stealing thieves and wondering if the man I love more than life itself will ever forgive me for keeping this secret and deceiving him.

It's our second morning in Kamala, the boys are in the gym at the end house and the girls and I are making breakfast. Actually, let me rephrase that. *I* am making Spanish Omelette while the lazy girls watch. Abbie is lying on the kitchen bench and Didge is sitting on a stool at the kitchen island. Apparently, they went to a karaoke bar last night and embarrassed themselves. What a surprise.

"I saw you on the dance floor, Bridget. Don't try and deny it." Abbie raises her eyebrows in question.

I look up from the frying pan. "Saw what?" I ask.

"Ben and Bridget had a moment." "Did not!" Bridget snaps.

I frown as I continue to flip the omelette. "Do you like him, Didge? You can tell me you know, I don't care."

Bridget bites her bottom lip as she thinks and shrugs her shoulders. "Not really," she mutters under her breath.

"Oh, please." Abbie rolls her eyes. "You are so into him."

"He's just a nice guy that's all. I like spending time with him but it's not romantically charged."

"Oh my fuck, did you just say it's not romantically charged?" Abbie frowns in horror.

I smile broadly and Bridget shakes her head as she smirks. "It's sexually charged, imbecile, not romantically charged."

Abbie scoffs. "If you are waiting for an attraction to be romantically charged you are going to be waiting for a lifetime. Shit doesn't happen like that."

"Does too." Bridget widens her eyes at Abbie to accentuate her point.

I nod as I agree. "It does, Abbie. With nice guys it happens." I start to lay out the cutlery and hand the bottle of juice to Bridget who starts to fill the glasses on the table.

"Blah, blah, blah, nice guys are boring. I want a bad boy to bend me over and I want sexually charged. Bang the romance shit you two go on about," Abbie replies.

"Nice guys bend you over," I mutter.

"Really?" Joshua coos from his spot at the doorway. I throw him a smirk. How long has he been standing there listening?

"You are a nice guy and yes, I am bent over regularly." My eyes hold his and he smiles sexily. He walks around behind me and kisses my temple as he wraps his arms around me.

"Stop it. You're all sweaty." I swish him away.

"You like sweat," he whispers darkly

"Eww, yuk, stop it,"

Bridget frowns. "You two are gross," she adds.

Joshua picks up an apple and takes a bite. "My house." His eyes dare her to reply.

She whips him with the tea towel and shakes her head.

"I'm taking a shower." Joshua kisses me gently on the lips and disappears out of the room.

My eyes flick to the two girls as their eyes meet. "What?" I ask.

"You two are really happy." Bridget shakes her head in disbelief. "I never thought I would see the day."

I smile warmly and nod. "Yes, we are." I have never been more in love with my beautiful man. Here he is how I imagined he would be if we hadn't had to put up with all of the crap in our lives. We are in a love bubble, one I don't want to pop.

"Who would have ever thought you would fall in love with a guy who is this rich?"

Abbie mutters as she takes a sip of her juice. "This whole resort thing going on here." She gestures around the room at our surroundings with her glass. "Could be half yours."

"It's Joshua's," I frown.

Her eyes hold mine. "Semantics."

"Anyway, so what happened last night?" I turn my attention back to Bridget to change the subject.

"Ben and I were dancing," she answers.

"Yes." I take a sip of my juice.

"And then the song changed so we were slow-dancing."

"Ahuh." I turn and start to butter the toast. "Then what?"

She goes silent and my eyes flick up to her from my buttering toast duties to see Ben standing at the door. Oh shit, did he hear us?

"Breakfast will be about five minutes, Ben." I smile.

Ben's eyes hold Bridget's, and she smiles softly at him. Oh, she does like him. I have seen that look before.

"Ok, thanks," he answers in his husky South African accent.

"Shall we go and wait on the deck?" Bridget smiles up at him.

He nods and smiles back gently. Oh, he likes her too. This is so frigging cute, and I feel my heart flutter a little as they leave the room.

Abbie gets up and walks over next to me. "This is stupid, how can she date Joshua's bodyguard?" she whispers.

I frown. "What do you mean?" I ask.

"Think about it. Every time Joshua needs him to go out at night, Bridget is going to want him to go out with her."

I frown as I start to dish out the omelette. "Not necessarily."

"Oh bullshit," she snaps. "Get a reality check."

"Just shut up and dish out the food, Abbs and keep that opinion to yourself. Don't say anything to Didge. She can like who she wants. I like Ben," I reply.

"Get this. She kissed him last night on the lips on the dance-floor and then he broke away."

I frown. "What...tongue kiss?"

"No, like a peck. But there was probably more that I missed."

"And he pulled away?" I frown.

"Yep, totally." She nods. "But then he was looking at her all doe-eyed all night, like he wanted more to happen but he didn't make a move."

"Hmm, I will ask Josh about it later," I whisper as Adrian walks into the room.

"Morning, ladies." He smiles.

I smile broadly at someone who is fast-tracking his way to being one of my favorite people. "Morning, Mr. Murphy, how was the gym?" I ask as Cameron walks in and takes a seat at the table.

"Yeah, okay." He flicks on the coffee machine.

"Go ask him now," Abbie whispers over the bean grinder.

"Shhh," I whisper. "Abbie, you are so punishing."

"That's why you love me," she replies.

Joshua returns from his shower and the seven of us all take a seat. I place the large Spanish Omelette in the middle of the table with the fruit and toast I have prepared, and everybody starts to dig in. Joshua is sitting opposite me.

"What's on the agenda today?" I ask.

Joshua swallows his food. "I thought we would go down and get you a motorbike license."

I look at him in horror across the table. "Why?" I answer.

"So we can go riding together," he states matter-of-factly.

I screw up my face. "Ah, no, not happening. I could think of nothing worse."

Joshua smirks. "What now? Why wouldn't you want to ride a motorbike?"

"Because I hate them and these roads here are frigging dangerous. I don't normally like to get killed on vacation," I mutter as I bite into my toast.

Abbie, Bridget and Adrian smile.

"Wouldn't you rather die doing something you love?" Joshua frowns.

"Exactly." I point my fork at him, and he smirks as he takes another bite of his food.

"How would you want to die then?" He raises his eyebrows.

I shrug. "So, doing something I love right?" I question.

He nods as he continues eating.

I think for a moment. "I would like to die in my sleep or eating a Big Mac."

Joshua screws up his face in disgust.

"I would like to die getting a head job," Cameron interjects.

"What a way to go." He shovels more food into his mouth. Ben laughs and Adrian rolls his eyes.

"I would like to die in Paris," Bridget says, smiling. "Underneath the Eiffel Tower."

Ben smiles warmly at Bridget and I drop my head to hide my smile at their interaction.

"What about you, Josh, where would be your favorite place to die?" I ask.

"Next to you," he replies quietly. I smile broadly and take his hand in mine over the table as I melt. The rest of the table breaks into moans of disgust at his gushy reply.

"What about you, Murph? Where would be your favorite place to die?" Joshua asks.

He shrugs and takes a sip of his coffee. "I don't know. I don't think I have a favorite place." He frowns. "Maybe here."

"Don't you dare fucking die in my house." Joshua shakes his head in disgust.

"That could be arranged you know," Cameron says matter of factly. "Ben and I could knock you off in your sleep." He drinks his coffee.

Adrian fakes a smile at Cameron.

"Can I get a motorbike license, Josh?" Abbie asks.

"Yes, of course. All three of you girls can. It will be fun and then we can ride around the island today." He smiles.

My stomach drops in fear. This is going to end badly. I just know it.

Turns out I was right. I told them to listen to me. After taking three hours to get my motorbike license Joshua was so appalled at my lack of prowess he wouldn't let me drive one anyway. So, I spent the afternoon on the back of his bike while everyone else had their own. We did have fun exploring the island, what a beautiful place it is...and the food is magnificent.

It's now 6 pm. We have stopped at Kamala beach and have been tubing for the last hour. Tubing. Being towed behind a boat on a huge inflatable tube, now this is what I call enjoyment. I keep falling off and have to be dragged into the boat by the poor workers. Joshua has even pushed me off a few times. It's every man for himself on this thing. The boys are doing everything in their power to push each other off at full speed. My stomach is sore from laughing, and I can't remember having this much fun. The boat drivers are getting in on it and doing zig zags in the water to try and throw us off. Abbie's bikini top even came off, much to Cameron's delight. The boat slowly pulls in and we swim slowly to shore.

"Hold onto my back, Presh," Joshua whispers as he goes under water.

"I can swim Joshua," I splutter.

His eyes dance mischievously in the water.

"I know." He smiles as he grabs me and pulls me onto his back, and the others all continue to swim into the shore. He grabs my legs and wraps them around his body.

"Let's fuck," he whispers over his shoulder.

I laugh out loud. "Let's not." I pick up a handful of water and splash him in the face.

"Did you just splash me?" he asks, affronted.

"No, it was a wave," I squeal as I start to make a dash for the shore.

Joshua grabs my ankle and pulls me back to him and dunks me hard.

I squeal with laughter as he continues to drown me. "I see nothing's changed." I giggle.

"What do you mean?" He laughs as he chases me through the water.

I cough and splutter as I laugh. "You used to try and drown me back in the day, remember? You are still a behemoth."

He raises his eyebrows as he smiles broadly. "Behemoth,

hey? I think I need to fill that smart mouth of yours with my dick to shut it up." He splashes me in the face.

"This doesn't happen in my romance novels." I laugh as I splutter and go under, his warm arms then go around me and instantly I can feel his arousal. The mood instantly changes, and we are both brought to silence.

"Is this more like your romance novels?" he asks as his lips drop to my neck and his hips grind into mine.

I nod and kiss him gently on the lips. "Yes"

He smiles broadly. "Nice try, Marx." He dunks me hard again and swims to the shore.

"Watch out for sharks," he yells over his shoulder. Oh, of all the nerve.

"You are going to cop it later, Stanton," I yell after him. "Promises, promises," he replies as he swims off in the distance.

It is true, this doesn't happen in my romance novels...and you know what? This is life exactly how I want it.

"Shit, look at the bruises on your body," Cameron gasps. I look down at myself. We are on Adrian's pool deck. Adrian is in a deckchair on the right and then Joshua, me, Bridget and Abbie are lying on towels and Cameron is on a deckchair on the other side to the left. I'm not sure where Ben is.

"I know, all Joshua's fault pushing me off that tube of death yesterday." I smile with my eyes closed and my face tilted to the sun.

Joshua leans up on his elbow to inspect the bruises on the insides of my arms. "It looks like fingerprints." He frowns.

Cameron sits up and takes a closer look. "Yeah, that would be where they were pulling her back onto the boat."

"Oh right," Joshua answers. "Look at your hipbones, for Pete's sake."

I smile again with my eyes closed. "I didn't even feel it. Hey, take a photo on my phone so I can send it to Mum." I hand Joshua my phone and he starts to take photos of the bruising.

"I think I can safely say I won the tubing challenge, Presh." He gives me a smirk and a wink.

"Haha, so funny," I mutter. "Name the photo 'Joshua's trophies'."

He smiles broadly and texts it over.

"How did you do last night, Cam?" Joshua asks as he lies back down next to me.

"No good," Cameron replies with his eyes closed. What are they talking about? Oh right, they are talking about hooking up.

"Do you like Thai girls, Cam?" I ask.

"Ahuh." he answers, still with his eyes closed.

"What is it you specifically like about them?" Abbie asks as she raises the back of her forearm over her face to shield it from the sun.

"I don't know, the natural thing," he replies.

"Natural?" Bridget repeats.

"Yeah, you know, the carpet matches the curtains."

"The carpet matches the curtains." I giggle as I decipher that mentally.

Abbie screws up her face in disgust.

Joshua smiles and starts to slowly rub my oil sunscreen into my hipbones. He discreetly pulls me closer. I smirk, he loves my hipbones.

"Oh, dear God, Cameron, please tell me you don't date girls who have a carpet?" Adrian murmurs as he screws his face up in disgust.

Cameron smiles with his eyes closed. "Yeah, I can work with a sixties vibe," he replies.

"Oh gross," Bridget sighs.

"Yuk. I definitely don't work with carpet," Abbie groans. "In fact, sixties vibe carpet is a deal breaker."

"Yeah, especially shag pile." Bridget giggles and I laugh.

"How about you, Tash, does the carpet match the curtains?" Cameron asks as he leans up on his elbow to see my face.

"Fuck off," Joshua snaps. "Get your filthy mind off Natasha's carpet."

I giggle. "I'm right here, you know."

"Market research," Cameron mutters as he lies back.

"Not on the fucking market," Joshua snaps. Adrian laughs as his phone starts to vibrate.

He answers. "Murphy." He listens and then stands up in a rush, and we all fall silent.

"Don't you fucking dare!" he sneers. Joshua sits up immediately at the tone of Adrian's voice. Who the hell is on the other end of the phone? The girls and I glance at each other and frown.

"Don't bother," he snaps. "I'm not listening." He narrows his eyes in contempt as he shakes his head in anger.

"Don't call me, don't email me and stay the hell out of my life, Nicholas. We are done." He listens again. "Too little, too late." He hangs up the phone and throws it on the deckchair with such force that it bounces and flies straight into the pool. Cameron immediately dives in after it and Adrian storms inside. Joshua's eyes meet mine.

I wait five minutes to see how the boys handle this. They all lie still and start to chatter as if nothing happened and nobody is going after him. Men are hopeless. I tentatively stand and walk inside where I find Adrian lying on his bed. I slowly lie down behind him and cuddle his back.

"Tash." He shakes his head as his anger steals his ability to speak.

"I don't want to say anything. I just want to lie with you," I reply quietly.

He lies silent and still while I troll my brain for the right thing to say. What did Nicholas say to upset him this much? He was only with him for a month...who am I kidding? I was only with Joshua for a month when we first got together, and I have been fucked over ever since. A lot of love can happen in a month.

"I want to go home," Adrian sighs.

I nod. "Okay," I answer. "We can go early. We are due to go in three days anyway."

Adrian shakes his head sadly as he rolls onto his back and puts his arm under my head. I gently kiss his chest.

"It will be ok, Adrian," I whisper. I know how a broken heart feels... it's lonely.

"I want to go home," he replies.

I nod and squeeze him that little bit harder. "Do you live near Josh?"

"No. I want to go to my parents' house," he replies.

My heart drops and my eyes close. I know both his parents are dead.

"I want to be depressed at my mother's house and have her fuss over me and make me fattening food and my father to tell me that Nicholas didn't deserve me in the first place. But no. They had to die, didn't they?"

He's angry that they died. It's a natural progression in the grieving process. I am still angry with my father for leaving me. I can't even imagine the pain of losing both parents at the same time.

"They would be here if they could, honey, you know that. It was a terrible accident, Adrian. They didn't want to die," I whisper as I kiss his chest again. He pulls me closer but doesn't answer. We lie still for another 15 minutes both lost in our own thoughts. Joshua walks in and sits at the end of the bed and grabs Adrian's foot.

"Want a drink? I'm making cocktails," he asks Adrian as he twists his foot.

"No," he replies flatly as he yanks his foot from his grip.

"Want to beat up Cam?" Joshua asks as he raises his eyebrows in question.

Adrian smirks. "Possibly," he replies.

"Get up and stop carrying on. If you want him back, go and fucking get him." Joshua stands and holds Adrian's gaze for a moment and then leaves the room. I smile at Adrian.

"Jeez, he has so much empathy," I smirk.

Adrian shakes his head. "That was Joshua being empathetic. Cameron is the soft one." I smile. My man is probably the worse communicator in the human world with me. It never once occurred to me that he is like that with everyone. And I didn't ever imagine that Cameron would be a soft-hearted communicator. I really am learning something new every day about these complicated men that have come into my life.

*To continue this story you can*
*download it now on Amazon.*

# AFTERWORD

Thank you so much for reading and
for your ongoing support
I have the most beautiful readers in the whole world!

Keep up to date with all the latest news
and online discussions by joining the Swan Squad VIP
Facebook group and discuss your favourite
books with other readers.
@tlswanauthor

Visit my website for updates and new release information.
www.tlswanauthor.com

# ABOUT THE AUTHOR

T L Swan is a Wall Street Journal, USA Today, and #1 Amazon Best Selling author. With millions of books sold, her titles are currently translated in twenty languages and have hit #1 on Amazon in the USA, UK, Canada, Australia and Germany. She is currently writing the screenplays for a number of her titles. Tee resides on the South Coast of NSW, Australia with her husband and their three children where she is living her own happy ever after with her first true love.

Printed in Great Britain
by Amazon

54733461R00314